ALSO BY SCOTT GARDINER

The Dominion of Wyley McFadden (2000)

KING JOHN OF

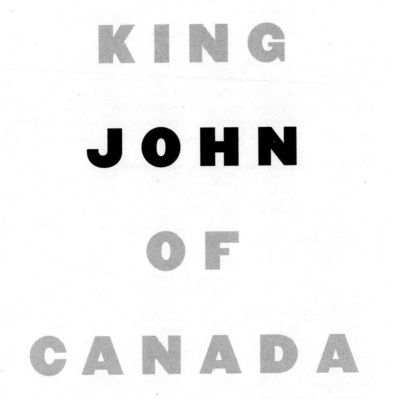

KING JOHN OF CANADA

SCOTT GARDINER

[A DOUGLAS GIBSON BOOK]

McCLELLAND & STEWART

Library and Archives Canada Cataloguing in Publication

Gardiner, Scott, 1959–
    King John of Canada / Scott Gardiner.

"Douglas Gibson books".
ISBN: 978-0-7710-3309-4

I. Title.

PS8563.A6244K55 2007   c813'.6   C2006-904293-4

We acknowledge the financial support of the Government of Canada through the Book Publishing Industry Development Program and that of the Government of Ontario through the Ontario Media Development Corporation's Ontario Book Initiative. We further acknowledge the support of the Canada Council for the Arts and the Ontario Arts Council for our publishing program.

Typeset in Garamond by M&S, Toronto
Printed and bound in Canada

A Douglas Gibson Book

This book is printed on acid-free paper that is 100% recycled, ancient-forest friendly (100% post-consumer recycled).

McClelland & Stewart Ltd.
75 Sherbourne Street
Toronto, Ontario
M5A 2P9
www.mcclelland.com

1 2 3 4 5   11 10 09 08 07

THIS BOOK IS DEDICATED TO MY CHILDREN,
FOR WHOM AND BECAUSE OF WHOM IT WAS IMAGINED:
TO DAYTON AND WILLIAM, WITH LOVE AND HOPE

Is it possible, after all this, you still wonder?
With the New World new again, such cost! – haven't I answered?
I'll say it, just in case. Who's king?

KING **JOHN** OF CANADA

DAY ONE

THIS IS THE POWER of storytelling.

A mile down the shore there's a boathouse. It's a white boathouse, classic Muskoka design with double doors swinging out across the water, bedrooms above, and a broad bay window overlooking the lake. Every time, *every time*, I pass this boathouse I gaze up at that window. Even now, in January, as I trudge across the ice dragging my toboggan like some halfwit habitant in an overpriced Krieghoff, with the cursed dog that's supposed to be pulling instead walking behind where the going is easier, even now – when I know there's not another living soul or burning light for miles – I gaze at that window because of a story. And here is the power of storytelling: it's not even my story, and it's not John's either.

A neighbour down the lake told him years ago, and John told me. It would have been summer when I first heard it, the only sensible time for people to be here, and John and I would have been out among the islands in his boat. It would have been dark, past midnight, and John would have been driving, leaning up against the gunwales, a gin and tonic in the hand that wasn't steering. We'd snuck out, I think. At least that's how I remember it because it seems to me there were no lights ahead or astern. Even back in those days the sentry must have taken a very dim view of John going out by himself, especially in the middle of the lake at night where any terrorist or lunatic could get at him, but John took a dim view of watchdogs, and after all, as he'd always told them, who exactly was monarch?

Still it was rare to actually manage an escape: likely through a window while he was supposed to be sleeping; tiptoeing down to the dock, unmooring the boat, and paddling around the point before starting up the engine, exactly, he'd said, like when he was a kid sneaking out after being grounded. You could never imagine an American president pulling off a thing like that, or for that matter a Canadian Prime Minister. But John wasn't a president, he wasn't a PM. And anyway, he said, people here don't assassinate their leaders, so he was entitled to a little time to himself.

That night, somehow, we'd snuck past the watchers – this was well before the Osprey Guard, otherwise it would have been impossible – at any rate we were out there in the boat, sipping gin and tonics with the engine running slow and leaving barely any wake. We were talking, as I remember it, just the two of us, but not about affairs of state. Anyone who's spent time on the lakes knows how voices travel over water in the still of night, and both of us were sensible enough to be aware of that. But that's part of the pleasure of moonlit cruises, the amplified silence, the rumble of the engine, understanding the significance of echo.

John pointed to the white boathouse as we passed and told me that years ago, long before all the changes, he'd been on another cruise in someone else's boat: a friend from down the lake giving him a lift from the mainland. The friend had stopped in front of that boathouse, John said, pointed to the window, and whispered that once he'd seen a naked woman there.

It was dark then too, the friend had said; he'd been driving down the channel with the motor barely idling when a light came on and the woman appeared. She was so beautiful, he said, so shockingly arresting, that without really thinking he'd pulled back on the throttle and hung there in the channel, staring. He said that after a moment the woman must have realized that the lights she was watching go by weren't going by any more. According to the story, she had smiled, waved the kind of wave that people give in daylight when they're sitting on their dock and a neighbour passes, then turned her back and disappeared.

John said the most interesting part of the story was how his friend admitted that since that night he could never drive by the boathouse without looking up at that window.

"And the funny thing," John said, "was that from then on, neither could I."

We were both staring up at the window as John told the story, gazing wistfully at the empty squares of glass. And now I, too, can record that there hasn't been once that I've passed that boathouse – even now, even yesterday with four feet of snow on the roof and not a breath of life but the deer mice – without glancing up, hoping for a naked woman.

That is the power of storytelling.

On the other hand, perhaps it's the power of naked women. Let me think about that.

Though we did see a lynx. Or should I say *I* saw the lynx. The dog, in his usual mindless oblivion, was too busy with his head in the snow. We'd just set out, it was early in the morning, not long after dawn, the dog in that canine state of idiot excitement at the beginning of anything new. On the return trip, with the toboggan loaded and a day's steady labour behind us, he'd be trailing along head-down in the path that I and the groceries had already beaten through the snow. At this stage, he was still too enraptured with himself and his crystallized muzzle of ice.

It's been snowing since I arrived. Nearly a week now, I think, but already I am losing track of time. Snow, snow, and more snow. The storm must have let up at some point in the night – with dawn arriving less as a sunrise than a gradual incarnation of cold.

There is, I've discovered, an oddly masculine quality in temperature like this, a willing suspension of attachment. It's the dampening of everything external, the self's insulation of self. Everything else, every twig and branch and fibre, was coated in bristles of ice. Muffled in my layers of garment, I could hear the movement of blood, the passage of air into my lungs: each breath an act of self-awareness. There's something about cold – a true cold like yesterday's – that diminishes emotion and clarifies thought. It made my mind up, at any rate, that I couldn't leave this any longer.

The lynx would have spent the storm holed up as well. He was padding in circles around what may have been an overturned boat, or a pile of wood, but now appeared only as a mound of undifferentiated white. I think he'd sensed a rabbit or a mouse beneath, and this was what absorbed him. The depth of snow must have silenced our approach because – suddenly – there we were: an unexpected human where no humans had any right to be, and an asinine dog. The dog, for his part, never did become conscious of the cat – I've often wondered by what means dogs are thought to be of use in hunting – while the lynx stared at us, inscrutable, then disappeared in a furrow of snow into the woods beyond the shuttered buildings.

It was the first lynx I'd ever seen. They're considered a northerly species and this, however it may feel otherwise, is the balmy south in relation to most of the rest of this country. Maybe our lynx had wandered down from the north, or maybe he'd been here all along, keeping to the back bush until after Thanksgiving. But there he was, and there was my heart so unexpectedly pounding. John, as far as I know, had never seen a wild lynx either, certainly not one right here on his doorstep. He'd have been thrilled, completely delighted. It was one of his favourite themes, how human nature leans simultaneously to wildness and civilization, and how government must always be aware of this. It would have pleased him immensely to demonstrate how his own territory could overlap with a lynx's – as fine a definition of boreal hegemony as any he could think of – that's how I'd have written it. Our lynx-in-metaphor would have had John smiling for days.

Beginnings are hardest, aren't they? I've always thought that. Heraclitus – I'm fairly certain it was Heraclitus – wrote that you can never step into the same river twice. This applies to stories too; the moment you start one, you've changed it. Every telling twists the tale, it's said: an observation especially true for those of us employed to do the twisting.

I mean to be faithful. That I can tell you. That has always been my intention. Even now, more so now than ever.

DAY TWO

I SEE I'VE BEGUN with reference to Cornelius Krieghoff. I'd chop him, if these were normal circumstances – it's possible you've not even heard of Krieghoff (another thing I'll never know) – but the business of editing is much more daunting without the cut-and-paste option. Already there's a pile of crumpled yellow paper by my feet beside the useless laptop. They're excellent tinder, admittedly. But I'm using them up at an alarming rate.

Krieghoff was a nineteenth-century painter, Dutch-born, who came up the St. Lawrence just before Confederation and set up shop painting Indians, mostly, and *Canadien* peasantry. Typically in winter. His canvases – and I think he finished thousands – now sell for small fortunes despite generations of trashing by the cognoscenti types. They're sentimental, somewhat in the Norman Rockwell tradition if you spattered his subjects in spruce gum and set them in a forest. John always kept one or two on display in the Silos' public lobby – for old times' sake, he liked to say – along with all the gaudy totem poles and abstract icebergs. Four times a year, like clockwork, Quebec's ambassador sends a note demanding their repatriation. It's the little ironies that make history so worthwhile.

If you could picture a typical Krieghoff, though, you'd

understand the allusion: a week without shaving (or bathing, for that matter), an old woollen sock I managed to stretch over my head to keep my ears from freezing (I'd brought a real hat with me, but the cursed dog has eaten it), and, God help me, a couple of blankets stripped off one of the beds, with holes cut in then, slung across my shoulders poncho-style. I didn't freeze on my trek into town, but I wouldn't have looked out of place in a Krieghoff, either.

I used to tell John that writing is only the task of rephrasing cliché. Even so, I'm amazed that I've just used up three pages of my precious paper on Cornelius Krieghoff. Paper's one of the things I failed to bring enough of. There were six yellow scribblers on the shelf at the store in town – I thought it wise not to draw attention to myself by buying up the whole stock, or should I say more attention than I was drawing already swaddled in blankets with a toboggan as a shopping cart attached to an idiot dog that wouldn't stop yapping. Luckily, the place was empty and the girl at the till was still at that age when they don't notice anything anyway – but for reasons that at that moment seemed logical, I bought only four of the available six. An error in judgment, I now concede. I've used up half a pad already.

The point worth making about Krieghoff, however, and the one that may ultimately save me a rewrite, is the fact that only Canadians know him. This allows me to mention how hard I laboured convincing John's public that a culture is defined simply as one group of people knowing things about themselves that other people don't. I can report that we made considerable improvement there. No, I'm being modest. We made huge, *gigantic* progress on that front. One thing I can say with confidence is that the inhabitants of John's erstwhile dominion are a great deal more bullish about themselves than they were when we started this monarchy game. There's another understatement.

DAY THREE

JOHN'S COTTAGE sits on cedar posts dug down to Precambrian Shield. It has stood this way one hundred years. John was very fond of explaining the engineering rationale for this, which involves fluidity of motion in winter. Ice moves, he liked to tell us – never in this country assume a condition of stasis. (Ice, as I'm sure his biographies will record, was a major motif of John's reign. We'll come back to that, but for now let me be the first to record that John's lifelong fascination with ice and all of its political ramifications stemmed from his study of its effect on this building.) An aluminum washtub – the very one he claimed to have bathed in as a child – has hung for decades from a nail hammered into a joist beneath the floorboards. Mercifully, no holes have rusted through its bottom.

I exaggerate when I suggest the cottage isn't heated. There's a wood stove, as you've read already, thank heavens, or I would not be still surviving. There is also water, a whole lake of it, once a hole is chopped through two feet of ice to get at it. It took me an hour this morning to hack my way through with an axe. Using a saucepan from John's kitchen, I dipped slush from the lake into a larger pot, then carried it up to the cottage and transferred into the abovementioned tub. This was then arranged, precariously, on top of a wood stove built for heating air, not water, braced with a broomstick that soon began to char.

John's cottage has a bathtub located, unfortunately, very far from the fire: an old enamel four-claw that sits, logically enough, in a shed built off the kitchen at the rear of the house. Not a lot of heat from the wood stove reaches this part of the building. Plumbing, of course, has been disconnected for the winter, which is to say that the pump was drained in the fall so as not to freeze and burst in another fine demonstration of the amazing expansionary powers of ice.

The plan was this: to fit a rubber plug into the bathtub, then, as quickly as possible, haul the heated water to the bath and dump it in, to be followed immediately by my naked self – which was to be scrubbed, also as rapidly as possible, before the water cooled and reverted to its solid state. I was gambling that once I pulled the plug, the dirty water (very dirty, amazingly dirty – where does dirt come from under all this snow?) would still flow down the drainage pipes and find its way to the septic tank, theoretically still functioning somewhere snug beneath the frost.

To quote a better-known bather: Eureka!

It worked. I am clean. The bathing anecdote is over.

It puzzles me, though, that I have done what I have done. Never before in life have I felt the slightest compulsion to set down events of the moment or, for that matter, events of the past simply for the sake of recording them. History, in my line of work, is a bank of arguments retained against the future. A reservoir to draw from, if you prefer, not add to. As to this strange new fascination with the present, this brazen obsession to inflict you with my day-to-day irrelevance, think of it along the lines of Julie Andrews's spoonful of sugar. I mean that from my perspective, you understand, not yours.

Whatever else, though, whatever else I might regret, I don't regret the bath. Cleanliness is worth the illusion.

DAY FOUR

I FIRST MET JOHN in Malaga. We were in our early twenties, which (though you may not know it) is the happiest age for people to be. My parents, having lived in America long enough to recognize the limitations of French, had sent me to Spain to learn Spanish. John, in that inimitable way of his, just stumbled on the place. He'd been backpacking through Europe, met a girl in Barcelona, caught a train to Malaga, and, somehow in the course of events, ended up my roommate at the Andalusia Institut d'Española. He told me that day, unfurling his sleeping bag, that he'd just had a good feeling about the place.

So you see, even then, John was nurturing that talent of his for staggeringly prescient banalities. At the Andalusia Institut, he and I became kings. Both of us. There's really no better way to describe it. In later years we'd try to put a finger on exactly how things evolved the way they did, we'd try to remember exactly what it was back then we did so right, but in truth it just wasn't something you could aim to make happen again. What it was was luck, timing: a favourable conjunction of the stars. Not to be repeated, at least not by me.

Admittedly, certain conditions worked to our advantage. For example the ratio of women to men. Language schools tend to attract more female students than male. (An interesting phenomenon unto itself, and one that seems to support the prevalent thinking that women are more communicative than men – John would always take that side of the argument, whenever we kicked it around, and I could never properly refute it, though I always wanted to.) At the institute, the girl-to-boy ratio must have been seven or eight to one. I can hardly remember other male students, when I think back on it, though there must have been some. But if so, they were irrelevant. Within a month, John and I were running the place like our own little seigneury.

It's tasteless of me to express it this way, but still I'm smiling as I write that the school was like a smorgasbord to us, a table of inexplicable exotica. It drew students from all over the world: an improbably large-breasted girl from Hong Kong named Desdemona; a Mandingo tribeswoman (I swear) from Guinea who to this day still makes me sigh when I think of her; more Germans than you could comfortably keep track of; a wide assortment of Swedes and sundry Scandinavians, as well as the usual array of Canadians, Americans, Australians, and one kibbutznik Israeli. Then, of course, the Andalusians themselves, hauntingly lovely, Catholic – difficult and therefore much pursued. All women. All – or almost all, and truly I am not exaggerating – looked upon John and me as an essential part of the curriculum.

Popularity is like money: the more you have, the more rapidly its interest compounds. Before we left Malaga, John and I were in such demand that it became almost embarrassing. Not to say that's why we left, but when the time came we departed almost eagerly, aware – even at that age – that something of this nature was too good to last. Wiser to leave at the pinnacle, mythologies intact. We learned hardly any Spanish (quite a lot of German) but, God, was it an education.

The other thing that worked so much in our favour was the calendar. Courses were always exactly one month in duration: Beginning Spanish I, Beginning Spanish II, Intermediate

Spanish, Intermediate Spanish II, and so on. Every month brought a fresh wave of enrolment. At the start of each semester, the administration held a fiesta introducing local food, wine, and music – and John and me. It got so that we could stand back at these parties and divide the new recruits between us. Sometimes we'd compete – often both successfully – for the same girls. This in no way undermined our friendship. If anything, it strengthened it. Soon it was common practice for us to be referred to in the collective, as in *Los Canadienses*, though I wasn't one, not then – but already I was under the umbrella. Often we were taken for brothers. John and I understood somehow, implicitly, that whatever was happening wouldn't be happening if the two of us hadn't been causing it together. Our rule in those days was bicephalous.

Near the beginning of our second semester, we were drawn into what came to be known as the Flamenco Incident. This was the final and finishing factor in our rise to local splendour.

The school employed a band for the fiestas. It had a name, this band, but I don't remember it. We called them the Flamenco Boys, and even from this distance of memory, I have to admit that they were top-notch instrumentalists. They played that eerie, wailing, wildly mesmerizing Moorish kind of music, accompanied by incredibly rapid clapping of hands and thrumming of Spanish guitar. As I've said, they were good, and accustomed to being so acknowledged. There were four of them.

It's fairly well recognized, I think, that musicians get more than their share of female attention. I believe this truth is universal. Factor in the brooding good looks, the nearly all-girl audience, as well as that lovely tendency of young women to judge propriety in degrees of distance from home, and you can see how the Flamenco Boys would have felt somewhat proprietorial. Let it be said that they came to resent our presence.

The incident erupted, appropriately enough, over a girl named Helena. Helena was a polyglot Norwegian, what you might call a senior at the institute. She'd been in attendance four or five months already, and was more than conversant in Spanish. Helena was seeing one of the Flamenco Boys – exclusively, so the word went out. She had a little *pension* off-campus, and the Boy in question was in the habit of spending the latter part of his evenings there before returning home to the bosom of his family. A few weeks after our arrival, he rapped at the door, as was his custom, but no Helena was present to answer his call. (She was, as I can testify, hand across my mouth, knees around my waist, while the door latch rattled and the knocking grew more and more insistent, then died away in wounded muttering.)

Two days later, a shockingly wooden and slow-stepping Helena appeared in class with swollen lips and the edges of bruise above her neckline. The story came out as stories always do. Flamenco Boy, manhood impugned, had reasserted it in the time-honoured method of his forebears.

Now I have to digress again and tell you something else about John. Much has been written, and more will be written now that he's dead, about the things John got away with. It's simply true that John was able to say and do what no other politician would have dreamed of attempting. (He himself always argued that he wasn't a politician, and that therefore any such comparison was invalid, which may have been true in a literal sense but false in a great many others – a more political soul than John's is hard to imagine.) Not to suggest for a moment that he didn't get into trouble. He did. But his implacable sense of morality simply rode over it. That was how it worked with the Flamenco Boy, and how it worked years later when John emptied his glass in the face of Sheik Bin Wahhabi, or pinned Fox Blotter live on EagleNews TV. He was just doing what he and everyone else knew was fundamentally right, and optics be damned.

As it happened, the day our battered Helena showed up for class, Flamenco Boy also had an errand at the school. Perhaps he was picking up his cheque from the previous show, or booking an engagement for the one to come, or simply pissing on fence posts. Whatever the reason, there he was, at the door to the principal's office no less, when John ran into him.

Please remember that it was not even John who'd slept with Helena (though I'm quite sure he did later). But it was John who first found him. It was John who grabbed a fistful of shirt front, and it was John who spat in his face in full view of the school's administration. It was also John who said, roughly (I wasn't there, so this comes second-hand, with allowances for translation), that only the most contemptible, craven, shit-eating son of a whore-mothered worm ever raised a hand to a woman.

Flamenco Boy – and the office staff too, I imagine – was taken so profoundly by surprise that apparently no one had time to react until it was over, and John, back turned, was marching down the hall on his way to Beginners Spanish II.

I stayed close to him after that. Malaga in those days, our corner of it at any rate, was still a small town, and I figured John to be a marked man. But it was only a matter of time before the girl I was chasing led me in one direction while John and his date drifted off in another. Here's the other thing you have to know about John: he was always lucky – so was I, for that matter. And luck, as Machiavelli himself points out, is something the fortunate must learn to rely on.

The Flamenco Boys caught John in an alley we'd used as a shortcut to our favourite tapas bar. It was his date's Germanic yodelling that got my attention, and this was the lucky part – I was only one street away and ambling home from the opposite direction. I came at the Flamenco Boys from their blind side, backs to me, eagerly hammering.

There's a political lesson here, I'm constrained to point out, one I've had occasion to put into practice on John's behalf several times since, though never quite so ostentatiously. If your opponent is foolish enough to present his backside, choose that moment to hit him with whatever you've got – in this case a goat bladder of low-grade Madeira. The Andalusian wineskin, filled to the neck and swung by its shoulder strap, generates considerable momentum.

The nearest F-Boy, I think, would afterwards remember only that suddenly his legs were no longer beneath him, taken out as they were at the knees by several gallons of high-velocity plonk. His fall was lucky too. He went straight into F-Boy number two, and unbalanced him as well, which seriously distracted F-Boys three and four. What with John taking advantage of the better odds – he was taller and significantly longer of limb – they absorbed some pretty hard punishment before they, too, were face down on the cobblestones. One of them started getting up, took a look at the state of his friends, and decided to stay where he was.

Years later, when Roberto Duran uttered his famous *no mas* at the end of the Sugar Ray Leonard fight, John and I shared an admittedly atavistic moment of pleasure. We'd heard the line before.

The story went through the school like a virus, mutating with every retelling. Both of us had the presence of mind to deny the wilder accounts, but after all there was a witness, and who were we to contradict? John's bumps and bruises (I escaped without a scratch) only added to his appeal. Even the teaching staff were smitten – this was Hemingway country, remember. From that point forward, we could do no wrong.

But more than anything else, it was John's spit that left the most lasting impression. When newcomers arrived at the school, learning the ropes, absorbing the briefings of those there before them, it was always John's spit they heard about first. I think it was the moral brazenness that left its mark, the sheer, ethical ferocity of that act. John never scrupled to call a spade a spade (and please, here, disregard what I said earlier about writing being simply the rephrasing of cliché – often no new phrase is necessary). There should have been repercussions, official ones, I mean. You don't spit in someone's face outside *el Principal*'s office and expect no rebuke. But John did, and received none.

This is the point I wish to get at:

There was discussion in the halls, that day, before our final bout of violence, about cultural relativism. When Flamenco Boy chose to raise his hand to Helena, there was talk that this was the expression of a culture that we, as outsiders, had no right to impose our own standards upon. If such was acceptable behaviour in this place, the thinking went, then it was not our place to criticize.

John was – and always remained – utterly, dismissively, intolerant of that notion. Years later he was famously quoted as saying that civilized nations, like civilized people, did not accept the intolerable in the name of tolerance. I believe that this is why he got away with so much of what he did. John's morality, intellect, and emotions combined to work in greater synchronicity than anyone's I've ever known. He always believed, he always *knew* – as in that day at the door to the principal's office – that all people distinguished between right and wrong. When prevailing culture and religion obscured that distinction, John allowed for no retreat into equivocation. He attacked.

And as we know he was adored for it everywhere. Americans – not just the Blue ones – ate him up. The day after savaging Blotter on EagleNews, John's approval ratings spiked the highest in the Red states – and I'm talking Gallup, not just Decima. And when he dumped his ice cubes over that fatuous sheik, even the Saudis secretly applauded. A few years later, when the revolutions swept the Gulf and all those bearded heads appeared on pikes above the royal palaces, I'm convinced that the revolution had its origins in the ordinary people seeing that their potentates were far more vulnerable in the real world than they believed themselves to be at home.

John sent flowers, by the way, a big bunch of Ottawa tulips. Canada's share of the global oil market shot from 2.2 per cent to more than 6 per cent.

DAY FIVE

My father named me Blue. It was meant to be a nickname, used only in the family, until John got a hold of it. We'd been assigned a list of Spanish irregular verbs, and that's what I was doing, conjugating *estar*, when John interrupted.

"*Blue?*" he said.

He was stretched out on his bed, reading a letter. Not until that moment did it occur to me that the letter he was reading was mine. This would have been early in our second month of residence.

"You *bastard!*"

"*Blue?*" he asked again.

"Mail is private, you know."

I'd had a letter from my father. In those days, people still used pen and ink. There was nothing shameful or secret or worrisome in that letter, just gossip from home. So it shouldn't really have upset me to see John reading it, except for the principle of not asking first.

"*Blue?*"

I decided to ignore him and go back to my declensions.

"I didn't really read it," he said. "Just the watchamacallit."

"Salutation," I sighed.

"That's right. It says *Blue*. Who's Blue?"

"It's a nickname, okay? Only my father ever uses it."

"Why?"

"None of your business."

"Yes, but why *Blue*?" He paused in that way that always let you know he was thinking, that a witticism was on the cusp. "Why not orange?" he said at last. "Why not brown? Green?" He mined this vein for several minutes, sifting through the spectrum. When he got to yellow, he made a point of ruling that one out. "Not appropriate at all," he said – this was not long after the Flamenco Incident – John's method of assuaging and assaulting, both. "Cranberry, though," he said. "Carmine. What about aquamarine?"

"Fuck off."

There really wasn't any reason not to tell him. The name had to do with a birthmark, one that disappeared while I was still a toddler. I have no recollection of it myself. If the subject had come up in other circumstances, I'd have given him the story.

But now the dye was cast, the pattern stamped. I wouldn't tell, and never did. It became one of those quirky, hard little edges of history. A secret, silly ritual. For the rest of our lives together, John never stopped pretending to obsess about the origins of Blue. My part of the game, and game it was, was to guard the secret. As with any contest, it evolved its own peculiar set of rules. In latter years, John had at his disposal quite a considerable intelligence network – he threatened, sometimes, to put the RCMP on the case. Once, he winked at me as we headed into a meeting with a former CIA director and muttered that *now* we'd get to the bottom of this. But according to convention this was not allowed, and in abstract matters like this John was a stickler for orthodoxy. He never cheated. At least, as far as I know he never cheated. Now there's a thought.

The upshot, at any rate, was that John – without forethought and in the absence of malice – detached me from one name and assigned me another. From that moment on he refused to call me anything but Blue; very soon everyone else in Malaga was following suit. Decades later, a different sort of throne beneath him, he did the same again on a global scale.

I must tell you that John was never a serious linguist. He learned things naturally, not by application. While I studied parts of speech, John would practise speech itself. In written tests, I got the better marks; in oral ones, he did. Although he often mangled syntax, John always had at his command whatever words were needed.

So it shouldn't have surprised me that he memorized the word for *blue* in at least a dozen languages. In class, he kept pretty much to formal Spanish. *¿Dónde está Señor Azul?*

Señor Azul est en la baño.

The other students were pleased to follow his lead. Soon the instructors had incorporated Blue into their lesson plans.

¿Porque Señor Azul está en la baño?

Porque Señor Azul no le siento.

Elsewhere, he'd adapt to fit the audience. Drinking with the Germans, I was *Herr Blau. Ich liebe dich wie ich liebe meinen hund, Herr Blau*, they'd say, brimming with Teutonic mirth. Or later, hiking boots off and under the bed: *Wo ist mein süsser Herr Blau?* (Mitigation, I learned then, often has a greater value than the thing it is intended to relieve.) But when we visited Barcelona with a pair of exchange students from Poland, it was *Niebieski* the whole damned weekend. Mandingo I've forgotten, likewise Finnish (though I recall it sounded like something to do with crushing gravel). But blue is *blå* in Norwegian, and *lan* in Cantonese. At one point I knew it in Hebrew as well. John would have remembered.

Only months ago, at an NI function we'd hosted in Toronto at the Silos, John presented me to Quebec's new ambassador: *Je vous presenté mon cher ami, Bleu.*

He was a bulldog, our John.

DAY SIX

I'M WISHING NOW I'd bought a radio. Also, I'm running low
on firewood. You'd be surprised how much it takes to keep this
place endurable. The stove, I think, is meant to be airtight but
is not. It burns out if I don't stoke it every three or four hours.
There have been some chilly mornings; the glass of water frozen
solid to my nightstand when I wake and probe my face for hardened skin. I've given up trying to keep the dog out of bed. It's
to our mutual advantage, he's convinced me, pooling warmth.

Last night I decided I've come around to the concept of
chronology. At least in theory. I admit it makes sense to tell a
story by beginning at the beginning and ending at the end.
The problem is that bits keep emerging out of sequence. When
I got up to put more wood on the fire, I couldn't get back to
sleep – it's so cold, the moments spent outside the blankets
shock my body into utter wakefulness. I started thinking over
what I'd written, specifically yesterday's little *virage* into the
nature of John's . . . nature, and realized I couldn't quite leave
it at that.

That segue touched on John's moral sense of balance, about
how far he'd spread himself to keep that balance, how willing
he was to strike if that balance was threatened. In case I forget,
or in case I don't get to it – in case something happens before
the end of this – I have to add that John more often than not
chose comedy as the agent of that strike.

As I've said, John was not tolerant of intolerance, particularly as it applied to intellectual dishonesty. He seldom took issue with dishonesty per se. The lie detected *always* defeats you, he said, but a tactical lie is forgivable if it achieves its intent. (It's just that the risks very often outweigh the advantages.) What outraged him was the lie that was dishonest to its own internal principles. Deliberate dishonesty, in other words, was forgivable – stupid dishonesty was not. John liked to say it was his principle to contradict contradictions of principle.

So he tended to come down hard on things like religious fundamentalism, ethnic entitlement, certain women's lobbies, and, of course, Quebec. While he was more than willing to take off the gloves with the first two – shockingly so, sometimes (and we all know what happened with Quebec) – his scruples prevented him from any such behaviour with women.

Very early on – and I'm talking very, very early; right at the beginning, when the whole idea of a homegrown monarchy was still something much closer to a joke – John was invited to present a Woman Writer of the Year Award. In those days, there were many publicly funded organizations dedicated to enhancing the status of specific groups. There still are, naturally. John was in every sense committed to government's role in defending minorities. The issue for him that day, however, was that women were not a minority, particularly in the estrogenic world of Canadian publishing.

We all know now that John would go on to become the greatest patron to the arts the country has ever known. (The Gold Leaf is – I say with some pride; I had no small role in its design – now without a shred of doubt the world's most esteemed award of literary merit.) But in those days all that was far in the future.

I remember that night with absolute clarity. It turned out to be an audition, though I've never been sure of who, precisely, was auditioning whom. Certainly, if I could point to a single event that changed the course of my life, that evening was it. I'd arrived in Toronto late that same afternoon. This would have been the first time John and I had seen each other in several months.

I'm getting ahead of myself again, but for this part of the story to make sense I have to tell you that John and I were seldom in the same place during the years between Malaga and Crown. We lived in separate countries and pursued separate lives. We'd write, occasionally. When e-mail came along, we e-mailed. But often months and sometimes years went by between visits. Truth be told, if either of us had married, the friendship would probably have withered. But both of us were single then, and every so often John or I would make the trip and the two of us would get together for a weekend of beers and reminiscence. On several occasions I came up to visit him here in this cottage. It would have been summertime, of course.

The year John won the Crown (God I love that phrase, so beautifully, reprehensibly precise), things changed dramatically. We'll get to that, but for now I have to say that John realized very quickly that if he didn't want a farce for a throne, he would have to act independently of the wishes of those who had placed him there. And he'd need unaffiliated allies. Being John, he was clever enough to look beyond his immediate options.

At that time I was in Vermont, making a small name for myself in communications at the Governor's office. I had heard, of course, about Canada's homespun venture into monarchy – it was the sort of item that TV stations were tucking into the back of their broadcasts for fun. The *New York Times*, I think, had run some whimsical pieces. But the name, when it eventually emerged, simply failed to register. Why would it? It moved more front and centre, though, a few days later when my answering machine took a message from my old friend John explaining that he'd recently been appointed King of Canada and that he was thinking that he'd probably need a chief of staff, or a royal adviser – he wasn't really too sure at this point what the position was called – but that he thought it would be a good idea for me to come up and talk to him about it. I learned later he'd had to pay the airfare himself. At that stage, royal travel budgets had not been envisaged.

Which brings me – circuitously, I know – to that evening in one of the smaller function rooms at the Royal York Hotel, watching John present an award to Toronto's top woman writer of the year. The reason he was there in the first place was that the actress who was originally supposed to present the prize had cancelled on account of the flu. That's how things worked in those early days. He picked me up at the airport, already wearing his rental tuxedo, and drove me directly to the hotel. Which is how I came to be present at John's first formal appearance as the newly minted King of Canada.

What he delivered, I have to say, was not the address I'd have prepared. Admittedly, it was close to what I might have come up with in the years to come, once I'd convinced myself the whole thing wasn't a fluke. But it sure as hell was like nothing I'd ever have put into the Governor's mouth. The usual format for this kind of function is fairly straightforward: be gratefully humbled by the talent assembled here this evening, say something witty about the person being honoured, drop in a policy plug if the circumstances permit, then get the hell off the stage, smiling at the wonderfulness of it all as you clap your way behind the curtain and out to your car. John did all these things – minus the exit to car, which was parked five blocks away where the outdoor lots were cheaper. Except that he failed to deliver on the two most important ingredients. D&R, I used to call them stateside – Deference and Reverence. Not that John wasn't impeccably polite; he was, very much so; he almost always was. What I mean to say is that the standard practice is to be extremely respectful with regard to the worthiness of the event itself.

This, John was not – or rather, he appeared to be but wasn't.

I forget now who the writer was – one of those mid-list, middle-brow, sari-clad women from the period when Mistry and Rushdie had made Indian writing so hot. And John was nothing if not congratulatory – he'd read her, of course, and thought her work was genuinely worthy – he just didn't think she or anyone deserved a prize that shut out half the competition. Not that he said as much, exactly, on stage. What he did instead was refer to her throughout his talk as the *authoress*.

In those days, you understand, a Hollywood celebrity could comfortably discuss her breast enlargements, she could detail the professional imperative of liposuction and tummy tucks, and would happily grant interviews on the topic of her latest hymen replacement – because, oh my, if she'd only known how precious it was she'd never have given it away in the first place – then boldly stake her ground on the honesty of nakedness (hers) in film, but she would be utterly, absolutely mortified to hear herself referred to as an *actress*. She was an act*or*. To suggest a sexual dimension to her craft was deeply demeaning, to say nothing of discriminatory in the eyes of the law. In those days, we had gender, not sex.

Likewise with the literary arts: a writer could be secretary-treasurer of the Society of Women Poets. She could make her career publishing exclusively in anthologies of women's writing. She could teach contemporary woman's literature at a university at which she was head of the department for women's studies. She could proudly point to her name on the syllabus of women's studies programs in campuses across the continent. But call her a poet*ess* and you might just as well have stuck your hand up her skirt at a Wicca convention. Some things just couldn't be done.

And yet John did exactly that.

His first use of the word was followed by a shocked, uncertain round of silence. The kind in which well-bred people glance at their neighbours, mutely asking if they'd really just heard what they thought they'd just heard. The next hit, moments later, confirmed to everyone that the first had not been an unfortunate slip of the tongue, and now the silence spread to every corner – then found its voice again in angry, anxious murmur as John struck with the suffix again and again, catapulting it into the crowd in unrelenting salvoes, launching it from harmless, happy sentences where it exploded like a stink bomb in the faculty lunchroom. He heaped praise upon the *authoress*, he congratulated the committee for its selection of the *authoress*, and expressed his sympathy for the difficult job they must have had selecting this *authoress* from among the pool of so many talented *authoresses*.

And something interesting began to happen. Something I was to witness many times in years to come, but that I watched for the very first time there that evening, as the room perceptibly began to split. One by one, from their scattered chairs across the floor, people suddenly and individually realized they'd taken the point. Part of my role, you understand, is minding the audience. Like a caddie who chooses the club then moves off to where he can see the shot land, one of my functions is recording the strokes my player delivers. Usually I'll pick out faces at random, and stand near the back of the room watching for a change in expression. I was studying a man with his wife sitting two tables over, and witnessed exactly the moment he suddenly got what John was about. The woman was still frowning when the man's eyebrows shot up. He started turning, mouth slightly open in the way we do when we're about to whisper, then caught himself, and squared his body back into his seat.

Without moving, without turning his head, he assessed his partner's reaction, and concluded she hadn't yet seen what he had. A little smile began to form and he looked down at his shoes, suppressing the smile, but not quite.

There's a game we used to play, a parlour game I guess you'd call it, the kind of riddle you can only have played on you once and then must play on others. We called it My Aunt Minnie, but I'm sure it goes by other names. The object of the game was to figure out why Aunt Minnie liked certain things but didn't like others. It was a logic game, with a very clear con-nection linking all of Minnie's preferences (*Aunt Minnie likes connections but not things joined*). You played it with a group so those who'd figured it out could help torment those who hadn't. (*Aunt Minnie likes puppies, but she doesn't like dogs.*) The first stage drives you crazy – then comes epiphany – and much glee afterwards in adding to the distress of those for whom enlightenment hasn't yet descended: *My Aunt Minnie likes the moon, but she doesn't like the sun. Aunt Minnie likes darkness, but she doesn't like dark.* Does she prefer the night over the day? *No, she likes neither night nor day – though Minnie's partial to the afternoon.* As individual players solved the puzzle, they'd begin to add their own contributions. *Minnie likes kittens, but she doesn't like cats. Minnie likes swimming, but she hates having swum. Minnie hates autumn, but she does love the fall.* And so on . . .

You've probably guessed already that Minnie likes any word with double letters. It's easier to spot in writing. If you haven't yet, I've robbed you of your moment of pleasure: that instant you realize you've worked it out – when you pause, mouth open – when you're just about to blurt out how obvious it is, now you've seen it, but check yourself because part of the plea-sure is the awareness that others haven't yet got to where you are. What I'm hoping you can capture is that moment when you smile and look down at your shoes – that moment of sudden awareness that now you're playing from the *inside*. (*Minnie likes winning, though she's bored with having won.*)

That's what I watched in the Royal York that night. I watched one face after another suddenly click. I watched individual moments of understanding dawning all over the room, and I watched the pleasure it brought, the sudden, secret understanding – and the instant bond among those who'd recognized themselves as insiders too. I watched *appreciation*. I watched people suddenly thinking, Now this is different . . .

God, he was clever, our John – he manipulated people by getting them *thinking*. Completely the opposite of how it's normally done. John won people over by tickling their brain cells, by sparking their neural connections, linking their synapses, engaging abstraction – the very faculties people in our business typically do everything we can to suppress. John's genius was in making people think they were like him.

And it wasn't just the men. His ratings, of course, were always higher with women, even after that global glam-fest of a wedding. But with an attack on affirmative action in a forum like that you'd think a larger number of women would have been offended than men. Looking around the room, I could see this wasn't so. The women who got it looked charmed – looked *flushed*, in fact – as if he'd touched their leg under the table and they'd decided that they didn't half mind. Thank God for women, I always said. It would have been a far more difficult journey without the polls we got from women. On the other hand, after Gwen . . . but I'm getting ahead of myself again.

Here's the caveat, and there always is a caveat: the ones that were pissed off were *really* pissed off. I'm talking about both women *and* men. There will always be those too fundamentally entrenched in their beliefs to admire cleverness of any sort.

There was a segment of ideologues in the room that night – there always is, and the literati has its dogmatists like any other group. These people were grinding their teeth well before John was done.

The thing to remember about ideologues is that the ideology itself doesn't matter. All that matters to the dogmatist is the cancellation of doubt. Believing relieves the necessity of thought. Part of the audience, I saw to my professional delight, stood up and stormed out of the room. Their departure did not go unnoticed.

There was, in the way of these soirées, a small contingent of media present to report the evening's events; a minor one, by national standards, but a potentially potent one nevertheless. Arts reporters tend to underestimate their own significance; people in my business recognize that they're often the first to pick up on new developments. It's valuable to know this. A handful of arts reporters, sent off to fill a half-column hole above the horoscopes, suddenly found themselves with news-worthy material. One of them, as it happened, was standing right beside me.

I can always spot the media types. There's a bicameral sort of quality to someone whose job is to report on the significance of others – a kind of splintering of personality, for want of a better image. It's as if their brains are divided into chambers. One part's listening, taking things in the same as everyone else, while the other part is processing *news* – information of profes-sional concern that may or may not be of interest to the more autonomous hemisphere. After a while, it shows in their expres-sions. Journalists have to school their minds to simulate concern about things they're not really interested in. The best ones – or should I say the most successful – cope with this by teaching themselves not to be interested in anything. Most brains, however, are not so biddable, and the average hack has trouble suppressing the buzz of excitement when something sneaks along and strikes subjectively.

That's what I saw in the handful of reporters present at the Royal York that night. John had engaged them on a personal rather than professional level.

I flipped open a notepad and pretended to be scribbling furiously. "Wow!" I said and scribbled some more. Understanding how to work the media is a matter of grasping one simple professional truth: *it doesn't matter if you miss a story as long as everybody else misses it too – but failure to report on what your competitors are reporting is disaster.* Hook one, in other words, and you've landed them all.

The guy beside me nodded distractedly, churning copy in his own head, flipping material from one side of his brain into the other part that paid the mortgage. He looked up and nodded, took me in and nodded again – more in confirmation of his own position than in response to mine. When I moved on to stand beside a woman fussing with a tape recorder, he was punching numbers on his cellphone.

And that's how it started. John went that evening from being a joke to – well, I'm getting ahead of myself again – and I moved my life to this country. Both of our lives – many peoples lives, if you want to look at it that way, millions of lives – changed that night. But that's another day's story.

It's dark. I'm cold. Tomorrow I'll have to see about getting some wood.

DAY SEVEN

THE MORONIC DOG has saved my life.

After all this – after everything – it comes down to the presence of a dog. How absurd, how bizarre to consider that if it had not been for the dog, I would now be dead and, with me, this narrative. It tempts me, almost, to take up metaphysics, or lay my head in the lap of the divine. (I must remember too, before all's done, to sketch out John's views on the role of accident in history.)

I don't even like the dog. It's sitting here now as I write, wagging its idiot tail, panting puffs of steam beneath the table, hoping, if it can keep up eye contact long enough, that maybe I'll take it for another walk like yesterday. The dog, at least, thought it was great fun. Or most of it. For a moment there, when it looked like I might pull him down with me, I saw the terror in his eyes too. But the second he was out of the water you'd have thought it was the greatest game invented – barking, chasing his tail, running in circles like the moron he is – and me still shaking and gasping on the ice, wondering if I'd freeze to death anyway. I would have too, if it had been much farther, or if the weather had been anywhere near as cold as it was a few days ago.

It was the thaw that put me in the water in the first place. I went through the ice, is what I mean to tell you, a quarter-mile from home on the far side of the island. Any farther and I'd be there still.

Now that I've had a bit of time to think about it, it explains some things that had been puzzling me. I couldn't figure out, for instance, why the snowmobiles never come near the island. I can hear them in the distance. When I walked into town, whenever that was – a few days ago – there were snowmobile tracks all over the wide parts of the lake. I've become a great fan of snowmobile trails; they make travelling so much easier. Snowmobiles beat down the snow; if you can find a snowmobile trail going the direction you want it's almost like they've built a sidewalk for you. But none of them come near the island.

There's a map of the lake on the wall behind the wood stove. It's an old map, yellow at the corners and cracking where the thumbtacks pin it to the panelling. But it's a good one, the kind that notes the water depths in two-foot increments. If I'd paid more attention to this chart I might have saved myself an early glimpse of cold mortality. What it tells me, now I've had the wit to look, is that there's a current moving through the lake. Water enters from the north and flows out over a dam at the southern end; beneath the ice it's always moving. Moving water, as John would have been the first to advise, resists solidifying. A look at the map shows that the channel I was crossing yesterday is one of the shallowest parts of lake, narrow too, to further increase the flow. Faster water, thinner ice. Snowmobilers don't come near the island because they know the ice around it is dangerously unstable.

The dog and I were out stealing wood. There's no other cottage but John's on this island; the nearer ones across the way we've plundered already. We had a small woodpile here to start with, stacked beneath the eaves against the back bedroom. John used to go up weekends in the fall, whenever he could get away. It's tradition in these parts to close up the cottage on Thanksgiving weekend – after that there's too much risk the pipes will freeze. But October nights are cool, and people with wood stoves keep a stack of fuel handy to help with the chill. John's supply was meant for weekend burning. Now, in January, with the fire going day and night and still barely making a dent in the cold, I burned up every stick the first week out.

The dog and I have been spending an hour or so before the light fades scavenging across the way. It amazes me how quickly a civilized, largely urban being can settle into what amounts to a hunter-and-gatherer lifestyle. Unless there are stashes still lurking beneath piles of snow I haven't yet been able to locate, I can say with confidence that I've used up all available fuel within sight of John's dock. If worse comes to the worst, I can start cutting trees, but at this stage it's still easier to go out and find wood that somebody else has already chopped.

John's cottage faces south. Until yesterday, the dog and I had done all our off-island foraging strictly on this side, directly across from the dock. It's much easier to walk over windswept ice than inland snow. Among the trees it gets up to your waist; out on the ice it's usually at knee level or less.

Unfortunately, most of the cottages directly across the way don't seem to be equipped with wood stoves. So yesterday we decided to go north and try our luck off the back side of the island. The deal I've worked out with the dog goes like this: he pulls the toboggan when it's empty; I pull when it's full. I'd prefer it the other way around, it goes without saying, but the dog lacks the necessary girth and gear to haul a heavy load. When huskies pull a sled, they're fitted with a harness that wraps around their torso. They pull with their bodies, in other words, not with their necks. All I have for this dog, alas, is a regular collar that chokes off his wind if he's straining at anything with very much weight.

An empty toboggan, however, is doable and has the added benefit of keeping him in the trail right behind me rather than running all over the place and making a fool of himself. At least he helps me tramp down the snow.

When we got to the far side of the island, I sat down for a breather. But not for as long as I'd have liked, because any time I put myself at ground level, the dog assumes he's being invited to play. After he'd knocked my hat off twice (or should I say the wool sock I use as a hat), I gave up and headed out across the ice. We weren't more than twenty steps beyond the trees when, suddenly, I was under water.

Just like that. One second I was on solid footing, the next under the ice. It says on John's map that the lake's only eight- or ten-feet deep where I went in. But anything over your head is enough to drown in, and I couldn't pull myself out. My clothes and boots filled up with water, and in a few seconds I could barely keep my head out. Funny thing is, I don't remember the cold. Only the water filling my mouth. When I finally got an arm out, the ice beneath it just broke and sent me under again. I came up, gasping – and there was the idiot dog with his nose in my face. Barking.

He thought it was a game. As far as he's concerned, we were just fooling around. It was his lightness, I guess, or the fact that a dog's weight is spread over four feet rather than two – whatever the reason, the dog was still on solid ice. I tried to stretch a hand toward him, but he danced away, yapping. With just my eyes and nose above water, I watched him do that crouch dogs do when they're playing, chin to the ground, tongue lolling, tail swishing circles in the air.

"Good dog," I said, and my mouth filled with slush. When I opened my eyes there he was again, with his nose in my face. This time I managed to get a grip on the rope around his neck.

I won't bore you with the rest, except to say that once I had the lead, I was able to draw up the toboggan. That let me spread enough of my weight so the ice didn't break. I managed to haul myself up like a streaming seal onto an ice floe. The dog went in too, at one point, and I was tempted to leave him there, but in the end I got him out as well. Idiot.

It was a nightmare walk back, that I will tell you, with every step getting heavier and my clothes freezing hard against my skin. Incredible sleepiness. I spent the rest of the day wrapped in blankets curled by the fire. There's still enough wood in the house, thank God, for another day's burning. It wasn't until some time in the middle of the night before the chills stopped.

I'm fine today. I've let myself spend the whole day indoors. Tomorrow, though, I will have to find a new supply of fuel. The dog, too, has been giving me grief about not getting outside.

Is he aware of how much I dislike him?

DAY EIGHT

TECHNICALLY SPEAKING this isn't Day Eight. I did no writing yesterday, or the day before either. For that matter, seven or eight other ones went by before I started. So much for chronology. Day Eight, it is. We'll only number the ones that count.

Yesterday, we hit paydirt.

I have to admit it's therapeutic, this survivalist's lifestyle. My head is clearer than it's been since . . . well, since John. Nothing like a little brush with death, my own I mean, to put life in perspective. As I've said, this was not intended as therapy, but a little on the side won't hurt. I'll get this done, I think. A bit of self-indulgence might even help move things along.

Leaving aside for the moment the breathtaking irony of that last remark, I want also to mention that John would have enjoyed the adventure. He had an affinity for winter, our John. My own relationship with cold and snow has always been somewhat more . . . theoretical. While it's certainly true that the image of John as Winter King was as much a part of my own efforts as his, it's only now I've come to understand what that was really all about. I mean by that the significance of winter to John personally, rather than its usefulness to me as a marketing angle.

I have not expressed myself well.

I don't wish to leave the impression that during all that time I helped John transform the consciousness of Canadians by means of their relationship to winter, I failed to understand the process. I understood what we were doing very well. It's just that it had always remained for me an intellectual exercise. Now I *understand* it. I *feel* it. Now that John is dead – now that I am living, in winter, here in his cottage, my presence here occasioned only *because* he is dead – now at last I can say I understand John's understanding of winter.

We uncovered the motherlode, yesterday, the dog and I.

The temperature had dropped again the night before, which I suspect helped thicken up the ice to our advantage. This time, too, I used the map. Rather than choosing the narrowest spot, we crossed where the lake was widest. It added considerable distance, but it worked. Neither one of us went through.

I took precautions this time. Before venturing onto the ice, I hacked down a sapling and made myself a safety stick, like the balancing poles you see with tightrope walkers. This I clutched by its middle – with several feet of trunk stuck out to either side – and, very gingerly, tiptoed across. The route I'd chosen must have been the right one, because as far as I can tell the ice never even cracked. Not during that first experimental crossing or in any of the nine or ten trips that followed.

The place we raided yesterday clearly belonged to someone who took his wood-burning seriously. My guess is a retiree, still youthfully fit, but with enough time on his hands to do things right. In terms of quantity – a full cord or more, at least – this guy had laid in enough to set him up for several seasons of weekend burning. Knotty oak and maple. It took us until nearly dark to haul the pile away. We also swiped his chainsaw, which is going to make life much easier in future.

I'm absurdly pleased with yesterday's accomplishments. This is what I mean by therapy.

Eight days, though – and three of my scribblers filled already – and still I've managed to avoid describing how John came to be King in the first place.

I can think of a number of factors explaining my reluctance, but let's put the main one down to habit. Like most Canadians (and I *have* become Canadian, in citizenship as well as in custom of thought), I've conditioned myself not to think too much about the pre-John era. A case of the physician healing himself, perhaps – but I am not being the least bit facetious when I write that by the latter part of John's reign it had become a sort of unwritten, unspoken policy in Canadian political circles not to dwell upon the nature of John's ascension. Too much reflection on that time leads to speculation of how easily things might have been otherwise, which makes for grim meditation. No one likes to look a gift horse in the mouth, as they say. All the more so now the horse is dead.

John's monarchy, not to put too fine a point on it, was a total, absolute, ridiculous fluke.

But as the King himself would also say, never underestimate the role of accident in history. Since Marx, I think – since Genesis, for that matter – we've been absorbed with the notion of historical determinism, that old idea that events unfold along a path of logical, if not predictable, ascent. Randomness – as it applies to human development – is too uncomfortable a notion to apply to ourselves. However grudgingly we've come to accept the role of chaos in the wider universe, when it applies to our own evolution – when it comes to human history – we just can't shake our infatuation with destiny, that firm and fond conviction that history moves from one stage to the next toward a higher, greater good.

Crap. All history is accident.

DAY NINE

I'VE SETTLED INTO THE HABIT, while the room warms up enough to thaw the ink, of rereading what I have set down so far. The more it accumulates, the greater its effect on what comes next – which does suggest a role for history in the process of evolution. Interesting too. But not what I want to talk about.

Today I wish to come back to some observations I made about the nature of ideology before I fell into the lake. John would often call its practitioners *ideologists*; a very pleasing word, I think, with a hint of other useful words within: *id*, *idiot*, *idolater*. Ideologists, according to John, were best described as people who willingly surrendered their thinking. They were a mixed blessing for us.

On one hand, the ideologists were extraordinarily useful – indispensable, in fact, as darkness is an essential quality for understanding light. On the other hand, they mattered far more to John than they really should have.

If John's great genius was in persuading other people that they were like him, his greatest shortcoming was his tendency also to believe in the flip side of this. John considered the rest of humanity perfectly capable of making the same mental connections he did. He refused to see stupidity as innate, something some of us are simply born with; he saw it as wilful, deliberate, self-imposed – a state in the domain of sin itself.

For John, stupidity was a genuine evil, an affront to the first principle of humanness – an enemy to be struggled against just as evil is meant to be struggled against. A thing to be conquered, or, at least – and perhaps more accurately – a condition never, ever, willingly surrendered to.

Any writer will tell you that a story needs conflict, that a story without conflict just isn't a story. John's life, John's reign, was *a story*. To make that story work, it needed conflict. The ideologists provided that. They were the antithesis against which John stood so brilliantly in contrast. That was their benefit.

The problem was that John took the conflict too seriously. He hated them. And his hatred wasn't theoretical. He hated them.

When I think about John and his reaction to the ideologists, I'm strangely reminded of Gwen and her reaction to the cold. Despite her marriage to a man the world would come to call the King of Winter, Gwen could never accept the weather as a simple condition of existence. She took it personally. Gwen was affronted by the cold. She would look up, scandalized, while listening to the news. "My God!" she'd say. "It's *minus seventeen!*" in exactly the same tone she might use to talk about an airplane crash or a multiple murder. It made for some awkwardness, let me tell you, what with John and his snow fetishes. But I'm digressing again from my digression.

I often reminded John that this blanket hatred of ideology was itself a form of ideology. This would always make him stop and pull up, shake his head and glare. He hated when I boxed him in a paradox. But the fact remains that for John it *was* an ideology. He was aware of the contradiction, and lived within it, but never reconciled it. John could be as selective in his approach to paradox as anyone else. Gwen, for example. Or, for that matter, me.

DAY TEN

HERE'S ANOTHER REASON I'm reluctant to write about the pre-John era: I was absent at the time. In those days I was still living in Vermont.

But there should be no lack of other resources. Now that John is dead, publishing houses all over the continent will be scrambling to be the first out with a royal biography. This material will not be unfamiliar. Yet perhaps there are one or two windows I can open. Yes, I suppose there are. The series of accidents that put John on the throne are only of significance for the ripples they created, and will continue to create, mind – that *is* important – long after both of us are gone. It's not the fluke I want you to understand, but the means of transforming the fluke.

Your histories will tell you that Canada, before John, was a country on the verge of collapse. You will know that Quebec – which was then, of course, a province – had been for several generations delivering to the rest of the country a brilliant tutorial on the merits of political extortion. You will also know how the remaining provinces (some were faster to catch on than others) and a variety of special-interest groups had gradually learned to apply the Québécois model of self-advancement. The Western provinces, by this time, were threatening to separate too, as were parts of the East Coast after happily discovering a fondness of their own for petro-dollars. Aboriginal groups, meanwhile, were busily carving out independent homelands from one end of the country to the other. All this, I imagine, is standard high-school curriculum. And of course you will know the apparent death knell to Confederation when Toronto – the awkward sleeping giant – finally woke from its servility.

But there are things that happened in Toronto that you won't know, that only John and I and Hester Vale could ever tell you. And both John and Hester are dead. Certainly, you won't know the whole story of Theodore Sapper.

I read not long ago he was trying to get himself into politics. He was running for the local chapter of the NRA, or something similarly Texan, but soon discovered that his background had reduced his chances pretty much to nil. Canadians just aren't popular down there these days, ex-pats or otherwise – even Red Revivalists as gaudy in their pedigree as Sapper. He'd applied for citizenship the very day he moved – and certainly he's proven himself as Republican as Republican can be – but folks down there still can't seem to cotton on to him. Strange, isn't it, that someone once so influential has been reduced to a footnote? But who am I to talk, swaddled in blankets in a wood-frame shack with snow blowing through the shutters.

For a time, though, Sapper was the Magus himself, the Grand Puppeteer. And it's unquestionably true that without him and his headlines nothing would have happened the way it did. It was Sapper who first came up with the idea that Canada should have its own monarch.

This was strictly a business decision, originally – a straight-forward, share-driven scheme to sell newspapers. Sapper owned a chain of them, the country's largest, and was the kind of pub-lisher to give himself a very free hand editorially. In one of his unsigned op-eds, he'd floated the notion that a nation as glori-ous as Canada should at least have its own head of state. The subtext was clearly understood to be ironical: the chief editorial philosophy of Sapper's papers was to mock the country. (It was very much a tradition among Canadians in those days to belittle themselves – a tendency Sapper's papers seized every opportunity to exhibit as typically Canadian self-loathing.)

The official head of state, pre-John, was of course the Queen of Great Britain. You'll be familiar with the history, although I expect that some of it still will seem very strange. The British monarch's authority was officially exercised by the Governor General, a political appointment made by Canada's Prime Minister. Surprisingly, the country had run smoothly enough with this admittedly peculiar system for more than a century, with the Prime Minister's Office making all the real decisions and the sovereign's representative ceremoniously rubber-stamping each one into law from the stately confines of the Crown's official residence in Ottawa. Rideau Hall, they called it, and still do to this day – although I think in recent years it's been redeveloped as a housing complex for retired civil servants. Sapper's editorial thundered on about how typically colonial it was that Canada should have a foreign monarch. This, too, was by no means revolutionary.

From time to time, editorial writers were inspired to take a poke at the Governor General. It stirred things up a bit if news was slow that week, and sometimes provoked a printable spasm of public debate. Sapper's papers often attacked the GG as functionally useless (and redoubled the criticism whenever one attempted anything of value). His argument for installing a *Canadian* head of state was actually fairly original, in that it took the old, familiar one step further (at one time, he reminded his readers, the notion of a Canadian Governor General was equally unthinkable: until the 1950s, they'd all been lords and viscounts born to English aristocracy). The article had coincided with an uptick of public interest around the GGs and their spouses – a juicy little scandal had been swirling over Rideau Hall for months, involving a nanny, if I'm not mistaken, and eventual proceedings of divorce (adding the *vice*, as Sapper phrased it, to *vice*-regal, and inspiring a frothy debate as to whether *exes* were entitled to be *Excellencies*). But no one – least of all Sapper – expected his rants to be taken seriously. There was no shortage of genuine crises facing the country already.

A few days later, though, an open letter from the Premier of Quebec appeared on the paper's front page. The letter strongly endorsed Sapper's proposal to immediately pursue the creation of a properly indigenous head of state.

Now *that* got people taking notice.

One of the reasons I've been so reluctant to start into all this ancient history is that I knew how difficult it would be to wrap up, once begun. The same used to be said about the Constitution – *if ever that file was opened, you will never be able to close it again.* Well, we did, John and I, exactly that. We opened it, and very successfully we closed it again. I promise the same again here. Before I go to sleep tonight it's my intention to finish with this section. I've wasted enough of my paper already on preamble.

But in all good conscience, I'll have to give you a page or two on Quebec.

Quebec in those days was run by a separatist government, meaning to say a provincial government that repeatedly went to the polls exhorting Quebecers to free themselves from the shackles of Confederation – and repeatedly won. At the federal level, it had elected a block of MPs equally committed to the goal of separation. By the time of Sapper's editorial, the Canadian Parliament was so regionally splintered that the Bloc had actually won the second-greatest number of seats in the House of Commons – and not for the first time. Meaning to say that Her Majesty's Loyal Opposition was sometimes a party committed to breaking up the union Her

Majesty technically governed. This, too, I think, will give you a flavour of how strange a place this must have been back then.

The important thing to understand is that very few Quebecers actually wanted independence. This is obvious now but was strangely opaque to Canadians then. Decades of separatist policy had been wonderfully good for the province. For every dollar Quebecers paid in income tax, they got back many times that in federal expenditures meant to bribe them into staying. Quebec voters had become uncannily perceptive in maintaining the threat of separation without ever actually committing themselves to the deed itself. There was a natural ebb and flow to the game, though, and Sapper's editorial happened to have come along at the bottom of an ebb.

Polls around that time were showing that Quebecers seemed to be easing up on the trigger. The optimum number, from a leverage perspective, was a 49 per cent response in favour of secession. At 49 per cent, the separatists could perpetually claim to be *almost within reach* of their goal, while the federal government – terrified that only such a slender differential separated *them* from disaster – could be safely counted on to cut whatever cheque was called for. If the polls were running at 45 per cent or less, however – in other words, if significantly more than half of Quebecers indicated that they did not want to separate that week – Ottawa might be tempted to relax a bit and consider allocating resources somewhere else.

At the time of Sapper's editorial, Quebecers had been peering beyond their borders and observing that the goose that laid the golden eggs was looking a little green around the gills. If they actually killed it – well, enough said. That concern was starting to show up in the polls. This was bad news for the Premier. A government whose stated purpose is separation could not afford to let enthusiasm for separation drop too low before this started to be interpreted as a lack of confidence in the government itself.

I have to admit here and now that Quebec, in those days, produced smarter politicians than anywhere else on the continent. The loss of talent to the country was truly appalling, when Quebec's ministers finally withdrew from the House, and the massive defections from the civil service very nearly crippled us. But that's another day's story. The point I want to make now is that only a master politician would have seen the opportunity presented in Theodore Sapper's editorial. It was genius.

I keep repeating, I know, but I'll say again that no one ever took those editorials seriously. With a single letter, though, the Premier made the country do exactly that – to his great political gain. It was a truly no-lose proposition, once you think about it, really no more than a logical continuation of established tradition. The real genius was dreaming it up in the first place.

Keeping Quebec in the country had become a national mantra by that time. Something so important that, for a great many years, Canadians had willingly granted the province exclusive rights to provide the country's prime ministers. Generations of separatist threat created a tradition whereby only Quebecers – or politicians sworn to uphold Quebec's special status – ever made it into Cabinet.

In his response to Sapper's letter, *Le Premier Ministre* was simply taking advantage of an abstract opportunity to advance this principle to a higher level. A made-in-Canada monarch, he reasoned, would have to be chosen from either Quebec or somewhere else. If from Quebec – which totalled barely a fifth of Canada's population – then *bien*, he could turn to his constituents and observe that now they had a monarch, as well as a PMO, serving to advance their own interests until such time as they embarked upon sovereignty.

If, however, the newly created monarch came from any region *other* than Quebec – well, this would be an outrage, a humiliation, yet another signal of English Canada's savage efforts to bury Quebec's unique way of life beneath the crushing weight of anglo monoculture. Whichever way the coin landed, you see, would work to his advantage.

But never for an instant did anyone in Quebec or anywhere else ever take this as anything but an exercise in political distraction. It was stirring the pot; a perfunctory jab at discomforting the enemy while reminding the troops at home that no opportunity was lost in advancing the cause.

Then the second letter appeared.

This one was signed by the Premier of Alberta.

Alberta, historically speaking, was the country's second hotbed of succession. Its brand of independence was largely a reaction to Quebec's. Alberta was passionate in its objection to the federal government's eternal surrender to Quebec. It truly and deeply despised Ottawa for the way it had allowed itself to be emasculated. So deep, in fact, was Alberta's antipathy for federal weakness that it unfailingly supported any initiative to further enfeeble the federation.

Quebec's letter in support of a dangerous and divisive notion to plunge the country deeper into acrimony, in other words, was exactly the kind of proposal Alberta could always be counted on to wholeheartedly endorse.

Alberta's letter caused an even greater stir than Quebec's. For one thing, it was well written, well reasoned, and diplomatically phrased, which in itself was unusual for anything originating directly from the desk of an Albertan Premier, a surprising number of whom were Baptist Creationists or former CFL linebackers. With the benefit of hindsight, it's difficult not to see the hand of Theodore Sapper behind this letter. There were famously close ties between Sapper's office and the Premier's:

Sapper was a notorious right-wing defender, the Premier a right-winger notoriously in need of defence.

In any case, Sapper was quick to capitalize on the public debate he'd so unexpectedly sparked. He was clever, was Sapper, the more so for being fundamentally a fool.

He instantly commissioned a series of polls to canvas Canadians on their views as to the merits of a made-in-Canada monarchy. These were not insignificant surveys, by the way, but large, expensive, and statistically valid cross-country sweeps. The questions were constructed so that their results could be broken down by province. What Sapper expected to see, I'm sure, was the same predictable pattern of regionalism.

Canadians, by this time, could be relied upon to never agree about anything. Whatever was favoured in the East was certain to be opposed in the West, and there were no limits at all on what might be construed as offensive to Quebec. This made for reliable copy, from a publisher's point of view – controversy, as any editor will tell you, is the heart and soul of journalism. Sapper's papers were particularly adept at teasing up minor disagreements until they became major enough to make front-page headlines, which could then be sent out to the newsstands and cable affiliates in advance of his competitors. Remember that the media swims in schools. If one fish dives for a morsel of bait, the rest are driven by instinct to descend even faster.

But the results of Sapper's polls honestly shocked everyone. So much so that every other media organization rushed out to do their own research. The numbers, though, all came in the same. A solid majority of Canadians *strongly favoured* the creation of a Canadian monarchy.

What was even more surprising was how this response held up across the country. Nowhere – *not even in Quebec* – did support for a patriated monarchy drop below 60 per cent.

I can't overstate how shocking this was to the pundits.

It crowded everything else off the front pages of every newspaper, nationwide. It was the lead story for every radio and television network from Whitehorse to St. John's. The country was suddenly abuzz with the notion of a domestic monarchy. Truth be known, it was more the fact that Canadians had *agreed* about something that made the story so hot. But hot it was. And Theodore Sapper was in it up to his chin. In one of those eerie demonstrations of the media's ability to feed on itself, Sapper was now appearing on talk shows and giving news-hour interviews, weighing in with his personal views on this startling development.

I used to keep a box of archival tape in my office. Every so often I'd roll some video footage of Sapper's pontification, just to remind myself of where we all started. There he would be, in his Savile Row suit, looking deeply meditative. "I think," he'd say and pause weightily, "I think that Canadians just want to be able to agree about something." (Here he'd look straight into the camera.) "I think Canadians have realized the jig is very nearly up. I think they understand that all the things they see dividing them are just about to do exactly that. I think – however abstractly – they are looking for something underneath it all to pull them back together."

It was bullshit, of course – an exercise in lobbying at its most manipulatively cynical – but Sapper had nailed it absolutely. He never did understand how accurate he was that day. Sapper was only out to keep his fires burning. He was only marketing. But John did understand. Later, when all this absurdity landed him – *deus ex machina*, if ever the term was applicable – on a stage where he could put that understanding to work, John became the physical incarnation of Sapper's own observations. But Sapper himself could never understand that. This is the problem with people who grow to be too clever, it gets in the way of their thinking. The country, though, was already seething with nervous excitement.

Until Hester Vale weighed in with her own little bombshell.

Hester was Mayor of Toronto. She died a few years ago in one of those freakish accidents that leave us all too cold to think about. As a gesture of respect and a symbol of the ties between Toronto and the Crown, John was scheduled to act as pallbearer. He had to cancel. I stood in for him that day. It would never have done for the public to witness their King so catatonic with grief. Or Gwen either, more pragmatically.

Hester was in a very real way as responsible for everything that happened in the early days as John himself. I had no role in what went on with Hester, or very little. That was John. John and Hester.

It's an imprecise analog, I admit, but in several ways it's useful to think of Toronto as a microcosm of the country. I mean this in the sense that conditions in that city provided a mirror to those of the nation as a whole. Toronto, at the time of Hester's election, had slid so low it was no longer aware it was sinking. Not that it wasn't still the economic heart of Canada – even then it generated nearly half the country's gross domestic product. It was simply that, as a city, it had lost all awareness of itself. If Quebec was the place where most money in Canada was spent, Toronto was the place where it was earned. But no one in the city cared. Its citizens were so habituated to the futile squabbling of their political masters that they envisaged no role for themselves other than that of the country's indentured provider. Toronto was the milk-cow of Confederation, a cow systematically starved into absolute docility.

Until Hester.

Toronto's duty was to be taxed. While the federal government pumped money from the city to pay for daycare in Quebec, Toronto's public schools were being closed for lack of funding. While parents in Toronto mortgaged themselves to send their kids to university, tuition in Quebec was subsidized by federal grants. While the provincial government was busy building golf courses for its constituents north of the city, and paving every second side road from Newmarket to Timmins, Toronto was selling its municipal parkland just to stave off bankruptcy. Everyone jokes about their potholes. But the cracks in Toronto's pavement had turned into craters; every summer, major arteries were washing out for lack of simple upkeep. Sewers had been leaking filth for decades. Toronto's previous mayor – the mayor before Hester – was a used-car salesman who dressed up in prison stripes for TV commercials and screamed at the camera that his cars were so cheap, people thought he'd stolen them. I'm not making this up. It stretches credibility, the depth to which the city's self-esteem had sunk.

Until Hester.

I could go on for pages about Toronto. For an outsider like me, there's just something absorbing about the evolution of a city's personality. John used to say that political entities are made up of people, so we shouldn't be surprised when they behave as irrationally as people. This was certainly true of Toronto.

Hester was at the peak of her powers the night she and John first met at the Royal York Hotel. That was the night John delivered his maiden speech at the award for Toronto's top woman writer of the year. She was the presiding official. It was Hester, as a matter of fact, who handed John the envelope containing the name of the winner.

As it turned out, Hester and John discovered they had quite a lot to talk about that night. One of my first responsibilities as political adviser to the new King of Canada was ensuring that no one – most particularly Hester's husband – had any notion of how late into the evening those discussions went. My Ukrainian grandfather used to say there was more than one way to peel a turnip, but the old way is usually best.

DAY ELEVEN

WHEN IT CRACKS, the ice makes noise like thunder. Think of cubes in your glass. Drop them in, pour the Scotch, and listen – that tiny crackling sound as the bond between the crystals snaps. Purists will tell you that whisky should be taken neat – and perhaps there is justification to that if your focus is strictly with the whisky – but purists tend to cluster at the dim end of the spectrum. There's something about the fracture and pop of the ice that enhances the experience. With ice, you feel it in your hand as well; that tiny, percussive vibration once the cold's been compromised. Ice adds. It increases complications; it mixes sound and touch on top of taste and smell. Putting ice in your Scotch represents an expansion of experience rather than a narrowing. It's the very opposite of Zen. That's what John would have said.

Only now, at this stage in my life when it's far too late to do any good, I've finally come to understand what's so fundamentally foolish about all those New Age spinners of self-help sophistry. The Buddha-hucksters are always at us to pare away complexities, but the point is, we *like* complexities. In fact, we need them. They define us. It's our perpetual search for complexity that *makes* us human. Any philosophy that urges you to sever your connections is only asking you to make yourself more stupid. You might just as well sign up with the Reds.

So fuck Zen.

I bought a bottle of Scotch while I was over in town. But that isn't what I wanted to talk about. Let me get back to the ice. Imagine those audible fissures in your glass amplified a hundred million times. Imagine standing on the ice cube when it's dropped into the Scotch. Imagine feeling the fracture in the soles of your feet. That's what the lake does. It rumbles like thunder. At first I tried to tell myself it *was* thunder, except that clearly it was coming from below instead of above. Scares the crap out of you, when you're standing on it. Even the dog had sense enough to cower. Suddenly there's this ripple you feel through your knees and it's moving toward you then under you and finally rumbling away and off into the distance. Then you notice this two-inch gap in the ice, crackling away to the horizon, and water welling out.

And you think to yourself, Now what?

The thing is, that's it. Nothing else happens. Eventually you realize the ice has cracked but also that it does that all the time, and you tell the dog not to be an idiot, and keep on walking into town to get your groceries.

And maybe you decide you'll pick up a bottle of Scotch while you're about it.

We were running low on food, but most of all what I needed was paper. I'd laid in what I thought was plenty to get started, but as it turns out it was nowhere near enough. (For some reason I also lugged in my laptop. But the battery's run down and with no hydro to recharge it – old habits die hard, apparently.) I got lucky in town, though, with the paper. The general store must have got in a shipment of school supplies, because there were boxes and boxes of lined yellow notepads. I bought out the lot. The salesgirl looked at me quizzically this time. But there isn't much I can do about that either.

DAY TWELVE

WON'T DO THAT AGAIN. The chills from a hangover are bad enough without waking up with a frozen foot. Seems I passed out last night and let the fire die. Lucky thing I had the sense at least to crawl into bed and get under the covers, but I guess one of my feet was hanging out enough for the skin to freeze. I don't think it's too deep, but it looks ugly, and hurts like hell. Serves me right.

It was nice at first, though. Sitting at the kitchen table with the bottle and thinking of all the other bottles we'd emptied over the years, John and I – gin in warm weather, Scotch when it started turning cooler – all the talks and all the ideas floating back and forth. Sometimes hard-assed politics, sometimes the squishiest of metaphysics. Sometimes just football, or women.

I got all maudlin, sitting there by myself with my bottle. Self-pity is detestable.

But I have to admit that today I just don't feel up to politics. And I'm in too much pain for frivolous abstractions. As for women – not now. So let's tackle football.

Football plays an important part of this story, the story I want to tell you of how John made good of being King. Football itself, of course, couldn't be less important, it's just a spectacle, a game, but in a political life any meaningless thing has the potential to suddenly blossom with significance. *That's* what I want to tell you.

Funny, but just this very moment I've remembered some-thing else John said. I can't remember where we were when he said it, or what brought it on. But I've just had this flash of memory of John wondering if there might ever have been such a thing as a political muse. Are you familiar with the Muses? In classical mythology, they were the daughters of Zeus, I think, and one of the goddesses, I've forgotten which – but they were said to be the origins of all poetic inspiration. The ancients believed that poets themselves didn't come up with their ideas, the Muses did. The poets only took dictation. I have this clear recollection of John asking if there was ever such a thing as a muse for politicians – it must have been after something that worked out particularly well, and it was just his way of being coy, you understand, of not taking credit for something espe-cially clever – but I also remember that it pissed me off because I thought if anyone deserved the credit, it was probably *me*. Strange, though, that I can't connect the incident to any partic-ular initiative. Stranger still that the memory would drift into my mind just at this moment.

In any event, if there ever was such a thing as divine inter-vention in the life of a political figure, it would have been John's decision to get involved with the Canadian Football League. John had been King a year or two, I think, at that stage: established, but very much still at the beginning of things.

Having been brought up American, let me admit straight up that I was hardly even conscious of the CFL. Who paid any attention to little-league wannabes except the little-leaguers themselves? That's what everyone thought in those days, including most Canadians.

At the King's Cup game a few years ago, I watched a reporter stick a microphone in John's face and ask him why he'd decided, way back when, to throw his weight behind football instead of hockey – which, after all, had always had the greater claim as Canada's national game. The guy was a sportscaster, you understand, trying to get philosophical, which is seldom a wise idea. But still I get a chuckle when I remember the look on his face when John laid a hand on his shoulder and whispered, "Same reason Champlain got behind the Huron."

This was classic John – in latter years, I mean, when he could afford to play the éminence grise – though I wonder whether he'd have risked it with a real reporter. On the other hand, he might have, at that; it was just the sort of riff he and the smarter members of the press corps got off on. (At some point I'll need to devote a few pages to the utterly – repeat, *utterly* – symbiotic relationship between government and press: horse and carriage, love and marriage – you can't have one without the other, that's what I'm getting at; it's amazing the number of pols who never get that equation.)

When Samuel de Champlain showed up hereabouts in the early 1600s, he arrived in the middle of a war between the Huron and the Iroquois. John remembered a woodcut reproduction in one of his grade-school textbooks, illustrating that Canadian History Event. Privately, very privately, he acquired the original and had it mounted in his inner office. I warned him that his sense of irony would get the better of him if anyone got wind of it, but that was John being John. And to be fair, the room was off limits to everyone but the two of us – and, latterly, of course, Gwen. The historical point of the picture, I mean from John's perspective, was to commemorate Champlain's political acumen, and to remind our sovereign of its lesson every time he looked at the picture. (*My* point was that it wasn't necessary to insist on putting it up right in the middle of the most sensitive part of the land-claim settlements – if anyone from one of the Aboriginal teams had ever got wind of it, we'd have been sunk. But no one peeked, and we didn't sink – and let me herewith accept the wisdom of trusting in one's own sense of irony. Or maybe there *is* a political muse, after all.)

The image shows a helmeted Frenchman with trumpet-mouthed blunderbuss mowing down a bunch of naked Indians, with another bunch of naked Indians jumping for joy beside him. The cheering ones were the Hurons, who up until Champlain's intervention had been the steady losers in their ongoing struggle with their Iroquois antagonists. Champlain tipped the balance, with the advantage now going to the underdogs. The rest, as they say, is history.

And history, as they also say, always comes back to bite you. Hence John's pictorial memo to self.

The point he was making with the sports guy was that he'd made the strategic decision to support football instead of hockey because football was desperate, whereas hockey was not. When it came to the Aboriginal negotiations, the message went a little deeper and quite a lot darker. Rulers from Genghis Khan to Julius Caesar have understood the merits of dividing to conquer. But John liked to have that woodcut up there on the wall, just as a reminder.

Being a sports reporter, the guy had no idea what John was talking about, but the King's instincts, as we know, proved true. The CFL was very, very grateful. Which is why we call it the King's Cup now, instead of the Grey Cup, and why for the last many years it's been the King's – and only the King's – function to kick off the first ball at the start of the game. Most years John would get a bigger cheer presenting the Cup than whichever team had actually won it, and all the players would take off their helmets and bow – which still astounds me, the bowing part – before receiving a handshake from their sovereign.

Of course, the players are all Canadians now – that was one of the rule changes John bulled through – but still I can't tell you what a bizarre experience it was the first time, watching a three-hundred-pound lineman with tears in his eyes, staring at his hand, mumbling how one day he'd tell his grandkids. No need to advise you what glorious television that makes.

John was the only head of state ever to make the cover of *Sports Illustrated*. Everyone seems to have that fact at their disposal, it's one of those little bits of pop-culture esoterica, a staple for TV quiz shows and trivia games. And now it's common knowledge how hard he worked training for that one kick. But back then – the first time, at the start of the very first King's Cup, back, I mean, when everyone was still calling it the Grey Cup – well, you just can't imagine the impression it made.

I admit, I'm not the biggest sports fan, but even I can still close my eyes and see it – John, standing in the backfield, rubbing his hands. It's snowing, just a little snow – not enough to cover the chalk or mar visibility – only an ideal sprinkling, to lend effect. John is standing in his cleats in the backfield, warming his hands, breath emerging from his nostrils in jets of Kingly mist. Everyone in that stadium is wondering what they're all doing here, outside in the snow three days before Christmas. The whistle blows, and John is taking those three long strides – that sound of boot striking leather – and suddenly the ball is sailing. Sailing. Sailing over the heads of the receivers standing with their necks craned, peering up, stunned to see the ball so far above them, then turning, turning, flat-footed still, watching that ball drifting down toward the end zone. What I remember is the absolute silence of those few seconds, every person in that crowd struck dumb. And then the roar, the rippling, thunderous applause of forty thousand fans surging to their feet having just watched a dignitary execute a kick any professional would have been happy to make. And the chant: that chant that's now become a King's Cup tradition – the chant that would unnerve so many kickers in the years to come: "John! John! John!"

"I was lucky," was what he said in post-game interviews. Yes indeed. We'll come back to that. Every year, every single King's Cup since, there has been at least one close-up of John in his seat in the stands, rubbing his hands and doing his best to look embarrassed while the crowd chants his name and some poor bastard down on the field, who's trained all his life for this moment, is coming to terms with the fact that forty thousand fans are telling him to step aside and let the King make the kick instead.

What John did was make Canadian football *Canadian*.

I'm too tired to go into the details, my foot is throbbing and I think I'm running a fever. It's all a matter of record: John got himself put on the board of directors and eventually had himself made chairman, then did an end run on the owners. What the CFL decided to do, ultimately, was retract, retrench, and turn its disadvantages into selling points. With this, I was able to be of some help.

The first and central part of the strategy was returning the game to the outdoors. This meant no domed stadiums, no Astroturf. Real sky, real grass, and real mud or, better yet, really frozen ice and snow. The second, and harder, part was returning the fans as well. This was more challenging, but the one idea worked hand in hand with the other. The whole point of the New CFL – or should I say the whole selling point, the so-called "brand essence" – is that it's a game for genuinely tough players not afraid to play in genuinely tough conditions. Canadian players, in other words, not Dixie Red poufs.

Everything about the New CFL is anti–prima donna. If it's raining, the guys go out and play in the rain. If it's snowing, they play in the snow. (That spirit most famously captured during the "Lightning Rod Game" in Calgary, when a bolt of lightning hit one goalpost and arched over to the other long enough for someone to catch the image on film – which made

Sports Illustrated too, as a matter of fact, and a fortune for the lucky shutterbug who happened to be fiddling with his aperture at just the right moment.)

As for the fans, the buy-in was this: if the players were tough enough to *play* in these conditions, then by God the fans ought to be tough enough to bundle up and watch. It doesn't work for everyone, of course (the vast majority still take in the games on television), but a proper CFL stadium isn't the monolith you see in the NFL – thirty or forty thousand fans will fill them up nicely. Which means all you need is thirty or forty thousand nutbars to go sit in the snow to watch a football game. And here's where having a King makes all the difference.

Sitting in the snow is one thing, but if the King is sitting in the snow and you're sitting with him, then you're not sitting in the snow – you're sitting *with the King*. Think of it as the Versailles effect. John got to be so popular, his presence itself was commanding. If the King was attending a football game, then you'd find an awful lot of people deciding they wanted to be there too. And not just ordinary folks. I'm talking about important people, the kind that other less fortunate people are pleased to call elites. CFL games, especially late-season games and, of course, the King's Cup, have come to be very much a see-and-be-seen event.

One of the interesting little historical wrinkles in all this was the extinction of cheerleaders. Cheerleaders, not to put too fine a point on it, did not fare very well when the mercury dropped much below zero. The league tried, during the first year or two, but pompoms in parkas just didn't cut it, and without the parkas – well, let's just say they tended to stiffen up and lose their bounce. Which meant the cameras had to find something else to aim at whenever the play was whistled down. So they started roving the crowd, picking out faces: actors, entertainers, celebrities of various stripes. As Canadians became more and more politically re-engaged, politicians began making regular appearances too. It didn't take long before your picture on the Jumbotron was a serious affirmation of status – which made the converse true as well. Important people wanted to come to the games to be validated as important people. And the King was the central, gravitational force around which importance revolved.

It was ordained, of course, that John would be in the royal seats down on the fifty-yard line for every King's Cup, and a good bet he'd show up for any playoff games in Toronto, but John was famous for flying to Winnipeg just to catch a Bombers game mid-season or unexpectedly turning up in Halifax to watch the Privateers. He really did take this part very seriously. The King was loyal to his covenants. The Osprey Guard hated it, naturally, but the fans adored it, and CFL events took on a significance among the upper strata of society that had never before been imagined. You'll see the same people at King's Cup games, these days, as you'll see at the Brazilian Ball, or the Gold Leaf Gala, or any of the more important embassy functions – except that for the Cup, they'll have spent a lot more for their outfits.

Permit me to take a measure of credit for the buffalo-robe craze that swept the nation some years ago. Though I'll admit that to start with it was nothing but a bout of snarkiness on my part. John was hectoring that day, as I remember it, trying to talk me into wearing one of those stupid hats for some function in Calgary – and I was refusing. Sometimes we could become quite heated in these little debates, and when he started in with the old respect-for-tradition argument, I shot back with my favourite *ad absurdum* defence. "Then why stop at cowboy hats?" I asked, cranking up the rhetoric. "Why not get ourselves some pointy-toed boots and those big brass buckles – and maybe a buffalo robe to throw over the saddle while we're at it?" (And yes, while

I'm the first to admit that a well-made Stetson is actually very efficient in keeping off the rain if you happen to be out on the range when it's raining, and I'll even concede that gestures like wearing a cowboy hat while visiting cowboy country can go amazingly far in smoothing out the cultural prickles, I won't wear silly hats indoors, and that's final.)

The buffalo thing was pure hyperbole – I was fairly sure I was going to lose this time anyway, because we were having trouble again in Alberta just then – but suddenly John was pausing in that way that let you know he was thinking, that he was about to be very clever – and then he said he had some research to attend to and wandered off and let the matter drop.

I forgot all about it, naturally, having more important things to think about. But John didn't.

That December, when the King's Cup came around, he showed up in a full-length, full-fleeced buffalo robe, sewn from the hides of genuine, erstwhile buffalo. He'd had one made for me too, the bastard. John was never one to underplay his sense of humour.

Thing is, the press went nuts. It was just the sort of absurdity tailor-made, if you'll forgive the pun, to take the chattering classes by storm. Textbook PR was what it was: charmed some, outraged others. Everyone started talking about John's buffalo robe. Suddenly fashion editors had an unexpected angle on the sports scene, and ran with it. Even the *Globe* and the *New York Times* found themselves commissioning think-pieces on the cyclical nature of style, printed alongside archival photographs of Teddy Roosevelt or Ernest Shackleton dressed up head to toe in fur – alongside contemporary shots of *GQ* models strutting the runways in haute couture knockoffs of John's buffalo sensation. The anti-fur lobby got its dander up, naturally, but John by this time had established himself so firmly as friend of the environment that only the extremists turned against him, and their defection was a good thing in the long run. The irony was that John himself was truly surprised by all the commotion (not me – at least not once I got over the shock of finding myself decked out in thirty pounds of pelt).

All of a sudden, though, everybody and his mother was pining for a buffalo robe. Now this could have been disastrous. Buffalo are fairly rare, you understand. They're less rare now than they were then, but even today the stocks wouldn't survive a year if we'd left the market to straight-up supply and demand. (It takes three buffalo to make one robe, believe it or not, which sounds wasteful until I remind you that the meat gets processed too – John was very keen to see the status of pemmican upgraded on the cocktail circuit, for exactly that reason – and although it never came close to outselling foie gras in most of Europe, it's caught on rather well in Asia; the Japanese import it by the ton. John hired a team of chefs to dream up recipes involving eiswein, I believe, and cranberries. Anyway, the stuff they came up with is delicious. We go though barrels of it at Silos society functions.)

The little Ma and Pa outfit that designed those first coats for John and me suddenly found itself fielding hundreds, then thousands of orders. Soon there were more requests for coats than there were buffalo to make them out of. It created quite a pretty little panic. There were hysterical editorials about a second rape of the plains, an environmental catastrophe set to blow up in our faces. But, in fact, exactly the opposite is what happened.

Turns out that buffalo don't do very well penned up in feedlots like cattle. They get bovine tuberculosis, or hoof and mouth disease, or scabies or some such thing. What they do need is big tracts of unfenced pasture, which, until the buffalo-robe craze, made raising them impractical. But when suddenly a single fleece is worth eight or ten grand, well, that loosens certain economic strictures. So now it paid to convert this marginal land – land that was formerly kept productive only by massive overgrazing or artificial irrigation – back to something a lot closer to pre-Columbian plain. And lo and behold, didn't some kind of prairie grass everyone thought was extinct start growing, and then that little burrowing owl that lives in gopher holes moved in, and those adorable foxes with the big ears that were also supposed to be at death's door – and now the environmentalists are getting hard-ons like they haven't seen since their first pair of Birkenstocks, and everybody's happy.

John was over the moon about the owls – we were able to delist them from endangered species status, though the foxes haven't done quite as well (maybe it's the other way around, can't recall) – anyway, he was more pleased about the owls and foxes than he ever was about the buffalo's bullish effect upon the royal treasury.

One of the things you have to soak straight into your bones, if you want to be a monarch, is that *there's never enough money.* Ever. This ranks right up there with death and taxes as one of those universal, immutable truths. So when I saw an opportunity to get in at the ground floor, as it were, it was only prudent to follow up. Shortly after our first buffalo-robed appearance at New Varsity Stadium, when orders for coats were starting to flood in from all over the continent, I acquired an interest in the little Ma and Pa outfit that manufactured them. They were – Ma and Pa, I mean – strongly in need of some seed money, understandably, and that's exactly what I provided. Or rather John did, through one of the many offshore accounts now connected to the Crown. He was a little pissed off, truth be told, about ethics. My own concern was more with optics – but both of us were seasoned enough by this time to deal with these – and at the end of the day I can tell you that we've done some very worthwhile things with our buffalo funds. It's attention to the little details like this that keeps a good monarchy humming.

The only way to keep the buffalo from being sent straight into extinction was to impose very strict conditions on their harvest. And the best way to do *that* was to grant an outright monopoly to a single buffalo-robe producer. But the only way to make *this* politically acceptable was to ensure that the monopoly-holder was Aboriginal. (People were long accustomed to Indians having special status back then, and the notion of Aboriginal groups as *stewards of the land* was clung to rather dearly, still, in popular imagination. This was well before the shooting, I remind you.)

By fortunate coincidence, the Ma and Pa shop that produced our buffalo robes happened to belong to the Blackfoot tribe. So when the government of the day announced that sole and perpetual rights to the production and distribution of all Canadian buffalo robes would be granted to the Blackfoot Nation, as proprietors of the hastily created Buffalo Robes of Canada Co., Ltd., no one was morally in a position to object very hard.

No one, I should say, except *other* Aboriginal groups. The family that manufactured the robes was connected to the Blackfoot's lead treaty negotiator, who in turn was the band chief's brother-in-law. The point that stuck in the craw of certain other tribal councils – say, the Cree, for instance – was that the Blackfoot were one of the first among the prairie nations to sign off on their land claims and agree to start paying taxes like everybody else. The Cree, at that time, were adamantly refusing.

And the moral of the story is this: good things happened for the Blackfoot; bad things happened for the Cree. There was never much love lost, historically speaking, between the two nations; they'd been stealing each other's women since long before the first Europeans showed up on the Prairies. In modern times, both bands had filed claims to great swaths of overlapping territory. It ought to come as no surprise that the Blackfoot now hold title to much of the land they wanted. And the Cree do not. It's also interesting to note that when a group of Cree decided to go into the buffalo business themselves, by way of poaching, the Blackfoot were extremely helpful – *zealous* might be a better word – in locating and prosecuting the malefactors.

There are only a few thousand buffalo robes produced each year, and their sale is strictly regulated. Because demand by far exceeds supply, the entire annual production is sold off each fall at auction. (It's too long a story to tell you how that came about, but Sotheby's supervises the bidding.) People routinely pay as much for a prime buffalo coat as they do for a luxury sports car, and it's the same kind of buyer – the same class of people, I mean – who buy up King's Cup tickets years in advance. Suffice to say the Blackfoot derive considerable income from their interest in buffalo, as does the Crown from its share, and federal and provincial levels of government by means of normal taxation.

So everybody's happy. Except maybe the Cree.

Which leads me back to football. King John's sixty-two-yard kick goes down in history as the stuff of sporting legend. In political circles, though, it's what went on *before* the kick that still leaves the junkies spellbound.

It was my idea to invest in some coaching – simply to avoid the worst-case scenario of John's missing the ball completely and looking like a fool on the news that night – but I have to admit it was *his* decision to behave like he was trying out for the team.

We found an ex-NFLer – a guy who'd never made it past fourth string in his playing days and had taken to drowning his sorrows in all the usual ways, but the moves were hard-wired, brain-to-muscle – and he was happy to come up from Arkansas for the pittance we were able to pay him. He was a good guy, our punter – I've forgotten his name; John would remember – and a surprisingly capable coach. We worked with him every night after dinner, moving around from field to field in schoolyards all over the city. We were still living in Ottawa, in those days, so training in secret was easy. The whole town closes up at suppertime anyway. I can't tell you, though, how often I hiked that ball, or set it up for the kick – or how many variations of Charlie Brown jokes we tormented one another with. But John started getting pretty good. And then he got better. This went on for *months*.

Thing is, when a dignitary kicks off the ball at the start of the game, no one expects it to go any distance. The receiving team plays way up-field, hands on hips, yawning. Sometimes they'll stand almost on top of the guy. They just want to scoop up whatever dribbles their way and get on with the match. So we had the advantage of surprise.

And there were certain other little details we could see to, for instance making sure that John kicked from the south end of the stadium instead of the north. Toronto enjoys what's called the lake effect. Meaning to say that Lake Ontario, to the south of the city, often creates a breeze blowing north. And sure enough the flags were standing straight out that day above the stands. No one had to tell John to lift the ball as high as he could and let the wind carry it for extra yards.

Now, do we call that luck, or something else?

Three kicks that day that went into the books as *shorter* than John's, kicks by pro-ball athletes (all of them into the wind, but no one recorded *that* fact), and John's CFL debut went down as one of the most memorable in sports history. Since the New Rules clearly disallow any alterations in the way the game is played, John's kick will be just as impressive a generation from now as it is today. You'll see. You will see.

Christ, though, my foot is hurting. It was ice-white to start with; now it's gone a splotchy red. It feels like it's been burned, which is strange because the opposite is true. I'm wishing now I had some of that Scotch left over, to help me sleep. Perish the thought. Also I'm wishing I had my buffalo robe. They're warm, I'll say that for them, and wouldn't a buffalo wrap and a jug of whisky nicely finish that Krieghoff allusion?

DAY THIRTEEN

I PROMISE TO GET BACK to how John got to be King in the first place, and I will, but first a postscript to yesterday:

Don't think that John deliberately set aside a century of Grey Cup heritage just to change the name to one that better suited his agenda. That was me. John himself was appalled when people took to calling it the King's Cup. (Officially, of course, it still *is* called the Grey Cup – just as Ottawa is still officially called the Nation's Capital.) He was adamant, in the early years, about correcting anyone – particularly me – who used the new name in his presence. But vernacular is as vernacular does, and common usage wears down the best of intentions in the long run. I was only doing my job in helping evolution along.

You would also be mistaken to assume that John was not a hockey fan. Witness the Olympics year – the year Team Canada was down 4–2 in the gold-medal final, with a period to go. Everyone knows how *that* game ended: how the King barged into the dressing room, kicked out the coaches, forced his own security from the room. Exactly what he said has never been officially recorded. Every player in that room was asked about it afterwards and every one of them refused to say – except the young defenceman, the one who won the Calder Cup that year, who later admitted that the King had whacked him on the helmet with his stick. Sports fans around the world remember how that series turned out, I promise you. And if you don't think the King had a hand in that day's victory, you didn't see the look on the players' faces as they swarmed back onto the ice – or understand what a leader can summon up when summoning is called for. That kind of history also counts, believe me.

It was through football, though, that John achieved his full brand status. He hated that, by the way, the notion that he was a product – like breakfast cereal or a compact sedan. But like it or not, all great public figures are representations of themselves. If they fail in this . . . well . . . they just flat-out fail. You can read it as a chicken-and-egg argument if you like, but there's no such thing as a celebrity without an image to reflect and refract that celebrity. John would pace and growl like a bear if I poked him with this particular stick, but he understood the truth of it.

Part of being a brand is having a logo – or, if you like, a motto – and if you want a handy way of understanding that, think of it as the phrase they pin you with after you're dead. Martin Luther King's was *I had a dream*; JFK's was *Ask not what you can do for your country*; Churchill's was probably *Blood, toil, tears and sweat*. Pierre Trudeau's was certainly *Just watch me*.

John's brand essence was fixed forever in his famous *Be brave* quip. That was the one that grew into his motto, his logo, his brand-attaining moment. In the days leading up to the funeral, the *Be brave* segment looped through the channels almost continuously. You couldn't turn on the television without running into it. As it happened, I was standing beside him when he stopped to utter those now-famous words. You can see me there over his right shoulder, or half of me, at any rate. Which means I had to look at myself all that week too, smiling. Or half of me.

It happened during the second or third King's Cup, I think, before people had entirely convinced themselves they were willing to buy into all this outdoorsiness. We'd just been driven uptown to New Varsity, and the weather *was* inclement. The decision to hold the game at winter solstice was wholly deliberate. And I've always acknowledged the marketing cache to that date, but I also have to tell you that it's always fucking, fucking freezing. I was probably grumbling during the drive up – I've never been as keen as John for these events – and it's possible that he was already thinking of what he'd like to say to me if he hadn't already decided he was going to be sweet that day.

It had become by this time a minor tradition for the King to field questions from the press corps during the walk from the car. These would be lightweight, low-grade sort of blather: Who was he calling to win? What was his thinking on point spread? How would the kicker fare this year? – that kind of bunk. A reporter from one of the trendier stations (easy on news, heavy on personality) had managed to position herself directly in front of the stadium doors.

To stake out that spot, she'd probably have had to get there fairly early, which means she must have been standing out in the weather for quite some time before we arrived. Clearly, her question was meant to be taken as ironic. It wasn't even a question, really – more in the line of a cheeky observation phrased with interrogative intent.

"But, *John*," she wailed, "it's *cold!*"

There was confusion, in the early years, over how the monarch should be addressed. *Your Majesty* was simply too absurd. Likewise *Your Highness, Your Excellency*, or any of those poncey, bootlicking anachronisms left over from the high old days of Rule Britannia. Very early on, almost right away, people settled simply on "John." There was something satisfyingly impolite about that name, something also profoundly democratic. Something splendidly, suitably, no-nonsensibly Canadian.

I'm quite certain that when this reporter had practised her delivery back at the station, it would have emerged in that laconic, lubricious tone we associate with television personalities in short skirts and shimmery blouses. But this was December 22 and bitterly cold. By the time John had passed through the rest of the gallery, she could barely keep herself from shivering, and her lipstick shaded more to blue than pink. So it didn't come out ironic, it came out as a squawk. You could almost hear the goosebumps. Whatever voice training she may have had by this time had abandoned her completely. There was something so fragile in the tone, so utterly opposite to what she'd intended, I think even the cameramen were given pause. John stopped dead. What followed was one of those unscriptable, unarguable, unpredictable moments of television truth. The kind that film can still sometimes record as real, despite the thousand ways we've learned to trick it. And I promise you, it was completely spontaneous.

The King took off his coat and draped it over the reporter's quivering shoulders.

The girl, I'm sure, was mortified; she'd fluffed her line and now was being treated like an orphan, on camera. Professionally, she must have been cringing, but the look she gave him was pure, unpractised woman – Eve regarding Adam on the ceiling of the Sistine Chapel – that kind of look. Too surprised to help herself, I think. (He could have whisked her off to bed right then, if he'd wanted, and in fact may well have later.) But it wasn't the girl's expression that made it to the archives, it was the King's.

He cocked his head in that way of his and raised one eyebrow. That famous John look, the look that almost always made a nation smile to see it. But this time, this first time, it carried a deeper note, an undertone – dare I say it – of paternal rebuke. Foolish girl, his eyes were saying, not to take yourself more seriously. He was smiling; John was always smiling. But it's impossible to watch that clip without picking up the gentle, fond yet mocking note of censure. His hands were on her shoulders.

"Be brave," is what he said, his lips beside her ear, but not so far away the microphones could miss his words. "Be brave," he said, then winked and moved on through the door.

It was *John's* irony, you see, that made the moment.

God bless the CBC. Of all the cameras present, it was the CBC's that perfectly captured the image, and it was a CBC intern somewhere in the bowels of the corporation who had the wit to file it away. Years later, when John was well and truly *Rex*, there it was. Ready to define an era.

As I write this, there are *Be brave* T-shirts cruising beaches and strolling shopping malls in their hundreds of thousands, *Be brave* coffee mugs and neckties, *Be brave* self-help books and billboards. In the wake of John's death, a *Be brave* graffiti campaign has swept the continent. While I was in town the other morning, I saw it spray-painted on the side of a delivery truck rumbling down the highway. It's everywhere, always with its twine of maple leaf and thorn. In the wake of John's death, the PVPV has reportedly added *Be brave* to its List of Un-American Expressions. You have to wonder, sometimes, whose side those guys think they're fighting for.

Be brave.

Here goes, then:

John was chosen King of Canada because he held the winning ticket in Lotto Canada's Be a Monarch! Sweepstakes. Simple as that. The advertising agency responsible for putting together that particular campaign decided to go with a monarch butterfly as its defining symbol, rather than any regal sort of imagery, reasoning that the ticket-buying public would identify more easily with a bug than with the arcane concepts of Canadian kingship. (If you look carefully at the print ads, you'll see the butterfly wears a tiny purple crown.) They were right too.

The draw that week sold a fraction of the tickets it normally did, when the prize was the usual millions in tax-free cash.

The lottery corporation was furious with the government for spoiling its take, complained of political interference, and threatened to sue for lost revenues. The minister in question had to promise she would never interfere like that again, and was later demoted regardless. But ministers, in those days, were dropping like flies in a cold snap.

As I've said, the times were desperate. Quebec was just gearing up for its fourth referendum (it may have been the fifth – I lose track). Advance polls were showing the usual even split between federalist and separatist supporters, but this time that hallowed, spongy group of undecided voters in the middle seemed to be trending in favour of secession. By tradition, at times of referenda, various organs of the federal government would flood *La belle province* with constitutional cash and various less subtle forms of economic incentive. That was just the way things worked. This time, though, time-honoured practice was threatened with a recent series of scandals over how many untendered contracts and dubious sponsorship programs were still being awarded as part of the bill from the *last* referendum. When all the various slush funds and special projects were tallied up, the total amount was staggering even by previous standards, and the government found itself having to withhold any new spending or risk a motion of non-confidence. This shocked Quebecers to the core – what use was Confederation if not to pay for things? – and hardened the hearts of those so-called "soft federalists."

Alberta, meanwhile, was scandalized – and in its usual fashion was blaming urban Ontario. Stalwart Ontarians, according to tradition, invariably supported the status quo vis-à-vis Quebec, which meant consistently rejecting the waves of reformers eternally stampeding out from the Prairies. It wasn't that Ontario approved of things as they were, mind you, it was just that the Albertan alternatives were always even uglier. John liked to quote what he called the Law of Perpetual Error, a rule that held that as long as the parties attacking an issue are more reprehensible than the thing they're attacking, the original problem will only get worse (I've seen him actually pulling out his hair, for instance, watching good environmental policy brought to ruin by the idiots endorsing it).

The irony – when it came to what should be done about Quebec – was that Albertan thinking was as often as not in the right, but that it always came freighted with so much tub-thumping, gun-toting Deuteronomy fanaticism it was impossible for civilized people to take any part of it seriously. What evolved was a condition wherein Albertan voters unfailingly entrenched Quebec's interests, all the while blaming Ontario – which they preferred to think of as Toronto, writ larger – for letting it happen.

So when our satirical friend Theodore Sapper proposed an all-Canadian monarchy, and when a surprisingly romantic majority of ordinary voters appeared to support the idea, a desperate Cabinet was quick to seize the opportunity for political diversion – to say nothing of a handy solution to the spectacle of the Governor General and spouse hanging out their private laundry in the tabloid press. The Prime Minister himself announced that his government would pursue an immediate investigation as to the feasibility of establishing an indigenous monarchy, complete with debate in the House of Commons, an all-party Senate committee, a full Royal Commission, several white papers, of course, as well as a series of town-hall meetings proclaimed from coast to coast to fully ensure transparent public accountability.

The problem, it turned out – once you'd decided you needed a monarch – was where to find one.

Nations with more ancient pedigrees could always dip into the bloodstocks for some descendant of a bygone royal line – if one could be found with the usual number of fingers and toes, and whose jaws met when they chewed. This was more or less what Norway did, last century, which in a roundabout way is what provided us with Gwen. For countries with established aristocracies, there was always the option of recruiting some healthy specimen from the current stock of blue blood. Canadians, as they discovered, had no such tradition – and were deeply charmed to be reminded of this fact.

There was, really and truly, no segment of Canadian society that qualified as anything even remotely resembling a real aristocracy. As John later demonstrated, this was one of the lingering glimmers of goodness Canadians still saw in themselves: a subconscious, subcutaneous bond that threaded its way across the land beneath the surface skin of rancour. (Interestingly too, and as a sidebar: the political classes in Quebec pronounced themselves culturally embarrassed by their lack of an identifiable elite. One of the first things the new President did, post-secession, was to create the order of the *Chevaliers Québécois* – most of whose members were lobbyists grown fat on federal disbursement, but never mind. *C'est la vie.*) To his credit, some of Sapper's editorials waxed quite poetically about what a splendid thing that was to say about a country, that it had no hereditary ruling class, though this was mostly marketing too.

It was also Sapper, with his customary irony, who first proposed the notion of choosing the new King by lottery. After months of debate – interrupted only by yet another change in minority government – Canadians felt no closer to actually having their own monarch than they were when the whole discussion had started. Everything else, meanwhile, was more of the same, or getting worse:

Quebec's referendum had ended with another miraculous 52 per cent in favour of the federation (clearly, increased investment was urgently needed to prevent certain disaster next time round). The federal government had again gone down to defeat – though this time to a coalition of angry Albertans. The West now controlled the PMO, but barely. Their fragile minority government was kept alive only by the support of separatist MPs from Quebec, who could be relied upon to agree with their Albertan counterparts about one thing and one thing only: how thoroughly they both loathed Toronto. All the excitement that surrounded the monarchy issue was dissolving back into that eerie mix of apathy and anarchy so characteristic of those times.

There had been, so far, not a single, sensible proposal for finding a suitable King (or Queen, I should say. I only use the word *King* because that's what I'm used to, but the rules were scrupulously clear on the matter of gender equity). Quebec had produced a very long list of *pure laine* candidates – the very same that later made up the *Chevaliers* – but the rest of the country balked at supporting a monarch who might very well refuse to speak English in public, which in turn outraged Quebecers and sparked riots next Saint-Jean-Baptiste Day. Alberta's legislature had unanimously proposed Alberta's Premier for the job. Not long afterwards, however, the candidate and several of his advisers were caught on film urinating over the charcoal at a fundraising barbecue, which even in cowboy country effectively drowned any rumours he was interested in a run at the throne. Ontarians, in principle, liked the idea of a monarchy but as individuals were uncomfortable with putting their own names forward. (When polled, they tended to spread their support among the more deserving Aboriginal contenders.) Quite a number of applicants came in from Newfoundland and Cape Breton, where it was argued that since many families had refused to learn anything but fishing or mining for ten generations, they had the necessary discipline for a successful career in monarchy.

Some of the strongest contenders, in fact, arose from the Aboriginal communities, all of whom traced their tribal authority back to the beginning of time itself. There were so many of these, however, representing so many different bands and organizations, that their petitions tended to cancel one another out over the long run. A handful, I believe, did emerge as definite possibilities – but all of these were men, which deeply offended the Aboriginal women's wing and pretty much scotched the Indian lobby as a whole.

The country, in all its many parts, was growing more cynical by the day. Then came the next big American terrorist scare, and a deeply Red president who circled the wagons and sealed off the borders and lifted his policy straight from the Scriptures. When newspapers here started into the new Prime Minister for failing to bring home the monarchy at a time of national crisis, people were in a mood to listen – not the least of them the PM himself, who by this time was desperate for something to lift his numbers in the polls and break the cycle of minority governments. This was when Theodore Sapper proposed a national lottery, and that was all it took to set down the path to where we are today.

John kept his winning ticket framed and mounted in his private office. Another excellent reason, I've always believed, for keeping people out of that room.

Tomorrow I'll tell you what I can about Hester.

DAY FOURTEEN

EVERYTHING SO FAR you can look up in any good encyclopedia or download from a reputable Web site. I'm glossing over
it lightly, mostly to refresh my own uncertain memories. I still
wasn't even in the country at this stage of events. And please
also bear in mind that I had to absorb all this myself, and
rather quickly too, upon arrival here. We'll skip forward to the
day I landed in Toronto. John's winning ticket had by this time
been officially verified, and John had just been declared the
monarch designate.

The shit hit the fan pretty much instantly.

It's an ancient joke among Canadians that the only thing
they could all agree about was how much they hated Toronto.
Torontonians themselves would typically chuckle at this, and
dip their heads politely and say ha ha very funny, and try their
best to treat the whole thing as if it really were an exercise in
good-natured familial bantering. But it wasn't. People from
outside the city honestly and unreservedly loathed the place.

There isn't the time right now to explore the underlying
pathology. And to be honest, I've never completely understood
it myself. What I do know is that it was Hester's success in edu-
cating Torontonians as to the astonishing depths of the
country's ill-will toward them that ultimately changed everything here, when first the city, then the nation, rose and shook
themselves of ancient servitudes. But that's another day's story.

What I will tell you is that, flying into Toronto for my first day on the job as John's royal adviser, I was half convinced I wouldn't be staying the week. Truth be told, if I'd read any of the Canadian papers before I left, I'd have never got on the plane in the first place. Canadian current events, though, were not much in demand where I came from so it wasn't until I was in my seat, buckled up with the plane taxiing down the runway, that the flight attendant handed me that day's *Globe and Mail*. I got my first taste of how utterly appalled the country was that the winner of the Be a Monarch! Sweepstakes turned out to be from Toronto.

It was axiomatic in those days that no Torontonian could aspire to political high office, at least not in the federal arena. A generation earlier, a slick Bay Street lawyer had actually managed to get himself made Prime Minister, very briefly, which so upset the rest of the country it all but amended the Constitution to prevent that ever happening again. By the time Hester came on the scene, ambitious young Torontonians had understood for decades that they should focus their talents on generating income, and leave the spending of it to properly accredited Quebecers. Canadians were so ingrained with the notion that nothing good could come from Toronto, transfer payments notwithstanding, that when it was announced the winner was – God forbid – *a Torontonian*, the country suffered a collective embolism.

Even the Toronto media were calling it a scandal.

I can't remember which minister it was in those days, but when the poor dear stood up in the House of Commons and reported that the new Canadian monarch would be – gasp – a Torontonian, she might just has well have rubbed herself with steak sauce and jumped into a tank of piranhas. Right off the bat she was accused of having helped to rig the draw (Toronto was capable of any such perfidy). Then – once she'd proven beyond doubt that John's winning number had popped out as randomly as any other might have – she was even more intensely vilified for having failed to prevent such an outrage. The chair of the Ontario Human Rights Commission was quoted as saying she'd never in her whole career witnessed such an egregious violation of democratic principle.

For some reason, it just hadn't occurred to my adopted countrymen that the computers would fail to properly correct the Toronto factor. To be fair, not all that many Canadians had bought tickets in the first place (by and large, most people here just weren't willing to waste two dollars on a draw you couldn't even take to the bank if you happened to win). But even so, it still seems strange to me that no one had worked out Toronto's percentage of the country's total population, then calculated the odds. There were more people in Greater Toronto, for instance, than there were in all the Maritime provinces combined. Statistically speaking, it was quite a lot likelier that the winning ticket would be drawn from Toronto than, say, Charlottetown. But the good folk of Charlottetown, as with elsewhere in the country, were so accustomed to a system of regional vote distribution that effectively cancelled out Toronto's influence that everyone just took it for granted the same would happen this time too.

Ironically enough, the only place where people didn't give a damn about Toronto was Quebec. Quebecers didn't care if the winner was from Toronto or Tofino, and likely had never drawn much distinction anyway. The simple fact that the winner wasn't Québécois was all that mattered there. A head of state from English Canada was no improvement on a head of state from England – worse, in fact – at least the British royals stayed out of sight on their side of the Atlantic. Quebec's Premier called an immediate press conference, flanked in fleur-de-lys. "Behold the New Colonialism," he thundered, waving a picture of John's face dramatically torn from that morning's *La Presse*. Support for secession increased by ten points the very next poll.

But this was more or less expected. It was also perhaps not surprising that the Premiers of the Western provinces, who just happened to be meeting that week to demand less federal interference and more federal dollars, called a press conference to jointly announce their condemnation of a Toronto-based monarch – or that Newfoundland's legislature should resolve to draft a letter to Westminster requesting a return of its protectorate status. What *was* surprising was how aggressively the government of *Ontario* reacted. Toronto, after all, was supposed to be the capital of that province.

But as Hester later explained, this should not have been a shocker either.

Provincial politics in Ontario were run according to the same principles as at the federal level, when it came to Toronto's place in the order of things, only more so. The city's population amounted to nearly half the province's, but electoral boundaries were set up to ensure that the rural and suburban regions elected far more members to the legislature than the urban ones. From the perspective of the government of Ontario, it was completely unacceptable that the country's new monarch should have close ties to Toronto, let alone be from there. This was nothing short of "a slap in the face," as the minister for agriculture swiftly pronounced, to the rural voters who kept them in office. The Premier of Ontario personally telephoned the Prime Minister, informing him that under no circumstances could he support the present candidate for monarchy.

You'll be asking yourself how Toronto tolerated this, and believe me, I've asked myself the same. It seems incredible, doesn't it, that a place so toweringly important to the rest of the country should be so utterly innocent of the shadow it cast? Torontonians were simply oblivious. I think they just didn't see themselves as different from everywhere else. Or, rather, they didn't see everyone else as different from them. As head office for most of the country, the city's focus was relentlessly, reductively, national. This applied to almost every economic sector, but most of all to the media. Toronto's newspapers, radio, and television served a demographic far beyond the city's own borders – and tailored their coverage accordingly. Even dedicated local programs were careful to appeal to commuters with roots in far-flung suburban municipalities. It seems like a case of far-sighted myopia, I know, but Toronto's first perspective was the nation, not the city. If people in other parts of the country might expect their news to reflect their own interests first, in Toronto the reverse was true. Which accounts for the incredible ineptitude of its local politicians: urbanite voters just didn't give a damn for municipal politics, and really didn't care which moron they elected. They were far too busy fretting over what was going in Charlottetown or Winnipeg.

As theories go, there's still a lot it fails to explain, I know. But it's the best I can come up with short of arguing that five million people were fools.

John liked to say that the best way to avoid a punch in the nose is a punch in the nose. Not so long ago I took a call from an editor at *Bartlett's Quotations*, who asked for a selection of the King's Epigrams, and the punch in the nose one was part of the batch I sent over. As it turns out, this wasn't John's line after all, it was Hester's, and John was furious when he saw it attributed to him. (I told him my concern was with *his* posterity, not his dead girlfriend's, and anyway, it was too late to change history now; these things have a way of coming back to haunt you.) What he meant – John, I mean – was that weakness is the number-one instigator of malignant behaviour. It's one of those simple, sad, but unassailably biological truths. If you dispute it, you've forgotten your time in the schoolyard. Meekness is the crucible of wrath, said John, the catalyst to violence. It brings out the worst in even the best. Which implies a certain moral responsibility in all of us to abjure from passivity in the interest of peace.

Good governance, according to John, is less a matter of preventing aggression than a means of preventing the weakness that provokes the aggression to begin with. Toronto's tolerance of the country's bad behaviour, in other words, only abetted that behaviour. What Hester did, on behalf of her city, was to stand up and poke the country in the nose. Once the blood was wiped away, everyone was the better for it.

But here again I'm hitching the cart before the horse.

The point I was making was that even the Toronto newspapers were up in arms about the choice of John for King; and the shrillest, most outraged voice of all was Theodore Sapper's. His papers blasted the minister for deepening the country's crisis with such a foolhardy foray in populist pandering (he loved a good alliteration, did Sapper) and demanded the minister's resignation. She lost her temper in a press scrum and hotly pointed out that the whole thing had been Sapper's idea to begin with. Headlines the next morning loudly wondered where the government would find its policy next. The poor dear found herself dropped from Cabinet before end of week.

But never underestimate the usefulness of enemies when it comes to influencing friends. Fools, too, serve their purpose. As with horseflies or mosquitoes, even as you're swatting them, it's wise to remind yourself they play their own part in the ecosystem. When Sapper's stable of newspapers so aggressively staked out the anti-monarch territory, it forced the more moderate publications to more or less begrudgingly tone down their own opposition, and steered them down an ultimately monarchist path. But this is all the future too.

All I'm trying to tell you now is how utterly, stupidly appalled I was by the time my plane hit the tarmac at Pearson – and how furiously angry I was with John for having dragged me into this absurdly comic opera.

"Blue!" he said, smiling and waving when he spied me in the crowd.

"*Bastard!*" I think, was the first thing that came out of my mouth.

In the car, John explained that we were going to the Royal York Hotel, where he would shortly deliver his first and probably last public address as monarch before presenting the Woman Writer of the Year Award. You might imagine this provoked another spasm of resentment on my part. Once this had petered out – around the time we passed the Leisuredome – I got around to asking John what he planned to say. He sighed, shrugged in that immensely irritating way of his, and told me that on the whole he'd rather be hanged for a sheep than a goat.

"If you're going to give them Aesop," I said, "why not the one about the dog in the manger?"

I've told you already about his speech that night – the night of his first encounter with Hester – I'm sure I've told you how John so adroitly played the clever fool and won over what should have been a deeply hostile audience. I think I may even have intimated that John was flat-out brilliant that night, which wouldn't have mattered a damn if the Mayor hadn't chosen that very same evening to launch her own historic coup. I haven't told you that part yet.

Hester always swore her decision was spur of the moment, which I've never believed for a second. "I was very impressed by the King's delivery," was what she told reporters afterwards, laying on the irony. Her Worship steadfastly insisted that she'd been inspired by John's performance, and decided then and there to move her own agenda forward. Which is possible. There was a connection between those two that went well beyond hormonal – they jumped at each other's brains as much as bodies – and it's certainly true that each was a whetstone to the razor of the other's mind. So yes, it's possible that something unexpected in John's presence triggered Hester's own political instinct that night. But she was a proactive thinker, not a spur-of-the-moment kind of girl. It's just too much of a stretch to believe she'd have let herself go off like that unscripted. On the other hand, everything that happened later was completely unforeseen, and she rode along with that without a backward glance. So who am I to say? Even so, I'm a skeptic. John's last-minute invitation had to have come from somewhere, and I'm betting that somewhere was the Mayor's office. I'm convinced that Hester planned the whole thing, clever creature that she was. At least the first part, certainly the first part.

When you think about it, the timing was brilliant. Hester always loved to take opponents by surprise. Remember, too, that she was pitching to the home team. At these sort of functions, there's always a pretty fair scattering of hard-core powerbrokers – Bay Street lairds short-leashed by literary wives, captains of industry attending in support of the arts (while furiously browsing their BlackBerries), as well as the small but tactically sufficient assortment of media – if it was spontaneity, it was serendipitous spontaneity. An interesting coincidence, too, I've always thought, that a female politician should choose an award of strictly female merit in which to stake her future. I've often wondered how she and John squared off on that one later.

My own theory, for what it's worth, is that she suspected a leak and moved up her announcement to head it off.

When John had finished his speech and smiled and waved to that segment of the room that was wildly applauding, and I was thinking that at least he'd gone out with the lions instead of the lambs, Hester walked on stage, took the microphone, and briskly announced that Toronto would be separating from the country.

People who were standing up and clapping sat back down. When the room was quiet Hester went on to say the motion had been passed at a session-in-council earlier that evening. And, since the physical embodiment of the Canadian government (she meant John) happened to be present on stage with her that evening, it was only fitting that she direct her declaration to his august person – namely that the independent state of Toronto would shortly be removing itself from the jurisdiction of said body.

Spectators gaped, photographers flashed. I think it's fair to say that this blew John's ironic foray straight out of the water. But somehow the room was silent again when the new King walked back to where Hester was standing and repossessed the microphone.

Three hours later, the two of them were locked together in the conference room upstairs, going at it like minks.

DAY FIFTEEN

WHAT IT IS ABOUT MINKS, I wonder? I ask this only because I saw one just a few minutes ago. While the fire's getting going in the morning I walk around a bit and try to work some circulation back into my leg. I happened to be looking out the window over the veranda when this black, humpbacked, undulating needle came plunging through the snow. It disappeared under the dock, reappeared on the other side, then vanished round the point. There have been trails of footprints other mornings. This explains them. But I wonder what's supposed to be lascivious about a mink? This one seemed a solitary soul to me.

John went through a phase of being quite obsessed with mink. It irritated him that an animal whose defining characteristic was ferocity should instead be identified with lust. I have clear recollections of his opinion on this matter, because I lived through his efforts to convince our new marine corps it should formally adopt the mink as its mascot. That was classic John – he often took on battles he knew he'd never win on principle (a tendency shared with the mink, he pointed out, which argued all the more for its appropriateness – at times he could be deeply irritating). When senior officers brought to his attention the fact that the soldiers themselves were not at all eager to be known as Minks, fearing, quite rightly, no end of barracks fallout, the King actually commissioned a zoologist to try to convince them. "Pound for pound," the zoologist told them, "there's nothing on land or sea any fiercer than a mink." The marines, to their credit, refused to be swayed – their choice was the osprey, which they neatly argued would evoke their unit's airborne capability in addition to its naval abilities. This stumped the King, though he continued to grumble that mink were clearly more intelligent than osprey – the one was a bird, the other a mammal – which really should count for something in a mascot. The corps utterly destroyed this line of attack by pointing out that osprey eat mink, not the other way around, which effectively halted any further rear-guard actions on the part of their commander-in-chief. Since that day, Canada's marine units – and the King's elite guard – have been known collectively as the Fighting Osprey. As history has proven, they're as proud of that name as they are fierce in defence of their King – having won their first victory over the monarch himself.

But enough about mink.

I need to talk about my foot. I'm admitting now that I'm worried. It's gone from white to pink to red to purple, and now looks like a bruise with the top layer of skin peeled off. It glistens, and it hurts like hell. What worries me more are the traces of yellow near the edges. I think it's infected. Correction – and who am I kidding? – I know it's infected. It's just that I'm concerned this might be more serious than I'm able to deal with at present. I have it soaking in a pot of salted water. It gets cold very quickly, the water I mean, though it stings like fire whatever the temperature. Luckily, there was a box of salt in the kitchen. And on the positive side the wood stove keeps the water hot – it's just that it doesn't stay that way once I've set it down on the floorboards. I have to keep inter-rupting myself to get up and refill it, which I'm loath to do because every drop still has to come from a hole cut through the ice. I've been using my new chainsaw lately, rather than the axe – which makes the job much easier – but still it eats up time.

On the other hand, because the throbbing now keeps me awake, I'm working much later into the night. You will note the last few entries are longer. Overall, my productivity appears to be increasing, though working when it's dark presents its own set of problems. For reasons that escape me now, I wasn't thinking candles when I last walked into town. Ditto batteries for the flashlight. I suppose that's because I was too busy contemplating my bottle of Macallan, which cycles neatly around to a pretty little moral lesson, does it not? I've scrounged through all the drawers and cabinets and located several working flashlights, but between them there wasn't enough battery power to keep one going for more than an hour. Better luck with candles. You'd be surprised how candles accumulate. Women love them, for some reason, or at least the idea of them, and are very fond of presenting them as gifts. It's my good fortune that John received a lot of candles before he was appointed King. Judging from current rates of consumption, I have many hours of illumination still available.

A candle, though, is much brighter than you'd think when viewed from a distance. That's the funny thing about them, when you've got one burning by your elbow in a pie plate, you find yourself forever squinting and moving it around the page: a candle's always casting shadows exactly where you want your light to fall. But leave it where it is and walk out the door onto the ice a hundred paces and you'd swear it was a search-and-rescue beacon. I'm fairly certain this single flame is visible from all the way across the lake. Before I light the wick, I have to make sure the windows are shuttered or covered up with blankets. All in a day's work.

You'll be asking yourself what I'm doing talking candlesticks when I ought to be constructing kings. And right you are.

Hester made John that night. Even I can't deny that. And it's true she rescued our nascent monarchy. But it's also true that John saved the country. There's no disputing that one either. There's just no arguing that without John on the ground that night to divert her, Hester and Toronto would have done it; they'd have skipped off into their own bright future and the country would have shattered. It must have seemed almost beyond belief, the sudden shock of it. Here was this so-called King, some nameless flake who a week before nobody had ever heard of, a guy whose only qualification was that he'd paid two dollars for a winning ticket in what amounted to a grotesquely political publicity stunt, yet here he was – and this became stupefyingly clear in the days that followed Hester's announcement, as a Parliament split, then fractured altogether along its regional divisions – the only thing that stood in the way of collapse and disaster.

You can imagine how the media responded. It was outrage, it was treason, it was completely unthinkable. Even worse, it was unconstitutional! The cartoonists had a field day. One showed John, "The Bingo King," sitting backward on a horse called CANADA dressed in armour with sword and buckler, and an empty space of bouncing bingo balls behind the visor of his helmet. Hester, naturally, was the dragon with flattened dollar signs in place of scales and a single horn shaped like the CN Tower.

But there was no escaping the fact that the country had been brought face to face with its own disintegration. For decades it had been accepted wisdom that Quebec's departure would spell the end of Confederation. Of course it didn't, any more than removing a porch means collapsing the house. *Renovation isn't demolition* (another line I came up with, albeit not quite so successfully). With Toronto, the analogy was very different. Removing Toronto was more like whisking away the building's foundation. It was architecturally inconceivable.

The thing about Quebec is that it sucked the money out of Canada. The thing about Toronto is that it pumped the money straight back in. Hester got as far as she did without concerted opposition for the simple reason that no one ever really seriously contemplated Toronto's being gone. As a concept, it was just too metaphysical. You could chop off a limb, say, for argument's sake, and amuse yourself debating how you might survive the operation. But you could not get by without the heart. There wasn't room for speculation there, is what I'm getting at. So no one did.

Though, clearly, they ought to have. When you look back after the fact, there was no shortage of warnings – starting with Hester herself and what she'd done with city council. But Hester was a new breed of animal. In that sense she was like John, except that whereas John appeared as if by magic, Hester was the product of natural evolution, and evolution is harder to spot until it's already happened. Hester was the first Canadian politician – the first in North America – to recognize that demographics would make the political system she'd grown up with unworkable within her lifetime. Again I have to say how obvious this seems now – but people then just didn't see it. We get used to things the way they are, I suppose, and can't help expecting them to stay that way. Hester was anomalous in this regard.

By rights she should have been a man. I mean this statistically, you understand, without reference to anything beyond probability. Figures like Hester are rare enough in either sex, but while history seems to throw up men of her stature once or twice a generation, it does so far more rarely with women. I can think of only a handful: Elizabeth I, or Catherine the Great; in modern times maybe Indira Gandhi or Margaret Thatcher. (Cleopatra, strangely, is the one that comes first and foremost to my own mind, but that's Shakespeare's doing, not history's.) What I'm saying is that when a person of this quality happens to be a woman – and appears in the world at a time when that isn't quite the liability it usually is – it makes for a remarkably formidable force.

History will remember John's accomplishments far more glowingly than Hester's – that's just the way of it. It's pointless speculating otherwise. I will tell you, though, that none of what happened would have done so in her absence. Hester was the planner, the designer. If John was Fortune, Hester was Fate. And like him, she was favoured with luck. It was only that the King was luckier still. And of course he had me.

She was the kind of figure you read about – the kind who early on in life decides she's going to be Prime Minister, and ends up exactly that – except that Hester chose mayoralty as the more ambitious goal. We were never close, she and I, but I do recall her once confiding that, from the moment she first set foot in city hall, she did so in the knowledge that Toronto's Mayor would one day hold power to eclipse the PMO's.

It's probably fair to say that if the city had been served by something approaching capable government, Hester's radicalism would never have gathered the momentum it did. It was her good fortune that the council before her was so utterly corrupt, so flagrantly incompetent, it destroyed not only itself but its own system of government – leaving the vacuum that Hester had fully prepared herself to rush in and fill. Both provincial and federal levels of government, meanwhile, had withdrawn from all urban responsibilities save extracting taxes. The city's governing structure was little more than a husk when Hester assumed it, and a bankrupt one at that. Hester climbed her way to office as the city's resentment slowly simmered. Once in place, she turned the flame to boil.

DAY SIXTEEN

Now THAT WAS QUITE the little lurid image, wasn't it? Original too. Hard to believe I used to get paid for copy like that.

What I've been trying to get across, *pace* the panting prose earlier, is that Hester saw it coming. Not to say that others didn't – there was no shortage of census-takers filing reports and elected officials purporting alarm at what they were reading – but Hester was the only one to actively plan for revolution. The natural reaction of everyone else was to try to avert it. Hester, being Hester, approached the problem from the opposite direction.

By the time she'd won her first seat in municipal council, most of Canada's population was already concentrated into a handful of city-regions, with Toronto's being by far the largest. Factor out Quebec, and Toronto's share of voters expanded even more dramatically. If the city and its suburbs were a province, its population would substantially exceed the others'; if it were an independent state, its economy would rival what remained of Canada's. Hester understood that the federation was in the process of rebuilding itself from within, but that the existing political structure would resist this at every turn. "What we have," said Hester, "is a new Two Solitudes."

This was a reference to Hugh MacLennan's defining novel from the 1940s – a fine encapsulation of the ancient Canadian divide of English against French. Back then, the country was indeed a string of small communities stretched out across a continent, with the anglo-franco issue as its single and defining knot.

"It isn't like that any more," said Hester.

The suburb of Mississauga now contained more people than all of Saskatchewan. Every last Prince Edward Islander could be comfortably housed in two or three blocks of uptown condominiums. Fewer than one in five Canadians spoke French. And yet, as the Mayor-Elect reminded her councillors, even as the demographic nature of the country was radically shifting, its system of governance clung more and more stubbornly to a structure put in place a century and a half ago. Quebec's concerns still dominated the national agenda, and the Premier of Prince Edward Island still held a permanent seat in intergovernmental meetings at which representatives of Toronto's millions were not even offered a chair.

"Time," she said, "to break the mould. The country's crisis isn't Quebec, it isn't Alberta – it's *Toronto*." (Here she would pause, in that airy way of hers, as if a stray thought had just occurred) "But maybe it isn't that the mould should be *broken*," she would say, slender fingers in the air as if to trace the line of reason, "perhaps *recycled* is a better word."

Thus was Hester the true architect of what later became known as mirror diplomacy. Although I gave it its name, and John its future, it was Hester who first provided the model itself. Alberta, true, had chafed for years with sullen echoes of Québécois demands, and other provinces in turn had aped Alberta, but no one came anywhere near the full-scale reproduction that Hester laid out. Under her guidance, Toronto's new administration carefully documented each of the demands Quebec had made, listed all of the privileges it had accrued over the years, then turned to the rest of the country – like a diner looking over at someone else's heaping plate – and said, "We'll have the same."

If Quebec could manage its own immigration, so could Toronto; if Quebec could administer its own taxes, so could Toronto; if Quebec could establish its own foreign missions, so could Toronto. I won't assail you with the details – there were quite an unconscionable number of pages before you got to the bottom – but it all led straight to the kicker: if Quebec could separate, so could Toronto.

This was where Hester's blueprint diverged from the original.

It's well understood now that Quebec never really intended to leave. This was how successive premiers had managed to promise that transfer payments would keep coming, even after Quebecers achieved their glorious independence. It was all delicious fantasy. Voting Québécois perfectly understood that much more was to be gained from the threat of departure than from departure itself. The central strategy, in other words, was to keep the process going indefinitely.

In Hester's Toronto, that thinking was stood on its head.

As the new Mayor made so perfectly clear, Toronto had every reason to ditch the country, and none whatsoever to delay the procedure beyond the minimum bounds of politeness. "The sooner we get this done," the Mayor advised her restless city, "the sooner we'll be spending our own money."

At first, and perhaps not unexpectedly, the business community reacted with horror. Hester's slate of councillors leaned to the left, which alarmed the old guard on principle. The previous council had billed itself as "defenders of business," but so shovel-nosed had they grown enjoying those interests, they'd eventually expensed themselves beyond even their sponsors' redemption. Hester's new council was younger, and much more amenable to the appeal of imagination – which the new Mayor served up in quantities equalling the pork passed around by her predecessor. It was all too much for the barons of Bay Street. The Toronto Chamber of Commerce bought up media time and aired a predictably dour campaign spelling out the disaster sure to follow the new Mayor's headstrong naiveté. But Hester had armed herself accordingly. Just as her support in the polls was beginning to waver, she sallied forth with some fearsome numbers of her own. In a blitzkrieg of business luncheons – impeccably backed by PowerPoints and pie charts – the new Mayor carefully tracked and tabulated the money that flowed out of the city in the form of taxes. Then she added up the totals that senior levels of government injected back in. The difference was staggering, even without the bells and whistles. Twenty billion a year, if I'm not mistaken, or something thereabouts.

"Imagine," said Hester, "what could be done if we pocketed the difference."

"*Imagine* what we could do with the money we send off each and every year, money that ends up building subways in Montreal, or subsidizing daycare in Chicoutimi. Don't you ever ask yourselves why your own kids don't get public daycare or their university tuitions frozen by federal fiat? Or why the thirty thousand commuters who travel every day to university at York *still* don't have a subway line to take them there? The students at Laval do, thanks to your generosity. Is it so revolutionary, this concept, investing in your own infrastructure instead of your competitors'? Or is there some secret altruism they teach you guys at biz school . . . ?"

By this time, the suits would be studying their shoes. There were reports of them shaking their heads, muttering, as Hester spoke, some of them actually wringing their hands. What they were hearing contradicted every precept of citizenship they had cherished since the cradle. But the Mayor was relentless:

"You are aware that we're closing schools. You are aware we barely have the money to staff the classrooms that are left. You are aware that our schools no longer have libraries because we can't afford the books, let alone librarians. You are aware this city is teetering on the brink. You also know that every year we send dollars in the billions out to the rest of the country, for which in return we receive nothing but loathing and contempt.

"I'm asking you to help me change that," said Hester. "I'm asking you to ask what if? *What if* the subsidies we give to Saskatchewan farmers were applied to revitalize our port lands instead? *What if* the capital we raise to widen highways in Cape Breton was diverted to fixing the Gardiner Expressway? I'm asking you, my friends, *what if?*"

Around this point, Hester would usually open the floor to discussion, which typically settled into a stunned round of silence. Eventually, some anguished CFO would find his voice. "But still," he'd say. "*What about* the farmers of Saskatchewan? *What about* the fishermen of Nova Scotia? Don't we have *responsibilities?*"

This was the cue that Hester had been waiting for: "Fuck the fishermen," she'd say. "They've been fucking you." Then she'd lay her hands on her hips and speak the words that no one else in the city could ever have dared:

"You want to know Toronto's role?" asked the Mayor, eyes blazing. "I'll tell you what Toronto is. Toronto's their *whore*, that's what she is" – she'd be leaning in close now, so close they could smell the perfume – "Toronto, my friends, is the great pathetic whore of this Confederation."

If the Mayor didn't have their full attention up till then, I promise you she had it now.

"With due respect to honest prostitutes," said Hester, "what I'm talking about is the kind of whore who turns tricks day and night, night and day, seven days a week, then hands over every cent she's earned – why? – because she's desperate to be loved, that's why, poor pathetic fool. But she isn't loved, is she? Very much the reverse. And when her dress gets torn and her shoes wear out and her earnings start to drop, do we know what happens next? We know this part too, don't we? What happens then is that she's made to beg. Because that's what whoring is, isn't it? Whoring means getting on your knees and begging for a new pair of stockings. And *you, you people want to talk about responsibilities?* Fine then. I'll tell you all about responsibilities! You have responsibilities enough *right here at home!*"

There was fury in her voice by this time, and genuine shame; her audience could feel it through to their tingling groins.

"And if you don't want to think about *those kind* of responsibilities?" The Mayor was rolling up her sleeves now, ready for the final stroke. "If you don't want to think about abstract obligations, I urge you to consider your real ones. What will you say to your shareholders? How will you explain your opposition to *tax reduction?*"

This was Hester's *coup de grâce*, her needle to the brain of the federation. The new Mayor's separatist campaign rested on the promise of the most extensive tax cuts in the history of the nation. Of course, the nation would no longer exist, but tax points were tax points after all, and who could argue that? The savings, said Hester, on both personal and corporate levies, would be counted in the hundreds of billions.

Now think about *that*, she'd say.

Later I would hear her (privately) suggesting that M.B.A. programs should really be administered by the athletic departments of their universities rather than the academic ones – in that what they delivered was far more in the nature of conditioning than education. John at times attempted to dispute this, if he was feeling in the mood for some bruising that day: there was simply no gainsaying Hester's point. When it comes to the lure of tax cuts, the business community's reaction is – then, now, and always – textbook Pavlovian. "Ring the bell of tax reduction," Hester would say, "and they'll slobber to heel every time."

And so they did.

Which leads me back to Theodore Sapper. Sapper was an ardent fan of tax cuts too, evangelically so, it might be said. The masthead of his flagship paper bore an inscription proclaiming in Latin that *governments are best which tax the least*, or something similarly exhilarating to the mercantile soul. Philosophically – insofar as Sapper had philosophy – he was predisposed to throw his full support behind the Mayor. Her liberal leaning troubled him, naturally, but the pheromonal pull of tax reduction annulled political preferment; he further reasoned that if ever she betrayed her promise, he'd have all the means he needed to destroy her. Sapper was a pragmatic believer in what I've come to think of as "the division dividend," which in a nutshell means he approved of anything likely to promote disharmony on the grounds that it sells more papers and generates more air time, and therefore more ad space. So his flagship paper in Toronto came out in furious support of the Mayor's proposals, demanding that the issue be immediately put before the people in the form of binding referendum. Its editorials framed the issue as a challenge to Hester herself. "FISH OR CUT BAIT!" read one headline, in a startling turn of original phrase.

"My goodness," said Hester. "What choice have I now?"

Some years before, the federal government had put into place what came to be known as the Clarity Act. This was in response to Quebec's last referendum but one, and spelled out the rules for future engagements. Before this, separatist governments had tended to fudge the central questions with so many double negatives and contradicting clauses that voters, in postreferendum polling, often admitted to being not entirely sure if they were meant to answer yes or no. There was danger of an accidental affirmation, which neither side wanted, so the new rule insisted that questions from now on would have to be unambiguously clear. More importantly, the act also required the federal government to recognize a yes-vote if it was fairly asked, and bound it to begin negotiations toward a genuine sovereignty. Strategically, this was a case of calling the separatist bluff. It worked with Quebec because Quebecers really didn't want to separate. For Quebec – which was all that anybody thought about – it was earnestly appropriate.

But for Toronto, which no one ever thought about, it left the door wide open.

Sapper's editorials explained all this. His business pages printed endless graphs with dollar signs and arrows pointing eternally up. Even the sports sections ran psychological analysis of the strengths Toronto teams would draw from representing a *nation* instead of only a town. Hardly a paper left the presses without fresh data supporting the manifold advantages of independence. In a truly eerie parody of Randolph Hearst ("You supply the question, I'll supply the vote"), Sapper one-upped his spiritual mentor and provided the question as well. One epochal Saturday, Toronto readers were jolted from their morning lattés with the following:

THE QUESTION, MAYOR:

Subject to the provisions set forth in the Clarity Act, are you in favour of the Region of Toronto seceding from the Dominion of Canada and becoming an independent nation state – yes or no?

PUT IT TO THE PEOPLE!

Three days before a federal government desperate for distraction formally proclaimed my friend John the new King of Canada, Hester did exactly that.

DAY SEVENTEEN

LEAVE 'EM HANGING, I've always said. Nothing like a snap in the arc to keep a narrative moving. Truth be told, my hand was cramping and the candle burned down to a nub. I've rationed myself to a half of one each night, which by my calculation allows me twenty or so more evening shifts. By end of day today, or tomorrow at the latest, I intend to have John on the throne. We're making progress.

There never was a throne, by the way. That's a figurative expression. (Excepting the fancy chair in the Senate reserved for the Crown since days of yore.) Anyone envisaging some rococo extravaganza with ivory treads and golden canopies was in for disappointment. I wish I had a dollar for every enthusiastic royalist, though, who offered to supply one. It's amazing, the number of people who wrote in demanding the King be installed on properly anointed upholstery. But John would have none of it. "The goodwill of citizens is all the lumbar support I need," he liked to say. (His own wording, I needn't tell you.) The same applied to crowns. There wasn't one. If John wore something on his head, it was a woollen toque, in winter, like everybody else.

And before we move on to those pivotal six days between the referendum and the Royal York, I need to mention a few things more about Theodore Sapper. You may have absorbed the impression that Sapper's media interests were focused primarily in Toronto. This would be another case of my misleading you. His flagship was firmly anchored in that city, yes, but the bulk of his media artillery was scattered in tactical deployments right across the country. Sapper's genius as a publisher was in positioning the pieces so they aimed at one another.

I shouldn't properly call him a newspaperman, either. Most of his empire, and certainly most of his income, derived from TV. He'd bought into newspapers later on in his career, capitalizing on the prestige-factor still associated with print, but his big money was made much earlier in the grand arena of television. Sapper was a master of buying low and selling high when it came to programming. And I mean low. He'd made the bulk of his fortune on bosoms and bloodshed, the kind that's cheap to film and easy to watch. As a business model it was brilliantly successful. So much so, he was encouraged to apply similar principles to the news component of his network too.

Over the course of his long career, Sapper had come to understand that ideal television – TV's most pristine product – was the nighttime soap. Indeed, he'd been an early pioneer of the massively popular reality TV, a form of episodic programming that put non-actors (at non-union scale) into soap-operatic situations and encouraged them to behave as badly as possible on screen. These were massively popular, and flourished for nearly a decade before audiences abruptly decided they'd passed the point of nausea and tuned out. Their themes varied according to setting, but all revolved around the central premise of maximized conflict. Some of them were really very clever in the way they forged contestants into groups and then, by virtue of teamwork, turned each member against the rest. The failure of one participant always resulted in the promotion of another, with the cameras carefully positioned to capture the humiliation in each inevitable succession. They were very deeply revealing of human nature, I admit, and politically educational.

And they pulled in millions and millions of viewers, while netting fortunes for their broadcasters. There was no practical reason, Sapper decided, why *news* programs should not operate according to the same formula and generate the same appeal. When he started buying into print media, he was merely advancing his business philosophy to its next logical step.

Sapper Enterprises embraced the doctrines of what we then called "convergence" – which was the marketing catch-word of the day for old-fashioned conglomeration and market monopoly. Television networks were absorbing print publications and building massive syndications of "multi-platformed content providers." Of great concern, in those times, was the fear that these media monopolies would in effect harmonize the news. And this, of course, is what happened. For a time, until the system collapsed, the words emerging from the anchor's mouth at evening news hour would be virtually identical to the text appearing in the syndication's morning papers. Stateside, Red broadcasters were particularly adept at this, which I think explains so much of their early successes.

Unbeknownst to all, however, Sapper Enterprises had taken the principles of "synergy" a giant leap forward.

What tended to happen, as news outlets were concentrated into fewer and fewer hands, was that reporters wound up tailoring their copy according to the sensibilities of their masters in the corner office. The process trickled downward from the masthead: managing editors got grief from publishers for running stories that earned *them* rebukes from the CEO. Assistant editors started spiking drafts they knew would bring the senior editors down on their necks. Writers, in their natural place at the bottom of the pole, simply gave up on pitches they knew weren't going anywhere anyway. From time to time, there were flare-ups when staffers quit or were fired for breaking rank, but all that resulted was the dissenter's replacement with someone who better understood due diligence.

The vast majority of journalists (and this is very, very important to remember) are no different than rank-and-file worker bees at any other enterprise. There's always more to be done than there is time available to do it. There's always more news happening than there is staff to cover it. Most important of all, there are always days off at the end of the week to justify everything else. If management wants a certain style of dance, well, truth be told we're dancing anyway – so get on with the music till it's time to go home. Corporate culture is exactly that, after all, and all culture imposes itself from within.

Conglomerates with old-time lefties at the helm therefore tended to unflagging support of unionized labour – unless it was their own workers striking. Right-wing establishments expected unceasing attack on any form of governance arriving from the left (if a liberal minister spoke approvingly of motherhood, headlines were to read: GOVERNMENT SLAMS DADS). Managements with a Christian bias referred to employees of fertility clinics as *abortionists*, while writers for publications belonging to Jewish-owned syndicates understood that there was no other noun for the adjective *Palestinian* but *terrorist*. And so it went.

Sapper, for a time, became the darling of the chattering classes because his far-flung empire resisted the trend toward editorial convergence. His various newspapers showed no sign whatever of marching to any institutional beat. Indeed, they seldom agreed about anything. More often than not, they vehemently disagreed. In fact, most of them seemed to be perpetually at one another's throats. Sapper let it be known that his properties enjoyed absolute freedom of political expression. He advanced a profound respect for the "trajectories of journalistic independence." Battles over public policy – fought from the editorial forums, say, of his Montreal, Toronto, and Calgary properties – were "simply the natural exercise of regional diversity." Not surprisingly, times being what they were, he was greatly admired. His thoughtful brow appeared on the cover of both *Maclean's* and *Time* – publications, take note, in which he himself had no controlling interest.

But Sapper was playing the game at a level no else had even imagined. While most of his peers expressed their egos by means of ideology, Sapper's ideology was ego itself. I suspect it troubled him, espousing philosophies he disapproved of from a business standpoint (and if you looked, you'd never see any of his fearlessly independent papers advocating higher taxes, for example). But for the most part, there was no principle Sapper would hesitate to overturn on principle – except the drive for deeper market penetration. He understood television more clearly than anyone I've ever known, and the fundamental formula it ran by: that conflict is to programming what water is to fish.

So Sapper approached the news as he would any other commodity – a source of revenue to be aggressively manufactured, not passively harvested. If conflict hastened growth of profits, then conflict should be encouraged by all means possible. While other media conglomerates faced public wrath for insisting that their component parts agreed, Sapper kept himself far, far busier making absolutely certain the far-flung fields of his estate *disagreed*.

During critical moments in national affairs, he would close his office door and compose half-a-dozen pieces simultaneously, then send them out across the country to be planted exactly where each competing seed would prosper best. Think of a system of cross-pollination designed to promote the growth of neighbours' weeds, and you'll have something like a useful analogy. This was the overarching philosophy of

Sapper's approach to journalism: News is whatever creates reaction, which then becomes more news, which then creates more reaction, which churns out copy *ad infinitum.*

So while his outlets in Toronto beat the drums in Hester's favour, his other properties were sowing dragon's teeth against her everywhere else across the land. He loved Hester for the countless opportunities she provided him for cross-promotion. Hester was almost as good as a war when it came to readability. Torontonians adored her – he'd helped make sure of that – but Sapper made equally certain all *other* Canadians looked upon her as some kind of Amazonian Antichrist.

If Hester was the spark, Sapper was the bellows that fanned her flame to maximum burn. Most of us love a good fire, after all, and can't help watching even when it's our own house that's burning. Although his motivations were strictly business, Theodore Sapper was as taken with the spectacle of arson as anyone else. Perhaps this was the key to his nature. Then along came John to smother the flame. I've always thought this explains so much of what happened later.

At first, though, as far as Sapper was concerned, the Bingo King was nothing so much as another useful stick of kindling. During the monarchy's larval stages, he was an ardent – if tongue in cheek – supporter (in Toronto, I should say. His other outlets were insisting that any draw that had picked a Torontonian must surely have been rigged). It went without saying that something as absurd as a Canadian Crown made for good ink on principle. And after all, Sapper himself had taken a distinctly creationary role in its pupation. I suspect he saw himself as a kind of Geppetto figure – there were traces of something almost like paternal pride in his early printed references to our nascent monarchy – until Pinocchio transformed into a real boy, that is. Then the puppet-master exercised his option to heave his project straight into the furnace. But by then it was too late, as I'm about to tell you – the strings were cut, the spell was cast.

Speaking of which, it's time for me to see to my own creature comforts. The wood stove's down to embers. The candle's almost guttering, and my foot is throbbing. We'll sit John upon his throne tomorrow.

DAY EIGHTEEN

WHAT I'VE BEEN TRYING TO GIVE YOU, over these last tedious pages, is a sense of how everything came together by suddenly falling apart. From time to time, you'll come across an academic analysis looking into the relationship between crisis and charisma. Research like this is usually back-page material, if it gets any mention at all, but for anyone with political proclivities, it's interesting study. Experts sometimes call it "the crucible moment." Charismatic leaders tend to rise during times of chaos because – so the theory goes – it's only then that they're worth the trouble. Without ill winds to justify them, heroes tend to create more problems than they solve. If voters have to think a minute before remembering the names of their leaders, that's usually a sign that things are quietly humming along rather nicely, thank you very much, with no need to rock the boat. But when the seas are rising and the hurricane approaches – when the ship of state is foundering and people fear they're sinking with it – that's when the prayer goes out for someone larger than life to seize the helm.

John's arrival coincided with exactly these conditions. Think of Hester's blitzkrieg of Toronto as something like the fall of Paris in the early days of the Second World War – a terrible warning of darkness to come. Then suddenly this ersatz King appears and takes command, and somehow the sun starts shining again. A debut like that is enough to give anyone a hero's dose of royal jelly, and John had charm enough of his own to keep the buzz going from there on in. The irony, despite everything, still makes me laugh. I can picture him – Sapper, I mean – scribbling away in his corner office, doors locked and bolted, labouring to create precisely the conditions that created John. How surprised he must have been when his Pinocchio sprang up from the workbench to shove his wooden fingers straight down old Geppetto's throat.

Enough nostalgia.

I haven't even talked about what happened with the House of Windsor, which, of course, had everything to do with what happened after that. The main thing to remember at this stage, though, is that as far as the feds were concerned, their toss at royalty roulette was never meant to be more than a diversionary sideshow. The idea was to work a little sleight of hand involving the office of Governor General.

Time-honoured custom permitted a sitting Prime Minister to devote as much attention as he liked to choosing the Crown's next representative. It was – according to tradition – a process involving much deep reflection, lengthy consultations, and a great deal of politely ruthless jockeying among the top-drawer contenders in the nation's cultural elite. This time round, however, the PM was responding to a situation none of his predecessors had ever imagined.

Rumours as to certain nap-time activities involving a nanny formerly employed at Rideau Hall – rumours only hinted at, initially – had by now erupted into full-blown, front-page scandal. The press corps was riveted, and Ottawa pink with embarrassment. Politically speaking, it was a delicate state of reserve – though there was no hint of delicacy on the part of the principals: in the weeks leading up to the resignation of Canada's last-ever Governor General, their Excellencies had barricaded themselves into opposite wings of the mansion, trading affidavits through their lawyers like knife blows in a tavern brawl. Then came the Governor General's tearful, prime-time resignation before an astonished nation. His wife was equally upset.

The Prime Minister handled the situation with inspired brilliance. Neatly turning the crisis to his own advantage, he summoned the press to announce that he would scrap his customary privilege and appoint the winner of the Be a Monarch! Sweepstakes instead. The move was positioned as an open, democratic, and resolutely Canadian response to a situation that – were it not for the PM's swift and steely resolve – might easily have cascaded into ever-more damaging farce.

Governors General were all pomp and circumstance anyway, so the thinking went. A few yards more red carpet, a little extra ermine here and there, maybe half-a-dozen trumpets added to the foyer of the House of Commons and Bob's your uncle – Your Excellency becomes *Your Highness*. Buckingham Palace would have to confirm the nomination, sure, and play along with whatever changes were inked into the job description, but the Royal Family was in no position to get shirty, just then. And furthermore, once everything had settled down, the dummy-king could be retired at the end of his term, and the whole embarrassing interlude laid to rest and forgotten.

It might have worked too, except for the ridiculous.

The next act was staged courtesy of the House of Windsor, which could not have timed its exit more dramatically: nothing so common as furtive encounters in the linen closet off the vice-regal nursery, no; *hereditary* monarchs understood the rules of misconduct better than that. But certain inconsistencies were stalking connubial tradition in Buckingham Palace too. Aroused by rumours of royal misbehaviour involving animals and national soccer stars, Londoners had begun taking their doubts into the streets, waving placards and hurling pointed accusations across the palace gates. The Royals, confronting issues of succession *en famille*, and increasingly fed up with being held to higher standards than everybody else – not to mention all the paparazzi – started slinging their resentment straight back into the faces of their critics in the hoi polloi. Their tactic did not go down well with the public. The sun may have set on the empire, but not on presumptions of stiff upper lips. Canada's request for John's confirmation as Governor General – together with some other provisions no one paid the slightest attention to – arrived just as the crisis had reached the point of no return. The papers were hastily signed by a monarch teetering at the edge of the unthinkable. Two days after the Sovereign of the British Empire had formally appointed John as Canada's Keeper of the Crown, the House of Windsor imploded as a family.

No need to go into the scramble this caused all over the world, as one former colony after another woke up next morning no longer certain exactly who was supposed to be their head of state. Canada, like all the other members of the former Commonwealth, was now a monarchy without a Crown – except the imaginary article that had just been settled on the head of my friend John.

The point I've been driving at, with the usual apologies for taking so long, is that John – however inadvertently, however accidentally – was invested with the same authority as a Canadian Governor General. Canadians were about to find out just how extraordinary those powers were.

The biggest explosion, though, came from Toronto, which thoughtfully chose that moment to launch its own assault. All the other problems would likely have been got around eventually, in that fine old spirit of Canadian compromise. But Toronto's coup was hatched without reference to this national characteristic. Hester fully intended the city to separate. The truth of this is often overlooked in later tellings of the story, which tend to portray Toronto's sovereigntist manoeuvrings in the same light as Alberta's or Quebec's. Some of her supporters may even had been lulled into thinking the same – that once their threat was forcefully delivered, senior levels of government would have no choice but to hand over a fairer share of tax points, etc. If so, they were mistaken. Hester wasn't looking for a bigger piece of pie. Not in those days. She wanted the deed to the bakery.

As ever, her timing was perfect. Just weeks before the final convulsion at Buckingham Palace, Hester had launched her referendum and won it overwhelmingly. The text was just as Sapper phrased it. There was no ambiguity. No room for misinterpretation. It was a straight-up *Do you want to separate – yes or no?* Sapper had made certain no voter in the city could be in any doubt whatever as to what the question meant. The choices were simple: prosperity and independence, or poverty and servitude. One or the other.

Overwhelmingly, Torontonians chose the former.

Next morning, the city awoke to the most perilous headline since declaration of the two World Wars: TORONTO PINK-SLIPS THE NATION: A STUNNING MAJORITY! VOTERS CHOOSE SECESSION!

Everywhere else in the country, though, Sapper's audience was being fed a very different message. "We've always known Toronto was a cesspit," screamed the *Red Deer Rattler* the day after the vote, "but we never thought that it could sink as low as this!" *The Revelstoke Rocket* wondered if Hogtown had finally out-Quebeced Quebec? "It's bold-as-brass blackmail – that's what it is, and everyone in this province knows it!" In St. John's, Newfoundland, meanwhile, Sapper's local news channel had convened a panel of spokesmen from the United Association of Unemployed Fisherpersons (UAUF). The panel agreed that Toronto had clearly lost whatever it may have had in the way of moral compass. "Oy've driven dat hoyway 400, one toime," confirmed a grizzled old trawlerman, "and dat tells me all oy needs to know about what koind 'a people dey's got der – t'inkin 'bout nottin' but makin' it ta work on toime, while we pore fellas here is cryin' on da shore, for lack o' work."

As for Quebec, the fact that Toronto was discussing separation was proof that Toronto was not a nation. Quebec *was* a nation. Ottawa must call a halt to this distraction from its singular priority and comprehensively address the historical grievances of the only true nation in the country.

It's tempting to suspect that Hester and Sapper had somehow cooked it up between them. Certainly, Sapper could not have been a greater promoter of Toronto independence. But it was accident, that word again. I can promise you this: There was never any possibility of collusion between those two. Hester possessed the weird ability to assess people at a level I can only describe as a chemical. She could *smell* character – there's no other way to express it. My own theory is that Hester was better able to read pheromonal information than most people and, because she was Hester, understood the value of her gift and cultivated it. What I *can* tell you is that I have never known anyone who commanded such loyalty from those who surrounded her. I think this is because she was able to recognize compatibility at some deeply biological level and nourish it. It stands to reason also that the reverse of this was also true: I'm certain Hester could somehow unconsciously identify potential enemies just by shaking hands. I remember her saying once that the very presence of Sapper in the same room was enough to make her flesh creep. Her instinct for self-preservation would never have allowed her to enter into conspiracy with the likes of him.

As for Sapper, he was perfectly confident that Hester's plans would end in ruin. It was the disaster he was promoting, not its architect.

But the net effect was a convergence of two opposing poles of magnetism, each generating vast quantities of political energy in an accidentally common cause. With Sapper's help, Hester forged and hardened her city's resolve. With Hester's complicity, Sapper convinced the rest of the country that Toronto was hysterically bluffing. Hester did her part – once the referendum was won – by moving to the next stage swiftly and in secret. Sapper, meanwhile, assured all non-Torontonians that the city's fit of pique was typical Toronto narcissism; that the whores of Babylon only wanted an even higher set of heels to prance around on.

I'm sure there were other factors at play – there must have been – because I still can't account for the country's reaction to the news that its largest city had just filed for divorce. There was no reaction. In fact, there was worse than no reaction. As Hester affirmed (and Sapper ensured), the famous Canadian spirit of compromise did not extend to Toronto. Rather than offering some gesture of conciliation, the provinces upped their pressure. The feds, or some of them at least, had the sense to try to defuse the situation. But the government's own back-bench rebelled. Two days after the referendum, a now-besieged Prime Minister called an emergency session of Parliament, where he tabled a motion to remit back a portion of the taxes levied against the city. It wasn't a lot, a few hundred million if memory serves, but it would have been enough to get the street-cars up and running again. His coalition partners from Quebec, however, refused to support the amendment on the grounds that any resources diverted to Toronto would necessarily be pre-vented from reaching Quebec, effectively subverting the purpose of Parliament. The Alberta caucus – now voting as a separate block much like Quebec's – on this issue supported the position of their francophone colleagues. The Prime Minister was forced to hastily withdraw the motion, or face the dire consequences of another vote of confidence – which was looking more and more likely, whatever he did.

Parliament's failure pretty much garrotted any lingering opposition Hester might still have faced at home in Toronto. She'd been banging away for months on the theme of the country's contempt for its major city – and here, at this critical junction in history, she'd been handed the most staggering proof imaginable. Not only Sapper's newspaper, but *all* of the city's dailies, raged at the injustice. Hundreds of thousands of straight-laced Torontonians took to the streets, picketing federal buildings wherever they found them – even, on two well-publicized occasions, tearing the flag from its standard and trampling the maple leaf.

Hester now had all the backing she needed to summon her own emergency meeting – in camera – at which she presented city council with a document it had never seen before. This was a declaration of independence, if you like, the fledgling constitution for an independent city-state. John let me read it once, a few days after Hester's death, while he was still not quite himself with grief. It's a stirring piece of writing: terrifying, actually, if you want my opinion. I expect you'll read it when the Royal Archives are unsealed. As the streets outside the council room swarmed with protestors, while the city's police force stood by in silent support, Hester asked each of her councillors to sign it. And sign it they did. Every last one of them.

This was the document Hester presented to John that night on stage at the Royal York.

Near as I can figure it, the plan was to position Toronto independence as a *fait accompli*. There were any number of legal barriers, of course – not the least of which was that, technically speaking, municipalities had no standing in the Constitution – but revolutions don't respond to legal niceties. And revolution was precisely what Hester was counting on – or should I say, the threat of it. She'd got Toronto's police force onside, tired of playing second fiddle to its weaker but much more influential provincial counterpart. The chief, a firebrand with political aspirations of his own, had quietly agreed to deploy his uniforms at all the major arteries in and out of town. The idea was to seal off the city to any external intervention – up to and including the Canadian Armed Forces, which at that time were so overstretched and underfunded that the local cops in fact outgunned them. Numerically speaking, Toronto's police force was the largest armed assembly anywhere in the country. But Hester was gambling that Canada's obsession with keeping the peace would prove to be its own undoing. For most Canadians, it was simply inconceivable that any government official would give orders to fire on other Canadians. The more determined side, she reasoned, would prevail on the strength of determination alone. Her side, if everything went according to plan.

It all hinged on the willingness of Toronto to alter its nature. And Toronto by now was furious – even the Chablis-and-canapés set who'd turned out for the Woman Writer of the Year Award that night at the Royal York when history changed its habits. Which explains why the audience reacted as strongly as it did to John's attempts at satire – there was a tension in the room that had everything to do with Hester's presence on the stage, and nothing whatever to do with Bingo King. This escaped me at the time, being so new to the territory. I did notice, however, that Her Worship was not pleased to see John receiving the attention he did. Hester was tapping her toes as John finished his turn at the microphone.

As I've said, I don't remember which meritorious writer took home the award that night, but neither does anyone else. When at last the winner was applauded off the stage, Hester returned to the microphone with more than a touch of eagerness and admitted that there was one small piece of business that ought to be cleared up before everyone went home.

Right away the audience sensed something was up and shushed itself into silence. Hester possessed a fine sense of theatre. She knew exactly when the moment was hers. "Subject to the expressed wishes of its citizens," she said by way of preamble, "city council today has unanimously passed a Declaration of Independence . . ."

If you've ever ended a love affair, you'll understand when I describe the feeling as being like the moment you realize you've reached exactly that moment – when history disappears into the vacuum of the boundless present. That's how it felt; a thousand chills along a thousand vertebrae, all breath arrested – for just that instant – then the sudden inhalation when all those lungs realized they had to keep pumping for life to continue.

Hester held on to that silence until she was certain she'd heard the room gasp.

"Toronto, as of today, is no longer subject to the Dominion of Canada."

As she spoke the words, she waved a regal finger in John's direction. (*Look what this relationship has become*, the gesture implied, *look what this country has sunk to*.) "By our good fortune," said the Mayor with all the fury of a city scorned, "we are this evening favoured with the presence of . . . ah . . . the federation's newly appointed head of state. It's only fitting, therefore, that I take this opportunity to apprise his august person that documents are at this time on their way to His Majesty's [heavy sarcasm] Parliament for immediate ratification by that body . . ."

There was something so audacious in her delivery, something so inherently comedic in its presentation, that a good part of the audience surprised itself by laughing. But the mood grew sober again, I can tell you, when Hester announced that, even as she spoke, Toronto police, including

SWAT teams on the major arteries, were sealing off the city.

"It is now the responsibility of Canada's Parliament," the Mayor concluded, "to swiftly pass the necessary legislation . . . or suffer the consequences."

Everyone by this time had forgotten all about John. Certainly, the Mayor was greatly startled when the Bingo King rose, gently placed a hand on her shoulder, and took possession of the microphone.

"Madam Mayor," said John, gazing into Hester's eyes, "I am sorry to inform you that Parliament will be unable to consider any legislation at this time because, ahem . . ." He was still unfamiliar with the proper phraseology, after all. "Well, because . . . by the powers invested in me, etc., etc., I hereby dissolve the legislature . . . *Parliament*, I mean. But I'm sure we can work something out . . ."

DAY NINETEEN

LIKE MOST MEN, John was unwilling to discuss his private relations in their application to women who mattered. I have
often in life been amazed at how willingly women surrender
the details of their love. We don't do that, we men. We'll table
stories, sure, the same as we might compare notes about the
lakes we've fished, the hills we've skied, or the courses we've
played. But when it comes to the important ones – the ones
who matter – this is simply not a fit subject for discussion.
John was a particularly manly man in this regard, which puts
me at a disadvantage when accounting for what happened
between Hester and him.

The fact of the matter is, it's impossible to know where the
boardroom ended and the bedroom began with those two. I'm
fairly certain they intersected that very same night. There's a
famous photograph – you've probably seen it; a close-up of
Hester's look of transcendent astonishment at what she's
hearing; the King's hand caught frozen, hovering above her
shoulder. It was taken by a Random House publicist, of all
people, who'd just got one of those instant-broadcast digital
cameras that were all the rage, sent out to cover this bookish
event. The shot is widely cited as an example of photography's
ability to capture the infinite variety of human expression – in
this case, unfettered surprise – which explains the iconic stature
it now enjoys among aficionados of such things. But look

down from Hester's face, next time you see it; take note of what the rest of her is doing. It may be my imagination, or just a trick of light, but as Hester's head tilts back away from John in consternation, her hips are clearly canting in the opposite direction.

I'm pretty certain they started that night. Though John, of course, would never say. I believe I've mentioned Hester's ability to decode compatibility. My hunch is that Madam Mayor was at that moment receiving a blast of pheromones the like of which she'd never felt before. Call me a romantic. But it's this, I reckon, that accounts for the look of slack-jawed astonishment. History, as you know, records otherwise. When I think back on it, it still amazes me – how they got away with it. No one ever knew the truth about Hester and John. Except me, of course, and now you. It seems incredible, though, doesn't it? That a fact so crucial to everything was missed by all the players but the principals themselves. Even Sapper never picked up on it. Which shows you the true depths of a cynic's credulity . . . and how fortunate John was in having me on hand to spin all that tension in more productive directions.

So I've always felt I deserved to know more about how things fell out that night – who proposed what, and how they worked it out between them. Gentlemen's code, however, is gentlemen's code, and everyone involved is now dead. I can tell you, though, that my first official responsibility as John's aide and spokesman was making sure that no one, not even the Mayor's own staff, got into that meeting room. For all I know, they *were* just talking. But I don't think so.

Here are the parts I can be sure of:

An hour or two before dawn, John and I slipped out through a loading dock overlooking an alley behind the hotel (Hester knew these covert byways, even then) and walked five blocks to the budget parking lot where we picked up John's battered Volvo and drove to Ottawa. We arrived before the Senate began session that day, which gave John enough time to find the seat reserved for the Governor General and from that chair to formally dissolve Parliament. His hastily assembled witnesses – to say nothing of the Speaker – were too surprised to do much more than blink around the empty room, which at this stage I didn't know enough to call the Chamber. John was still wearing his rental dinner jacket, which lent an accidental air of *gravitas*. All this is recorded history, so I won't waste time repeating it. What I don't think has been noted is how fast we got out of there afterwards – pretty much at a run, I'd say – while all the politicos and press gallery types were still swallowing their ham and eggs, blissfully unaware of the turmoil about to engulf them.

What I can also tell you, repeating a nugget John permitted himself to confide, is that at least part of their time holed up in that room was spent hunched over Hester's laptop, madly browsing the Web for information as to how – technically speaking – a Governor General goes about dismissing a government in session. It had never been done before in this country, not in that fashion at least, but there had to be a protocol documented somewhere. John would laugh when he described the two of them, bickering already over what sites they should visit. Whichever they found evidently did the trick. John somehow discovered the right words and put them in the right order, and formally dissolved the Parliament of Canada – all of which would have counted for nothing, of course, had the Prime Minister not been so sagaciously obliging.

But there were a great many things John and I *did* talk about during that four-hour drive (he slept the entire trip back, and who could blame him?). By the time we reached the Nation's Capital, I'd begun to have some sense of the monstrous scale of what we were attempting. I can tell you that my heart was thumping well before the Peace Tower came into view, as it has been ever since.

Still, I'd love to know what he did to talk her into it. Those first few minutes, I suspect, must have been critical. Hester would have been raging, and John . . . well, I at least have a better sense of what John's frame of mind might have been. But how did he do it? In the space of merely hours, how did those two move from total strangers to lifelong collaborators? My natural bias inclines me to think of John as the initiator, but for all I know it was the other way around. Maybe it was Hester who made the first move. It's perfectly plausible that the Mayor realized how the deck was now stacked irredeemably against her and commenced reshuffling on the fly. She was a quick study. Hester would have understood from the start the length of the odds she was playing. It's even conceivable she was bluffing all along. It's possible that – with John's sudden appearance in the deck – she saw an unexpected opportunity to strengthen her hand, not weaken it. But again, I don't think so. In later years I had ample opportunity to witness how those two minds meshed, and I think the discovery of their compatibility stopped everything else in its tracks and set them both off in a wholly new direction. Hester was brilliant. But, of course, so was John.

For me, that has always been the most marvellous part of this story: of all the possibilities to randomly select from, the country ended up with the one-in-a-million combination actually fit for the job. John is on record as having said he learned everything he needed to know about politics from reading the *Globe and Mail* (a statement that, if I may say so, played a definite role in that newspaper's increasingly pro-monarchist leanings, but never mind, it's still true). John absolutely insisted on reading the best paper available cover to cover every day of his life, even all those years ago in Spain. For him, politics *was* religion – John defined hell as the place where people don't think about what happens after they're dead. As a private citizen, he was keenly, obsessively interested in the nuts and bolts of governance. It was this shared fascination, I think, that cemented our friendship as far back as Malaga. I believe it had the same effect with Hester.

Which is all a long-winded way of telling you that at some point that night, John and Hester agreed on a set of common goals that bound them to each other for as long as they both lived. Your history books, of course, say something very different. Conventional wisdom has it that the two were locked in bitter conflict, only resolved much later through the King's prodigious talents in negotiation.

For Hester, everything hinged on her ability to entrench the notion of an independent city-state. Crossing this threshold was her Rubicon, if you like, the most formidable barrier against all her hopes for the future. Even in the best-case scenario, she knew that Parliament would never just declare Toronto independent and, *voila*, it would be. Cities, remember, had no standing at all in the Constitution, none whatever. They were the lowest of the low in the federal pecking order, without even a mechanism for their leaders to be heard. Hester's objective was first and foremost to get the process formally begun. Once started, she was certain the momentum would take on a life of its own. And this is the point that historians have missed: Hester understood that introducing Toronto independence to the nation's legislature – even merely as a topic for emergency discussion – would be enough to free the genie from the bottle. Once out, the cork would never fit back in again.

I've mentioned earlier that Hester's blueprint was Quebec. That conceit has been discussed ad nauseam, of course, and now fills libraries. There are half-a-dozen volumes here in this cottage, as I noticed the other morning while looking for something to get the fire started. Each and every one of them has completely missed the point. Hester's plan depended on the *differences* between Torontonians and Quebecers, not the similarities. They've made excellent tinder, though.

While John and I were on the highway bound for Ottawa, Hester was working the phone. Speaking through her aides, she announced an emergency press conference scheduled for later that same morning. This event was delayed, however, and then delayed again as more and more media scrambled to establish links while the Mayor – still communicating at one remove – let it be known that negotiations were far too delicate at this time to interrupt.

What negotiations? screamed the press. But the Mayor's office was maddeningly tight-lipped. By midmorning, it was clear the Prime Minister was not involved. The PM, unbeknown to all but his closest advisers, was meeting that day with petroleum executives at a secret location deep in Texas. According to his Ottawa spokesperson, he was unavailable for comment. Panicked phone calls started going in the opposite direction, with government aides frantically telephoning their contacts in the media asking them if *they* knew what was going on. As the first tide of Toronto's morning commuters were waved through silent police checkpoints that had ominously sprung up during the night, dial-up information centres were swiftly overwhelmed with the sheer number of terrified callers and obligingly crashed. By the time most people got into work, all the country was aware there was a national emergency. But nobody knew what it was.

Then suddenly from Ottawa came unbelievable reports that the Bingo King, sitting in the Governor General's chair, had somehow suspended the nation's government. Details at this point were still extremely sketchy. Moments after his surprise appearance in Parliament, the King had vanished. The PMO, still, was issuing no statements.

Rumoured insurrection in Toronto by this time had already wiped everything else off the morning's news agenda. When the incredible story from Ottawa broke, the national media was faced with a situation it was incapable of comprehending, never mind reporting. Breakfast television and morning radio dropped all regular programming, leaving their hosts floundering for what to say next. Talking heads across the country were dragged out from wherever talking heads are stored when not in use. It was soon apparent, though, that even the experts were flummoxed. Producers fell back on the tried-and-true stopgap of panel discussion – which succeeded in filling up the nervous airwaves but only added to the levels of B-Roll confusion.

The big question – was this legal? – seemed increasingly unanswerable as the morning wore on. Satellite hookups linked constitutional savants coast to coast. The experts debated one another rather than the question. A retired judge from Manitoba insisted that yes, on balance, the Bingo King probably, technically, had the authority, constitutionally speaking, to do what he appeared to have done, assuming – and in the absence of any contradictory evidence – prime ministerial consent. But a senator from Nova Scotia argued that it was criminally irresponsible to issue any such statements until a Royal Commission was struck to examine the question in the first place. Newfoundland's Deputy Premier, fresh out of bed and obviously still working from yesterday's brief, kept insisting that everything came back to the scandal of foreign overfishing, while a Stetson-headed lawyer from Calgary, filmed behind the wheel of his late-model Hummer, declared that if parliamentary suspension meant smaller government, then parliamentary suspension could only be a good thing. As the clock ticked on, a secondary issue began to take on greater prominence: Where *was* the Prime Minister?

During all this time, Hester was alone in the hotel room,

pacing the carpet, awaiting the signal to launch the next stage. John reached her on my cellphone from the car at just about the time that we were skidding out on to Wellington Street from Parliament Hill. I was privy only to one side of this conversation, you understand, but it was clear that he was letting her know things in Ottawa had gone more or less according to plan.

It would have been shortly after this, then, that Hester announced to the nation – again through her bewildered aides – that King John, as commander-in-chief of the Canadian Armed Forces, had just ordered the military to stand down.

In a prepared statement read to the press by one of her spokespeople, Mayor Vale grimly acknowledged the wisdom of the Canadian government, as represented by its head of state, and the courage of the King's decision. "Despite our many differences," she said, "and many still to be resolved . . . I am deeply heartened by King John's assurance that – no matter what the outcome of this day's negotiations – not a drop of blood on either side will be shed."

And there we had it. Instantly. John established as a public presence.

As *King*.

Within thirty minutes, all signs of roadblock disappeared. Melted away completely. I don't know how she managed it, but whatever markers she had with the chief of police, Hester must have called in, and then some. When John and I passed the Welcome to Greater Toronto sign just a few hours later, there was nothing but a few flattened cartons of Tim Hortons Timbits suggesting a police presence had ever existed.

He told me later (privately – Hester was prickly about this sort of thing) that the Mayor had not indeed been aware he was commander-in-chief until the fact emerged on Google. John always maintained that *he* knew the GG was also commander-in-chief of the Canadian Armed Forces – as any properly educated citizen should – but that he'd simply not appreciated the *significance* until Hester was kind enough to point it out. It's still a mystery to me how they got hold of the general's phone number. Hester's organization, somehow, must have opened the lines of communication. But I was sitting beside John at a red light on the outskirts of Ottawa when he placed a call to General J.B. Bennett and commanded him to stand down the army.

The general, with commendable self-discipline, I must say (he had one of those booming telephone voices that make eavesdropping easy), advised his commander-in-chief that the army had not actually been stood up, sir.

"Excellent," said John.

"Excuse me, sir," asked the general, who'd been appraised of the situation on breakfast television, like everybody else. "But . . . sir . . . how do I know you're you?"

"What do you mean by *you*?" replied the King, soon to be famous for his philosophical approach to governance "and for that matter, how do I know you're you?" While the general pondered this apparent weakness in the chain of command, the commander-in-chief severed the connection.

They had agreed, he and Hester, that at this stage it would be better for her to do most of the talking. Which was precisely what the Mayor continued to do, at neatly calculated intervals throughout the rest of that morning. John was sleeping by this time while I, one hand on the steering wheel, switched back and forth between radio stations. The airwaves were buzzing with "the situation in Toronto." Even the jock-shock guy from some Mojo outfit in Cincinnati was lamenting how screwed up those poor Canadians were, what without having a Second Amendment and a properly armed citizen militia to fall back on. On CBC-One, an announcer with a Caribbean accent gravely compared present events to the October Crisis, while on CBC-Two the scheduled Brahms recital was pre-empted with a crackly replay of a broadcast made the day the War Measures Act was proclaimed in 1970. Even MunchMusic found a retired history professor willing to draw comparisons with the Upper Canadian Rebellion of 1837 – though he was having a hard go of it with his giggling host, who couldn't sort out the difference between Mackenzie King, Prime Minister, and William Lyon McKenzie, rebellion leader. ("*King*, though," she kept saying, "*King* . . . I mean, isn't it just too weird that word keeps coming up? I think it's karmic!")

The pundits were all telling one another that nothing like this had ever happened in Canadian history, which was another way of admitting they really didn't know what else to say. Producers were making the best of things by flogging whatever bygone crisis they could dig out of the archives.

I've said before that Hester was brilliant. She never liked me and I never liked her, but that won't stop me admitting straight up that the Mayor's bloodshed reference was the most inspired piece of media manipulation I've ever been party to. John's sixty-two-yard kickoff was a credible example, sure, but that one took months of preparation and still doesn't hold a candle to Hester's spontaneous performance. Much as I'd like to, I can't even give John a share of the credit. He was in the car with me that morning when she pulled it off. It was Hester being Hester, and when she was in form there was no one better. Such a shame she's dead.

There was never the remotest possibility of actual bloodshed. That goes without saying. The cops weren't really blockading the city, and the army in those days didn't have the transport available to move troops into Toronto even if it had been aware of any need to do so. But Hester planted the seed, and in the media hothouse that morning, the image of violence took root right across the country. People adore being frightened. Ask the average Canadian, even today, to name the most perilous moment in Canadian history and eight out of ten are still likely to tell you the "Toronto Crisis" – and that's *after* having lived through the constitutional revisions that, believe you me, were a hell of a lot more dangerous. More to the point, ask who defused the situation: I guarantee they'll tell you it was John, of course. King John.

He liked to say it was because Hester was a woman, and women are more inclined to selflessness than men. Bullshit. It wasn't selflessness (to be honest, I don't think John ever believed it was, he just liked to see me roll my eyes when he got going in that vein). What it was was calculation. Women can be more calculating than men, I'll give them that. Hester had a woman's talent for making the best of things, John included.

By the time we made it back downtown, Front Street was choked with news trucks. The sidewalk outside the Royal York was a forest of mobile antennas. I'd shaken John awake somewhere past Port Hope; we'd stopped at a roadside McDonald's, where the King shaved with a disposable razor and men's room hand soap. For the rest of the drive, he and Hester talked nonstop by cellphone. In fact, the phone was still against his ear as we parked the car and pushed our way through to the doors of the hotel. I think it helped that John was wearing a tuxedo. My guess is, the image of a man in a tux striding through the foyer talking on his cellphone must have lent the impression of importance somehow, because we had a lot less trouble making our way through the crowd than I expected. (People thought he was senior hotel staff, is my opinion.) We took the stairs and made our way to Hester's floor without incident, but the press of bodies was thickest in the hallway just outside her door. I could hear John murmuring as we elbowed our way through the pack. The door jerked open the instant we reached it. *"Hey! Isn't that the king guy?"*

someone shouted – but by then we were already through and the door slammed closed behind us.

With a glance at me that was decidedly unfriendly, and a look at John that was very much the reverse, Hester put her finger to her lips and pointed to the television. A news presenter was summarizing events to date. There was a banner at the bottom of the screen with the words "*Crisis in Toronto*" blinking on and off in blood-red type. Nothing new was being reported – that I did take in – and I was just about to say that we were up to speed on this already when the broadcast was interrupted with a piece of breaking news: *King John* (note the title, *King John*) *has just been spotted entering the Mayor's conference room* . . .

"They work fast, I'll give them that," said John, standing in the middle of the room.

Hester smiled the smile I've only ever witnessed in his presence. "Let's just say I laid a little groundwork." For a moment I would have sworn she was just about to kiss him. But then she glanced at me.

"This is Blue," said John.

"Hello, Blue," said Hester.

Such was my introduction to Her Worship.

DAY TWENTY

I WISH I COULD SAY I'd ever liked Hester. More to the point, I wish I could say she'd ever liked me. Gwen and I understood each other, right from the beginning. With Hester that just never happened. She reconciled herself to me, I think, by simply pretending that I wasn't there. I don't mean to suggest that she was rude. And I'm not implying she ignored me in any socially deliberate way. What I mean to say is that Hester imposed on herself the discipline of behaving in my presence as if she were alone with John. There were physical limits, thank God, for which I'm still grateful. They never embarrassed me. It must have been hard for both of them. Certainly, it was not easy for me.

You should understand that John and Hester were seldom physically together. This is not a euphemism for anything more or less than what it says. Hester as Mayor and John as King both lived intensely busy lives external to their relationship with each other. As far as everyone else was concerned, too, that relationship was hostile. And, of course, Hester was married. Later on, John embarked upon commitments of his own. Their worlds were circumscribed by politics, and for political reasons it often was necessary for me to be present when the King and the Mayor conducted their affairs of state. Hester came to appreciate my talents. She was smart, everything comes back to that, far too smart to overlook Blue's usefulness.

It was Hester, for example, who cured John's dread of speechwriters. That just wasn't in the cards, he'd insisted – hiring someone to put words in your mouth was like contracting a stand-in to have sex with your wife. "It's a surrender of competency," said John. "For the life of me, I don't know how anyone agrees to it." Hester surprised us (John more than me, I think) by laughing out loud. "You overestimate your own resources," she told him. "And it's the *writer's* function to absorb his patron's thinking – not the other way around. It's not a question of someone else putting words into *your* mouth. It's a question of *you* infusing *your* thoughts into your commissioned instrument." For the first time in that conversation, Hester looked me in the eye and sighed. "I suppose that will have to be you," she said.

Speaking to me, Hester conversed with John indirectly. I absorbed this that first morning, when Madam Mayor gazed at me and imparted to John how from now on we would be managing the press. The game is called accessibility, and soon enough the three of us were playing it like masters, though perhaps I ought to say the four of us, because Theodore Sapper provided us the board to play on. For a time, at least.

Hester had already made her decisions as to which media outlets we would deal with and which we would not. Sapper's local franchise stood at the top of her list. Our hotel-room television was tuned to Sapper's Toronto channel: I watched with Hester as John experienced for the first time the strange sensation of making and breaking news simultaneously. Sapper's newsroom, she explained, had been the first to accept the Mayor's conditions, and therefore was the first to be granted privilege of access. Certain rules, in exchange, would be observed henceforth: There were to be no further references to *bingo*, no more snicker-quotes around the "King" in John's title, an end to disrespectful qualifiers. Hester's thinking, as she explained it to her bureau chiefs of choice, focused on simple pragmatics: the present situation was far too explosive to risk the consequences of irresponsible reporting. *Both* parties involved in these negotiations must therefore be referred to with appropriate respect. Any media not abiding by this request would find themselves on the wrong side of the briefing-room door. It was not a lot to ask.

"I have no fondness for either the man or the institution," confessed the Mayor during her tension-filled press conference late that morning, "but like it or not, the King now speaks on behalf of Canada's people. That in itself must command our attention." Most commentators were not precisely certain what to make of this. But they reported it.

Sapper cherished no such uncertainty. By midafternoon, his properties (all of them, this time) had firmly sided with the King – at least insofar as the legality of his activities in Ottawa were concerned. Throughout the morning, there was frenzied debate about whether John's suspension of Parliament had actually been legal. Here again Sapper's outlets – though with widely different interpretations – concluded that intentionally or otherwise, the new King had been constitutionally invested with the same powers as any Governor General, which included the authority to dissolve a sitting government. When reports began emerging of John's intervention with the army, Sapper's panels of experts again found themselves obliged by point of law to conclude that – insane as it sounded – the King was indeed constitutionally commander-in-chief and *ipso facto*, entitled to command . . . and a lucky thing he was too, because by midday a series of leaks began trickling out suggesting that King John had, somehow, succeeded in brokering a peace.

Just before noon, Sapper's CityNewsTV broke the national lead story that day when it announced that Mayor Vale had been persuaded to dismantle her roadblock of Toronto. (No physical roadblocks were ever erected, I remind you. But all politics is optics, and all optics is refraction.) As midday gave way to afternoon, the bulletins took on ever-more hopeful tones. Then – in a stunning development – an obviously furious Mayor appeared at a dinner-hour news conference, bitterly conceding defeat. Denouncing the King for his constitutional intransigence, a clearly shaken Mayor Vale apologized to the people of her city for failing to deliver on their independence. "It was so close . . . ," the Mayor was heard to whisper before visibly controlling her emotions. "This is not the end . . . ," she said, lifting her shoulders and staring straight into the camera.

Though the text of her address was brief and tellingly short, the Mayor's tone and even posture supported the impression that she'd been badly outmanoeuvred. "I have been prevailed upon to endorse this agreement," she read from a prepared statement, "only by the prospect of a greater future for Toronto . . ." The text was as hollow as the voice that pronounced it.

This shocking image of a Mayor overwhelmed was broadcast simultaneously with equally striking footage of a tired but jubilant King assuring his country that disaster was averted (CityNews, in fact, won a National Television Award that year for its innovative use of multiscreen technology: at the height of the crisis, John's and Hester's faces appeared side by side on screen, tabloid style – speaking as if to each other – though the actual footage was shot at separate times and locations).

Hester retreated to the caverns of city hall to acknowledge her surrender. The Mayor spoke from behind a curtained table, reading a prewritten speech in a hushed and darkened conference room. John, in classic *contrapunto*, addressed the nation live from between the pillars at Union Station – train whistles blowing, taxi horns blaring, commuters bustling in the background: the very picture of a man in motion. Praising the Mayor for her forbearance and the courage and conviction of the people of Toronto, King John reassured an anxious country that the worst was now over . . . and that although there was much to be done and many obstacles yet to overcome, the nation could rest assured it would remain a nation.

I think I've noted earlier that the media tends to travel in schools – if you can get the fish out front swimming in the direction you want, odds are the rest will turn and follow. Sapper's coverage established the optics through which the Toronto Crisis is still perceived to this day. In the weeks to follow, the country's news organizations devoted most of their attention to speculating what *would* have happened had Toronto not been stopped, rather than analyzing what actually *had* happened on the day itself. But by then too, of course, they'd been given even more spectacular material to divert the lens.

Those were the days of virtual reality. I remind you that computer technology had only recently evolved to the point where it could present credible versions of what people assumed to be true. The application was mostly commercial, needless to say, and predictably adolescent in scope. But during that era, we were fascinated with the notion that reality itself was relative – that narrative was viable only within a limited reference to itself. I always think of Hester when I ponder that abstraction. What Hester engineered was a virtual coup. Or, more precisely, a virtual failed coup, and a brilliantly successful one. The line of John's narrative carries on through me to you: from the present by means of the past and on into the future. How is that for reality? Or virtue either, come to think of it.

Hester positioned John as the man who'd subdued her. If you've not yet grasped the political potency here, then already I am failing you. She was post-feminist, our Hester. Which meant she understood how television had combined with affirmative action to focus the power of sex more blindingly than ever in history. Hester won John instant admiration, and not just from men. She keenly understood the King's appeal to other women – in this one respect, at least, she was in line with Gwen. Women as a polling category were always John's staunchest supporters. Even the lesbian sector was smitten. John insisted on marching with the girls, not the boys, every Pride Day, which never failed to inspire the bolder among them to whip off their tops. Pride Parade coverage invariably presented the image of a virile King attended by a host of naked Valkyries, which I don't mind saying suited my own purposes very nicely.

But none of this would have happened in the first place without the assistance of Parliament. If the Prime Minister – or any of his ministers – had acted against her, Hester's gambit would inevitably have failed. But none did. I remind you that the House of Commons was chronically, fatally, divided. Governments of that era teetered perpetually on the brink of disaster. It's human nature – not just grimy politics – for people to do whatever it takes to survive. I believe that every member in that legislature saw in John a means of ensuring personal survival, while simultaneously annihilating the opposition. Tuck that one away, if you like, as a memorandum worth remembering. Every politician in that House invested our manufactured King with the magical properties of some exotic virus: a latter-day smallpox they themselves were immune to, but a poison destined to lay the other side low.

The Prime Minister had come to office as a bright new force in politics. For starters, he was a non-Quebecer – Canadians under fifty had little experience of prime ministers from anywhere other than Quebec – so he was a novelty item on that score alone. Furthermore, he was Albertan, and widely regarded as the cream of the Calgary intelligentsia: a new breed of politician nourished in the creative ferment of Western dynamism. He was said to be deeply intelligent – yet another departure from his recent predecessors. Staffers in the PMO let it be known that the Prime Minister was invariably the smartest person in the room, which in hindsight simply illustrated how much time he'd spent cooped up with them.

To be fair, history had put him in an impossible situation.

His party was an offshoot of an earlier coalition, one forged in resentment of a system of government eternally controlled from Quebec. But after a decade in the political wilderness – during which time it proved itself unelectable beyond its home base on the Prairies – its leaders had evolved a progressive new strategy. Thoroughly convinced, by now, that Quebec was essential to victory (the Constitution, in those days, assured Quebecers a guaranteed number of parliamentary seats, whatever their share of population), the party devised a plan to out-Quebec the Quebecers when it came to federal largesse. Hindsight, of course, demonstrates what a difficult proposition this would be, given the party's founding principles. But mark what I said earlier about survival plotting its own course of action. The new platform promised Quebecers a series of inducements the likes of which would have sent the party's charter members running for their shotguns had they been advanced from any other quarter: Quebec was to have an independent voice in international affairs – there was talk, even, of its own seat at the United Nations. As for transfer payments – well, these would rise to heights unimagined in previous budgets.

It was just a question of time, naturally, before loyal voters in Alberta (rapturous at first about their win – *The West is in! The West is in!*) could no longer ignore the fact that *more* of their petro-dollars were flowing to Quebec these days than ever before.

By the time that Hester launched her coup, the PM must have been at his wit's end. His Alberta caucus had erupted into full-scale mutiny, while the band of Québécois MPs that kept him in office – aware that pressure only works by way of increase – relentlessly upped the price of their support.

Hester's insurgency was timed to catch the government in the jaws of its very own Cerberus. Indeed, the Quebec imperative explained the Prime Minister's mysterious absence from the nation's capital that day – the monster needed feeding, and he was fresh out of means to appease it. The larder was down to barest bones – at least in terms of normal parliamentary procurement: Cabinet was certain to tear itself to pieces at the suggestion of any further allocations for Quebec. And raising taxes was, well – suffice to say that that was not an option for this particular administration.

Desperate, the PM turned to his tutors in the Calgary oil patch, who secretly passed him on to *their* mentors in Texas. What he was aiming for, I think, was ready money now, in exchange for open spigots later. Nurtured as he was in the politics of petroleum, the give-and-take of macroeconomics was as natural to him as gas flares and suburban sprawl, though Canadians with roots outside that sector patch would doubtless have advanced a less supportive view.

He was desperate, as I say.

I've often wondered how much Hester knew – she had eyes and ears in the PMO, I'm sure of that. Her timing that day caught the Prime Minister not only out of the loop, but out of the country – and for clandestine reasons at that. The PM, for his part, responded with initial panic, which accounts for his silence during the early hours of what's now known as the "Toronto Crisis." Isolated from the more nuanced thinkers in his Cabinet – staffers not from Alberta had been left to mind the store at home – and surrounded by a school of barracudas whose tender solicitations even he – perhaps especially he – would have had the wisdom to suspect, he simply had no idea what to do next.

The news from Toronto was simply *inconceivable*. I can picture him, surrounded by flinty-eyed oilmen, banging on his cellphone, certain he'd misheard. I wonder how long it took him to talk his way back to the airport, perhaps in a borrowed limousine, cursing Houston traffic. Maybe someone offered him a private helicopter. He would have been in a terrible rush to get back to Ottawa before questions as to his whereabouts started getting hotter than they were already.

Then, out of nowhere – deliverance!

Toronto – that Sodom of a cesspit he disliked even setting foot in – had up and surrendered, only hours after launching its lunatic revolt, and without a single shot fired! Initial reports were suggesting – and this was almost as unbelievable as the actions of its anarchist dyke of a Mayor – that his court-jester King, somehow, had taken a hand in bringing her down. If the news was true, or even partly true, it would shine credit on his office for wisely appointing the man in first place. But be that as it may, the crisis in Toronto – already safely in the past – would serve to cover up his business in Houston. Better than anything his press secretary could ever come up with, that was certain.

The more he thought about it, the more he must have liked the possibilities. The media, by this time, had learned he was in Texas, though not what he was doing there. This was bound to cause some headaches down the road. But the collective IQ of Ottawa's press corps, in the Prime Minister's opinion, was equal to less than his waist size – and he'd been dieting since the last election. Undoubtedly, the boys in Calgary would find a workaround to take care of that little problem, not a difficult challenge given all the nonsense being served up in Toronto as distraction. And if there was one thing that could be counted on to bring Quebec and Alberta into any kind of alignment, it was that Toronto needed to be brought to heel – the scales were tipping in his favour. He'd always known the Lord was on his side.

Then – and, truly, this was the most astounding news on this astounding day – came word that the Bingo King had somehow made the country believe that *Parliament* had been suspended!

The PM's first reaction was probably resentment – he was known for his short fuse when it came to minions over-stepping their authority. But that initial anger must have settled very quickly into a kind of gloating jubilation. Dissolving Parliament meant going to the polls – in the present situation, an option decidedly worth the gamble. His minority government was trapped in perpetual nightmare; every vote in the House a high-wire act. What could be more divinely inspired than an election he himself could not be blamed for calling? Lord knows, a spell of pounding the pave-ment on the campaign trail would be good for everybody's disposition. Nothing like a month or two of kissing babies to paste a smile back on a party's face. The Opposition was no better organized than he was, after all. Worse. He might even gain some seats if he could leverage Toronto.

Come to think of it, maybe he should focus there, this time, pump the money he'd promised Quebec into Toronto instead. One sink's the same as another, after all, and they'd been whining for it long enough to be grateful, God knows. If he could pick up some urban seats, that just might offset his losses in backwoods Saguenay. What a pleasure it would be too, not to have to listen to those bastards frothing away in French. His backbench had been simmering for months, but a snap election would set them on the straight and narrow.

They'd have no choice but to rally behind him now, or risk losing their own constituencies. Could the possibility of *majority* be within his grasp?

Addressing the nation that evening, the Prime Minister lavished praise upon the country's new King for his unfaltering strength at a time of national emergency. Events like this served only to show the true depths of Canadian resolve. While he deeply regretted the necessity to prorogue the nation's business – artfully implying that he'd had a guiding hand in John's performance – the Prime Minister called upon his fellow citizens to take this opportunity to embark upon a new beginning – particularly the worthy citizens of Toronto, whose era of disappointing government he personally promised to bring to an end. With that in mind, he would shortly be visiting the Governor General – er, the King – requesting permission to call a general election at His Excellency's earliest convenience.

And that was how his government ended. Not with a bang, as they say, but a fervent whimper.

What with all the excitement in Toronto, the Rest of the Country (ROC) had foolishly taken its eye off Quebec. Which was a mistake, because the function of ROC was at all times to envy and admire the supremacy of the francophone culture it was oppressing. *La belle province* immediately expressed her outrage. The sovereigntist brain trust was truly, brutally insulted that anyone would have the temerity to poach on its separatist preserve. How dare those insipid Torontonians speak about separation? Separatism was a *Quebec* issue, for *Québécois* alone. This was nothing more than a farcical anglophone joke, and a reckless one at that. If Ottawa could call a snap election without consulting its properly elected Québécois parliamentarians (which was how *Le Devoir* translated events), then Quebec City had every right to call a snap referendum too.

History, as we know it, then fell out in the following sequence:

The Prime Minister, reacting with well-concealed delight to the dismissal of his government, announced his intention to call a general election six weeks from the day of Parliament's dissolution.

The Premier of Quebec, reacting with no delight at all to the transparent machinations and callous betrayal on the part of the so-called Prime Minister, declared that the nation of Quebec would refuse to participate in a federalist election. Rather – and on the self-same day – it would hold its own national referendum. Quebec would ask its people if this latest Canadian outrage was not, finally, too much to bear. Was it not time, at long last, to declare inevitable sovereignty?

Lastly, and most memorably, the new King of Canada – responding to the previous two announcements and facing his third national crisis in forty-eight hours – found himself again standing before a microphone in a rented conference room in downtown Toronto. I was on the job, by now, so his hair was combed and a Canadian flag was draped appropriately behind him. As anyone who watched the news that day will tell you, the King's announcement trumped the other two in spades.

In light of the present challenge arising in Quebec, said the King, and with apologies to the Prime Minister, he was regretfully obliged to inform Parliament that the Prime Minister's request to call an election could not be honoured at this time.

Rather – and in what he hoped would be taken as a *suggestion*, nothing more – the new King felt it was his duty to sketch out an idea he had personally been wondering about. As no more than a figurehead – he had no authority at all in this matter, of course, none whatever – yet he sincerely felt it was his obligation, as an ordinary citizen, to respectfully suggest that perhaps, this time, *all* the country might want to be involved in discussing the future of Quebec.

And so the King made his famous proposal. Which, as we know, galvanized an era and reshaped a nation. Maybe a continent, we'll see – or you will. But I have to tell you it didn't seem so radical to me, standing off in the wings that day, listening. Then again I hadn't been brought up here, and lacked the almost supernatural reluctance of Canadians to put into words the heresy that John was articulating. The King's proposal came from so far away, so far beyond the norms of Canadian discourse, that all the traditional mechanisms that normally would have sprung up to smother it somehow failed to trigger. I figured this out later, once I'd had time to absorb the weirdness of how things were done here. At the time, John's idea didn't strike me as all that revolutionary – given so many other things here that did.

On the same day Quebec held *its* referendum, proposed the King, the Rest of Canada ought to organize a referendum of its own – advancing the self-same question. If Quebecers were to be consulted about their wishes with respect to Canada, it seemed only reasonable that the Rest of Canada should be consulted about its wishes with respect to Quebec.

It was just a matter of complementary interests, wasn't it? Which was what a federation was meant to be all about. Wasn't it?

DAY TWENTY-ONE

ON TOP OF JOHN'S BOOKSHELVES is a stuffed merganser. Red-breasted, with a crest. Over the last few days, I've been staring at this duck, trying to catch its eye. At some point in the recent past it was fashionable for people hereabouts to collect stuffed waterfowl. This was a form of accessorizing, as I understand it – there have been other, similar expressions of taxidermic art the dog and I have come across in our neighbourhood raids. For all I know, John's merganser was part of a flock shot down half a century ago and scattered into every second cottage on the lake. I wish it were a real duck, though, I'd eat it. No wonder it's staring.

Have I mentioned that John was very fond of William Blake? Not the longer poems, as much. But he was a great fan of the lyrical ditties you'll find in *Songs of Innocence*. *Songs of Experience* too. (The one about the rose always reminds me of Hester, as a matter of fact, but no need to go into that here.) John said that everyone should reread the *Proverbs of Hell* at least once a decade, for the pleasure of picking out lines that failed to register last time round. Having just done exactly that, I concur. There's a copy of Blake's *Complete Works* on the table as I write. This cottage, of course, is crammed with books. The shelves go back to before John was born, and he himself filled several more before kingship took him elsewhere. Books and bookshelves are so much a part of the place I tend to overlook their presence.

This morning, though, while waiting for the ink to thaw, I limped over and ran my thumb along the spines while the merganser glared down from above. There's no time for reading here, and I have not let myself give in to that temptation. But I was hoping – still am hoping – to find some reference to frostbite. John and his ancestors weren't much for alphabetization, or even grouping books according to size, let alone subject. The shelves here appear to have been filled organically; you'll find Descartes next to Dickens, alongside Margaret Atwood, propped against Drs. Johnson and Seuss. Somewhere in here, though, I'm betting there's a medical reference text. I did find an elderly copy of *Gray's Anatomy*, but no mention of frostbite.

I also found this volume of Blake:

He who desires, but acts not, breeds pestilence.

Or,

Drive your cart and your plow over the bones of the dead.

Or,

The bird a nest, the spider a web, man friendship.

You can get hermeneutical to your heart's content with William Blake. But the line that strikes me hardest is the one I recall John quoting during the Quebec disputes:

As the air to a bird or the sea to a fish, so is contempt to the contemptible.

He would sigh as he recited it; I remember him actually standing in front of a mirror watching himself repeat the words. Mirror diplomacy, you see, involved our side's embracing the contemptible too.

The fox condemns the trap, I threw back at him once, *not himself.* Meaning to say stop mooning and get on with it. John always appreciated a dose of your better-class irony.

There are chairs of political science departments now entirely devoted to the concept, so very likely you're sick of it already. Generations of high-school students will, I'm certain, have cursed John for his contribution to their workload (though it was me who actually coined the term – pithy, isn't it?). In a nutshell, mirror diplomacy amounted to our side's decision to conduct all negotiations with Quebec in the same spirit as Quebec pursued its negotiations with us. Doesn't sound particularly draconian, does it? But at the time it was heresy. Your high-school essayist wouldn't be too far off the mark in describing mirror diplomacy as the simple strategy of returning Quebec's ill-will. That's what always troubled John about it. One region of his brain understood the logic, agreed with the ethical appropriateness, but the other part kept telling him this was something no civilized Canadian should even think about, let alone do – a barbarism on the order of striking one's wife.

A hundred and forty-odd years of two-nations protocol had been based on the premise that Quebec would look out for its own interests exclusively, while the federal government (ROC) was expected to retain Quebec's benefit within its own range of objectives. In practical terms, this meant that Quebec negotiators never gave a thought to anything but their own advantage, while across the table their opponents were committed to working for both sides equally. You can see how this might have tilted the surface, strategically speaking. Mirror diplomacy was just a shorthand way of saying that Canada, from now on, would apply the same aggressive self-interest with regard to Quebec as Quebec had always applied to Canada.

As I've said, it gave everyone on the Quebec side seizures, but to the rest of us it suddenly made sense. It clicked. I'm very proud of the term, to be honest. It said exactly what it was meant to say, it summed up everything in two tidy little words. Within days of John's introduction of the term, people in coffee shops from Moncton to Medicine Hat were discussing the policy as if they understood it. And they pretty much did. Not in minutiae, of course – as it turns out, we ourselves didn't realize the full breadth of its repercussions – but in broad strokes people got the concept and suddenly, wholeheartedly, approved. It really did change everything. Once Canadians took the bit between their teeth, they raced with it, demanded more of it. *Damn right!* they said. *Why didn't we get here sooner?* Before the end, we couldn't have stopped them even if we'd wanted to, and believe me when I tell you we did everything we could to slow it down. But the hardening of attitude was so swift it took not only us but the rest of the world by surprise. *The Economist* magazine, known for its exaggerated British boredom with everything Canadian, ran a cover showing a map of Canada with a jagged hole where old Quebec had been and the tag: "WHAT HAPPENED?"

You know what happened, so there's no point in rehashing it. I wish I could tell you, though, that we had something to do with the beautiful symmetry of those final numbers. Truth is, we didn't. We nudged. We pushed. We manipulated, sure – we did everything we could to herd both sets of voters toward the same conclusion – but that numerical coincidence was really just another of the happy accidents that blessed John's reign. Or maybe the work of his tutelary muse, who's to say? In any case, the papers had a field day. It was a headline-writer's dream: TWO SOLITUDES JOIN IN AGREEMENT TO SPLIT! QUEBEC AND ROC VOTERS CONVERGE, 72% OF QUEBECERS, 72% OF CANADIANS VOTE FOR SEPARATION!

Of course we knew, going in, that we were likely to get a majority on both counts. (And by the way, the question to both groups was a straight-up "Do you agree Quebec should form an independent state – yes or no?") John still hadn't much in the way of technical resources, at this stage, or any loyal staff except me. But the media groups were all polling madly, and we could read as well as they could.

When push came to shove, the two sides had agreed by an unassailable majority. What could be more harmonious than that? What more fundamentally Canadian? Voters in Quebec and the ROC woke up next morning realizing they'd done it, they were splitsville. From that point on, it was just a matter of drawing up the paperwork.

George Orwell – who I also note is well represented on John's shelves – wrote somewhere that a nation's continuity is like that of an individual's from infancy to adulthood. They're still the same person, yet wholly different. That's something like what happened here. Canada without Quebec was still Canada, but a Canada utterly changed. I'm going to argue that Orwell's analogy is insufficient. What happened with Canada was more like full-scale metamorphosis. Perhaps you've read about those creatures that spend years, decades, sometimes centuries wedged into precise little crevasses, waiting for the right environmental signals to hatch from their pupas and emerge transformed. That's the more appropriate analogy. Canadians of John's reign – or should I say what used to be called English Canadians – tore out of their cocoons different animals than they had been before.

It's tempting to suggest the transformational spark was John himself, but that would be like saying mirrors make images. They do not. They only reflect them. Better to say that John was the glass. The change, the energy that fuelled that change, always originated in Quebec. If John was the lens, though, it was Hester who directed the light.

She was the first Canadian I met who'd openly admit to resenting Quebec. Once the dam of public sentiment broke, post-referendum, it got to be popular, Quebec-bashing. Unpleasantly so. But when I first arrived in Toronto – or let's say as early as two or three months before that time – anyone who publicly expressed reservations about Quebec's special status, never mind bilingualism, tended to be grouped in with the guys in white sheets and burning crosses.

You should appreciate that Hester *was* Toronto. The successes and failures met with by her city were experienced directly and emotionally by the Mayor herself. This was what made her so beloved by her constituents; Hester really was the city's heart. I am not trying to be literary. Hester's supporters, I believe, could physically feel the force of her devotion. Her enemies, I can tell you from experience, registered exactly the opposite.

Second only to John, Hester's great political success was in defining Quebec as *foe*. I myself have always thought this was not quite so great an accomplishment as people later made out. On the political plain, admittedly, the rift was epochal. But at the emotional level, where Hester always held her firmest grasp, it really wasn't so much of a stretch.

The so-called founding nations had been on the verge of breakup since they'd got together in the first place. Despite the centuries of coexistence, the fabled rapprochement was always more suspicious détente than joyful union. Put your finger in at almost any period in Canadian history and you'll see French and English in conflict, not harmony. *Never* harmony. It's a miracle the marriage held up as long as it did; it was an uneven, unhappy wedlock kept alive only through the bitterness of obligation.

If you've ever watched a couple break up, or witnessed the rush of malice that so often follows in the wake of a divorce, you'll have some sense of what happened. Litigators feast on these emotions, and their repercussions clog our civil courts. The difference for Quebec, as its benighted citizens soon discovered, was that the civil courts no longer pertained in their case. Quebec's interests had always been protected by federal sanction. With its withdrawal from the federation, its protection under this umbrella was also rescinded. International law, as I can advise you, works only as long as the parties agree to it, and even then always favours the stronger claimant. When the time came for dividing the assets, post-divorce, post-two-nations, we took them to the cleaners, pure and simple.

From Hester's perspective, this was political necessity. She'd just lost the biggest gamble of her political career. Or appeared to have. Toronto had been hammered in its bid for independence. Disasters of this magnitude almost always spell the end for whichever politician takes the blame for having caused them. But then Quebec took over the spotlight and attracted to itself all the hostility that rightly should have focused on Her Worship. There's nothing like a common enemy for cementing friendships. Which is why it's good advice to choose your foes far more carefully than you do your friends.

If Hester made John, John repaid the favour by saving Hester. That's how they worked it out between them. It still makes me squeamish, though, remembering Theodore Sapper's role. Worse for John. He turned on us later – Sapper, I mean – which in a way is consoling. But John's conscience was never quite as malleable as mine. Many times I reminded him that if Sapper had ever found out about Hester and him, he'd have destroyed both of them without a moment's qualm – that was just the nature of the beast. John would nod. He always agreed on that.

Sapper was no fan of Quebec to begin with. This was for purely business reasons, as I'm about to explain – but even the bilious pen of Theodore Sapper found itself restrained by Canada's rules of two-nations etiquette. If you read Sapper's pre-John editorials, you'll find in them a notably harsher tone toward Quebec than was usual for commentators of that era, but nothing remotely like the savagery that filled his pages once John let loose the dogs of referenda. Quebec, in those days, already enjoyed many of the advantages of an independent state. It had its own "minister of international relations," for instance, and operated a network of pseudo-embassies abroad. For decades it had relied on its complex language laws to discourage non-Québécois corporations from leaving footprints in the province. This was how it ran afoul of Theodore Sapper.

But before I get to that story (and speaking of ironies), here's a different one, more sidebar, really, but pertinent. I'm just remembering a little anecdote of Hester's:

From time to time, the Mayor was called upon to attended conferences abroad. I don't remember the topic of this one and it doesn't matter, except that it took place in Mexico City, where Hester found herself being introduced to Quebec's then-minister of international relations. *Le Ministre*, it turned out, was in town that day courting Latino businessmen. He was fresh from delivering a hard-hitting speech to an audience of Mexican industrialists, emotionally comparing their lot to Quebecers': The world's downtrodden must help *each other*, the Minister urged, not their oppressors. Marginalized nations should conduct their business only with *other* marginalized nations; Latin Americans should make common cause with Quebecers – "*los Latinos del Norte*," as he'd shamelessly described them – not anglophone Canadians. I remember her telling this story several years later, not long after some well-meaning coalition of church groups had informally broached the subject of readmitting Quebec into Confederation. "That would be difficult, I imagine," replied the Mayor, hiding her smile. Canada's economy was by that time already far, far too dependent on Quebec's pool of cheap labour. There were too many Québécois gardeners, nannies, and pool boys in circulation for middle-class Canadians ever to consider giving up their *Northern Mexicans*.

Sapper's own pet issue was protectionism. Midway through his campaign to establish himself as top dog in the media kennel club, Sapper's acquisition of certain francophone holdings had been blocked by Quebec's government. The case was based on language laws, as I recall it: Quebec wielded astonishing power in the interest of defending its culture. The sanctions brought to bear against Sapper ought to have been unconstitutional and, if memory serves, would have been in any other province. But because Quebec was guaranteed perpetual veto over such matters, his lawyers had advised him not to even bother taking it to provincial court, never mind appealing to a Supreme Court where Quebec-appointed judges were certain to rule against. The budding mogul contented himself with printing a seething editorial about Quebec's uncanny reliance on a Constitution that it hadn't brought itself to actually sign, and bided his time. (Financially speaking, by the way, it turned out that the setback worked to Sapper's advantage over the long run. He got less than he expected for the value of the shares he'd purchased, but far more than they were worth a few years later when the Montreal stock market crashed. The rich never really suffer, do they?)

Point being: it didn't take a Metternich to nudge Theodore Sapper into outright hostility toward Quebec. He had a grudge to start with, and a personality well adapted to the exercise of grudges. All we really needed was that first set of poll results suggesting John's speech had struck some serious resonance with English Canadians. Once that note was sounded, Sapper was ready to back it with the full force of his orchestra. Pretty soon he had the whole country tapping in time.

There's a psychological term for what happened: *transference*, if I'm not mistaken. Everyone's anger suddenly channelled straight into Quebec. In Toronto, citizens were already gnashing their teeth. Remember that Hester had spurred them to the point of wanting to abandon the whole damned country. Independence had been squashed as quickly as it had taken flight, which only made them more resentful. Then John stepped in and told them – without actually saying it – that what they really should be mad at was Quebec. In his unsigned editorial the very next morning, Theodore Sapper was quick to expand upon the new King's understated theme.

Toronto had every reason to be bitter, Sapper wrote. But it had no one to blame but itself. Torontonians, after all, had always been Quebec Inc.'s principal underwriters. It was never any secret where their money went, but they just kept on paying regardless. Always had, always would – until folks here woke up and took responsibility for their own stupidity. How typical of Toronto that it should suddenly decide to flee its own table, rather than eject the one guest spoiling the feast. Torontonians deserved every ounce of scorn they got from the rest of the country. Quebecers were right all along: the city had no soul, and no guts either.

After that, he rolled out the same message right across the country – carefully tweaked according to the local tastes and prejudices. Province by province, city by city, town by town, Sapper visited each region's relationship with Quebec and picked the scabs. In Alberta, he publicized a study investigating "the federal fiscal imbalance." The paper tracked how much money each province contributed to the rest of the country, then measured it against what each got back in return. Over a twenty-year period, so the authors concluded, Alberta had been drained of several hundred billion – while Quebec, coincidentally, had been paid out precisely that amount. Albertans always enjoyed this kind of reading – even in normal times when they'd had to hold Ottawa responsible – but now they could savour their ill feelings communally, knowing the rest of the country was doing the same. This was a feeling unfamiliar to Albertans – this sense of collectivity – and they found to their surprise that they enjoyed it.

Suddenly, no one felt guilty about resenting Quebec because, suddenly, everyone else was doing it too. Newfoundland was already bitter over its deal with Quebec's hydro monopoly. Many Newfoundlanders believed that fast-talking Québécois negotiators had got their own Premier drunk on red wine and coaxed him into signing a deal that – forty years on – was still allowing Quebec to buy Labrador hydro at rates established back in the 1950s, electricity that Quebec then turned around and sold to New York at a scandalous profit. Sapper dusted off this ancient carbuncle, hinted that there was more to the red-wine angle than meets the eye, and also reminded Newfoundlanders that Gaspé fishermen had been plundering their cod stocks since, well, since before Cartier, let alone Confederation.

Around this time, Hester weighed in with an emotional interview – televised live – during which she revealed exactly the moment she'd realized there was no hope for Toronto in Confederation as we knew it. It was the morning after Quebec MPs had voted down the Urban Renewal Bill, she said – she remembered it like it was yesterday – that was when she understood her people would always be hostages. "As they still are to this day," said the Mayor, gazing sadly at the camera. The segment went out coast to coast on national feed.

And the beauty of it all was that exactly the same thing was going on in Quebec.

Quebec's francophone media was infuriated with English Canadians' presumption to be annoyed with *them*. *They* were the oppressed ones. What empty-headed anglophonic sophistry was this, that the violators should insinuate themselves as victims? Had everyone forgotten the Plains of Abraham? This vicious rise in anglo chauvinism was surely final proof of English Canada's colonial hegemony.

I have dipped my pen into the ink of irony a shade too often today, I know. But it's hard to avoid. (It's ballpoint, but you take my meaning.) Suddenly, Quebec's sovereigntist government – led by the very party that had come to power on a platform of Quebec independence – found itself desperately reminding Quebecers of the benefits of federation. They'd been in office long enough to understand, even if their supporters did not, what really was at stake if things were permitted to go too far. But their backpedalling was seized upon as evidence of treason by the cadre of committed secessionists who had always formed the core of the independence movement, and who now watched with glee as Quebec's great mass of soft nationalism suddenly turned hard.

It all came down to hurt feelings, in the end.

Quebecers had grown so habituated to their special status that they had ceased to be aware of it. They were not exceptions to the rule, as they saw it – they *were* the rule – and rules were just and fair and equitable, by definition. When the rest of Canada suddenly began shouting that it no longer liked the way the game was played, Quebecers saw *themselves* as victims of the cheat. I think I've mentioned before that a state is nothing more than the individual, extended. It is subject to the same range of emotions. I'm convinced that this explains everything.

In the final analysis, Quebec drowned in the flood of its own ill-will. Hester always held this view. John, I think, resisted it but ultimately couldn't overcome the logic. I've mentioned that Hester was not a woman willing to place herself at the disposal of her emotions. She was by nature a pragmatist. But I think I'm safe to say that Her Worship's anger usefully defined an era. It certainly informed my own strategies.

John eventually was brought around to the view that Quebec's attitude to Canada had poisoned Canada's vision of itself. Non-Quebecers were perfectly aware of Québécois disdain – there was no shortage of evidence – but they'd taught themselves to respectfully ignore it. Beginning with John, Hester systematically reversed that way of thinking. It was the little things, at first, that she succeeded in reading most into. There was never any shortage of billboard-sized examples of Quebec's contempt for English Canada. You could start with the respective perspectives on bilingualism, for instance, and work your way from there. On one hand, here was the federal government spending tens of millions encouraging anglophones to learn French; on the other was Quebec, defying the country's own Charter of Rights in its determination to suppress the use of English in the province. I have to admit I still can't figure out how this was tolerated in a so-called just society, but for John the story was so ancient his natural indignation had long ago been calloused over. What incensed Hester – and through her John and then the rest of us – were the smaller, sillier things; those low-weight snippets of back-page filler she would seize upon and thrash us with. I remember her pouncing on a poll showing 80 per cent of Quebecers could not identify the country's first Prime Minister. Things like this would set her pounding her fists. "Can you imagine eight out of ten respondents even in Mississippi not knowing George Washington?" (As a matter of fact, I could well imagine nine out of ten Mississippians not identifying their biological father, let alone any abstract constitutional ones, but I held my peace.) John pointed out that the very same survey showed that three out of ten *English Canadians* couldn't name Sir John A. either.

"There's stupidity," she answered, "and then there's *wilful* stupidity. I'll concede there's always going to be a certain percentage of innocent morons, but for the numbers to get that low, it has to be deliberate." Hester was convinced that most Quebecers knew damn well who Macdonald was but wilfully informed the surveyors they didn't. She said it was just another way of flipping the *Alouette's* middle digit.

But what affected John most was the gradual understanding that this wellspring of loathing spilled out beyond Quebec's own borders and infected the thinking of Canadians across the board. It took me a while to grasp this, but once I'd lived here long enough I believe I came to understand it. There was something self-defeating in Canadians' attitudes *about themselves* in those days, something that shaded beyond modesty and well into outright self-abnegation. It seemed to me that my adopted countrymen were constantly assuring one another they had reason to be proud but could never quite bring themselves to be.

It was a puzzle we solved with Quebec.

Official bilingualism guaranteed that for several generations, Quebecers had dominated the upper strata of government. Unless they were bilingual, civil servants were barred from advancing beyond certain levels of seniority, which effectively meant that only Quebecers reached the top. (Students in Montreal or Chicoutimi studied English for the same reason people in Malaysia and Madagascar did – it's a global language, after all – but for a rancher in Saskatchewan, say, or for that matter an engineer in Toronto, the only reason you'd want your kids learning French was to give them a leg up into the civil service – which I needn't tell you was not at that time especially high on most parents' list of hopes and aspirations. That being said, an astonishing number of Canadians did dutifully send their sons and daughters off to French-immersion schools. But unless they lived in border towns like Ottawa, there was seldom any opportunity outside the classroom for most kids to practise the language. Hardly any retained sufficient skills to shine in the civil service exams.)

So for a span of nearly half a century, the country's top decision-makers were drawn mostly from Quebec. Remember, too, that Quebec looked upon itself not merely as a province but as a national entity equal to the sum of the other nine provinces combined. By John's time, Quebec's population had fallen to roughly 20 per cent of Canada's, but those two out of ten felt perfectly entitled to halvsies with the rest of the country. This was particularly true when it came to cultural capital.

On the matter of Québécois cultural sovereignty, the Canadian state was intensely protectionist. Francophone arts and letters were understood to be in constant peril, and Ottawa remained fully committed to defending them. But in the event of *English* cultural institutions requesting defence from outside interference – this was answered with a much more laissez-faire approach to policy. Indeed, many Quebecers were embarrassed by the ROC's insistence that it had a culture to begin with. One of their premiers had famously stated that there was no such thing as Canadian culture at all, outside Quebec. To whatever extent it did exist – and insofar as certain English-language institutions might perceive themselves to be at risk from American competition – this was more a reflection of market economy than a case for governmental interference. Besides which, there was nothing to be done about it anyway.

Some years prior to John, the Prime Minister of the day had decided he was going to put an end to the Canadian Broadcasting Corporation, which as you know was mandated generations earlier to ensure that Canadian concerns were expressed in Canadian voices. Reverently Canadian in structure, the CBC was divided into two equal parts. The French half was called Radio Canada. It received 50 per cent of CBC's yearly funding and after the Quiet Revolution came under the control of the separatists. The Prime Minister, a Quebecer, as usual, but of necessity a federalist one, resented the constant attacks from his state-funded broadcaster. He resolved once and for all to end the absurdity by slashing the CBC's operating budget, stem to stern. But this being Canada, that wasn't how things worked out. The budget was, in fact, dramatically reduced, but the cuts ended up coming mostly out of the *English* operations not the French. Despite the PMO's intentions, Canadian cultural prerogatives kicked into force when it came time to actually wield the knife: It was unthinkable that a francophone institution constantly threatened by the anglophone culture should suffer destabilization. Radio Canada preserved its funding. The CBC's English service, on the other hand – traditionally condemned by the likes of Theodore Sapper as an institution no self-respecting market economy could allow itself to support – was slashed to the bone. It would have died altogether if John hadn't come along when he did.

(After the referendum, the King lobbied openly for Radio Canada's entire budget to be injected directly into the English network, which effectively brought an end to his honeymoon with Sapper, but which also accounts for the CBC's aggressively monarchist loyalties from that point forward.)

Where was I?

Canada's long experiment with official bilingualism was, and I still believe this, one of the noblest gifts of deference the world has ever seen. It failed, of course, and in the end achieved exactly the opposite of what it intended. But I think Canadians should still feel proud for trying, and after all they did try – for the span of two entire generations. John had nightmares about it afterwards. I mean it, honest-to-goodness nightmares that woke him from the dead of sleep – Gwen described them once. That's how emotionally committed your average Canadian was to the concept – English Canadian, I mean.

It's hard to explain. Think of official bilingualism for the average, mainstream Canadian as something in the nature of toilet-seat etiquette for the average married man – a habit shaped, in other words, not so much from personal preference but from the certain knowledge that to do otherwise was to invite recrimination without end. As analogies go, it's a trifle overheated, maybe. But what I'm trying to get at is the bedrock acceptance on *both* sides that this was a condition long since agreed to, unconditionally, as a fixed requirement for happy marriage.

And there was the rub, of course.

Because the marriage wasn't happy, and never was. When the dam burst, the flood of resentment pent up all those years was truly frightening to see.

The country's acquiescence to Quebec had encouraged stupid policy – enshrining a system of regionalism, for instance, that rewarded confrontation and penalized co-operation. Hester proved that one well enough. But the deeper harm was more psychological than structural.

Years ago, when John tasked me with establishing the Gold Leaf Awards, I had the opportunity to plunge myself into Canadian literature, past and present. What struck me was the almost total absence of political fiction. There was no such tradition in Canada, at least not in the modern and postmodern eras, and precious little before. Can you imagine the American canon without Robert Penn Warren, or Britain's literature without the likes of Graham Greene? Canada had no such writers. Not so in Quebec. Quebec's artists had no qualms about tackling politics, and clearly saw no compromise to their artistic integrity in doing so. ROC writers blushed at the very thought. When the separatist Premier accused them of having no culture, I believe he touched a more sensitive nerve than he knew. I think this also explains CanLit's long-standing tradition of narcissistic self-denial. The country knew whereof it spoke.

Dip him in the river who loves water.

Enough! Or too much.

DAY TWENTY-TWO

I'M CERTAIN NOW the duck is staring back.

It may just be my foot, which might be bringing on a touch of fever. Or maybe it's that all this policy wonking has got the better of me. At any rate, John's merganser clearly belongs to the waterfowl category (phylum? genus?), which reminds me of geese, which is all the segue I need to launch into the topic I've decided to recuperate with today. This represents yet another betrayal of chronology, admittedly, but I'm discovering that history has greater flexibility than even I'd suspected. Besides which, that postmodern flight of fancy yesterday has tempted me to experiment with form.

It had always bothered the King that his country offered the world so few distinctly national dishes. (There was maple syrup, true, but that was not so much a food as a flavouring.) Throughout his reign, John devoted a great deal of time and energy to increasing Canada's contribution to global gourmandise. He longed to do for his country what Artusi had done for Italy's gastronomic nation-building, and definitely succeeded in raising the profile of certain agricultural sectors and wineries – there's no denying the globalization of our pemmican trade, for example. But aside from those advances, John's goose initiative was his only out-of-the-park home run. Some of his wilder notions – I'm thinking, for instance, of his plans for woodchucks on Groundhog Day – were pretty much doomed from inception. The goose campaign, though, was a smash hit.

It was, if you'll excuse the pun, a classic example of the King's uncanny ability to kill any number of birds with a single stone. To begin with, there was the long-standing problem of the geese themselves. Canada geese had for years been making a terrible nuisance of themselves all over the grounds of the Silos, all over King's Island – all over the Great Lakes, for that matter. John's goose campaign started, fairly innocently, with the goal of reducing the quantities of goose droppings on the King's new green roof.

But then some hunting association, I forget which, invited John to a wild-game fundraising dinner for wetland rehabilitation or some such thing. John was always keen to bridge the gap between environmentalists and their natural enemies, so he accepted – on the condition that he could bring along a couple of the moderate members of the anti-hunting lobby, just to make the conversation interesting. He also sent ahead several cases of a very decent Niagara Riesling, with the same intent.

As it turned out, Roast Canada Goose was served that night, which – surprise, surprise – paired exceedingly well with the wine.

Unsurprisingly, since everyone was eating it, the talk came round to geese: how good they were when properly roasted, not greasy at all, how very well they went with this excellent Riesling, Canadian too, take note, how incredibly many geese there were all over the waterfront downtown. By this time, John's anti-hunting friends had topped up their stemware often enough to admit that they disliked the goddamn geese as much as anyone, but, really, there wasn't much that could be done about them. Someone said (as someone always did whenever city geese were discussed in any gathering of two or more) that we should eat the goddamn things, that's what we should do, and the environmentalist agreed that the goose tasted better than his mother-in-law's Thanksgiving turkey – that was a given – but, realistically, what could you do about that?

"*Eat goose for Thanksgiving!*" came the reply. "That's what you do!" And so was born John's Thanksgiving goose campaign, its official campaign slogan, and the nucleus of a coalition group already mustering in pro-royal support.

That first year, the King's Thanksgiving Levy served roast Canadian goose to a skeptical but curious gathering of two hundred carefully picked celebs. (We were sure to engage the city's best chefs, by the way, to ensure that the guests – pounced upon by hungry media as they left the dining hall – all pronounced the meal superb.) The next year, John conspicuously played up the lottery angle, ceremoniously presenting five hundred dressed, drawn, and frozen birds to the winners of the first Annual Canadian Goose Draw – which very cheekily invited pundits to make whatever inferences they liked about the King's own ascendancy.

After that, the Goose Draw went national. Every second year it still comes back home to Toronto, but in each and every alternating year since, John and several thousand frozen geese have flown off to Moncton or Winnipeg or Whitehorse (you'd be amazed how vicious the municipal lobbies get, fighting over who gets the birds next). It's absurdly popular, and the dinner event that follows it is always a who's who of local kingpins.

I'm wishing now I had the time to tell you all about John's plans for Groundhog Day. That one I had to talk him out of. Suffice to say, the major obstacle to making groundhog a national dish to be served on a February 2 statuary holiday was the geo-zoological fact that groundhogs were not a genuinely national animal; turns out they're not found much west of Ontario. "What about prairie dogs?" was the King's response.

From time to time, our monarch let his enthusiasms run away with him.

But Thanksgiving goose was a triumph. Many people still prefer turkey, mind you, and a lot more serve the regular store-bought domestic goose. But when you start to see marketers using goose imagery instead of turkeys for Thanksgiving ad campaigns hawking cars and computers, you know you've chalked up another cultural paradigm.

There's another thing about the Goose Campaign I need to tell you, and this is the most important thing. Think of it as a parable, if you will: a lovely, silly illustration of kingliness. An example of the kind of thing an unelected monarch can take on and accomplish that an elected politician cannot – or, more fairly, would never attempt. At the heart of this story is the singular and salient fact that the majority of interested citizens wanted something done about the geese. Goose shit, if you haven't experienced it, comes in little green logs about the length of your finger and sticks to your shoes. There were so many geese in Toronto that they were actually hampering the waterfront renewal. The city tried everything from border collies to birth control, but nothing worked, and the geese grew bolder. But the one thing they never tried – the cheapest, easiest, and most sensible solution – was ordering a cull. That option was never pursued because the moment it was even hinted at, the Save-the-Goose lobby sprang into action in all its savage righteousness.

Near as we could figure it, the Geese Defenders never numbered more than a few dozen hard-core specialists. But they were dedicated, and marshalled an arsenal of quasi-religious fanaticism. (Which, of course, earned them John's antipathy right from the beginning. John, as I think I have mentioned, inclined toward fanaticism himself in his dislike of fanatics.) The Save-the-Goosers always, inevitably thrashed the majority opposition because they brought to bear a focused zeal the other side could never muster. The simple truth was that, for any elected official, coming out in support of killing off a bunch of geese just wasn't worth the gunpowder. There were too many other, more important battles to fight. For Elspeth Blanc, on the other hand – and her cell of media guerrillas – opposition to the goose cull represented everything they stood for.

Elected officials have only so much political capital, is what I'm getting at, and a limited time to invest it. Special-interest groups can throw everything they've got into a single cause, take to the trenches, and win by attrition. But so, too, can monarchs. "A king can poke his fingers in democracy's neglected corners," I think is how we later phrased it, though perhaps a little overlyrically.

That was from a speech I wrote for John in the middle of the constitutional crunch. I quote the line here because it's every bit as applicable to geese as it was to the much larger issues of the day. And though I'm reluctant to draw comparisons linking Canada geese to Catholic schoolchildren, or Elspeth Blanc and her band of Save-the-Goosers to Archbishop Harper and the separate school board battle, the parallel applies. In the case of the Goose Defenders, a small minority had successfully promoted its own interests over those of a majority too busy defending other, bigger things. It was the same with the separate school boards.

Almost everyone (even most Catholics, according to our polls) recognized the inherent unfairness of public money being used to fund one religious group over others. But because of nineteenth-century constitutional provisions written to satisfy ecclesiastic interests in Quebec, several provinces were still obliged to educate Roman Catholic students separately from everybody else. I'm sure I don't have to explain the tremendous cost involved in maintaining parallel school systems – not only in duplication of services (Catholic school on one side of the street, public school on the other), but also the sense of grievance it caused among other religious institutions demanding equal preferment. It was colossally stupid, monstrously expensive, and immensely resistant to change.

Of course, there were vested interests perfectly happy with things the way they were. Successive provincial governments had mused about amending the act, and successive governments had been swiftly brought to heel by wrathful bishops threatening to mobilize the entire RC vote in opposition. In actual fact, there was never any certainty the church could deliver. Unlike politicians, religious leaders don't tend to poll their constituents, but no politician with a view to next election was willing to risk it. And always there were other, more immediate concerns. So for more than a century, untold billions in tax dollars flowed into a system the majority of ratepayers considered a direct violation of democratic principle – while the Constitution itself perpetuated the injustice.

"If you want the word to sum it up," John thundered from his own unelected pulpit, "if you want the word to describe this situation most exactly, that word is *blasphemy*! This is a blasphemy against the very spirit of the Charter of Rights, nothing less, and shame on you who seek to perpetuate it!"

Archbishop Harper, no slouch himself in the oratorical line, shot back that it was *John* who should be ashamed, confusing divine institutions with earthly affairs – and never had he witnessed such blatant and unconstitutional attacks on the very heart of religious freedom. John quite publicly rolled his eyes over that one and then delivered one of his more memorable quips:

"Will no one rid me of this meddlesome priest?" he said, deadpan, gazing straight into the cameras, then winked.

Much to my surprise, several of the reporters recognized the quote and laughed out loud. John's reference, of course, was to England's King Henry II, whose use of the same words was said to have provoked the assassination of Archbishop Thomas à Becket in 1170 or thereabouts. The joke caused a mighty buzz, I can tell you. The archbishop was outraged, as well he might be, and the papers had a field day printing cartoons of John in sackcloth and ashes. But by the end of the discussions, the act was expunged as surely as Quebec. Legislators drafting the new Constitution, while delighted to see John taking the flak, were even happier to walk through the door the King pounded open.

"Attack the fundamental wrongness of anything," John always said, "and eventually it cracks." To which I will add the proviso: "Ensure yourself the leverage to maintain the assault."

But back to the geese.

Elspeth Blanc was chairperson of the Animal Activist Movement (AAM), which was one of those small-in-stature, high-in-profile protest organizations that specialized in media. The AAM staged demonstrations at steak houses in support of cows, boycotted shoe stores to protest the villainy of leather, and occasionally raided rural mink farms in order to break open the cages and release the inmates so they could starve to death in their natural state of liberty, after killing off the local fauna. In one especially memorable campaign, they dramatized "the colonization of innocent insects," demanding an end to the oppression of bees through the forced-labour production of honey. Their star-quality candidate, though, was the Canada goose. Unlike the case against beef or leather – which most people either ate or wore – a broader constituency of animal rights supporters were able to get behind the goose campaign without denying themselves anything they were likely to miss. Canada geese were a popular cause among the armchair variety of AAM supporters, is what I'm saying, and Elspeth Blanc could always be relied upon to put extra effort into the promotion of her most recognizable brand.

John hated her.

I have to say it was unusual for John to truly hate a woman. His ingrained courtliness generally prevailed, when it came to what used to be called the fairer sex, and although there was no shortage of powerful females ranged against him over years – including both Hester and Gwen, at various times – John was by nature much more forgiving of women than men. But, God, he truly did hate Elspeth Blanc.

I believe I have mentioned that John was a serious environmentalist – you've absorbed that fact by now, I'm sure. You'll grasp neither King nor Crown, though, unless you fully appreciate the fundamental consequence of this connection. It was a component-part of John and his thinking – physical and metaphysical, dare I say – inseparable from both the man and his legacy. John's lifelong goal was to stop what he called the "fraternal war" between environmental interests and commercial ones. He was unwilling to accept the traditional division of left against right in its application to air and water. "Who picked the sides?" he'd ask, often pounding one fist with the other. "How did socialists come to be responsible for the environment? How did conservatives find themselves in opposition?"

John argued that of all the sad developments of the twentieth century, the saddest was this inversion of what ought to have been the natural order of things. Socialists, after all, were philosophically concerned with distributing capital. Conservatives were supposed to be preoccupied with keeping it. Environment was capital. So how did we find ourselves in a world where socialists were the hoarders of resources and conservatives its wanton spenders? The words *conservative* and *conservation*, he liked to point out, were etymological twins. What malignant force had driven two such philosophical siblings into opposite camps?

For John, the answer was obvious: Elspeth Blanc, that's what. Or, rather, the collective effect of people like her. If you wanted to target the single biggest obstacle facing the environmental movement, John always said, you needed to look no farther than the flakes within the movement itself. His point was that every time an average, open-minded, small-c conservative type – your basic backbone of society – started thinking seriously about environmental issues, up would pop an Elspeth Blanc to hiss in his face and chase him straight back into the arms of the Frobisher Institute.

Remember the Law of Perpetual Error? I think I talked about it a few days back – the one that holds that whenever an idiot gets hold of a good idea, the idea is doomed by the company it keeps? It's a very useful little formula, if you don't mind my saying, and one that cuts across a depressingly broad spectrum of practical reality. (Hester always complained, for instance, that the greatest barrier she faced in getting Toronto to debate the merits of separation was the fact the Mayor before her – the used-car salesman – had at one time proposed the very same thing. The problem was that everybody knew this Mayor was an idiot, and that therefore any ideas he had must also be idiotic, which effectively crippled the most potent force in Canadian politics until Hester came along to pull it out of the ashes.)

John despised Elspeth Blanc not so much for the woman herself, but for the discredit she brought to causes much worthier than geese. At least at the beginning, I should say, before the brown envelope. After that, his feeling took on shall we say a more personal note.

The brown paper envelope is – short of outright murder – by far the most effective anti-personnel device on the battlefield of

contemporary politics. Receiving a brown paper envelope is like
having Prometheus hand you the ingredients for your very first
firebomb; it's like what Moses must have felt watching the seas
wash over Pharaoh's army. It's like manna from heaven, if you'll
forgive the mix of mythic metaphors. Getting a brown paper
envelope is being blessed with something approaching divine
intervention. I've always suspected Hester was somehow behind
the E. Blanc e-mail, though it clearly originated with someone
much closer to Blanc herself.

Doesn't matter. We got the goods is what matters. And the
goods we got on Elspeth Blanc gave John the knife to gut her,
the hook to hang her, and the gibbet to suspend her carcass as
a warning to those who stray from the path of virtue, which I'm
bound to say he did with unseemly pleasure for so normally
good-natured a sovereign.

The secret to good dirt is that it comes in kind. The ideal
brown envelope (or anonymous phone call or blind e-mail)
contains information specifically and ironically appropriate to
its target. Its coin is hypocrisy. For the purpose of illustration,
consider the classic Right-to-Lifer caught arranging an abortion
for his teenage Bible-study partner. (And as a further aside, let
me add that I was aware of at least two such specimens in
Hester's game bag; clichés don't get to be that way out of
nowhere.) The ideal brown envelope contains information that
not only destroys the individual, but also expands to devastate
the wider cause the individual represents. When you happen to
loathe the individual herself, though, the secondary benefit can
be as great a pleasure as the prime.

For Elspeth Blanc, the end came in the form of a letter out-
lining her participation in the destruction of one of the last
remaining habitats of Canada's northern shrike.

Now I have to say that until that day, I'd never even heard
of shrikes. These days, everybody knows all about them. In

terms of national icons, shrikes now rank right up there next to beavers. But back then, they weren't exactly hot on anybody's radar. Except for people like John. John understood right away the significance of the information we received. It took a little while for him to calm down enough to explain it, and even then I didn't fully appreciate why he was getting into such a lather. Only someone with John's peculiar mix of ethical purity and practical ferocity could have succeeded in building such a fine mountain from the apparently insignificant molehill we received. But that was John. I could help, once the thing was underway, and did. But I have to admit that John was unique in his ability to get something like that going in the first place. I'll admit that.

Elspeth Blanc owned a piece of land north of Kingston. It was a farm, a hundred acres or so, that she'd inherited from some distant relative. Blanc herself lived downtown in Toronto like most environmental activists, and used the rural property for weekend retreats. Our secret e-mail informed us that an Elspeth E. Blanc had just completed a transaction of sale, with the buyer identified as development corporation intent on building a golf course on the property. Several of her neighbours, it turned out, had signed similarly lucrative agreements.

Now John had nothing per se against golf. It's true that four hundred acres of fairways and sand pits sucking water from the local aquifers is not perhaps the most environmentally sensitive form of land use. On the other hand, the quantities of pesticides and fertilizer spread around on golf courses are likely no worse than what gets dumped on your average potato field, with quite a few more trees left standing. John liked golf. And so did I. We both had fairly decent handicaps, and our games were sincerely competitive. A well-connected foursome, moreover, is every bit as useful in furthering a kingdom as it is any other corporate entity. You can't be a King in this country,

John liked to say, and not play a decent round of golf. What he did object to, though, and very vocally, was the practice in those days of developers establishing golf courses simply as the nucleus around which to anchor subdivisions.

A golf course surrounded in field and forest is not that terrible a blight on the landscape, for the most part; nature can more or less pass right on through. A golf course that's merely the hole in a doughnut of suburban development, on the other hand, might just as well be asphalt too. It was that kind of group to which Elspeth Blank had sold out the farm.

But it wasn't that that got John's passions flowing. What brought the killer out in him was the fact that she'd done it in full knowledge that not one but *two* pairs of northern shrikes were nesting on the property. I'll have to tee this up:

At that time, there were only a few dozen nesting pairs of northern shrikes left in the country. That's not quite true. There were similarly tiny pockets hanging on in other regions, but it's certainly fair to say the handful of specimens just north of Kingston represented a significant percentage of a deeply threatened gene pool. I can tell you a lot about the shrike because I became very interested in them myself later. We'll come to that. But for now let me just say that because of habitat destruction, pesticide proliferation, and all the usual by-blows of twentieth-century appetite, the northern shrike was well on the road to extinction. They're an interesting bird. In retrospect, I'll confess that if there was ever a bird to take an interest in, the northern shrike's the one you'd want to choose. But at this point it was all just coincidence.

Shrikes are predatory songbirds. Which in itself is an intriguing combination of notions. They have hooked beaks like hawks, but lack the curving talons to grasp their prey. Shrikes catch and kill mice and other birds, but because they can't hold them with their feet, they impale their prey on thorns or barbed wire before eating them. For this meat-hanging characteristic, they are also are called the "butcher bird."

Take note of the symbolic possibilities, please, in that name too.

When John went public with his accusations, Elspeth Blanc tried to argue that she was using the money she raised in selling off her farm to help save the geese. That yes, she was indeed aware that in converting shrike habitat to townhouses she was contributing to the further reduction of a species already at the brink of extirpation, but it was all in the name of a very good cause. (Subtext: Nobody's even heard of shrikes, but everybody knows about me and my geese.)

John's point – and you can imagine how forcefully he made it – was that the Canada goose was in no need of protection. There were millions of them. Literally. Destroying the shrikes to save a few geese was not a case of robbing Peter to pay Paul, it was a case of slaughtering Peter and using his flesh to fatten Paul's house cat. What it was – apparent now for all to see – was Elspeth Blanc selling out on every principle she should have had as an environmentalist, simply to heighten her profile.

John's emotions were contagious. This was one of his most shining assets as a public figure. He had the knack for channelling passion, our John. His indignation over Blanc's betrayal rippled out across the country like some biblical trumpet blast. It resonated in the imaginations of people who'd never even heard of shrikes the day before. (Also, the average person wasn't really much inclined to be too fond of Elspeth Blanc to start with, having been prodded for years with irritating barbs of guilt.) In short, it cooked Elspeth Blanc's goose to cinders.

But it did all kinds of other things, as well. The goose affair won John allies from both sides of a long-standing philosophical divide. With its more dubious elements purged, the environmental movement grew stronger – strong enough, eventually, to earn unqualified royal patronage, and through that national focus. On the other side of the equation, with a stupid little gesture like coming out in support of a goose cull, the King succeeded in gaining the ear of the hunting lobby, which bridged the gap to rural Canada, which in turn gained him ground in Alberta and the West. Down the road, when he started seriously lobbying for intelligent gun control, the boys around the Legion Hall were willing to set aside their arguments and listen.

It worked out very well for me and my private little project also. I'd been pestering John for some time to formally adopt a royal coat of arms. John had been resisting. The King was always wary of his social standing, and rightly so. The paradoxical success of our new monarchy rested on the genuine absence of an aristocratic class in Canada. It was truly (and I mean this sincerely) the thing John loved best about his country. And yet a monarch is of course by definition an aristocrat – the ultimate aristocrat, in fact, the *ne plus ultra* of aristocracy. Pressure inevitably mounted for John to begin accepting the symbols and privileges of his calling. People wanted it. So did I.

John did not. "If you start taking titles," he'd say, "next you'll be wanting little outfits to go with them, and before you know it you'll be living in the kind of country where people call themselves marquees right out in public." On that particular occasion, the King was airing his views on recent developments in sovereign Quebec. But he was very much concerned that the same sort of thing could happen here. I did not share that concern. Or more precisely, it was not my function to share it. My job was to enhance by every means possible the monarch's power and authority – and if that meant hectoring him to adopt a proper heraldic device, so be it.

Canada's official coat of arms was, and still is, the image of a lion and a unicorn pawing the air while supporting the nation's shield of state. According to heraldic tradition, symbolic devices tend toward large and powerful animals representing majesty and strength. All well and good, said I, but what did unicorns and lions have to do with Canada – or Mother England, either, for that matter? John agreed that our coat of arms was historically ridiculous and zoologically absurd, but would not agree to asking Parliament to change it. He preferred to err on the side of tradition, in this case, and was doubtless correct in his instincts. It was my view, however, that we could get around the problem by institutionalizing John's *own* coat of arms, stylistically appropriate to both sovereign and domain. This seemed to me a perfectly Canadian compromise – but the King's innate distaste overcame his better judgment.

The shrike, I am happy to say, tipped the balance. Our serendipitous shrike presented me with a royal emblem too perfect even for John to rebut. Which is how I came to know the taxonomy of *Lanius excubitor* so intimately well. A rather handsome bird, our shrike – charming, in many respects. Robin-sized, dove-coloured; a bird with an interesting voice of his own, but perfectly capable of imitating the songs of others. A predatory songbird, take note, a handsome, singing, dovelike bird that overcomes its prey by sheer ferocity and bloody-mindedness. A butcher bird whose call goes out in many voices.

It's hard to miss the symbolic possibilities, heraldically speaking. Could there be a better emblem for both the man and his dominions?

The design we finally settled on shows a shrike perched above a thorn bush, thorns empty of prey for the moment, but very much present, very much available should the need arise. Its eye is glittering, its hooked beak slightly gaped. There is the suggestion that the bird is singing.

See how a little thing like roasting geese can wing a way into so many new possibilities?

That's kingship.

DAY TWENTY-THREE

A LITTLE THICK with the avian metaphor, earlier. Apologies.

I'm prone to it – metaphoric overstatement. Hester kindly pointed this out early on in our association. And John, typical John, was pleased to give it a name. It amused the King to call this my *Albertanism*. If ever I carried on a shade too long on any subject, John would put it down to Blue's *Albertan* tendencies emerging (never in the company of real Albertans, mind). Ironically enough, though, the term was coined as a result of the King's own peculiar obsessions. Our sovereign was a closet ornithologist. Not the certifiable kind who tally up their sightings like baseball players tote their RBIs, but John was not at all above screaming at the driver to stop the car if he spotted some unfamiliar specimen cavorting in the ditch. It was all part-and-parcel with his zoological proclivities. I admit that to some degree it's rubbed off on me as well. The other day I spotted what I'm fairly certain was a black-billed magpie – a typically western species, according to the King, one that's recently been expanding its territory east. The sighting would have pleased him; John subscribed to several ornithological journals and made a point of keeping up on esoterica like that. I recall him reading an article on songbirds, one day, and letting out that hoot of his which served as warning that something of interest had caught his attention.

"Did you know," he said, "that even the birds out there are consistent?"

"Where, specifically, is there?" He was, of course, expecting me to ask.

"Alberta," said the King. "This explains a lot."

Then he read aloud a passage describing the differences in singing strategies between prairie birds and forest ones. The gist of it was that forest species tended to communicate in complex, multinote themes because of all the trees, which make sound more difficult to broadcast over distance. Out on the flatlands, however – with nothing but air to get in the way – prairie birds were free to hammer away on the same note all day long.

I had to admit that as a political pronouncement, it had a certain resonance.

My parents were Albertans – have I mentioned that? – Prairie Ukrainian stock, though they'd immigrated to the States before I was born. But that didn't stop John from referencing my *Albertan* roots whenever he caught me repeating myself. It annoyed me, though I also know he never meant it to. Hester's take was quite another matter. Hester never meant it kindly. *Albertanism*, at any rate, became their private codeword: a synonym for what the French call *idée fixe*. John was guilty of it as much as anyone, more. Returning home from the Sudanese campaign, that first time, he was downright Albertan himself on the subject of Gwen.

I think Hester knew before he did that everything had changed.

DAY TWENTY-FOUR

AND SPEAKING OF DIDACTICISM, I've haven't totally abandoned the idea of presenting this in sequence, but the days are
slipping by – twenty-four already – and I'm duty bound to pass
on what's important. Yesterday, I mentioned guns. Gun control
was one of the important things, one of those crucial hinges
that swung out so much of what happened later. I'm going to
tackle guns this morning, I think, and do my best to backtrack
history with whatever time is left.

Canadians of that era liked to think that a universal health-
care system was what set them apart from Americans. They
were, as in many other respects, mistaken. The big difference
was guns. This is something I've given a lot of thought to over
the years and perhaps am better qualified than most to
measure. I've lived both sides of the trigger, if you like. John
and I agreed that one of the nicest things about being King was
having the opportunity to put pet theories to the test. As a
quasi-non-Canadian, I was in a little better position than he
was to see more clearly on this particular issue. We conducted
some very clever polls that bore this out. Americans' obsession
with their Second Amendment and the right to bear arms was
certainly familiar-enough territory, but what wasn't so clearly
understood (at least not this side of the border) was the respective attitudes to the arms themselves.

The surveys we conducted pointed to a very clear distinction:

Americans saw their guns as armaments, as *weapons*; Canadians regarded them as something more in the nature of *tools*. If the Canadian government had understood this, pre-John, it would have saved itself a world of grief.

Around that time, the Department of Justice had launched an ambitious and disastrous program to register all firearms in the country. Its motives, politically speaking, were honourable. There had been a particularly brutal shooting that year, which sparked a tide of nationwide revulsion: a fairly textbook case of psycho-killer run amuck – the kind Americans were all-too familiar with, Canadians less so – but this one came with a particular twist. The killer had armed himself with an assault rifle (mail-ordered, it turned out, from a warehouse in Fort Lauderdale, Florida) and taken control of a university lecture hall where he methodically separated the male students from female, then shot all the girls. A suicide note found in his pocket blamed "the feminists."

The story was played all over the world in the days after it happened, then died away as local dramas do. A decade later, though, it was still being talked about here. The most immediate result was a public call for greater gun control, which might have gone smoothly enough if left to its own evolution. But of course there was a viciously sexual component of this crime to factor in as well.

Yesterday, I wrote about the joys of linkage. Today, I'll talk about its perils. It's all to the good if you can use one issue to shift another, so long as you control the lever. God help you, though, if your own momentum starts to tip against you. Sometimes, too, an avalanche will happen all of its own. I've said before that history is random. You can ask yourself if I'd be writing if I really did believe that, but I'll also say that you should never, ever, underestimate the role of dumb-ass accidents in human affairs. Particularly when it comes to the wisdom of yoking one piece of social engineering with another.

In the aftermath of the Lecture Hall Massacre, the linkages went haywire. Violence in general became narrowed down to violence against women. The call for gun control was taken up by the same voices calling for an end to spousal abuse, into which crept the notion that gun ownership itself was sexually deviant, which oddly encouraged the animal rights lobby, which in turn outraged hunting groups and opened a rift between urban and rural sensibilities, widening the traditional split of left against right.

The legislation was a decade in the making. Understandably, as you might imagine, the field-and-stream set felt itself besieged from the start. Very soon, hunters were refusing even to take part in the discussion. This only increased the influence of the more extreme elements from the opposite side. Before long, groups like Animal Activist Movement and people like Elspeth Blanc were influencing the wording, while rod-and-gun clubs were boycotting the initiative wholesale. Even John – who until he became commander-in-chief of the Canadian Armed Forces had never fired a gun in his life – was as a normal private citizen ashamed at how stupidly things were working out.

The final result ended up costing Parliament more than a billion, further discredited an already shaky political system, and did absolutely nothing to reduce the use of firearms in crime. The day the act was proclaimed, three people were murdered with handguns in Toronto. That same day, in Canmore, Alberta, a group of middle-aged farmers went to jail rather than register their single-shot gopher guns. If there was a spilt between urban and rural before, it was a chasm by the time the legislation came into being.

The great irony was that the average gun owner would not really have minded registering his hunting rifle if the request had only been made politely – his car was registered, after all, and did that prevent him from driving? What he truly did hate was the original assumption that owning a gun made him deviant.

We fixed the problem, when it came our turn, by looking more closely at the guns themselves. This was where our polling data came into play. It turned out that the average *urban* Canadian non-gun-owner saw little distinction between one kind of gun and another – a gun was a gun, in short – which ironically was identical to the position taken by the U.S. gun lobby. The National Rifle Association, an incredibly powerful force in American politics – utterly dominant in Red states – insisted that American citizens were entitled to possession of *any* kind of weapon, from a single-shot .22 to military assault rifles that could blast a thousand rounds per minute. A firearm was a firearm, was the NRA's position, and citizens of the republic had as much right to pack Uzis as air guns.

This was not at all the view of gun-owning Canadians. Not even remotely close. Canadian hunters understood – as their anti-gun counterparts clearly did not – that there were two very different kinds of guns in manufacture. One kind was made to kill animals; the other, people. Amid all the animosity and recrimination, pre-John, this distinction had somehow been lost. We revived it and made it the centrepiece of our proposal. Canadians, as we phrased it, were entitled to kill animals, and therefore were entitled to the kind of guns designed to kill animals. They were not entitled to murder, and therefore had no business owning weapons created for that purpose.

It was really that simple, once the basics were exposed and articulated. And, of course, our cause was greatly aided by the wellspring of anti-Red state hostility erupting just around that time. I'm pleased to say I did everything possible to encourage that eruption, though I'll also admit that with all the help I was getting down south, this was not much of an accomplishment.

Funny, though, how different times can cherish different values. When the first gun legislation was introduced, pre-John, it faced a massive resistance clearly and unabashedly sponsored by the NRA and an active Red lobby. Theodore Sapper and his papers recycled endless op-ed pieces originally published in *USA Today*. His editorial boards, of course, revelled in the fiasco. This was the kind of ongoing disaster that virtually wrote its own copy, and endlessly comforted his subscribers on the anti-government Right.

Ten years later, those same readers had vanished and all we had to do was *suggest* that other side had fallen under the influence of Red propagandists and that was enough to have the few MPs who opposed the bill turn up absent on the day of the vote. As John was pleased to phrase it, Canada's role in the twenty-first century was to help guide the policy of its neighbours, not the other way around.

I should leave it at that, I know, and move on. Like for instance filling in the background of how an unelected figure-head came to have such influence over Parliament – but I can't bring myself to drop this quite yet. There's an hour of daylight still. My hand's not cramping and my foot is hardly pulsing at all today. I'm going to press this forward just a little further.

It's worth exploring the disconnect, in politics, between the reality politicians see and the reality that exists. Politicians are as fickle in their own attitudes as voters are in theirs. The relationship is symbiotic – that's easy to say – but which feeds which is harder to pin down. What I can tell you for certain is that the go-between, the broker, if you like, is the organism that broadcasts the news. Voters use the press to influence the politicians every bit as much as politicians use the press to influence the voters. There's a constant exchange, a constant swirling mix of theses and antitheses moving back and forth between these poles.

But the medium through which this exchange takes place can have its own agenda.

What had happened, during the era leading up to John, was that the media had taken on the role of producing information, rather than simply distributing it. This was particularly true of Theodore Sapper's web, but by no means exclusively so. Years of political deadlock had led to the enfeeblement of politicians, which led to disenchantment of the voters, which opened a void to be filled with the media delivering itself.

In those years, Sapper was more and more able to make the *politicians* believe his voice was the same as the public's. He had always excelled in promoting his own pet theories, primarily by vilifying whichever ones he disapproved of. But because the politicians at this time were as weak and confused as the public they represented, he began convincing them *the people* were onside with him too. And some, of course, were. Sapper was a great admirer of Red Republicanism. Through the accident of political vacuum, he found himself in a position to convince both sides of the equilibrium that Canadian values, taken together, were tilting Red-ward.

It keeps me warm at night just thinking about it, how bitterly Sapper must regret the impulse that led him to publish that first mock-monarchist editorial. John's arrival – which Sapper himself had inspired – created a new power: a super-politician, so to speak, a fourth and balancing weight to the political system. The greatest irony in all of this is that he had quite the opposite affect upon the American Union. I entertain myself, waiting for the chills to pass, wondering what Theodore Sapper makes of present history. But what am I saying? Sapper has his millions and his Texas spread; it's me that's living off canned wieners and beans. Still, his legacy is dust, and mine, well, we haven't finished with that yet, have we?

The new gun bill outlawed people-killing military hardware and all handguns. Not just restricted their ownership, outlawed them altogether. If you were caught with one, you went to jail. Simple as that. A fair number of people did go to jail too. But there was a lot more room in the jails by then because we'd decriminalized marijuana, so the hapless idiots who'd gone to prison for smoking pot were now out on the streets paying taxes, which freed up lots of cell space for the ones who tried to shoot people. Insofar as the average farmer from Canmore, Alberta, was concerned – to say nothing of the hash-heads in the malls of Mississauga – this was a fairly respectable turn of events.

DAY TWENTY-FIVE

JOHN WAS SHOT by Indians.

Not the most sensitive of segues, admittedly, but natural enough. Any discussion of guns leads fairly enough to John's shooting, which in turn reintroduces the U.S. factor. Say what you will about my former countrymen, they know how to deal with heroism, and nothing gets a higher ranking in the land of the brave and the true than taking a bullet, especially one that's fired by an injun. People like to recognize their genres.

It helped here too, of course. All in all, I'd say that John's getting shot proved useful in virtually every category you'd care to examine. You will want me to place the events of that day within their larger context; a story needs its setting, after all, and John's story is not so much John's story as the story of how John's story is told. How's that for postmodernist cant? No wonder all those silly girls in black stockings lapped it up like licorice. The problem with postmodernism, over and above the preternatural silliness in the name itself, was always its issue with beginnings. You can safely assume that the roots of John's shooting go back to the pre-postmodern era. (Pre-PoMo?)

I amuse myself.

Aboriginal Affairs are much quieter now than they used to be. I expect they'll be quieter still by the time you read this – though perhaps I shouldn't say that. "Events cast their shadows before them," writes Euripides, phrasing the counter-argument better than I ever could. I've no idea where the shadows will be falling when it's your turn to approach them. But I have a hunch the K'oha Crisis will still be looked upon as a watershed event. It was. Following on the heels of the split with Quebec, and arriving at a time when so much else was in flux, with the Constitution itself laid out on the gurney – events at K'oha exposed the nerves of another long-standing Canadian ailment. There was ruthlessness afoot in those days, a hardness unfamiliar to Canadians before, I think, or since. Those of us who lived through it – people of my generation, I mean, and John's – prefer to think of it as necessary ruthlessness. Your times may not agree. History is all in how you tell it.

Once people decided they'd had enough of Quebec, it was hardly a stretch deciding to do the same again with Indians.

That's how I interpret it.

We'd decided – Hester, John, and I – that having punched so far above our weight already, it might be wise for John to keep a lower profile for a time and leave the politics to politicians. During the long days of turmoil immediately following the referenda, Canada's new King more or less disappeared into the woodwork. The Crown still resided in Ottawa, back then, so remaining invisible was easy. Rideau Hall was pleasant enough, and John could mingle with the tourists any time he felt the need for company. Every so often we'd arrange for Hester to make some particularly egregious demand, then manufacture an opportunity for the King to speak out against it – merely as a reminder of his presence. But for the most part, until the K'oha Crisis, John quietly tended his knitting. He did a lot of reading. We all did; there was a lot to catch up on.

But one thing he could safely do – mostly because no one else was giving it a thought – was to explore his connections with the military. This, again, was Hester's inspiration.

Hester believed, and firmly believed, that no government could make secure decisions without full confidence in its enforcement agencies. She was furthermore convinced that for such confidence to exist, it had to be reciprocal. Because she was smart, because she was charming – and possibly also because she was a woman – Hester was extremely successful in winning over the support she needed. As a civic politician, it was essential that she have Toronto's police force securely in her corner. At the many social functions she attended, the Mayor was often to be seen on the arm of Toronto's Police Chief, or one or the other of his senior lieutenants. It seemed to me that Hester was on a first-name basis with half the city's uniforms. Certainly, all the ranking officers were regulars at Hester's house for Sunday evening pot roast. (John or I were never invited, but of course John couldn't be.) Safe to say there was always room in Hester's budgets for a little extra spending when it came to law enforcement. More than once she'd found herself in political hot water for having intervened on individual officers' behalf, when they'd found themselves in trouble with civilian boards. This was a calculated gamble, but one well worth the cost if it meant solidifying her most important alliance. Toronto's cops, in return, were protective of their Mayor. When Hester shocked the nation by asking the police to barricade her city, no one on the force itself was surprised by their willingness to answer her call.

The King, she argued, should cultivate the same relationship with Canada's Armed Forces.

There were differences, to be sure. But there were also levers John might pull that Hester could never have dreamed of. First of all, he was titular commander-in-chief, which had to count for something. Indeed, he'd made it count already. However artificial the rank was meant to be, it was still, technically speaking, a command position.

Second, and more importantly, the army was desperate.

The Canadian Armed Forces were far and away the most depleted agency in the federal government. Canada's Department of Indian Affairs, for instance, received a budget four times larger than the annual spending on its Army, Navy, and Air Force combined. Stories of the army's mistreatment were so familiar during those days that even university students were embarrassed to mock the soldiers called out to supervise their demonstrations. A little extra funding had been thrown into the pot, in recent budgets, but this was more than swallowed up by lethal new commitments in Afghanistan and the Middle East. Soldiers in the field had ended up with even more responsibilities, which netted out to even less support back home. Hester reasoned that any official who showed the slightest spark of interest was likely to be warmly received by military brass. As ever, her assessment was dead-on.

What she didn't foresee – none of us did – was how warmly John embraced the army in return. He loved it.

You have to try to imagine the times to understand how surprising a development this was. In those days, the vast majority of Canadians would sooner have seen their sons and daughters take up professional panhandling than enlist in the military. It just wasn't done. John grew up as contemptuous in this regard as everyone else of his generation. But the very first time he sat down for drinks with General Bennett and a handful of his senior staff, they clicked. That was how the King himself described it. John liked to joke that his interest in the Canadian military was simply an extension of his sympathy for all endangered species, but the fact of the matter is, the soldiers took to John as much as John took to the soldiers. I watched it happen. It turns out John had all the makings of a military man. Who knew? He was as much at home with barracks grunts as he was among the top commanders at HQ. If you'd ever watched John yucking it up with a troop of Osprey Guard, I'll guarantee you'd see them grinning and bobbing their heads – and the King would be doing the same. He was in every way the opposite to what you'd think of as an army type, but John got soldiers. And soldiers got John.

So while the country came to terms with its incipient partition, John spent his days consorting with a deeply disenchanted soldiery. It's a safe bet they gave him an earful. General Bennett – the same chief of defence staff that John had spoken with by cellphone the day of Hester's ersatz putsch – turned out, by very good fortune, to be an anglophone. Rules of promotion in Canada's Armed Forces were much the same as for the civil service. Bilingual francophones rose more rapidly and were disproportionately represented throughout the command structure, so the odds of senior officers being Quebecers were better than good. But Bennett was an anglo, and a bitter one at that, with a clear view of what he saw coming.

Without going into the tedious detail (I refer you again to your source books), Bennett succeeded in convincing John of what would happen if things were left up to the bureaucrats in the Department of Defence. He was an expert on the malignant neglect of his Ottawa masters. John, for his part, helped Bennett to convince his own junior staff that they would not be in dereliction of duty – very much the reverse, in fact – if they obeyed any orders formally issued by their commander-in-chief.

The King then instructed selected officers to advance into the field and strip off every asset in Quebec that wasn't bolted to the bedrock. Quietly and quickly, they did exactly that.

It was a time of turmoil, I remind you, when individual soldiers were having to decide which nation they served. Things in the end sorted themselves out for the most part, as you'd have expected. Québécois personnel remained overwhelmingly attached to their roots and refashioned themselves as the new nation's Force d'Action de Québec. Pretty much everyone else stayed with their units here in Canada. Geography being what it is, Québécois personnel stationed in places like Fredericton and Wainright required transportation home. Anglophones operating in the former province of Quebec received similarly peaceable repatriation. Each side compensated the other for expenses incurred as a result of these relocations. It was all very civilized.

Less civilized, truly, was the division of non-human assets. It turned out that quite a number of these – most tanks, for instance, and artillery and helicopters and fighter jets, and almost all the Navy – had, by the time the Department of Defence got around to counting them, also been relocated well outside Quebec's newly demarcated borders. Possession being nine-tenths of the law, as they say, particularly where international relations complicate the niceties of ownership, it took quite a while – what with all the claims and counter-claims – for such equipment as was judged to be the rightful property of Quebec to actually find its way back there. Which also turned out to be for the best.

For a while, Quebec's collapsing government found itself inclined to bellicosity vis-à-vis its former co-confederate. Diplomacy, thankfully, prevailed, and the threat of armed conflict between the two new neighbours subsided fairly quickly. It's difficult to rattle sabres when they're stacked up in the other fellow's armoury.

People later questioned John's authority to have issued the orders he did. But these questions arose well after the fact, and came mostly from Quebec, which no longer had a say in things anyway. General Bennett went on to an extremely distinguished career reshaping the Canadian Forces, and now leads the New Internationals. The King, throughout his reign, continued his tradition of drinking with the troops whenever he could.

It was during one of these fraternizing sessions that news reached John of the standoff at K'oha. Here's a historical fact unlikely to appear in your history books: the King was more-than-mildly hungover on the morning he was shot.

I admit the irony appeals to me. The press devoted quite a lot of coverage to the quantities of drugs and alcohol discovered at the K'oha encampment; cameras lingered lovingly on the cases of Labatts piled up beside the stacks of AK-47s. And, of course, the blood-alcohol levels recorded by the detainees were widely reported. All I can say is, it's a lucky thing nobody thought to ask the King to blow a Breathalyzer any time that morning.

I've alluded already, I think, to the doctrine of the un-requited shove. John loved the phrase and so did I; I wrote it, and to this day I still take pleasure in its twisting symmetry. It's probably the most widely quoted of his repertoire and indeed has formed the basis for the New International's operational mandate. General Bennett quotes it often, and ranks of political scientists have savoured its self-conscious irony. "The unrequited shove, which King John of Canada has contributed to the lexicon, very neatly characterizes the danger of failing to respond to aggression." (*The Economist*) That was from an article on the situation in North Africa, I think, but the line that followed originated in a speech John delivered at The Hague some years earlier, so I can quote it verbatim: "Like love, we never seem to learn from it – aggression demands its reply; failure to acknowl-edge it is often more disastrous than returning it in kind."

I could hardly have said it better myself.

Everyone thinks K'oha was the underpinning for John's now-famous dictum. But of course the deeper inspiration was Quebec. What K'oha had was bloodshed and bullets, and intensely immediate repercussions. Philosophically, though, the lessons we took from Quebec were by far the more potent. But K'oha's case was so decisive – so blatantly, publicly physical –

that people assume John's thinking sprang from his experience there. It makes no difference; one is good as the other to stand as exemplar. Origins were never meant to be certain.

While it's true that the Aboriginal people of this country had been treated very badly in the past, it's also true that so had everybody else at one time or another. When Columbus made his landfall here, my own ancestors were winding up two centuries of rape that started out when Kublai Khan came calling with his Golden Horde, which makes our family, come to think of it, as much Mongolian as Slav, but never mind; John's Loyalist forefathers were tortured by Americans during the War of Independence; Hester's faced the pogroms, and even Gwen's proud Viking granddames had been made to drop their flaxen knickers for the Wehrmacht. If you add up the Somali refugees, the Vietnamese boat people, the concentration-camp survivors, to say nothing of the ragged Scots and starving Irish who came flocking to these shores, you have quite a lengthy list of shit-kicked. There's even evidence suggesting that the nomadic hunters who crossed the Bering Strait and settled the continent may have first displaced some earlier inhabitants. What I'm saying is that ill-treatment is endemic to the sweep of human history. This was the argument, at any rate, that John hoped to make in K'oha. That the past should be taken as a caution, not an inspiration.

But as I've said, he was hungover that day.

The warriors on the barricades at K'oha, not unexpectedly, took a different view. Their fortunes rested on the memory of past misdeeds, not on future reconciliations. K'oha was an interesting case. Aboriginal rights groups had been expanding their influence for decades as the central government lost ground against the regions. K'oha had enjoyed particular successes in facing down colonialist authorities, and served as inspiration to native independence movements all over the country. But K'oha was unique.

It was the one piece of Quebec's former territory that Quebec's negotiators argued tooth and nail *not* to keep. Quebec was more than happy to have our side administer K'oha. Our negotiators, for their part, tried just as hard to pawn it back off on Quebec. But there were fiduciary responsibilities and so forth – if we kept James Bay it was incumbent upon us to accept our responsibilities in K'oha too – so the long and the short of it was that we ended up with it and all the trouble that went with it.

The crisis at K'oha emerged from a mixture of guilt and overlapping jurisdictions. K'oha lands overlooked the St. Lawrence and traversed the borders of both Ontario and Quebec. Directly across the river, forming the reserve's southern boundary, was the state of New York. So if you counted the federal jurisdictions in Canada and the United States, there were five different governments competing for which could turn the blindest eye to what was going on there.

The problems started with shipments of cigarettes, which weren't taxed on the American side and so were much cheaper to buy on the river's south shore. The K'oha were fond of cross-border shopping. They argued that boatloads of cigarettes landed on the Canada side were not smuggled; tobacco was a *healing* substance in their culture, sacred to their ancient rituals. K'oha forefathers had sprinkled tobacco on the waters of the Big Waters since the beginning of time – the odd carton tumbling from the back of present-day speedboats should be interpreted as modern adaptation of those ancient rites, not contraband.

In any case, the K'oha did not recognize artificial borders, or the sovereignty of colonial aggressors.

Canadians felt extremely guilty about Indians in general. They also felt guilty about smoking. So no one wanted to make an issue of a group of disadvantaged Aboriginals improving their lot with a little black-market entrepreneurship. Trade became increasingly brisk. Before long, the operation got to be so lucrative that the big tobacco companies started taking a cut, rerouting their distributions systems to funnel Canadian brands of cigarettes to shippers on the American side, who sold them to the K'oha, who ferried them back across the river and undercut the market here. Before long, it was a multimillion-dollar enterprise.

Recognizing a moral quandary when it saw one, the Quebec government struck a blow against illegal smuggling by lowering its cigarette tax. The anti-smoking movement was incensed, naturally – the whole point of the tax was to encourage people to quit – but Ontario soon followed suit and changed its laws as well. Cowardly, maybe, but the strategy worked. Price-point advantage was lost to the smugglers and the volume of trans-border cigarettes sharply decreased.

But K'oha had a system going by this stage, and the headmen had picked up some expensive habits. Cigarettes now being less profitable, they switched to booze. Rum-running, too, was a time-honoured Canadian tradition, and for sentimental reasons – in addition to all the political ones – the authorities again found themselves inclined to look the other way.

But by now the money had got too serious to be ignored by bigger players. An untaxed, unguarded pipeline between two such major markets was simply too attractive not to catch the eye of more ambitious syndications. When two provincial governments chose to rewrite policy rather than intervene, the K'oha – and their new transnational partners – interpreted this as an affirmation of their territory's independent status. The reserve was now operating more like an international free-trade zone than an Aboriginal community, complete with its own armed border patrols. At a well-attended press conference in the slow-news days of summer, the K'oha announced that their land was now completely off limits to all but invited guests – which certainly did not include the Sûreté du Québec, Ontario's Provincial Police, the RCMP, or any of the various Aboriginal-run police forces that had been trying to bring some semblance of order back into the place. Uncooperative officials ended up run out of town. Band members who opposed the smugglers came home to find their houses burning, and the fire departments busy on the other side of town.

Before long, the community was entirely in the hands of organized crime. Traffic in booze expanded to include a booming trade in pharmaceuticals, which opened up the global markets and a steady flow of other merchandise. In due course, boatloads of illegal migrants were being ferried back and forth across the river as the trade in human contraband began to prove its worth.

The clash at K'oha began, of all places, in a massage parlour in Saskatchewan. Police in Regina had raided a local rub & tug and netted the usual crop of stupefied young women from the dismal corners of the Earth. Two of these, Romanians if memory serves, were so young and so exhausted that when an interpreter was found for them, they forgot they weren't supposed to talk. Their story, for the most part, was the usual – the promised jobs, the stolen passports, the isolation, the rapes, the solace of narcotics, and the further debts incurred obtaining them – but what caught the attention of the local, then the national media was a reference to a particularly brutal three weeks they said they'd spent in an "Indian camp."

They said they'd reached this place "by crossing a river at night." They were in America, they believed, when they got into the boats but were given to understand that the place they landed was somewhere else. They'd been warned that the men there would cut off their hair and their ears and their lips if they didn't do what they were told. After a time, they were taken to Toronto and dispersed from there. While they were with the Indians, they said, a man with hot wires had burned a brand into their skin so they would know who they belonged to. The marks were crudely done and badly healed, but a sharp-eyed reporter from CBC Regina noticed that the design looked the same as the one that flew on the flags above the band council office at K'oha. Once this hit the news, the story went national.

Confrontation was now inevitable. The officers dispatched to the reserve were met by a group of armed men crouched behind a barricade thrown up across the highway. Appeals for solidarity, meanwhile, had gone out to native bands across the country and reinforcements came pouring in. Soon the barricades were bristling with "warriors" in painted faces, bandanas, and camouflage fatigues, all of them armed to the teeth. The cops parked their cars, closed the highway, and settled in for the standoff.

John was enjoying himself while all this was going on, taking part in a training exercise somewhere north of Peterborough. Really what he was doing was riding around in a tank pretending he was a soldier. The Army was severely ill-equipped, but not so badly off that it couldn't schedule a few days of combat practice once or twice a year. John had managed to get himself attached to one of these as an "observer." Manoeuvres had just wound up, I believe, when word of K'oha reached his unit.

He was always a little vague about connecting the dots that led to his arrival at the reserve next morning, mounted in the turret of an overheated LAV III. What I can tell you is that he called me from the road somewhere north of Lindsay, saying he was en route to see what he could do to help defuse the situation. This was before five in the morning, and when I was awake enough to find the phone all I could manage was something like "right, but try not to get yourself shot." He liked to remind me of this.

To be fair, once I'd had the chance to shake myself awake, I jumped in the car and headed out after them. But it was rush hour by that time and a longer drive for me than him. Everything was over before I arrived. Hester had it worse. She didn't know a thing until she turned on the television and saw John face down in a puddle of blood.

He'd put himself in the vanguard, and so was the first to arrive on the scene. Police assumed that the sudden appearance of army units had to be the result of some decision taken at the very highest levels of the government, which in a sense was true. Anyway, they made no attempt to interfere. The media, of course, was present in force – they always were for K'oha confrontations – so what happened next was brilliantly recorded from half-a-dozen angles. John – whom no one recognized at this stage – got down off the LAV and started walking toward the barricade. He really did believe that if he could just talk to them, he would make them see that theirs was not a tenable solution. I don't think he got more than three or four steps before the bullet hit. It came from a heavy assault weapon – a few inches over and it would have blown a hole through his chest. As it was, it struck him on the arm below the shoulder, spun him around Hollywood-style, and crashed him flat on his face, gushing blood. All hell broke loose then.

"King's hit! King's hit!" came a frantic voice from inside the armoured vehicle. (I should mention that in those days, any soldiers' references to John as "the King" was taken as ironic, not patriotic, although things change.) But there was no trace of irony in the young corporal's voice that morning; and suddenly the LAVs were rolling up in battle formation with infantry pouring forward from the rear. These troops had been in combat mode for two or three days, remember; their blood was up and their man was down. The relationship had not yet grown to what it was in years to come, but these were many of the same men who later formed the Osprey Guard, and they were fond of John already. It would have been a bloodbath. You can watch the footage from that day and see for yourself.

Some fool behind the barricade let off another round. It hit the armoured plating, I think, and zinged off into the trees – that's audible too, on the tapes. The LAVs started their advance, another shot was fired, and that would have been that except, suddenly, there was John on his knees holding out his good arm like a demented crossing guard yelling at the Indians to stop their goddamn shooting.

And they did.

Then the King spun around the other way, streaming blood, and screamed at the soldiers to halt.

And damned if they didn't too.

The Army took a lot of ridicule during that era, and we still remember its combat capabilities in those days as something closer to a joke. But it's worth noting also that many of those men had served missions in Kosovo and Kandahar. They knew how to fight when it came down to fighting; they also knew how to deal with a rout. Most of the Warriors took the opportunity to high-tail it for the river. There was no more shooting after that.

While we remember K'oha for its violence, in actual fact the only blood spilled that day was the King's.

I set out this morning intending to briskly outline the significance of this episode. The sun's gone up, the sun's gone down; it's pitch dark and freezing both inside and out and I'm writing by candle – every few minutes I have to stick the nib into my mouth or wave it over the flame to keep the ink from thickening – it's well past midnight, and I've only just succeeded in getting John shot.

He carried the scar to his death. It fascinated Gwen, which in turn fascinates me, but Gwen doesn't enter into this part of our story. This was well before her time. The bullet ripped a hand-sized flap of skin off his shoulder. Just skin, pretty much. But I'm sure it hurt like hell over the months it took growing back. I'm also sure though that John would have tolerated quite a lot more pain in exchange for all the good we took out of it.

K'oha was a turning point. I guess the sharpest one of all, in retrospect. You can't imagine what incredible television it made – of course you can, the tapes are in the archives – but for today you'll have to take my word on how convincingly it snapped the country's vaunted mood for tolerance. There was a hardness in the air already; I've been trying to describe it: a clench-jawed willingness to let old orthodoxies slide. When millions of Canadians watched John bleed that day on television, they discovered two things: One, they liked this guy, whoever he was and however foolishly he'd got there. And two, they'd really, really had it up to here with the bastards who'd shot him.

It was K'oha that gave Parliament a free hand to abolish the Indian Act. The Constitution was already open, bigger things were on the table; there would never be a better time to fix this problem once and for all. Most significantly, people were willing. Those who kept up the argument for Aboriginal entitlement were literally shouted into silence. There was spirited opposition from the Council of Chiefs as well, of course, but several of its most vocal members were badly discredited if not actually in jail. Many of the more militant chiefs had joined the barricades before John's arrival, expecting a whoop-up and lots of good ink. What they got was very much the reverse. As so often happens when old taboos are lifted, the media rushed out with a flood of previously unpublished items chronicling the incredible corruption in Aboriginal Affairs – including some extremely damaging financial statements belatedly obtained under the Freedom of Information Act.

On balance, there's little doubt that conditions for Aboriginal peoples improved once the act was eradicated. New legislation redefined the tribes as corporations, with each status member awarded an equal number of shares. Treaties are now negotiated by corporate litigators rather than public-relations personnel. Each side's responsible for its own court costs, so claims that had been dragging on for decades – decades! – reached settlement stage in record speed. Every band member got a tangible slice of the pie, so when it came time for choosing who managed the assets, voters tended to take decisions seriously. Some chose well and others badly; some increased holdings, others cashed theirs out. Certain shareholders became very rich indeed, others sank even deeper into poverty. But as a group they ceased to be governed under different rules from everybody else, which led to smoother relations all around. In terms of costs to the taxpayer, the difference was incredible. Nearly $10 billion a year went into Indian Affairs, pre-John. Billions more flowed out litigating land-claim disputes, but now the settlements were strictly one-time payments. Total savings were enormous. With transfer payments to both Quebec and Aboriginals eliminated in one fell swoop, a reconfigured nation emerged into the world on sounder financial footing than most of its citizens could ever have imagined – and with a genuine celebrity as head of state.

For John, getting shot meant stardom.

He'd been in the news already, sure – the dismissal of Parliament, the order to stand down the Army, the public feud with Hester – but all of this was politics, and a great many Canadians had stopped paying attention to politics.

But getting shot by Indians, well now, there was something you could stand up and take notice of.

After K'oha, a picture of a blood-soaked and defiant John holding back the bullets appeared on the cover of *Time Magazine*. Within a month, there was a photo shoot with *Vanity Fair* and after that a salty interview with *People* establishing Canada's "Sexy New Monarch" as one to watch. Even stodgy old *Maclean's* pulled out the stops and commissioned a cross-border survey showing – incredibly – that John was not only outpolling the Prime Minister, but also scoring higher approval rating among *Americans* than their own President. CNN couldn't leave that one unbitten. Over the span of just two hours one memorable afternoon, I took calls from David Letterman, Oprah Winfrey, and even cryogenic Barbara Walters, all of them politely wondering if King John of Canada ever did TV.

DAY TWENTY-SIX

I WANT TO WRITE SOME MORE today about the distinction between what we think of as story, and what we think of as *news*.

As a starting point, let me mention that there's no distinction. All news is gossip, which means all news is reducible to the nuts and bolts of *story*.

We like to think of hard news as belonging to a different category than entertainment. It does not. It's neighbours talking over the fence, that's all it is, and all it ever was, and Mrs. Abercrombie cheating on her husband will always trump Mrs. Abercrombie being reconciled with same.

What people talk about breaks down into two basic categories: things that are important, and things that are interesting. The problem with the former is having to rely on your audience's ability to recognize importance. Not so with what's interesting. Deciding what's interesting is easy: sex and conflict (which in my experience amount to pretty much the same), that's what's interesting. Sex and conflict, therefore, are the primary ingredients of any story. Likewise, any news item.

Over the years, John and I worked out fairly elaborate theories evolving from this point. (See how your ears have perked up, by the way, just because I've mentioned sex? Here's something to remember: throw sex into the mix whenever you can, whether it fits or not, because it always does. But for now what I want to talk about is conflict.)

We need it, it's as much a part of our nature as the sexual imperative, and every bit as reproductive. Conflict is like oxygen; without it, we expire. It is the wellspring of human contentment. In its absence we are driven to create it. Every storyteller knows that conflict is the wriggling sperm of creativity. So should every politician. John was fond of saying that politics, like literature, exists to make us wiser. Good politicians, in other words, like good writers, serve best by confounding expectations.

Another way to look at this is biologically. We humans are a species programmed to adapt. Forget opposable thumbs, forget bipedal locomotion, forget brain size and lifespan and language – these all are just responses to that singular, most human of characteristics. *Adaptability* is what defines us. John would argue that even our name is misleading. *Homo sapiens* just isn't inappropriate. Given even the briefest perusal of human history, it's hard to disagree with that. *Homo adaptans*, John believed, would be far, far closer to the mark. It is the act of adapting that makes us wise. Somewhere, deep in our DNA, lies the certain knowledge that should we ever cease adapting, we would cease to be wise, and therefore cease to be human.

You're asking what this has to do with politics.

Only this: people think that politicians exist to solve problems. They are in error. Politicians exist to *create* problems. Human beings require a constant supply of things to adapt to. The function of politics is to supply this demand.

John liked to say that politics is "the practical practice of paradox." Sometimes the King had quite a way with words, other times not. I will rephrase it. If political *practice* might be defined as the ongoing effort to legislate heaven on Earth, political *practicality* is the certain knowledge that heaven is not only legislatively unattainable but logically impossible. In our heart of hearts, in our souls of souls, we humans understand that heaven itself is a contradiction, if for no other reason than if we were ever to achieve it, our profoundest nature would insist that we destroy it. (Which explains why people get so crazy with religion – zealotry is not the soul's expression of religious faith, it's the mind's diversion from religious truth. But I digress.)

Good news sucks, is what I'm saying, and is better left to PR firms and in-house auditors. Good news is bad news, from a political perspective. It needs to be fixed. If you want to make good news truly good, you've got to make it bad.

My own preference is the culinary model. Plants develop toxins that make them taste horrible to animals that try to eat them. We humans harvest those toxins, mix them with our food, and call it *spice*. There's human nature in a nutshell. Journalists have always understood this: Theodore Sapper absorbed it to the point of self-destruction; it's a fine balance, knowing how much to add and when to stop adding; for Sapper, the spice became the food itself. But if you want to understand how the greater news machine works, there's a simple rule of thumb: media coverage contracts with harmony and expands with controversy.

The more tasty a news item, in other words, the greater its measure of unpleasantness. Or, in the more familiar phrase, bad news sells.

There was a time in the dim beginnings of journalism when the temperature was recorded according to what it said on the thermometer. Someone would look at the glass and see that the mercury stood at, say, two degrees, and the weatherman would report a "chilly two degrees outside today." Then we invented the *wind-chill* factor – a brilliant innovation that allowed that same two degrees to be authoritatively presented as feeling more like *minus seventeen*. Minus seventeen, according to the formula, is a far more satisfying reportage than plus two. More recently we've come up with the humidex, which boils down to a way of reporting a hot day as even hotter than it really is.

There's merit to all this, I'm not denying – a cold wind will always make a winter's day seem colder, and a close, muggy afternoon definitely feels hotter than whatever the mercury is telling us. But what I am saying is that – meteorologically speaking – there are an equal number of days in which the reverse effect must also apply: sunny days in winter when the thermometer says zero but the weather feels much milder; breezy days in summer when a cool wind off the lake makes air-conditioning a waste of energy.

My point: Have you ever heard the weatherman announcing that the temperature today reads zero, but with the *sun-effect factor* it really feels more like ten above? Have you watched that perky, pug-nosed child on Channel 17 advising you it's thirty-one degrees outside today, but taking into account the *balmy-breeze index*, it really feels more like a pleasant twenty-six? Of course not. And you never will. This would contradict the core of journalistic principle.

Same again with politics. Politicians make enemies when they persist in describing the glass as half full when they could just as easily present it as half empty. The smart ones do. Or should I say, the successful ones don't. The smart ones have people like me who understand how much more important it is to make the glass *interesting* than to calibrate its contents.

I've just returned from an exploratory expedition with the dog, which explains today's penchant for things meteorological. We're enjoying a thaw this morning – I'm referring to the weather, by the way, not the dog and me; that relationship remains unchanged – out there, however, beyond this cabin's walls, it's become downright balmy. It's now warmer outside, I think, than it is in. Water's dripping off the roof. Tonight, when the temperature dips again, there will be icicles. For some reason, I have always had a fondness for icicles. The dog appears to like them too.

He was a gift from Gwen to John, which ended up with me like certain other of Gwen's conferments. She'd wanted a Norwegian elkhound, but we managed to avoid that. A Norwegian elkhound, according to John's description, resembles a truncated husky just back from the dry cleaner. (An *Irish* wolfhound you can visualize chasing a wolf, a *Scottish* deerhound you can picture chasing a deer, but a *Norwegian* elkhound is impossible to imagine chasing anything bigger than the neighbour's cat – John took me aside and explained that elk in Norway are actually the same animals we call moose, which makes the image even more amusing. He was laughing as he said this, but that didn't stop him from asking me to intervene with Gwen.)

In the end, we managed to convince her that for political reasons, John's dog would have to be a mongrel. That yes, a Norwegian elkhound indeed would reflect the Queen's proud Nordic heritage, but that John was after all the King of Canada, not Norway, and Canada was a nation built from the mingling of bloods. Gwen was nesting just then – in that difficult stage when everything must be made precisely right in anticipation of the whelp. After converting half the Silos' space to nursery facilities, and remodelling the rest (and let me just mention how glad I am that none of us will be around to justify those items in the budget), Gwen announced that no child should be raised without a dog. Evidently there were Norwegian elkhounds wandering the fjords where she grew up, and the Queen insisted on nothing less for her own issue.

Fine, countered John, but it's got to be a mongrel. John had strong opinions on most things biological, including the dubious virtues of pedigree. ("Bad enough that people segregate themselves by bloodlines. Even more ridiculous with pets.") There was political capital to be extracted here too, of course, and it fell to me to explain the finer points of this to the Queen. I needn't have worried. Gwen understood.

Like so much of what we did in the latter stages of John's reign, what came to be known as the "doggy op" was a masterful display of tactical profiling. At least a hundred members of the Silos press corps came traipsing through the Humane Society behind the royal couple, snapping photographs and sowing terror through the cages while the King and Queen promenaded from gate to gate, shaking paws and sniffing ears. It made for some terrific images. There's one in particular of Gwen, I recall, laughing as a squirming beagle licks her face. The Queen's head is thrown back in youthful delight; her coat brushed slightly off the shoulder to expose a marvellously innocent expanse of royal breast. That one made the pages of *Vogue* too, if I am not mistaken.

Rumours circulated for weeks afterwards that the Humane Society had scoured the countryside for puppies of every conceivable variety. If that's true, I can only credit their foresight. Personal donations went up something like 900 per cent following the royal visit.

The walkabout had gone on just long enough when the King reached into a wriggling mass of white and black and brown, pulled out the one that caught his eye, and announced, "I think this is him." Flash cubes exploded, kennel-keepers flushed, the Queen smiled and blinked her cobalt eyes, and all present erupted in spontaneous applause. There were pictures in all the dailies, next day, of John formally signing the adoption papers. What came home with them was the individual that now lounges on the floor beside me, gnawing his fleas by the light of the stove.

The mongrel theme, as it turned out, had legs beyond what even I could have hoped. Everyone from local sportscasters to the presidents of Yale and U of T found themselves referring to – and reflecting in – its invigorating symbolism. I like to think that even Theodore Sapper would have been forced to find something positive to say, but by this time he'd already pulled up stakes and removed himself to Texas. The *Globe and Mail* that weekend ran a lovely editorial, which the *Boston Globe*, the *New York Times*, and several other sympathetic outlets reprinted verbatim. *Salute to the mongrel*, I think it was slugged or something like that; a lovely little mutt-as-metaphor concoction, linking genetic diversity with plurality of thought and freedom of conscience. A bit of a stretch, in normal times, but contemporary readers took the meaning well enough. Washington had just announced the creation of the PVPV, once and forever clarifying its notions of Homeland Security. Our King was more and more perceived as representing the opposite political pole.

Prettily done.

John, of course, is dead. Gwen and the baby flown home to Oslo. And I'm here with the dog. The moving fingers write and, having writ, move on. Something like that.

DAY TWENTY-SEVEN

It rained last night. There's something unconditionally shocking in this. Not the rain so much as the thunder and crashes of lightning. It poured and poured. The dog scrabbled under the bed, and I was happy to keep the covers up above my chin. There is something preternatural about thunder in the dead of winter. Especially after all this intensity of cold. Every morning here you see your breath, but today, with so much moisture in the air, it leaves trails of vapour dangling like clouds. They drift below the ceiling, moving as we do. The dog pants, the mirrors fog.

And the lake has reappeared. Blue water, shore to shore. How is it possible so much ice has melted in a single night? I hobbled outside to fill my bucket. The snow was heavy and wet, slumping in against itself and sucking at my boot like porridge. In all this time I'd never used the dock. A dock is redundant when the lake is solid too. But this morning I edged out along the planks and lowered my pail, which clanged and stopped just below the surface. The ice hasn't melted, you see, it's simply been covered with accumulated rain. Liquid water has pooled above itself in solid state. Our lake is now one vast puddle, two inches deep.

The dog, in his idiocy, adores it. This new delineation of one element from the next has sparked some sense of canine wonderment. He dashes out, slipping and skidding, sending up spray like a boat. As far as he's concerned, any change is for the better.

But for me it's freakish. The thermometer's still above freezing. Water drips and drips. For the first time since I've been here, these papers feel damp. There's a wetness inside that chills more deeply than the honest cold I've grown accustomed to. Contrary to all principles of fuel efficiency, I have opened the doors to the wood stove wide: a roaring blaze seems more effective in combating the damp. It may be psychological, I admit; John would know the physics. I will tell you, though, that in the farther reaches of this building there are snowflakes falling from the ceiling. The moisture wafts into unheated nooks and crannies, crystallizes in the corners, and drifts back down again as snow. John's cottage, perversely, retains the cold more effectively than it does the heat.

Which reminds me of something else I've been meaning to tell you. I have been referring to this place as John's – because that's how I think of it, and because in every sense but one that's what it is – but technically speaking it belongs to me. Not long after K'oha it became obvious that he would have to give it up. Tour boats started appearing off the dock, hoping for a glimpse of the King in swimming trunks. Sometimes dozens would anchor out there in the channel, or just drift along the current like rafts of floating sheep. He was seldom here – life was already too busy for that – but the boats came anyway. After John's debut on the U.S. networks, and especially following the incident with Sheik Bin Wahhabi, you'd be as likely to encounter paparazzi scampering among the woods here as chipmunks. It got to be ridiculous. Eventually the King quietly notified local authorities that he would be selling, which made the Toronto papers next day. In due course, word was put out that the property had changed hands, and the King was never seen here again.

With the passage of time, the place has faded back into the woods where it belongs, its brief link with royalty forgotten. Once or twice a summer we'll arrange for someone to stay a week or three, as renters. There's a telephone number they can give to anyone who might inquire; a machine at the other end answers with the name of a property management firm. The calls, of course, are not returned.

John couldn't bear to let it go. It was a connection, I think, to normal life – to the normal person he was before – a reminder of heritage to set against the demands of posterity. We flipped it five times altogether, bouncing it back and forth among an unrelated set of holding companies. The deed is now formerly registered to a numbered corporation of which I am, at some remove, proprietor. And just so you know, it's willed back to the Crown. When I'm dead, this property reverts to John's heir and his estate.

Did you know that frostbite is the same thing as trench foot? I had no idea. Not precisely the same, exactly, but close enough. For a true definition of frostbite, the deep tissues must actually freeze; crystals of ice need to form and burst the cells, which plug up the capillaries causing oxygen depletion, then further cellular disruption. It's the clots that do the damage, from what I gather, more so than the freezing itself. Trench foot is more or less the same, except that it happens at higher temperatures: prolonged exposure to cold and wet causes blood vessels to contract; living cells starve for want of oxygen and die. It's the dead cells that cause the problems, I've discovered, in both cases. They become infected, which invites the gangrene.

I've been trying to talk myself into trench foot because to my mind it sounds somehow less serious, but I'm afraid there's no escaping frostbite. The only thing now is deciding on the degree of severity. According to John's encyclopedia:

> The outlook is best, when the frozen state is of short
> duration; thawing is by rapid rewarming; and blisters
> develop early, pink and large, and extend to the tips of
> the toes . . .

Can you believe it's taken me all this time to think of the encyclopedias? There's been a set of elderly *Britannicas*, all this while, staring me in the face. That's the downside, I suppose, of transitioning to the Internet Age – you lose track of old habits. My guess is, John's parents got him this set when he was a boy. Or maybe they were second-hand to begin with, they're a generation out of date. A whole shelf of them has made their way up here, at any rate, at some point in the past – you never know when you're going to want to look up things like "trench foot." Maybe that's what the merganser's been ogling about.

> The outlook is poor when: thawing is delayed; thawing is
> by excessive heat – e.g., greater than 46° C (115° F); the
> blisters are dark or hemorrhagic and do not extend to the
> distal tips; and when freezing then thawing is followed
> by refreezing. The last condition is disastrous and almost
> invariably requires amputation of the affected part.

On the positive side, I can say for certain that the foot only froze the once and has not been frozen since, so that's definitely to the good. Though I'm not so confident about the temperature I thawed it out at. That I can't remember. I remember my breath was steaming hot and the room was freezing cold. My foot felt like a block of cement at that stage. You could have hit it with a hammer and I wouldn't have known the difference. So I can't be sure.

In the matter of the blisters, these weren't clear fluid, like the kind you get from breaking in new shoes, but they weren't dark and bloody either. More pinkish, I'd say. Gwen would have called them chartreuse, or carmine, or something on that order. I am concluding from this that the damage done was more than superficial, but that there's also a reasonable hope the freezing didn't go down as deep as all that. They burst, a few days back, the blisters, I mean. Now the area is covered in what I would describe as a leathery sort of carapace, like a hard shell made from bull's hide. It's far from pretty, but so far it doesn't smell, which I assume is also to the good. When the blisters started bursting I ransacked the place for any old prescriptions of antibiotics but, not surprisingly, found none – John, of course, was deathly allergic to penicillin, so they'd never have been allowed in here to begin with. I debated attempting the hike to some of the other cottages to see if I could find something there, but the swelling was too much for my boot, and the pain – I can tell you now because quite a lot of it has subsided – was, well, the thought of walking very far was more than I could bear, if you want the truth of it. Also I believe that sealing my foot into a boot for any length of time would have just have further encouraged the infection. I did find an old tube of Polysporin and tore up some bedsheets, and that's what I've been wrapping it with. Every morning I boil the bandages in a pot to disinfect them. But in the last few days I've stopped having to do this because, as I've said, it's hardened off into this blackish leathery cast. It hurts less too, though it's impossible to tell one way or another what's going on underneath.

"Decision to amputate," notes John's encyclopedia, "is usually postponed for several months until the area has had time to heal."

I'm interpreting this as good news also. Despite the setbacks, things are coming along reasonably well. I expect to be finished before any such need arises. And if you think it courageous of me to have ignored the swelling and the sweats and shivers, I remind you that mental concentration is a kind of opiate. Somewhere earlier I said that writing is a form of therapy. John always said this was bullshit, but it's true.

So – and since there's nothing to be done about it anyway – I propose we use infection as the starting point for today's more topical discussion: John's impact in the United States of America. The Reds, of course, referred to *John* as the infection, and to be fair – if you change perspective for the sake of argument and look at things from the bacterium's point of view – the appearance of a white blood cell into their midst must have felt very much like contagion. (Art is everywhere, is it not? And point of view is everything.) John arrived from outside the system, is what I'm trying to get at, appearing like a shot of penicillin injected straight into the bloodstream of American body politics.

At first, almost everyone's response was positive, Reds as much as Blues. In fact, it might have been the Reds that admired him more to start with, for the simple reason that getting shot by Indians has more appeal to that demographic in general. John's earliest appearances on the talk-show circuit focused far more on the King's considerable charm and wit, rather than any notions of serious politics. And his appearance. You can be sure we made the most of his looks. There was money available, by this time, so when he went before the cameras he was quite elegantly turned out.

A brief aside on clothing: only fools and women think about what they wear beyond the time it takes to zip a zipper. But since fools and women make up the majority, it's even stupider ignoring this reality. The simplest of all human achievements is being well-dressed. All it takes is a credit card and a competent tailor. With women, I'll grant you, things are more complicated. When Gwen came along, the sartorial focus went over the top, but most of the attention was now on what the Queen was wearing rather than the King, so it didn't much matter. My job, as I saw it, was to ensure that John was presentable – that his hair was cut and that his clothes were well made and appropriately fitted; the cameras always liked him anyway, and he was the kind of public figure who preferred to make his presence felt in words, so it worked well enough for us. Leave the sartorial statements for those with nothing else to offer, is my advice, unless you have nothing else to offer, God forbid.

The other nice thing about the Americans was the fact that for them, royalty was *royalty*. It didn't much matter that John's claim to the Crown was completely artificial, because most of them didn't know the difference anyway. Certain viewers were vaguely aware that Canada's head of state had been, until quite recently, the Queen of England. But this obvious distortion of nationalist principles had always confused them. If they remembered it at all, people tended to file information of this variety alongside other bits of game-show trivia, like knowing that the language of Brazil is Portuguese not Brazilian, or that penguins come from the South Pole not the North one. A flesh-and-blood King right there in the studio, on the other hand – in an elegant but unassuming navy blue suit – now this helped ease the strain of keeping up with geopolitics. People appreciate their television more when it confirms their intelligence.

And John was entertaining, that you could rely on. More so later than at first, but even back at the beginning, audiences took to him.

During most of those first few interviews, the discussion seldom strayed beyond the details of the shooting. *As King, how did it feel, the moment you realized you'd been hit? Were you taken to a hospital, after, or does the Royal Palace have medical facilities on site?* I have to say that John handled this stage magnificently, smiling and ignoring the greater inanities, frankly and honestly answering such questions as could be replied to with modest panache. Inevitably, attention would be drawn to the King's vibrant good health – him so recently having taken a bullet and all. John would bow, a stiff and self-depreciating bow, and everyone would afterwards recall how attractively *regal* the King's demeanour was. That word started showing up in weekly listings of the *TV Guide* – *regal*, along with frequent references to John of Canada's refreshingly open nature and frank accessibility. That's another one that kept recurring, *accessible*.

A substantial number of U.S. viewers, as it turned out, were under the impression that Canada had had its own King all along, and that his appearance on their televisions was more the result of an enlightened shift in public relations than some complicated transformation in structures of governance. True, this King did not possess quite the same interesting accent as some other monarchs they might have heard, but on the other hand, he seemed a lot more likable – which counted for so much more in this day and age. No wonder he was where he was, right there in their living room where any A-list celebrity would certainly desire to be.

It was around this time too, I think, that we first began to recognize the true depths of America's monarch envy. It surprised me more than anyone. You didn't have to have been brought up among them to recognize how worshipful Americans were of their Republic. Yet almost without exception, all the people we came in contact with on those early U.S. tours – the producers, the cameramen, the makeup girls, and green-room caterers, to say nothing of the hosts themselves – were clearly over the moon with the opportunity of using phrases like *Your Highness*. It embarrassed him at first, especially as the folks at home were equally pleased never to use such expressions. (I say never, though of course there were occasions when pomp and protocol were unavoidable – Throne Speeches, for example, or similarly ceremonial affairs when everyone involved would have to make an effort not to chuckle and wink.) But Americans were beside themselves with eagerness to wrap their tongues around a title. John politely tried to stop them, but they were having none of it. Even after things turned so sour with the Reds, even when the majority of Southerners had decided that John was the Antichrist incarnate, even after they'd determined they wanted him flat-out dead, they still couldn't seem to help themselves from trotting out John's formal title whenever the King of Canada came up in conversation, which was astonishingly often, believe me, especially in the months leading up to his death.

I'm going to stop myself here, I think, and back us up a page or two. A few lines above I mentioned the Throne Speech. This was on my list of things I need to talk about too. Sorry, housekeeping.

One of Canada's quainter institutions has always been the Speech from the Throne. For people like me – those of us educated outside the British parliamentary system – traditions like this one were hard to come to grips with. A Speech from the Throne, pre-John, was a public document prepared by the Prime Minister but delivered by the Governor General who in turn read it out loud on behalf of a monarch from a foreign nation. Imagine if you will an American-style State of the Union Address delivered by an alien android and you'll have something like a fitting model.

But Throne Speeches were, and still are, very big news politically. Governments use them to outline their agendas at the beginning of every parliamentary session, so they're always significant events. Invariably, they're televised live and inevitably, pre-John, they qualified for the year's most boring newscast. Even hard-core policy wonks popped a handful of mondafinil before settling in to take in a Throne Speech.

When I say that John injected the tradition with an element of fun, I'm being slightly disingenuous. Throne Speeches in John's day were often not fun at all for certain ministers; worse for whoever had to write them. For those guys, in fact, they must have been a nightmare. But for the rest of Canadians, Throne Speeches became something more like a guilty pleasure.

According to custom, Governors General were expected to take no actual interest in politics. A GG's function was to stand up in the House of Commons and read the long, long list of portentous clichés that formed the government's legislative priorities for the year to come. Although the circumstance of his arrival had somewhat altered convention, the King remained scrupulous, or mostly scrupulous, in fulfilling his functions according to the precedents of history. He loathed the red cape and gown he was expected to wear on these occasions, but he put them on regardless. Publicly, no comment ever passed his lips in reference to the policies contained in any speech that he presented. When John proclaimed a Speech from the Throne, he read it verbatim, like every GG before him. Try as they might – and believe me, they tried – the media never succeeded in tempting the King to offer any form of verbal judgment on the document he'd just delivered. Still, he had his own opinions. And everybody from the Prime Minister on down was perfectly aware of them.

Which is what made John's speeches so entertaining to watch.

John was blessed with one of those faces that talked without speaking. He would raise an eyebrow, just a notch, above a certain passage, and that was all it took to start a buzz that the King had his doubts about that segment of the text. If he inclined his head a little – just the slightest hint of nod – this would be interpreted as an indication of support for whatever initiative the bob had coincided with. He'd do things with his voice as well. An extra pause here, a change of inflection there; analyzing and interpreting these gestures provided the press gallery and our chattering classes with truckloads of material. And always, there was that smile, or at least the hint of one. If it vanished, even fleetingly, lobbyists cringed and journalists sharpened their metaphors. By the latter stages of John's reign, Cabinets were known to be shuffled based on how much tooth he showed during the part of the speech that dealt with their portfolios.

You can understand how this drove the PMO insane. All the more so because John would brazenly deny it. He would smile and tell the press that he was just the reader, that's all he was. It was the government's role to write the speech, and Parliament's to assess it. The King's function was merely to read it out loud. What he was, he said, was a public address system in a pretty red cape. Despite what anyone will tell you, it's human nature to admire pointless complications. Especially when they're easy to understand. Everyone knew John had his own agenda, and people valued John's agendas all the more for the artifice with which they were presented.

The King had made the rules more *interesting*, and – as with any other kind of game – one player's penalty meant another player's gain. If John's opposition to any given point tilted the field against, it was also true that his support presented an advantage to the opposite side. The smart ones chose to work with gravity. Politics, after all, is a game where downward force accumulates.

From the spectators' point of view, more importantly, John made the sport a pleasure to watch. While the King delivered his speech, the cameras took to roving the faces of the government's front bench, hunting out the squirms. Yes, perhaps it did incline to *schadenfreude*, but people enjoyed seeing their elected leaders obliged to sweat. It brought the politicians closer; it made them more human, somehow, and therefore more understandable. If John's game was a charade, believe me when I tell you that the country loved to play along. And they trusted him. John was their man. If the King saw a problem, there likely damn well was a problem. His famous *twitches* took on a life of their own in political vernacular. The term soon came to be a synonym for *dubious*. Over time, its meaning broadened; these days it's used to describe almost anything likely to cause a government grief. Policy-makers seriously debate a clause's likelihood to cause *a twitch*; pundits count how many *twitches* an administration might get away with before losing traction in the polls. I can't help wondering, by the time you read this, if the phrase will still carry the currency it does today. We can only hope. Language has its fads that come and go, like politics. I understand that. But the useful ones tend to stick sometimes, don't they?

It's why we play.

John's kingship added to our system of government a whole new category of influence, an extra check if you like – an added balance to the body politic. And if his efforts occasionally lurched into silliness, well, the gains by far outweighed the costs. There was a scandal some months back – you won't remember, but it was big news while it played. Italy's prime minister had up and vanished. For weeks the Italian press was full of anxious speculation: Was he sick? Was he hiding? Was his government about to crash? At last the news leaked out: *Il Primo* had been holed up at a private clinic in Miami, recovering from plastic surgery. Afterwards – as you can well imagine – the cameras buzzed like flies around a downer steer, targeting the eyes and ears. One reporter hid behind a statue of Brutus and nailed a close-up of the back of the prime ministerial skull. Was that a scar, there, in the fold behind the auricle? Could that be traces of a suture? *La Republica* ran grainy reproductions of before-and-after headshots, superimposed with calibrated grids. The freckle displayed in picture to the left was clearly half a centimetre lower than on the image to the right? For the Italians it was great sport, which goes a long way to explaining Mussolini.

John's theatrics never came anywhere close to this degree of farce, but there was in them the same flavour of spectacle. People caught themselves taking an interest, despite their better judgment. John got people talking. And that was his point. What they were discussing was the pros and cons of better governance. Once he'd got that going, it wasn't that much of a stretch to get them voting again too. Which was good news for the politicians who supported the things John supported, and bad news for those who did not.

Now back to the U.S. of A.

Phase Two of John's emergence into the arena of American politics began with the Saudi water-toss incident. It's fair to say this event came along at exactly the right time for us, in that his currency as a celebrity bull's-eye was beginning to wane. Like the shooting, the Saudi water toss also garnered high approval ratings among the Reds. It was furthermore the true beginning of his feud with Theodore Sapper. Everyone knows what happened to Sapper, but few can point to where the end began. We'll get to that.

John's marketability in the news cycle had pretty much wound down by the time we'd reached the water-toss interview. The show itself was definitely bottom-flight in terms of ratings. In fact, I'd given some thought to cancelling and taking us home. But John and I had mulled things over and decided that this program might be just the place to begin shaping his public personae into something more substantial. The broadcaster was one of those left-leaning subscription outfits, the kind committed to wholesome public service. Originally, I think, the scheduled had called for King John of Canada – still recovering from gunshot wounds incurred while mediating a dispute with his country's hostile natives – to participate in a frank discussion with the interviewer on the wider issue of Aboriginal disenfranchisement. Platforms like this one were generally accepted as an opportunity to bemoan the sorry conditions endured by Native North Americans and to condemn all past participants for their tragic lack of cultural sensitivity. John and I had evolved some ideas of our own, by this time, on the subject of disenfranchisement; we decided that a quasi-intellectual, low-ratings, non-Canadian production aired by private broadcasters might be exactly the place to begin to quietly airing some of them out.

But then a junior producer screwed up the schedule and double-booked us with the sheik. To be honest, I can't remember what Prince Bin Wahhabi was in town that day promoting, another oil-for-tolerance campaign most likely. In any case, the production company decided both guests were too important to simply reschedule – the sheik was a member of the royal family after all, they all were, and John was a full-fledged King. So neither could properly be asked to come back some other day. Then the producer got the bright idea of presenting them *both* on air together – they had royalty in common, didn't they? – and then someone else decided the show could be repackaged as a discussion on the social obligations of *monarchy* itself: a kind of point-counterpoint, with a royal spin.

It didn't go well. John and the sheik did not take kindly to each other, as history records. The sheik made his unfortunate observation about the numbers of mothers with children using food banks in Toronto, and John, resenting the comparison to a society that dealt with its single mothers by recruiting them to brothels, tossed half a glass of water in the startled princeling's face. It would have been worse – I mean, for the sheik – but there was a table between them.

The event marked the beginning of Phase Two of John's American ascendance. It was also a very valuable lesson in national and international diplomacy in that the former – as we so usefully discovered – always counts far more than the latter. There was an international outcry, it goes without saying: the Saudis threatened to recall their ambassador, *Aljazeera* ran some screaming editorials, executives of several transnational investment firms predicted that the sky would soon be falling while diplomatic notes went whistling in and out of Ottawa like hailstones in a blizzard, but – and this is the important *but* – just as with most other storms, this one blew itself out with hardly a trace of lasting damage.

That was the lesson we learned. In international relationships, ascertain the bottom line, then reason outward from there. Bottom line with the Saudis, at least as far as most Canadians were concerned, was *who cares?* So what if they severed diplomatic relations? So what if their ambassador flew home to his Sudanese slave girls? Good riddance. It might have been different, say, if we'd been Europeans and dependent on Arabian oil. It would certainly have been different if we'd been like the Americans, with a fragmenting empire to hedge bets over. But we weren't. We had our own oil, our own knitting to attend to, and our own foreign policy too. I'm simplifying things – of course, there were consequences and, yes, some investors took a hiding – but the losses were tiny when compared to global gains. Polite little Canada had said fuck you to one of the world's most brazen tyrannies and discovered that the consequences were practically nil. I would say it surprised our side as much as anyone.

Then came the new rounds of terrorist bombings, which everyone remembers as having changed everything, though not quite as everyone recalls. Even before the first attack, the average American was not all that comfortable with Washington's coziness with Riyadh. All that came out afterwards – we remember that part – the millions of petro-dollars the Saudis used to bankroll al-Jihad, the funding of religious schools turning children into traitors against their next-door neighbours, the billion dollars paid over to Pakistan and then Iran to assemble their Islamic bombs – none of this was exactly top secret before New York, it just wasn't discussed. Afterwards, it was.

And now the thing everyone was talking about was why it was only brave King John of Canada (and by extension the country he reigned) who stood alone among Western leaders as having the courage to stand up for his country's convictions. While American manufacturers sold the Saudis $100 billion in military hardware, and while U.S. Ambassadors and Secretaries of State and Defence lined up like pigs at the trough to get themselves on Saudi payrolls after they'd retired out of office – while the President himself was a senior adviser to the private investment firm that brokered all those cash transaction – King John of Canada, alone among all public figures, was willing to take a stand and call a spade a spade.

If John was favourably received among Americans as an Indian fighter, his approval ratings soared off the chart once the water-toss video went winging its way across the Internet. As armies of bloggists gleefully noted, the most intriguing thing about the clip was how clearly it had captured Bin Wahhabi's reaction – not anger, not indignation, not even embarrassment, but *fear*. As if he really did believe, for those few seconds at least, that the King's fingers were about to close around his bearded throat. The scene was downloaded I don't know how many million times during that first week alone, and of course got endless air time on all the commercial broadbands. Quite a number of Americans admired John even before the bombing. Afterwards, he was elevated to the status of national hero.

Which is why it's my own preference to characterize this period as the Mary Pickford Phase – though you can't fault John for disliking the name. Whatever you chose to call it, it was during this era that Americans did with John what they had always done when they looked beyond their borders and beheld their heart's content. They claimed John for their own. Canada's crowned King became our latter-day America's Sweetheart.

Naturally, this had instructive implications here at home. It's an ancient truth that no Canadian can ever know real fame unless it comes up from below the border. This applied to John as much as anyone, though John in his usual way evolved the tradition. From Pickford to Gretzky, they'd all gone over to America – or raised their children there, which amounts to the same. But John never signed on for the house in Santa Monica. He couldn't, could he? That was the beauty of his vocation. Others before him had charmed the star-machine by returning to Americans what it was that moved them most: an enhanced reflection of themselves. John did it differently. Or should I say it was his differences that did it. This may have been a symptom of the times – yes, of course it was – but the fact remains that John's greatest attraction to Americans at that time was their perception of him as an outsider.

Of all the ironies, in a life replete with irony, this one's always been my favourite. Having earned his laurels in the only place where Canadian garlands could properly be gathered, the King returned home from America more triumphantly Canadian than when he'd left. It was really from this stage forward that Canadians truly began adoring him. Later, if you'd asked what it was they loved about John best, most folks would have told you it was his stand against the PVPV. But it was America's embrace that made Canadians want to love him in the first place. Flip perspectives, and the paradox is even more bewitching. Canada's Crown may have unmade America, yet it was America that fixed the Crown to begin with.

I'm getting ahead of myself, as usual, and skipping over details. John's trajectory was a good deal less vertical than I've been making out. Perhaps it shouldn't have surprised us – it didn't surprise Hester – but it was from hometown Toronto that we got the roughest ride at this stage. And it was in Alberta, of all places, where John registered his strongest support. Alberta, remember, was far more American in character than any other part of Canada, and shared with the Americans their tendency for unqualified endorsement of whatever met with their approval. (I think it was the shock of seeing their Republican model imploding, as a matter of fact, that sent them retreating back into Canada – but that's my own opinion, and premature.) It was a safe bet, anyway, that if Americans approved of John, Albertans would likely do so as well. But more important was his role in finessing *La Libération* – that beautifully ironic phrase the West had coined to summarize Quebec's decampment. Despite the many awkward battles in the months to come, Westerners never lost sight of John's role in bringing them back into Confederation. It was a lever we were glad to lean on more than once, believe me, during tenser moments in the constitutional debates. To its very great credit (and the country's enormous benefit), the West was always willing to cut John just a little more slack than it otherwise would have, simply because he was the guy that pulled out for them the chair where Quebec used to sit.

Fey Toronto, on the other hand – though it would profit from *La Libération* far more than anyone – was now experiencing one of those spasms of post-colonial rectitude that so nauseated the rest of the country.

Torontonians couldn't take back the part they'd played in ousting Quebec – mercifully – but now that matters had moved on to an issue more in keeping with their city's cosmopolitan persona, they could safely sidestep up to higher ground. John's louche behaviour with the sheik had deeply disturbed Toronto's liberal intelligentsia. They could sympathize with his initial sense of outrage, true – who would not? – they might even find something commendable in the new King's readiness to defend their own forward-thinking policies concerning child poverty and gender inequalities. But wider issues were clearly at stake. It was a form of violence, after all. Definitively so. The King's impulsive behaviour, furthermore, was a serious breach of diplomatic protocol. Not only had John savagely offended the most fundamental rules of statesmanship, he'd also insulted the dignity of a peace-affirming global faith. The Saudi state, as the world knew full well, was governed by the precepts of its own religious law. Disrespecting the state, therefore, was tantamount to disrespecting the state's religion, and thus clearly an egregious expression of religious intolerance. Toronto was firm about the sanctity of all religious bias. The various guardians of the city's enlightenment flooded local media with stern warnings about how it was exactly this kind of cowboy diplomacy that invariably led to the worst possible consequences.

Which played out very well for us, west of the Lakehead. When editorial writers in Calgary and Edmonton heard phrases like "cowboy diplomacy," they were more inclined than ever to declare themselves for the King. The more Toronto criticized, the more the West convinced itself that John was looking out for Western interests.

With the notable exception of media outlets controlled by Theodore Sapper. In Toronto, Sapper's flagship began attacking the King for all it was worth. "A mature periodical," intoned one editorial, "like a mature polity, recognizes mistakes where they have been made. While it may be true that this newspaper initially supported the creation of a Canadian Head of State, recent behaviour by the individual regrettably chosen to occupy that position has left the editorial board with no choice but to withdraw its support." Knowing what we know now about Sapper, it would have made sense to expect his *Western* outlets to weigh in with equal vigour on the opposite side. But that's not what happened.

While Sapper's Toronto editorials fanned the flames of local outrage, his pages in Alberta recycled ancient rants about the unelected Senate. The entire western half of Sapper's media empire, in fact, ignored the Saudi water toss completely.

No one but his bankers knew it at the time, but Sapper was caught in a dilemma. The real story came out after the events we're discussing – so once again it's hard for me to anticipate how familiar you'll be with the background. Sapper, as it happened, was deeply in debt to a financial institution controlled by Saudi interests; I can't be certain if you'll know this part. The Saudi state, a tyranny unchallenged at home, preferred to use its resources to bribe the citizens of *other* countries rather than its own. Its oil reserves generated hundreds of billions in capital, which the royal family reinvested in the economies of whichever states purchased their crude. It was an excellent strategy, in many respects, and if they'd paid just a little more attention to their backyard they'd likely still have their heads as well as their chateaux in Switzerland. Money buys influence, and the Saudis had a lot of that to go around. Too much for their own good.

By the time you read this, I'm sure the world will have a clearer picture of why it ran on petro-carbons for so many more decades than it needed to. Apologies, and all that. From the Saudis' perspective, the strategy was simple, really, as the best systems usually are: identify the economies you want to target, choose influential people inside those economies, then lend them money at rates so favourable that they borrow more than they can afford to pay back.

In Sapper's case, the great irony is that he likely could have covered his initial debts. Most of his holdings outearned their competitors. His business model worked – I'll give him that. But Sapper was always more interested in expansion than fortification. Rather than ploughing his revenues back in, he refinanced and borrowed more. (Did I mention he was an M.B.A.? Which means he studied Lipsey, Sparks, and Steiner, not Madam Bovary – otherwise he might have had more sense.) Unlike most lenders, who generally rely on interest payments for their own security, the Saudis pumped all the income they needed straight up from the sands beneath their royal estates. Riyadh's method of calculating interest was therefore rather original. Let me also mention that Sapper was by no means the only mogul of his era who wound up servicing his mortgage through methods he had never foreseen. Bottom line, shall we say, was that Sapper – to say nothing of the White House – was finding himself less and less motivated to investigate irregularities concerning Saudi commerce.

So when Theodore Sapper received a quiet message from Riyadh, he couldn't disregard it. As I say, I'm simplifying: the pressures brought to bear were subtle enough to have gone mostly unremarked for decades. But King John of Canada, it seems, had got under Saudi skin – the water-toss incident was perceived in Riyadh as more blatantly offensive even than the recent spate of bombings they'd been dealing with internally. The princes threw their usual caution to the wind when it came to John, and this was their undoing as we know, and, over the longer term, Sapper's also. It must have been hard for him. If I had the slightest shred of fellow-feeling for the man I might even entertain a scrap of pity. On one hand, here was an issue tailor-made for his divide-and-profit approach to storymaking. But on the other, there were his Saudi backers, warning that they'd call in his loans if he didn't do as he was told.

Po-faced Toronto was holding up its end of the plotline. While the city's cultural establishment stroked itself along the thigh, Toronto's Chamber of Commerce was lining up its most authoritative voices to express the concern – the deeply held concern – of the city's business community. It was all very well and good, they said, to claim the moral high ground in attacking the appearance of misogyny in foreign localities. And although forward-thinking citizens of Toronto would undoubtedly disapprove of sexual exploitation wherever this practice might regrettably occur, these same stakeholders might wish to consider the security of their own standards of living. The beating of butterfly wings in one part of the world, they warned, could cause the price of heating oil to spike in another. Any such increase would necessarily render Toronto's – and by extension all of Canada's – position uncompetitive in the present global marketplace.

It all came down to oil. The Western provinces, although they had sentimental reasons for admiring John's insult to the sheik, most of all delighted in the possibility that the Saudis might retaliate by driving up the price of crude. Industrial Ontario, meanwhile – and Toronto, in particular – was chiefly motivated by an equally intense desire to see the cost of bunker oil stay low. Although it was unlikely that the Saudis could affect them directly – we imported very little Gulf oil, even then – the business community worried that any disruption to the global flow of capital was negative on principle. John responded with his now-famous line about civilized societies not accepting intolerance in the name of toleration – which to their credit shamed the less doctrinaire of the arts crowd but, more importantly, went over like gangbusters out there on the Prairies. The Maritimes, meanwhile, with their keen sense in detecting prevailing political winds and a growing interest of their own in the value of off-shore crude, sided with Alberta. Rural Ontario opposed anything Torontonian as a matter of habit. So once again Toronto found itself in isolation.

But for every action, as Newton pointed out, there's an equal and opposite reaction. Enter Hester Vale – who chose exactly this moment to extend a thorny olive branch.

Everyone knew that Toronto's renegade Mayor had been at odds with the country's fledgling monarch from day one. Hester's low opinion of King John, personally, was a subject of much repetition among both Toronto's business community *and* the po-faced, PoMo, anti-colonial cultural set. She had the knack for cranking out an assortment of quotable quotes: ribald satire for the tabloids, pungent wit with interviewers from the *Report on Business*. Hester made very certain that Torontonians never lost sight of who'd been responsible for shooting down their city's bid for independence.

So no one was more shocked than Hogtown itself when the Mayor announced that King John would shortly be coming to live in Toronto.

Her phrasing, to be sure, was expressed more in the nature of a demand than an invitation. But still, the notion took everyone completely by surprise. Including, very obviously, the King. John was delivering an address at Massey Hall when CityNewsTV reporters caught him, clearly flat-footed. What was his response, they wanted to know, to Mayor Vale's insistence that he move his official residence to Toronto?

"I beg your pardon?" replied the King, so at loss for words that his customary wit deserted him entirely.

When informed about the Mayor's offer, the King's jaw, quite literally, was seen to drop. The cameras were on him, of course, so there was no disguising the evidence. We got copies of the tape; John and I replayed the segment half-a-dozen times that night, worrying that he might have overdone it. The jaw does drop. The King's mouth does gape. But as I told him, you can only overact if you're playing in the movies: in politics, it's hardly ever noticeable.

Did it surprise you, by the way, that Canada's Crown once resided in Ottawa? Most people these days have forgotten. It's hard even for *me* to remember, and I lived there. The monarchy is now identified as closely with Toronto as its predecessor was with London Town. But at the start of things, everyone expected John would set up shop in Ottawa because that's where the GGs had always resided. Rideau Hall was very nice, as I remember it, and I have pleasant recollections of our time there. The problem was more with Ottawa itself. With Quebec no longer in the picture, you see, having Ottawa as the country's capital no longer made sense.

It never really did. Queen Victoria chose it back in 1857, chiefly for its virtue of being equally insignificant in both official languages – and the fact that it was so far away from anything, American troops would likely never find it in the event of an invasion. Parliament Buildings were erected on a hill overlooking a remote stretch of water between Ontario and Quebec – and a little northern lumbering community became the nation's seat of government. A very pleasant place it is too, particularly for admirers of outdoor activities such as hunting and fishing, and sports involving frozen water. John did quite a lot of cross-country skiing while we were there and often remarked on how convenient it was having all those woodland trails right there at his doorstep. The tulips are lovely too, when spring arrives.

But *La Libération* had made Ottawa's bicultural advantages, politically speaking, redundant. Canadians began asking why they needed a capital attached to Quebec when Quebec was no longer attached to the Canada. This being Canada, though, others argued for preserving tradition – to say nothing of a century and a half of architectural investment. Quite a few parliamentarians, and thousands of civil servants, had bought up property in the area – much of it at bargain-basement prices after the francophone decampment. A surprising number claimed they wanted to stay. French proficiency was so ingrained in the bureaucracy, too, that many of its senior members knew no other way of doing business. Ottawa's faithful could continue to cling to the status of bilingualism at the municipal level, at least.

Besides which, fierce debate had sprung up among the other regions about where the new capital should go instead. Lobbyists in Halifax insisted it be relocated there, because Halifax was robbed the first time around in 1857. Then the mayor of St. John's, Newfoundland, pointed out that St. John's, as the oldest English-speaking city on the continent, had every bit as good a claim as Halifax – and what with the fisheries collapse and all that, the local economy could definitely use a boost in seasonal employment. Various western municipalities including Biggar, Saskatchewan (*New York is big, but this is Biggar*), demanded that the nation's capital be immediately transplanted to the West in compensation for all the years of alienation. Even Kingston, Ontario, which had been another of the original nineteenth-century contenders, officially proclaimed the renewal of its Capital Campaign with a squadron of Golden Gaels in leotards playing "Danny Boy" on matching golden bagpipes.

Of course the only logical move was to Toronto, which by virtue of its hatred by the rest of the country was out of the running from the get-go. Hester made quite a lot of hay with this, pointing out how – once again – the country was shafting the engine that drove it. Rumblings of separatism began to re-emerge, and the King was forced to make a nationwide appeal to *all* Canadians, pleading with them to come to their senses, honour tradition, and leave the capital where the hand of history had placed it.

He spoke directly to the people of Toronto – over the head of their Mayor, as it were – urging them not to split the country now, not now, not after so much ground had been gained in rebuilding. The road to the future, said the King, was through the creation of *new* symbols – not the revision of old ones. Subsequent polls suggested that his words had made some impact, and the sigh of relief coming off the Hill in Ottawa could be felt all the way to the Prairies.

Then Hester let fly with her counter-proposal.

Fine, said the Mayor. Toronto would agree to leave the capital in Ottawa. But only on one condition – that the Crown move its headquarters to the city. "You can house your Parliament wherever you like," she said, "but Toronto gets the Royal Residence. It *is* a matter of symbolism."

John tried his best to dodge it. He really did. He let it be known that he was fighting Mayor Vale tooth and nail on this one. And – so intense was the nation's dislike for Toronto – the country believed him. *Poor John*, they said when Hester dug in her heels and threatened to set another referendum date. *Poor John*, they said when Hester's advisers cunningly twisted the King's own arguments against him. And when at last, for the sake of the nation, the King conceded his defeat, *Poor John*, they said, appeasing the bottomless egos of Torontonians at the cost of having to wallow there with them. *It's a sacrifice.*

It did seem exactly like that, believe me. When he showed me Hester's plans to drop us on top of a derelict grain elevator amid acres and acres of the most squalid no man's land imaginable – I confess I was as appalled as the rest of the country. We went on what he called a "site visit" shortly after this. I'm not kidding when I tell you that we had to take with us a troop of guards as a security escort. Large parts of the building were being used as crack houses and shooting galleries in those days. The residue of homelessness was everywhere: fetid sleeping bags and rusty shopping carts, broken bottles, recycled condoms, cobwebs glazed with dust trapped back in the Diefenbaker era, shapeless detritus clinging moistly to the walls like fungal stalagmites. But when we got to the top – filthy and panting from the climb – there it was: the blue, blue lake away to the south, and to the north, east, and west, the city, sparkling, marching on as far as the eye could see.

"This is where we'll live," said John.

And so we did.

What's now known as King's Port, according to the real-estate agents, and The Silos District to everyone else, had for decades been the symbol for everything wrong with the city. The so-called senior levels of government controlled most of the port lands under constitutional authority, and repeatedly thwarted the city's plans to develop it. (Hester, by the way, passed a motion in chambers banning the word *senior* in any reference to the provincial or federal legislatures. "The senior party in any relationship," she said, "is the one who *gives* the allowance, not the one who gets it. And since it's us that's always paying, I'll be damned if I'll have *them* calling *us* the junior partners.") For most Torontonians, the waterfront was nothing so much as a source of endless corruption. When beat cops from the downtown divisions needed a quiet place to conduct a certain kind of interview, they drove their suspects down to Cherry Street, where none but the rats could monitor the flow of give and take. Toronto's prostitute community, in fact, was more familiar with the area than anyone, but even then only the tracts they were likely to glimpse from the back of a cruiser. A surprising number of suburban residents were not even aware the city *had* a waterfront. There had been so many plans, over the years, to revitalize these lands – and so many failures – that Toronto had long ago turned its back to the lake. It had ceased to think of itself as a port at all.

The Silos.

Even the name is music. As John was fond of repeating during his many, many interviews on this topic, grain has characteristics of both solid and liquid. Loose grain pushes downward, like a solid – but like a liquid it also pushes *out*. "That's why these structures were built the way they were," he'd say, running his hand along the concrete. "That's why these walls were made so massively thick." I researched quite a lot of this material, once we were committed, so I can recount this verbatim: *The silos' shape was in response to downward and lateral forces, together with the need to take up relatively little space on the ground.*

John would pause here, letting the implications sink in. "Now I ask you, is there a better metaphor for modern architecture? Or monarchy, either, for that matter?"

They're changed almost beyond recognition, these days, with the immense flying buttresses plunging down into the lakebed and the veils of mica-flecked granite – to say nothing of all the excavations to the north that made us part of the new archipelago – but the original structure was just a bunch of giant concrete cylinders, with us plunked down on top. What Hester needed (besides an excuse to keep John near, let's not forget) was a catalyst. The Mayor desperately wanted a project that would cut through all the intersecting squabbles and get something actually built. The one asset she had at her disposal, the only parcel of land on the water that wasn't tied up in encumbrances, was an abandoned grain elevator the city had acquired years before through default of taxes. The Silos had been sitting empty for decades –

too massive to tear down and too decrepit to refurbish.

They were built back in the 1940s, fifteen-storey tombstones to the city's glory days as a Great Lakes port. I'm not sure what gave her the idea, and I have only the sketchiest background about how all this evolved between John and her, but at some point Hester proposed the notion of donating the site to the monarchy as a place to establish its residence. It was packaged as a gesture of goodwill from Toronto to the nation – the irony apparent for everyone to see – but that's how Hester positioned it, and continued to position it until the deal was done.

The original plan was to use just the roof as a kind of platform, on top of which some sort of modest superstructure would be erected. They were *elevators*, after all, and the principles of elevation could be put to use transporting John as effectively as soya beans or barley. No one gave much thought to the cylinders themselves until the Osprey moved in with their corps of engineers. But that's another day's story.

It *was* symbolism. Hester was right about that. And symbolism is the means by which we communicate – the only means, come to think of it. That's how she understood it, and the King after her.

Theodore Sapper, according to his function, fought the project from the day it was announced. His Saudi paymasters had no objection to his position on this particular issue. Sapper was now committed to opposing everything to do with the monarchy, and remained so until the end. But already the market forces he had championed had begun to work against him. His Toronto flagship pounded John so savagely that its competitors – who at least in part defined their demographics as belonging to whatever categories Sapper's did not – found themselves incrementally driven to support the concept of a Toronto-based monarchy. Sapper's attacks were so personal that the left-leaning *Toronto Star*, for instance, known for defending whatever the right wing opposed, shifted from proletarian distrust to bourgeois benevolence on behalf of the initiative. The same Newtonian forces eventually prevailed even with the editors of the *Globe and Mail*, who in due course proclaimed that, all things considered, it likely was a positive development – in principle – for a country to headquarter its head of state in a location geographically removed from its legislature and that, national symbolism notwithstanding, the arguments as put forward by Mayor Vale and King John did indeed have overarching merit.

We worked very hard, John, Hester, and I (Hester mostly by behaving responsibly, with respect to the rest of the country, once she'd got what she wanted), and played up the symbolism for all we were worth. There was a fair bit to work with, to be honest.

Nowadays – as the lines of tour buses broadcast every thirty seconds – the Silos are celebrated as a triumphal blend of historic and modern architecture; the King's Verdant Roof has its own public elevator to accommodate the throngs who come to pay homage to the site where the Toronto School of Architecture is said to have been born. But all that came later. In the beginning, we focused on the simpler allusions – how the structure itself could be interpreted as a living symbol of a monarchy upheld by pillars of Western grain; how its inherently maritime nature paid homage to Canada's proud nautical traditional; how the crystalline nature of the concrete itself bore mute witness to the indomitable strength of the Canadian Shield, and so forth and so on. Never fear clichés, as I've said before, their status is hard-won.

One by one, the regions dropped their local claims. Little by little, by its sheer audacity, I think, the project began capturing the imaginations of people in places like Saskatoon and Dartmouth. Over time it came to be perceived as less and less a Toronto concern, and more and more a national one. I read not long ago – just before I went into seclusion – that the Silos now outdraw the entire Rocky Mountains in terms of weekend visits by domestic tourists. Even more incredibly, and I still find this one hard to believe, more *Americans* came to see it last year than visited Mount Rushmore (and wouldn't it be interesting, breaking that one out by percentage of Reds against Blues? I'd love to see those figures).

The Silos are to Toronto what the Eiffel Tower is to Paris, or what the Opera House used to be to Sydney before the waves took it out. But I don't think that even Hester could ever have imagined the renaissance it set in motion. Who would have believed that within a decade the United Nations would be eclipsed by a New World Order centred here in her city, or foreseen the blocks and blocks of embassies lining the elegant canals, or the Royal Dockyards either, for that matter . . . to say nothing of the blitz in civic building launched in preparation for the wedding of the century?

I've often wonder what Hester thought of that part.

DAY TWENTY-EIGHT

THAT WAS TOO LONG, yesterday. Far, far too long. I can only say that if you think it was tough for you to read, imagine what a bitch it was to write. Much closer to dawn than dusk, this morning; a writing hand still cramped around the shape of a pen. But I had to take advantage of this extraordinary weather. It got so warm last night, I let the fire die; candles and blankets were enough. No chills, hardly any bed sweats either.

I'm marooned.

John's island, this morning, is an island again. The genuine article this time, or very nearly. There's still a layer of ice below the water, but dangerously thin; the dog crashed through not five feet off the dock. I had to fish him out with a boathook. Quid pro quo, and all that, but if it was any farther out he'd have been a goner. If there's no way off the island, though, there's no way onto it either, which I see as a positive development. Twenty-eight days already. Someone's bound to have noticed. Amid all the recriminations, afterwards, with the Blues blaming the Reds and the Reds desperately alleging that the Blues must have done it to implicate *them*, it wasn't hard to disappear. There was that very public breakdown at the funeral too – having to be helped out, weeping; Gwen held up much more admirably, everyone said so. There are advantages in grief. Even so, it's been four weeks. More. Someone's bound to start thinking I've been out of sight an awfully long time.

On the other hand, why would they? It helps that Gwen's bug-gered off too, bless her. I wonder how long she'll stay in Oslo. There's a wild card.

Though it's very possible I'm overestimating my signifi-cance. They're all too busy now, beating ploughshares into polling data, to give much thought to me. That's my hope.

If you want to understand the difference between Reds and Blues – and who knows what difference will exist by the time you see this – frame your thinking according to how each of them interprets their pursuit of happiness. The Reds believe that happiness is something you can reach, something you can lay your hands upon and grasp. Blues are more aspirational. Reds are the believers, if you like, Blues the wishful thinkers – which, of course, requires a deeper generosity of mind. I've never been certain which is more dangerous, but I know which I belong to. Belonged.

Have I mentioned my parents? There's another on the list of things I've been meaning to tell you.

They were Ukrainian, second-generation Canadian, from a little town no longer on the map in central Alberta. My parents were what you might call different – both of them – and how two people of such complementary oddities were set down together at the same time, into the same improbable place, was a coincidence of such statistical unlikeliness their rational natures jointly agreed the signal was too profound to overlook. My father was a master of the crossword puzzle; my mother the kind of woman attracted to a master crossword-maker. There you have it. You might imagine how warmly this skill was appreciated by the dust-bowl sod-busters among whom they were set down. These were farmers, hard-core farmers, barely a generation removed from the oxen that broke the land before them. Abstract cleverness – the kind of interest to my parents, at least – was not looked upon as anything resembling virtue.

They married young, left early, and were gone forever. There was bitterness, it may not surprise you to learn – some of which I might have absorbed. I never met my grandparents.

The first time I set foot in Alberta was with John. I rented a car one morning and excused myself from meetings. Among the documents in my father's estate (they're both dead, by the way, both by natural causes) was a postal address: a lot and concession number. I drove out looking for the place. It's utterly gone now, no trace of any human habitation. A town had sat there once, sure enough. I checked and double-checked the census records. What I found was fallow field: a vast, dry ocean of dirt and a tractor with a mile-long trail of dust behind it creeping along the horizon. That set John blazing. He hated what the agricultural consortiums had got away with in those days, pretending to be farmers – "fucking robber barons" – and more than once I heard my own story retold at agri-environmental hearings. But as for me, more selfishly, it proved the wisdom of my parents' choice. Something to cherish wherever applicable.

Dad's first job was with some little paper just across the border in Montana. They paid him for the crossword puzzles, but I think he had to do the obituaries and wedding announcements on his own time. Then it was a bigger publication in Billings, then Sioux City, and, in due course, Chicago. Eventually they settled in New England, by which time my mother had me, and Dad had built himself up a national syndication. He used to say that making crossword puzzles was simply a matter of fitting words into patterns of your choosing. Definitions, ditto.

This I set down in explanation of my Americanness.

One of the interesting things about the Reds is how pragmatically identical they are to their Communist hobgoblins – down to colour coding, even – though the irony's as lost to them as it would have been to their Stalinists forbearers. Both access a well of ideology so deep it may be perpetually drawn without debit, both are so convinced in the rightness of their cause that all notions of wrongness applies only to the other side, and both, therefore, embrace a total willingness to subvert their principles in the higher interest of defending them. I get windy on the subject of Reds. I was raised American, as I say – albeit the New England variety – and despite my parents' in-bred skepticism, I absorbed its values.

And I know my enemies. John was always fascinated with how much more furiously I despised the Reds even than he, whose enmity was a natural response, as he saw it, to material threat. That's how he described it, but John was fond of debate when it came to self-analysis and often argued merely for the sake of it. My anger arises from the heart; his was more testic-ular in origin. But they amount to the same thing. I hate the Reds like a man hates a cancer in his lungs. Better to say I lament their existence, bitterly, and bitterly regret not having had the strength to stamp out the malignancy before it wormed so deeply into vital tissue.

The simple truth is that to beat the Reds we've had to fight the same fight they do. I suppose this is the nature of warfare, ideological and otherwise. *Homo adaptans. Homo politicus adap-tans.* John would say it's all on account of human nature.

The Reds had decided that liberalism was draining the soul of America, and that they had been sent forth to redeem it. Not that liberalism doesn't have a lot to answer for (see my notes, please, whatever day I talked about John's Law of Perpetual Error), but the Reds achieved a pitch of zealotry that even the looniest fringes of the American Left could never have envisaged. Or, more appropriately, were never permitted to put into practice. There's the difference. Yes, the other side allied itself with radical feminism, animal rights, affirmative action, and the self-neutering quagmire of moral relativism.

And yes, it did do damage – especially to academia, which ought to have been the strongest bulwark in the coming battle. But the Reds whored God Himself.

It's been said that American conservatism was taken over by religion. Truth is, it worked the other way around. Americans never did make much distinction between self-promotion and evangelism. "American Values," the export, had always had more to do with commerce than conviction. Likewise religion, and all those lofty visions whispered into the ears of nervous trading partners were mostly just distraction from the knee between the legs, which did the real convincing. But as the walls between church and state began truly to disintegrate, the nation's leading spokesman became more and more identified with the Lord Himself. You can't beat God's endorsement when it comes to product placement. When the Reds began to openly acknowledge that their president was a function of divine intervention, it wasn't that much of a stretch to suggest that members of the business community who'd supported his campaign were similarly blessed. Likewise, the goods and services they marketed.

An ecumenical spirit had been afoot for decades. Religious leaders of various stripes had long been arguing that since they shared so many common values, they ought to pool their efforts. But the process always bogged down in quibbles over doctrine – until the business community stepped in and offered up the M.B.A. approach to transcendentalism. An expert dose of market research, it turns out, had strongly indicated that there was one particular value, one *fundamentally American* value that practitioners of all denominations could happily agree upon. This was the founding father's notion that God sincerely wanted Americans to be rich. It went right back to Jefferson, didn't it? The Constitution made it perfectly clear that happiness was every American's inalienable right. And

God, after all, demands that his goals be pursued with a view to achievement.

So the newly refashioned conservatives abandoned the notion of conserving things, except their assets, in fealty to the Lord. And since God wanted them wealthy, it was equally true that whatever presented a barrier to wealth stood in contradiction to heavenly will. Government, for instance. Governments taxed income, diminished the return on investment, and succoured the forces of Satan. Or should I say governments headed by anyone other than one of their own.

Remember I said some time back that it's not a politician's job to keep things balanced; it's his job to keep things interesting? You have to hand it to the Reds, on that score. We've just emerged from a phase – here in Canada, I mean, the other side's still in it – during which politicians were running for government on a platform that governments should not exist. (Which always puts me in mind of the PoMo relativist crowd, who were similarly true to their commitment to the truth of truth's non-existence.) A healthy dose of paradox is always good for flushing the system, sure, but the effects are meant to be transient.

With God's right arm in the White House, it was increasingly difficult for the mere mortals of Congress to veto His intentions. And since the Lord's Disciples arose mostly from the South, it soon became apparent that the Almighty especially favoured this part of his Dominion. The flow of wealth into the Red states, therefore, was not the outcome of any economic strategy but simply the invisible hand of Jehovah, working as it should.

I believe it was this, as much as anything, that got the Blues so interested in John.

We like to think it was the lofty principles of secular democracy and so forth, but I'm convinced it was the cities of the

East, watching their powers bleeding into Texarkana, looking for a little intervention to call their own.

Like I say, the thing about the Reds is that they play for keeps. They're organized, they're committed. And they pay attention. The Blues, it's true, started seriously noticing John right around that time too, but for very different reasons. With the Blues it was still more fantasy at that stage. John's achievements with Quebec had conjured up a Bluish spark of wishful thinking: if Quebec's hammer-lock on Ottawa could be released, then maybe there was hope of somehow diminishing the South's control of Washington. The Dixie Reds had been enormously successful in cultivating the same sense of cultural grievance that had worked so brilliantly for Quebec; and there were those handy conquests, too, in both cases, to keep the fires of humiliation burning. Federal governments on both sides of the border responded by handing over larger and larger shares of national entitlement.

Like Quebec, the Red states ended up wielding far greater influence than their populations and economic contributions warranted. By this stage, you pretty much had to be a Southerner if you wanted to be president. This had been going on for decades, of course, but with God having sanctified the process, stateside, New Englanders had come to the reluctant conclusion that this was no longer just business as usual. They were frightened, truth be told, and had good reason to be.

For their part, the Reds had decided they'd better start keeping a more watchful eye on Canada after its upstart monarch's celebrated wager for Maddox Merere's left testicle.

The word *propaganda* is itself a cliché. True enough, but you have to acknowledge that the Reds were very good at it. We've talked about *American values*, about how the dissemination of these had always been a central plank – some years the only plank – of U.S. foreign policy. The Reds were especially keen on exporting their political beliefs. They were equally committed to doing their part to discourage the proliferation of un-American ones. Gun control, for instance, or taxes. Far-sighted Reds could not help but observe that Canadians were brazenly tolerant of these particular impieties. And while it was certainly improper to meddle in the affairs of a sovereign state, there was, on the other hand, nothing in a free society to prevent non-government organizations from supporting Canadian institutions that shared similar visions of global well-being.

The Frobisher Institute, by way of example, billed itself as a think-tank (this was the great age of tanked thinking) dedicated to the better interest of Canadian taxpayers. What it was, in fact, was a lobby group of CEOs sincerely convinced that their authority was more deserving than the state's. Its chairman, the wonderfully named Maddox Merere, preached relentlessly for greater integration of the Canadian and American economies – beginning with Canada's adoption of U.S. tax law. Critics accused him of being pro-American, but he wasn't. He was simply pro-Merere. The American system taxed less and thus was preferable: Q.E.D. Notions of sovereignty, one way or another, had very little resonance with Merere and his followers. They were interested in capital: American executives were allowed to keep more of theirs and were therefore better governed. It was in respect to this orthodoxy that the views of the Frobisher Institute intersected with those of the Reds. Though Merere himself was at pains to assure Canadians that the relationship was strictly non-denominational.

Maddox Merere was a regular panellist on Theodore Sapper's round-table economic discussions and a frequent contributor to his newspapers' business pages. Insofar as Sapper had principles, his and Merere's pretty much exactly overlapped. John always said he felt sorry for Merere: he belonged to that sad category of executives who'd simply lost sight of the fact that some things had value beyond what markets could index. When foolish people tried explaining how they sometimes preferred things the way they were – rather than changing them in order to be richer – Merere was simply incapable of understanding.

John was struggling to get this point across one night at the TK-Club, which in those days was the it-spot for the country's movers and shakers, a members-only kind of place that John had been recently been inducted into by virtue of being King. Merere was an aficionado of single malts, and the two of them had nosed their way through quite a swath of Highland before I arrived in time to hear the King loudly wondering, for instance, what value Mr. Merere placed upon his testicles? Was it ten thousand dollars? A hundred thousand? A million – name a figure? Or would Mr. Merere be willing to agree that certain things were beyond the comprehension of the marketplace?

I got him out of there as soon as I could. But the damage was already done. There must have been someone taking notes, because the story hit the news next morning, along with a snarling editorial in Sapper's flagship demanding the matter be properly explained to the public. Both John and Merere, I promise, would have been happy to see the story spiked and their hangovers with it, but by this time Merere's supporters were making things uncomfortable, and he allowed some foolish comments of his own to escape into the record. Sapper seized on the notion that Merere had suffered a public and personal insult originating from the Crown. Again his paper fired off a demand that the King come forward and apologize.

John had no choice now but to clarify.

In an open letter (which Sapper declined to publish but which the *Globe and Mail* and almost every other major daily was only too happy to print), the King explained to the country at large that he and Merere had been engaged in a *philosophical* discussion examining the nature of *value*. Mr. Merere, he said, had during this conversation maintained that all value was ultimately reducible to economic worth. The King, for his part, assumed the contrary position, contending that some things in life were beyond calculation by that limited measure. By way of example – and example only – he had suggested that Mr. Merere's testicles might ably serve to demonstrate his point. The King sincerely regretted any misinterpretations this remark may have caused. Indeed, and since the wider discussion was very much of concern to all Canadians at the present time, he felt it was his obligation to engage the country in resolving this very important point of order.

To that end, he had created a Web site solely for the purpose of establishing a definitive value for Mr. Merere's testicle (the left one only, in consideration of any future Mereres and with respect to professional scruples on the part of the requisite surgeon). Concerned Canadians were invited to make pledges of whatever amounts they wished to contribute. When the accumulated sum reached a dollar-value that Mr. Merere judged to be commensurate with that of his testicle, Mr. Merere had only to book the procedure, validate his argument, and collect his winnings. If, on the other hand, Mr. Merere conceded he'd lost the bet and acknowledged that the marketplace was *not* the ultimate decider of worth, all funds raised would be transferred to a registered charity of the King's choosing – tax-deductible, naturally.

Canadians, he had no doubt, would be grateful to see the matter fairly and squarely resolved.

I think it was that last point – the mocking tax deduction – that tickled people more than anything. Certainly it caught the fancy of Merere's opponents. One of his companies had been playing hardball with its unions just then, and their chief negotiator mounted a savagely hilarious campaign urging workers of the world to unite by means of collective contribution. The effects spilled over the borders and the anti-globalists got involved globally. Individual donations were seldom that large, but they poured in by the thousands. Worse, from a personal standpoint, was the reaction of the people Merere golfed with. Some of his former business associates were not terribly fond of him either, evidently, and discreetly contributed significant sums. Still others – purportedly friends – just couldn't resist the hilarity factor. His ex-brother-in-law was said to have made a four-figure pledge, as did several board members he sat with on various committees. (John's tax incentive was assumed to be a factor with these transactions in particular.) Then the former Mrs. Merere gave an interview in *Chatelaine* admitting that the article in question had, in her personal experience, significantly less value than a working set of double-d batteries. But even so, she'd have dearly loved to make a contribution – except that Mr. Merere was in arrears with his support payments again and she could barely afford to feed the children. (Grossly untrue, by the way, but crippling regardless.)

At first I think Merere reasoned he could just make the whole thing disappear through applied nonchalance. He was under no obligation to claim either defeat or victory. He could simply let the money pile up and ignore it. But that was the problem: The money did pile up – kept on piling up – and soon achieved sums that made ignoring it impossible.

Within a week the tabloids started printing updates on page two – right next to the girl in the bikini where no one could miss them – posting that day's figure as of print-time. New sites popped up all over the Internet providing convenient links so interested observers could track the increase minute by minute, and of course make donations of their own. Merere's life became a misery. Reporters hounded him. They called him at home; they called him at work; they waited by his car, and twice succeeded in ambushing him in restaurant men's rooms. He changed his cellphone daily, but they always somehow got the number. Grinning strangers stopped him on the street and pretended to pull out their billfolds. Paparazzi were dispatched onto his neighbours' rooftops. An enterprising escort service promised that for a fixed percentage of his winnings – if he elected for the surgery option – they would absolutely guarantee to keep the remaining testicle in tip-top working condition. A Milanese textile consortium approached him with a view to promoting its new line of extrabrief jockey shorts. Before the month was out he was getting calls from TV talk-show producers offering ever-greater fame and fortunes if he agreed to announce his decision live on their program. (Sapper, being Sapper, made the largest bid indirectly through his At Home Channel.)

In the end, Merere quietly got in touch and between us we brought the circus to a halt. I liked him, to be honest. So did John, though despite their later displays of camaraderie the two of them were never what you'd call bosom buddies. He was far from a fool and confided in me later that his attorneys, as lawyers always do, had urged him to pursue the matter through the courts. But Merere was intelligent enough to conclude on his own behalf that this was something he could never win, at least not without losing even more. John was too great a force by this time.

From our own perspective, the episode provided a sobering lesson on just how much power the Crown now had at its disposal, and how careful John must henceforth be in wielding it. Truthfully, he never meant to cause the man the embarrassment he did. And to his credit, Merere understood this – though it took a bit of convincing. With one hand, the King had brought his subject low; Merere was wise enough to recognize that with his other hand the sovereign must now raise him up again – or the story line would suffer. Think Book of Job.

The final tally was a staggering $22.7 million, and the only intelligent option was to put Merere in charge of it. He resisted, initially, but in the end he allowed his business sense to overcome his pride. With much fanfare, John announced that the entire $22.7 million would be used to fund the world's most lucrative literary prize – and Merere was right there beside him at the press conference, both of them grinning like brothers, slapping each other's shoulders and giving the impression that they'd cooked the whole thing up between them, the clever dogs. The highly regarded Mr. Maddox Merere, henceforth, was placed officially in charge of "growing" the Gold Leaf Fund. I shouldn't disparage. He did grow it, and very much to everyone's advantage including my own. And each and every fall since then, Merere has shared the stage with the King in what is certainly one of the most socially charged events of the calendar. It's true the arts community needed a while to get over its snickering, and even now there are those who still prefer to call it "the Left Nut Award" (though never the recipient, and certainly never in print). But the fact of the matter is, it's just too much money to mock. Merere deserves the credit he's collected.

At the time, though, very powerful interests were extremely displeased on Maddox Merere's behalf, which leads me back to the Reds. Despite his earlier appeal as an Indian fighter, John had revealed his true colours during the Merere affair. Canada's nascent monarchy had in effect declared itself for the Blue team. From this time onward, John was squarely in Red gun sights. It wasn't long before someone decided it was time to pull the trigger.

Though, in all candour, the first attempt might be better called a botched execution than failed assassination. Worse than botched – backfired. But up until that time their methods had been shockingly successful. It may be that I'm belabouring the point – I've watched them get away with it so often, though, and still I shake my head at how effectively it worked. All right, I *am* repeating myself. Even so, I'm going to tell you that it all comes down to the difference in how Blues and Reds think. It rests on the distinction, in fact, between thinking and believing. The beauty of believing is that it relieves the believer of the burden of thought. Believers are inoculated against infection by ideas contrary to their own, is what I'm saying.

There's nothing original here, but it helps sometimes to state the obvious. If belief is immune to the attack of reason, then reason is defenceless against the assault of belief. Understand where I'm going? To beat the believers, you must adopt their methods. That was John's strength.

Although he didn't do it consciously, not as the Blues did – intelligently plotting their attacks against intelligence. For John it was visceral, involuntary; John could supersede his thinking and move to strike with the blind conviction of any true believer. That's what happened that day at the door to *el Principal*'s office so long ago in Andalusia. It's what happened when Prince Bin Wahhabi tripped the hidden mechanism. And it certainly explains the day he called out Fox Blotter live on EagleNews TV.

Hester used to argue that the Red's logic of un-logic was standard biz-school curriculum. Cut-throat Capitalist Christians – as she liked to call them – tended to have backgrounds in business, and transferred into social policy the same skill sets they'd learned as marketers. You can't walk into a sales meeting with the news that your shares are falling because your competitor has introduced a better product. That's not the job you're paid to do. Your job is to make people buy it regardless, and the best way to make this happen is to fuck the other side over in every way conceivable. I'm not being the least bit facetious when I tell you that this requires enormous mental effort, though having God in your corner makes it all a little easier to bear.

The Reds had been triumphing on television, utterly. By this stage, a three-minute broadcast was considered the maximum allowable for anything unscripted. Many stations still encouraged genuine debate, but the ones that turned a profit kept these as brief and partisan as possible. Public service was all to the good, sure, but it had to be entertaining or advertisers wouldn't back the program. Guests representing opposing sides of a given issue were therefore sat down in-studio and given three minutes to win or lose – and the Blue side always lost.

The Red contestant was invariably the Platonic ideal of what a Red contestant needed to be: a consummate expert in the three-minute public execution. Blue guests seemed to come in one of two varieties: Type 1 was the fire-breathing nutbar whose role was self-immolation; Type 2 was the thoughtful academic denied a speaking part. If the Red Executioner was facing off against a Type-1 fire-breather, then the strategy was simply to offer up the necessary tinder and politely work the bellows. Properly stoked, the Elspeth Blancs of the world could always be relied upon to burn their bridges faster than their opponents could ever hope to fire them.

For Type 2s, the strategy was reversed. In this case, the Red would lead with an outrageous accusation, follow up with a welter of disjointed anecdotes, then acidly demand an explanation. Having no idea what was being asked, the Blue's reply almost always emerged as a question, which neatly invited a new stream of blistering invective. Right around the time the Blue contestant started realizing that he hadn't got a word in, the segment wrapped.

The idea was not to win, you see, it was just to make the Blue side lose. And lose they did consistently.

My hunch is that John perplexed them – I think at first there must have been some argument, in the EagleNews production room, over which category their guest belonged in. On one hand, there was clear-cut evidence of fire-breathing: he'd been shot by Indians, after all, and his behaviour with the sheik certainly argued for volatility. But on the flip side, John had been publishing some fairly thoughtful essays by this time and was known to hobnob with established eggheads. Furthermore, he was Canadian – and who ever heard of a Canadian that wasn't a dork? I suspect this must have tipped the scales in favour of the Type-2 filibuster. I'm guessing that Fox Blotter, lead pugilist for EagleNews, had pretty much convinced himself he had a weenie intellectual in hand, and was gearing up for what was fondly known in Red circles as the *Blott's-kreig*. But he hadn't yet committed himself. His lead would be the same in either case, and he could play it by ear from there.

"Gun control!" he barked before John was fully settled into his chair. "What do you guys up there know about *guns*?"

This was John's cue, as Polite Canadian – indeed the King of Polite Canadians – to begin framing a typically thoughtful Canadian reply, at which point Blotter would cut him off, turn to camera three, and chant: "I'm speaking today with His Majesty King John of Canada, who has graciously consented to appear on our show today and tell Americans why we should act more like good Canadians . . ." Except that John didn't say anything. He just nodded and smiled, and Blotter had to go ahead and deliver his monologue without having interrupted anybody first. But when that was over, he jumped straight back in:

"So, Your Majesty" – with a wink toward the camera – "what *do* Canadians know about guns? I'm sure there's the odd polar bear or moose that needs shooting up there, but I'm given to understand you folks don't even have a Second Amendment. So what exactly are you up to, if you don't mind me paraphrasing Lyndon Johnson" – shifting to back to look head-on at camera three – "coming down here and pissing on our rug?"

This time John did begin to reply, and this time Blotter scored his first direct interjection: "But before we get into that, I confess I don't understand how such famously polite people would even want to *talk* about guns. C'mon, Your Highness, everyone knows you guys hold the world record for politeness. What's that old joke? Hey, Sarah" – peering off-camera – "what's that great joke about the Canadians in the swimming pool? Oh yeah. How do you get a hundred Canadians out of a swimming pool?" – Slapping the table – "You say, '*Hey, you Canadians, get out of the swimming pool!*' Isn't it great? It's perfect! And you know it's dead on the money. Seriously. I was up there in Toronto one time and I bumped into this guy in an elevator, and he says to me, *I'm sorry*. It's *me* bumping into *him*, and *he's* the one apologizing! Your Highness, I mean Your Kingship, you have to admit that your subjects are the most apologetic people on the face of –"

But he didn't finish his sentence because John, while his host was talking, had hiked his chair over and casually dropped a hand over Blotter's wrist. John had big hands, very big hands, and a very long arm. "I'm sorry," he said.

He was smiling.

And at that very moment, I knew – I could tell it was happening – I'd witnessed it before, I guess, and recognized the signs. Though if you asked me what they were, I still would not be able to describe them: something in the face, something in the angle of the head and the tilt of the shoulder. Anyway, I knew right then that Blotter had tripped the switch and that John had launched into attack. Most of all it was the smile. John smiled. He smiled when he was being kind, of course – kindness gave him pleasure – but in John's moral architecture, being kind and punishing unkindness amounted to one and the same. The rewards were identical, as far as he was concerned: they both made him happy. And here's the deeper truth: he knew it too. He was aware of that trip-switch somewhere in his cerebellum; he counted on it, in fact, and deliberately manoeuvred his opponents until they set it off.

Sure, it was a gamble. I don't have to tell you that appearing live on EagleNews TV was the sort of thing royalty was not normally disposed to do. But that wasn't the gamble; John was a new brand of royal (or a very ancient one) and played by a different set of rules – all these pages I've been filling have been about exactly that. It wasn't the radicalism of agreeing to a format like this, that's not what had me worried. It was the very real possibility of John's coming off badly. A great many very clever people had gone up against the likes of Blotter and come away hemorrhaging. Intelligence is scant defence against the kind of assault that doesn't value it to start with. But then again I knew my man. And more to the point, my man knew my man. We both went into that studio with our fingers crossed, but I was dancing in the wings from the moment John started edging over with his chair.

Though – and to give some credit where at least some of it is due – I'd managed to help things along. I had made certain, for instance, that the Canadians-in-the-swimming pool joke had made its way into Blotter's in-box. And while negotiating with his handlers before the show, I'd innocently mentioned how highly my guy valued politeness, a Canadian trademark and all that. I could still trade off my Americanness, in those days. Blotter's people were reassuring, very reassuring, but I could see their lips a-smacking.

And it was true. John *did* have a thing about politeness. It was one of his quirks, specifically the notion that politeness was weak. You might call it a particularly pet peeve. It irked him –

sometimes rather more than irked – that outsiders mis-interpreted his country's notions of civility.

Blotter's strategy was not to talk about gun control at all, of course. His game was to cut off any real discussion from the outset by linking the whole idea with candy-ass Canadians who wouldn't even stand up for themselves in their own ele-vators, for God's sake. You should also understand that both sides that night were playing to the home team. The audience for EagleNews was overwhelmingly Red, and Blotter was only giving them more of what they liked to hear. For his part, John was betting that Canadian viewers – who always paid far more attention when their leaders appeared on U.S. TV than to any-thing they ever said at home – would tune in to Blotter's cable network that night in record numbers. We'd decided it was time for the King to begin making his presence felt in domestic policy; Canada's gun control legislation was up for parliamen-tary review just then, and there was no better platform for the King to put his stamp on the debate than on a U.S. broadcast of EagleNews TV.

Like I said, it was a gamble.

So when I saw that John had physically taken hold of the dis-cussion sixty seconds in, I was blowing kisses through the Plexiglas. Blotter, on the other hand, was startled. Physically, I mean. I don't think he understood what was happening.

"When I say, *I'm sorry*," said John, leaning in, very close. "I don't mean to say that I *apologize*. Saying I'm sorry is not an admission of wrongdoing, it's an expression of goodwill. When people bump into each other – when they do it *accidentally* – they say they're *sorry*. They're saying they regret this momentary interruption of each other's business. When we *mean* to do harm, then something entirely different happens, doesn't it? We don't say we're sorry then. But when it's accidental, when it's unintentional, only a fool would come away thinking he'd won something. An intelligent person could not regret goodwill, could he? Could he?"

Blotter was trying to free his hand, but this was less evident on-screen. "Are you," he started to say. "*Are you calling me a fool?*" I think that's what he was about to say. But he didn't, because suddenly he realized he had no idea what would happen after that. Furthermore, his hand was still pinned to the table, but he couldn't try to wrestle it free without acknowledging the fact. He was distracted – all the more so as John was talking to him reasonably, smiling politely, peering into his face with that genial hawkishness that defined so much of his being. Blotter really didn't know what he was dealing with.

"Now, when it's *intentional*," John was saying, angling in a little closer, "when someone bumps into someone else *deliberately*, then that calls for a different response. Wouldn't you agree?"

And just then Blotter flinched. Physically. Right there on camera. John had clenched a fist with Blotter's hand inside it, hard enough to make a knuckle pop. But that wasn't what the camera saw. What the lenses framed that day was Blotter leaning backward and away, while Canada's King moved forward and in. What the cameras caught was retreat. Then John asked if his host thought Canadians were somehow, oh . . . somehow less . . . *forceful* than Americans. "I only inquire," he said, "because that would be a regrettably simple-minded explanation for some very genuine differences . . ."

Here his grin grew wider and he raised a hand, the one that wasn't crushing Blotter's, as if to emphasize his point. "Why don't we talk about those guns –"

"Yes!" cried Blotter. "Let's –"

But then he stopped. Because at just that moment John's other hand released him. He looked wonderingly at his throbbing knuckles, which had scuttled back into his lap involuntarily: a soft, dimpled spider retreating from a predator more malignant than itself.

"For instance," John said, "did you know that your murder rate with handguns is fifteen times higher than ours? Gunshot wounds are the second leading cause of death in the United States, after car accidents. Did you know that? Thirty Americans are murdered with guns every single day. It boggles the mind, really, when you consider it."

"It does no such thing!" shouted Blotter, struggling to regain form.

"Doesn't it? Then maybe it should. Maybe it's time to think about the difference. Maybe you should stop convincing yourself you're somehow more prone to violence than I am and simply admit that you're more frightened of your government."

"Frightened! *Of my government?*"

"Then why do you arm yourselves against it?"

"We do not –"

"I'm sorry, but isn't that what your Second Amendment's all about? Unless I'm very much mistaken –"

"You *are* mistaken!" spluttered Blotter, now purple in the face. "The Second Amendment protects the rights of honest citizens to hunt, and –"

"Hunt!" For the first time John had raised his voice. "*Hunt!* Hunt *people*, you mean, that's what your amendment protects –"

"Now just you –"

"No, *you* listen," roared John, smashing his fist on the table and causing Blotter to really jump this time. "There are two kinds of guns: guns made to kill people and guns made to kill animals. Animals are another day's argument, but for my part I have nothing against shooting rabbits. I eat too. But *people* are another matter, and guns made for killing people are something else again. I don't think even in Mississippi you go out hunting rabbits with an AK-47." Here he paused a heartbeat, shook his head, then shrugged. "Then again, maybe they do. But they damn well don't and never will where I come from!"

It was said that night – north of 49° – that you could hear the cheering from the Grand Banks all the way to the Queen Charlottes (south of the Mason-Dixon Line, however, several television screens were reportedly shot out in fine displays of Dixie discontent). John did more in those three minutes to secure his own country's gun legislation than all the previous ten years of parliamentary commissions combined. He worked wonders for his personal approval rating too. The *Globe and Mail* ran a cartoon next morning showing a frightened, shrinking eagle – one of its talons pierced with a thorn – shying from a fiercely predatory shrike across the frame. I fielded dozens, no, hundreds of requests for interviews, but we granted only one. The following evening King John appeared on prime-time CBC Television, at home. Beautifully dressed and with the Maple Leaf standing stiff behind him, the King apologized to Mr. Blotter for having become, well, perhaps a little enthusiastic during their otherwise very pleasant conversation. He was indeed very sorry for that. All the more so as he'd meant to end his time in that good company with a quotation from one of Mr. Blotter's countrymen – who, John believed, had made some worthy observations on the point they'd been pursuing. "Always," quoted the King, tapping his copy of Thoreau's *On the Duty of Civil Disobedience*. "Always," he said, "you have to contend with the stupidity of men."

I can hear the water lapping outside.

Such a strange, strange sound. Not unwelcome, really, just out of place. Like finding vines of ripe tomatoes growing through a snowbank. A wind must be rising. Perhaps a cold front's blowing in. The shifting air disturbs the water; when I put down my pen I can hear the lake. It's extremely disconcerting.

Focus. That's what they teach them in the Madrassas and the business schools. Focus.

I noticed my foot was smelling this morning. There's the downside of balminess. Until this warmer snap, the cold had mostly done away with odour. Silver linings, and all that . . .

I'm focusing.

It's fair to say that John's outing with EagleNews TV was the modern equivalent of the raid on Harpers Ferry – an allusion Americans would grasp more readily than Canadians, but I know you'll understand. And it was from this time forward that Blue America started talking about the Canadian Model. There'd been a Canadian Model under their noses for the better part of two centuries, but now there was a face to go with it – that week John's appeared on the covers of *Time* and *Newsweek* both. I'm simplifying, as ever, but from about this time forward when Blue Americans looked at John they began wishing he was theirs. Which really isn't all that great a distance, is it, from wishing they were his?

I *can't* smell my foot, now that I'm concentrating. It must be getting colder.

DAY TWENTY-NINE

I WAS RIGHT. The temperature's gone down this morning and
the lake's transformed anew. This is almost as bizarre as when
it was water. I had grown accustomed to the snow. Snow piles
in drifts and riffles. It lends itself to shape, assumes its own
relief; a lake with a proper coat of snow feels more like a
pasture than a body of water. Now it's a vast sheet of glass, perfectly flat, scrupulously smooth. Solid, but deceptively so.
When I stepped out to cut a hole for morning coffee it spurted
water at the first touch of the blade, then gave way completely.
(If this lake were a woman, I would say she wanted me.)
There's still unfrozen water beneath the surface sheet, sand-
wiched by the original layer of solid stuff below. I broke
through the thin ice, but was held up by the thick. Point being
that I started my morning (again) soaking wet and freezing
cold: so today I have burned my first book.

I'd been considering this option, before the thaw, but that
spell of warmer weather postponed the necessity. This return
of winter has spurred me into action. Hamlet comes to mind,
or better still his father's ghost. And as it turns out, a pocket
edition of that particular play is presently holding up one
corner of my table – I cut it down this morning with the chainsaw but one of the legs came out too short. *Hamlet* (a Bantam
paperback) provides a perfect width of shim – and has thereby
saved itself from the fire. It's a tragedy, though, isn't it, when

all's said and done? No one really ought to hold their breath.

I haven't the strength to go ploughing through the snow any more, scavenging for wood. There's very little food left now as well; I will need to concentrate my energy. John's library, volume by volume, is my last remaining source of fuel. Of course, I knew this was coming. The final dregs of the woodpile disappeared days ago; I've been designating bits and pieces of furniture ever since (the merganser went in late last night, and reeked worse than my foot). But the books I'd been postponing as long as I could. There's something sacrilegious, isn't there, in the very idea? *Bücherverbrennung*, and all that. Never pictured myself as the Savonarola type, either.

Bundled up in what turns out to be my last night in a proper bed, I pondered through the wee hours, wondering if some form of ritual might serve to mitigate. I'd seriously considered starting with *Finnegan's Wake*, ceremonially, if you like – a sort of wilful exercise in taboo-breaking. It's said that archaic cultures worshipped insanity, that the incoherent barking of mouth-foaming lunatics, among Stone Age peoples, was revered as a sign of divinity. Over the course of my dealings with Gold Leaf juries, I've become convinced that our own culture adopts much the same perspective with respect to certain categories of lyrical prose. It would have been a blow struck in the name of art, I think, consigning Joyce to the flames ahead of everyone else. But literal counts the same as figurative, at this stage, and burning by quality presents its own set of problems. Sure, I could ease into it with the Danielle Steels or Helen Fieldings, but down the line what happens when I get to Alice Munro and Carol Shields – who'd take precedence? Better just to bundle them all in together.

I did try them in batches, as a matter of fact, but it was shockingly uneconomical. You'd think the collected works of Jane Austin, combusted together in a handsome boxed-set edition, would yield as much heat as a kitchen cutting board. Well, you'd be wrong. Whatever sweat she roused in English 101, Austin's just another flash in the pan when it comes to British thermal units. So I've abandoned completely all pretence of critical theory, and incinerate them as they come to hand. Some will linger, though. Despite my better judgment, I can't help a little browsing:

> My youth is spent and yet
> I am not old,
> I saw the world and yet
> I was not seen.
> My thread is cut and yet
> it is not spun,
> And now I live, and now
> my life is done.

That one's from "Tichborne's Elegy" – did you recognize it? – I'd not read it myself since university. It was in an anthology of English literature (a relic from John's undergrad years, I'm sure): onion-skin paper, well over two thousand pages – Beowulf to Beckett, that kind of scope. Cheap binding, but still exceptional burning. Half an hour plus.

It turns out that the most efficient way to heat with books is to fire them one at a time, briskly, on a small bed of embers with the damper tightly clamped. If the pages curl individually – one after the other, no faster – you know you've got the draft functioning near optimum. It goes without saying that the fatter the book, the better the burn, which is all that need be said with respect to the minimalist school. It's the most efficient method I've devised so far, but even so John's library was going up in smoke at a frightening pace, and the ink still freezing in my pen.

Then I had my Eureka moment.

It occurred to me that far too much heat was being wafted away into regions of the building where it wasn't needed. The attic, for instance, or for that matter all the other rooms but this.

So I have built a house within a house or, more appropriately, a hut within a cottage. The notion came to me when I discovered how much warmth was radiating off a little stack of paperbacks I'd piled beside the stove. These appeared to have an insulating property: the air was noticeably warmer on the heated side than the outer. I returned to the bookshelves, slogged over several armloads of wisdom-from-the-ages, and built up a sort of knee-wall encircling the hearth. Archimedes was never so pleased with himself. Unquestionably, my wall reflected back the fire's warmth.

After that it was only a matter of improving the design, which has ended up looking something like a giant beehive, or a shrunken igloo – or one of those conical pots the Moroccans use to make lamb stew. It's amazing how easily books can be made to support one another. Encyclopedias and similarly sturdy reference texts provided my foundation, interspaced with little volumes of modern poetry, as filler, wherever gaps required plugging. Then a layer of thick-bodied hardcovers, followed by trade-paper editions of similar heft. All finished off with an admittedly more precarious dome of mass-market best-sellers. As much as possible I have tried to arrange all the volumes spine-in, the better to reflect the light.

My door frame is an end table pillaged from the bedroom. Its top provides the lintel – the dog and I wriggle beneath it on our bellies. Inside is a mattress stripped off the bunkbed, with my cut-down coffee table set athwartship. I'm pleased to say that I had the presence of mind to move the furniture in *before* the wall went up; they would never have made it through the door. I sit on the mattress, lean my elbows on the coffee table, and commune with you. It's hard on the back – and I wish I hadn't burned all the dining room chairs, because one with the legs removed could have been slipped seat-first under the mattress and provided some lumbar support – but the dog curls up behind me sometimes, and I lean on him. Every book in John's cottage is now carefully stacked in concentric circles around where I am sitting, with the wood stove an arm's reach away. I've started with the five-by-seven paperbacks, intending to work downward and outward from there.

And yes, of course, I am conscious of the image. John would have judged it perhaps a little overworked, but as for me I rather like it, to be honest, when I can cut it back to abstraction. Quintessentially Canadian. I'm betting that if any one of several mid-list rural authors that come to mind had sent in a manuscript with a scene such as this one, odds are better than even she'd have made it to the short list on the strength of those pages alone.

Ha! I *am* delirious. Enough pathetic fallacies for one day.

Officially, John was a permanent member of all Gold Leaf juries and – officially – he read every book submitted. In practice, though, he'd seldom get past the first dozen or two before the Spanish fleet would start poaching too far into the Grand Banks, or a dam would burst somewhere in the Red River Valley, or another war would break out in Africa, and the King would be off with his Osprey putting things to right. He always read every title on the long list, certainly, even if it meant speed-reading in the bowels of a submarine or in the hold of one of his new Windigo-class helicopters – but most of the rest got delegated to me. I never minded. Fiction's a useful resource in my line of work.

Thoreau's phrase, by the way – the one I quoted John quoting at the end of yesterday's session – evolved into a kind of the guiding principle for working through the list. John's interpretation of the verb *contend* (as in *with the stupidity of men*) was a little sterner than is usual in modern times. In that sense, his thinking was more in line with Thoreau's. For John, stupidity was not merely something to be dealt with, shrugged at, put up with, *tolerated*. It was a malignant force, as Thoreau imagined it, a presiding evil to be ceaselessly, ruthlessly *opposed*. John conceived the Gold Leaf Award as very much an active agent in that battle.

I have said that the King was political to his deepest soul, so it should come as no surprise that the Gold Leaf was forged in a similar spirit. Artistic merit, for John, was judged not according to how it advanced any notions of art itself, but on how well it succeeded in retarding the forces against which it stood. John envisaged the GL as part of a wider return to a more muscular, testicular approach to fiction, which in the opinion of the Dead-Derrida school had become far too French and feminine in its self-regard. (He lobbied fiercely, a while back, for a submission entitled *The Lost Journals of John Moodie* – a historical novel set in pioneer times. The book had tickled John's sense of mischief by deliberately reversing the standard precepts of Canadian literature: far from being oppressed by the wilderness, its nineteenth-century narrator could hardly wait to slip away into the welcoming woods – if only to escape his embittered shrew of a wife. Not surprisingly, the jury overruled John's pick that year. But in honour of the King's memory, I take the opportunity to recommend it here. Read it, if you can find a copy, it will make you smile.)

Glory, though. That's the theme *I* always aimed for. The Gold Leaf Award reflects glory – of human achievement, of the Crown that bestows it, and (by extension) the body politic it represents. It's among the legacies I am certain will survive our departures.

A stem of curling leaf, amazingly real, as if set adrift from its branch in September; solid gold with a hint of copper to mirror the colours of autumn itself. (Though I admit the seven-figure cheque that wafts along with it adds a certain highlight to the lustre.) But the thing itself is lovely. John insisted that the design incorporate our maple leaf – one of the most universally recognized brands in all the world already. Foolish, he said, not to make the most of it. But beyond that requirement, he left the design entirely to me. I tracked down an artisan who begins the process with a living leaf, leaches out the pulp, somehow, and infuses what remained with layers of atomized gold. The final product looks *like a sugar maple would* – as one reviewer put it – *if its sugar transmuted to gold.* That was the effect I wanted, and that was the effect we got.

Glory.

One of the doyennes of that first year's short list – a CanLit stalwart who'd survived the previous cuts but didn't carry home the Leaf – let it be known that she was just as glad not to have to find a spot on her mantle for a trophy that would clearly be so difficult to dust. (The Dead-Derridists described her as *the True North's celestial whine*, but never mind.) Judging by the sales the winners rack up every year internationally, I don't think any writer has ever regretted the stardust. Our timing was ideal too: the launch coincided with the Orange sex scandal, and Lady Booker was by then already deeply compromised in the service of her corporate clientele. But of course, more than anything, it was the cancellation of the Pulitzers, just last year, that turned the world's despairing gaze so yearningly in our direction – that and all those ranks of previous honourees, solemnly tearing up their Homeland Security Cards. Terrific television. And God bless the PVPV.

Thoreau's useful little trope found its way into last fall's speeches again, not surprisingly, and nicely served to underscore the evening's theme: that literature (like politics) exists to make us wiser. Which leads us ever so gently back to my intentions for you. Although it's well beyond my scope to offer any wisdom, I can at least equip you with a sprig of context. Today's slice of unrecorded history is the tale behind the tale of Theodore Sapper's spectacular collapse, with full disclosure of my own involvement in same. Don't mess with Blue (*Cuckoo Blue*, as he was pleased to call me), that's the moral of this morning's tangent. What goes around comes around, cliché most essentially.

It was known across the land that the King had set Maddox Merere in charge of earning money for the Gold Leaf Fund. Theodore Sapper made it a matter of equally public record that yours truly was held accountable for how that money was spent. He had no business doing that, in all fairness. It wasn't his money. It wasn't public money either, but it was publicly *scrutinized* money, which amounts to the same thing. Canadians were never entirely at ease with me, I'll concede that too. My American origins were cause for suspicion; this fellow Blue's connection to the Crown had always been something of a mystery to the general public. Most of the time they were content to ignore me. Or would have been, except for Sapper's plastering a bull's eye on my forehead every time he spied my head above the ramparts. He couldn't go after John directly, you see – by this time no one could – but he could take aim at *me* whenever he saw the opportunity. If it was true (as it was) that the King's popular esteem had grown beyond reproach, then what this meant in practical terms was that anything royally *reproachful* must necessarily be laid at someone else's feet. Mine, as it happened, wherever Theodore Sapper was concerned.

Honestly, I don't even remember which issue he was on about the day he nailed me with the *cuckoo* peg. (And I'm convinced the name had more to do with his fondness for rhyme than anything related to current events.) Sapper's general policy was to attack everything that fell under my authority, and this occasion was by no means the only time he'd flung his gobs of mud my direction. But that one stuck, and stayed stuck. It also didn't help that the King laughed out loud when he read the editorial. John's sense of humour often got the better of me, and things of this nature tended to amuse him. Though to be honest, if the roles were reversed, I'd have likely found it funny too. It wasn't meant to be hurtful – John's laugh – just the good-natured amusement of one friend at the consternation of another. In any case, the label stuck, and in the collective imagination of Canadians, Cuckoo Blue I remain to this day. As a moniker it's unique. I'll give them that.

So I'd be lying if I told you my dislike for Theodore Sapper was not sincerely personal. I hope I've also made it clear, though, that he was, in the military argot of the day, a clear and present danger. That being said, I must also concede that Sapper was less of a menace latterly than he was in the Crown's more formative years. The King had raised the bar of public discourse, and, as that level rose, Sapper's stock in trade was correspondingly diminished. Here in Canada, Sapper's empire was by that time already in decline. "He who lives by the bored, dies by the bored," quipped John in a fine example of the King's prodigious talent for reconstituted kitsch. (And since I've gone tangential already, let me also point out what a useful device this is to keep handy: People think in patterns. If you can offer them original material dressed up in familiar cant, they'll thank you by repeating it. Pepper your lines with twitchy reversals: "a barefaced truth," or "sheep in wolves' clothing" – John's assessment of the Janjaweed, following his first raids in Sudan. Train your public mind to think in country-and-western lyrics, is what I'm advising.)

But if Sapper's reach was shrinking here in Canada, it was spreading tumorigenically beneath the great cranial dome of the American Southwest. Theodore Sapper, remember, was first and foremost a marketer. He had found – in what was once fondly known as Heartland, U.S.A. – the ideal consumers for the kind of product he excelled in manufacturing. In the Southern Red states, Sapper's willingness to publish lines like "New York Jews and other faithless neighbours" was working wonders for his market penetration.

So he was by no means neutralized – by no means at all. Even so, it would be ridiculous to claim that when the opportunity to harm him dropped (shall I say literally?) into my lap, my motives were purely impersonal.

Not to put too fine a point on it, I seduced his secretary. Although it's just as fair to say that she seduced me. My conscience is clear on that score at least.

It began at another Gold Leaf function – not the inaugural one we've been discussing – not this past fall's either, with all the Pulitzers, but the one before that. Gwen was ignoring me and I was standing by the oyster bar, surveying the room. I've always found oysters extremely difficult to eat with dignity, but still I have a weakness for them and was contemplating discreetly downing two or three before moving on to another vantage point across the room.

"You know what they say about them?" said a pearly little voice beside my elbow. Pretty, and prettily inebriated. I made the obvious reply, and we raised a toast of oysters on the half-shell and looked each other over.

Now I have to tell you something else:

Remember, days ago, when I told you about Hester Vale's knack for reading people? I believe I said that Hester possessed the uncanny ability to recognize compatibility at some profound, instinctive level. Hester could *smell* if a relationship would work, just from shaking hands. No need to tell you what a powerful advantage this must be for any politician – I'd have given almost anything to grasp the full potential of Hester's gift. But I do understand it, or at least a corner of it. What I'm saying is that I share a bit of it myself. Alas for me, it only works with women, and then only in matters pertaining to sex. I mean that in the active, verbal sense of the word. I can't explain it other than to tell you that an awareness comes over me sometimes, like a finger trailed across my spine. I just *know*, usually before my about-to-be partner is aware of it herself, I think. It's something I discovered back in college. I'd be sitting in the library, say, making small talk, and suddenly I'd realize that the girl I was chatting with was going to go to bed with me. And, almost always, she did. It has to do with pheromones, I suspect, and that's enough for me. Over the years I've learned simply to trust it rather than question its origin.

My point is that I had exactly that experience with the freckled woman standing by the oyster boat. She clearly didn't know me from Adam, which I have to say was also nice. All the women wanted John, it goes without saying, but often they'd content themselves with lesser luminaries – and there were plenty of these on offer too. It was the Gold Leaf Gala, remember, with giants browsing through the canapés everywhere you looked.

"*Blue*," she said, wrinkling her nose, "what a funny name!" She confessed to me later that she was very embarrassed at this, once she'd made the connection. Hers rang no bells with me either, but she was lovely and freckled like a sparrow's egg. I do recall her prattling on at one point about what an animal her boss was, but of course that was by no means an unusual form of neutral conversation either. I've fallen back on it myself from time to time. It wasn't until next morning, or perhaps a little later, that it occurred to me to ask her for politeness' sake what kind of work she did. Even then, when the name popped out, it emerged as much by accident as otherwise.

She was fixing her hair, I think, or touching up her lipstick –
a gabby creature she was, when she was running late – "If
people only knew," she said, "how much a person like me has
to *know* – especially for pricks like Sapper who expect things
before they even tell you what they want – most people would
be completely shocked." Shocking for me too; like the feeling
a lottery winner must have at just at that moment he's realized
the numbers he's reading are real. "Did you say *Sapper*?" I
asked, keeping my voice as level as I could manage. "As in
Theodore Sapper, the publisher?"

We sent him invitations every year, of course, as a matter of
form. The Gold Leaf Gala was always a who's who of media
contenders, and like it or not Sapper ranked at the top of the
heavyweight class. But he never did put in an appearance. It
irked him, I think, to see John so clearly *maître chez lui*. In all the
years I ran it, Sapper never once attended the party. Though, of
course, his various agencies all covered it according to their
bias. I think he made a point of handing off the invitation every
year to some deserving underling – like season-ticket holders do
midseason when the Cubs are in town, or opera buffs who'd
rather give away their seats than listen to another contemporary
Dane. That year, Theodore Sapper had off-loaded his GL invitation, still in its gold-leafed envelope, as a backhanded bonus
to his long-suffering personal secretary. I'm sure he told himself
that she'd be tickled pink. And indeed she was.

We men so often presume the allegiance of women under us,
don't we? It's a constant peril. I won't trouble you with details.
Suffice to say that with the judicious application of champagne,
good meals, two weekends in the Gatineaus, and one four-day
stint in sunny St. Lucia, I ended up with the contents of
Sapper's entire hard drive – along with all the necessary pass-
words he could never be bothered to remember. Infallibility
contradicts itself, remember that. Sometimes it's just that easy.

And what a treasure trove it was, may I say. And how perfectly positioned his old friend Blue, to trickle-down its riches.

It was the accountants who nailed him in the end, just like with Al Capone. Misleading shareholders, misreporting income, appropriating dividends. Then all those nasty antitrust investigations that gnaw through assets like a nest of lawyers in an unbequeathed estate. One thing led to another, as these things usually do, and in due course the Saudi connections began to emerge. After that, Sapper was more than ready to cut a deal, take his twelve cents on the dollar, and start a new life raising horses in the land of the brave and free where folks are more inclined to sympathize with the downs as well as ups of macroeconomics. It's a thousand acres, from what I'm told, so don't shed too many tears.

And before you think unkindly of me, let me mention that the young lady was well provided for. The affair was permitted to run its natural course, toward the end of which an offer came from the Office of the Cultural Attaché, in London: an offer just too good for anyone to turn down – "You'll understand, Blue. I *know* you'll understand." When last heard of, she was engaged to be married, or perhaps already wed, I've forgotten. At any rate she's living well and happily.

Which leads to another Polonius moment:

Although it may be wise sometimes to abjure from punishing your enemies, never, *ever* fail to reward your friends. This is the first and great commandment of political survival, and the second is like unto it: Smite your enemies too, once you've had a chance to think it over, lest your friends end up disappointing also.

Hamlet? he says. Machiavelli, more like. Good night, Sweet Prince. I'm fading.

DAY THIRTY

THE DOG FOLLOWS wherever I go. If I crawl to squat above the salad bowl that now functions as my toilet, the dog crawls with me. When I scrabble through our portal to the great outdoors of John's defurnished cottage, the dog scrabbles after. It's tempting to interpret this as love, but I am not deluded. This is merely what instinct instructs him to do. The dog, I am certain, loves me no more than the remora loves the shark, the raven loves the wolf. Its nature impels it to follow. It is a case of evolutionary symbiosis, this, and I'm the accidental co-determinate.

Yes, yes.

Why then should I love the dog?

He was assigned to me by Gwen, as I may have mentioned, and his presence curled around my feet reminds me that Gwen cannot be ignored much longer. I've been dancing around that topic, haven't I? I've been saving Gwen for last.

They met *before* the Sudanese campaign, you know. John always said it was Darfur, the second Darfur. But I remember. I remember very well. It was at that Polar Nations conference in Reykjavik. Europe's royal families had been closely following our ever-widening experiment with monarchy. When it was announced that Canada's King would attend the meeting in Iceland, many of the other royals decided that perhaps they ought to show up too. Then Japan agreed to go, which irritated both the Russians and Chinese, and set off another round of global monarch envy. A few of the royals hadn't met John yet – or their families hadn't – so he was busy being introduced around the room. When the King of Norway presented his middle daughter, John bowed and took her hand and moved along. It has always struck me as remarkable – for anyone – to have shaken hands with Gwen and not remembered. But he did have a very full agenda that day and the aquavit may have helped to hurry him through. In any case, John always swore he had no memory of Gwen until Darfur.

She sought me out that night, instead. I remember. Brightly curious, ferociously informed, Gwen peppered me with questions from the moment her supple fingers touched my wrist. It was by then common knowledge – at least in certain circles – that a movement was afoot to see John married. Gwen's information on this topic was remarkably precise – whether through that deeply female intuition or a much more active Norwegian embassy than I'd imagined – she seemed to take my role in this for granted. I denied all knowledge, naturally, and we enjoyed that charade for a time: the princess beautiful and brilliant, the courtier obligingly obtuse. She, of course, had the right of it.

Setting aside all the homilies about a public figure being twice as effective with a wife at his side as without, there was the very real and vital issue of succession.

I needn't remind you that the country had been, shall we say, a little haphazard in the formation of its monarchy. The rules for what would happen *after* John were still decidedly unclear. A few forward-thinking people had begun to wonder if perhaps it wasn't time to clarify matters on that score, and certain interested parties were suggesting that a union with a more established royal family would take us a long way toward that goal. The benefits, truth be told, were so numerous and obvious they hardly needed spelling out.

John chose instead to be indignant. The King took the earliest opportunity to publicly shake his fist and let the country know he'd stay a bachelor as long as he damn well pleased, or marry the checkout girl at Loblaws if that was where his own heart took him. Canadians sighed, and smiled and nodded in profound approval. But by then they'd got used to proper royalty, liked it, and wanted more. The notion of a royal wedding, particularly a royal-*royal* wedding, with all the bells and whistles and pomp and circumstance, took on a splendidly appealing sheen. I commissioned some polls; the numbers were eye-popping. John was furious about this too – the data was never released, it goes without saying, but even so he was extremely upset. And of course from his perspective, there also was the matter of Hester to consider. It must have been an uncomfortable topic, between the two of them. Not my business either.

Gwen radiated understanding. As a leading light of Europe's glamouratti, she'd accepted since adolescence that her love life would never be her own. The press had followed her as avidly as any pop star, long before she made her way to North America. And like John, too, she'd vowed that when she married – *if* she married – her choice would be made from the heart or not at all. At Reykjavik, Gwen made it plain that she understood what John was going through, and was deeply sympathetic. "We could form a pact," she said and held me with those cobalt eyes.

This is awkward. By the time you read this, the Queen will be advanced in middle age – I smile at the picture – but the fact remains that you will have no proper memory of Gwen in youth. I must now tell you that although she was in every sense the perfect opposite of *flirt*, Gwen achieved precisely that effect. To stand beside her was the same as being teased. We've spoken of pheromones. (Yes, I said this would be awkward.)

You will have seen photographs; you will recognize that the Queen was a beauty. But I'm certain it will be as hard for you to think of her in youth as it is for me to envisage her in age. You'll have no way of understanding, I think, how *comprehensive* Gwen's beauty was in my time. How exhaustive, complete, how all-encompassing. I will tell you, though – standing there among rosy royalty, tipping champagne and icy flutes of kir, smiling primly as if we were exchanging pleasantries about the weather – that already there was no doubt Gwen would extract from me whatever she needed to extract. Or that I would marry her to John, if she would have him.

I console myself still that our interests – then as now – converge.

But for John, the memory begins in Sudan. And of course it would, wouldn't it? She flew there to create it. Norway was one of the earliest supporters of John's intervention, one of the first to abandon the old United Nations and commit to our New Internationals. Already there were airlifts moving humanitarian aid from Oslo to Khartoum; Gwen attached herself to a shipment of medical supplies and caught John in the field all sweaty and victorious and randy as a goat. (You'd be surprised, he told me once, what an appetite killing people gives you. It's true.) She was never shy about this either. "You are a student of such knowledge, Blue," she informed me. "You are in pursuit of human nature." Gwen took pleasure in explaining things like the subtleties of buttons. "Much can depend on which are made open and which are made closed – amazing, truly, what difference a button can make." She was referring that day to her plans for a photographer from *Elle*, but the same applied with larger game.

For John's appreciation, in the shimmering deserts of Sudan, Gwen had outfitted herself in the obligatory khaki shorts and cotton top that accessorize humanitarian missions everywhere, buttons obligingly taut. She'd have made a point of landing hot and sweaty too. Glistening, no doubt. John would have greeted her in battle fatigues – it wasn't quite war, not full war, but there had certainly been killing. Hester was half a world away and armed guards patrolled the perimeter. No paparazzi in the deserts of Darfur, no enemies that weren't already dead or very distant. John, in his way, was right. Sudan is where the memory begins.

A few weeks later, the King paid his formal respects to Norway and her people. It was a three-day tour, and of course Gwen hosted the reception. On the second day, I think, history records the first official photograph of the two of them taken together. Not long after that, Gwen made her own royal visit to Toronto and pronounced herself enchanted. Later, I scheduled John for a peacemaking congress in Johannesburg, which, as it happened, Gwen was attending also in a semi-official capacity. And of course their paths crossed again when John received his Nobel Prize in Stockholm.

By that time I am certain Hester must have had a sense of what was happening – John never mentioned – but in any event her car went off a ramp around that time, plunged into the hole just where the New Gardiner Tunnel was being dug, and exploded. So we'll never know for certain, will we? Dead mistresses forever hold their peace. He couldn't grieve, of course, not publicly – and certainly not in the presence of Gwen. But her abiding presence must have helped. I'm sure of it. By this time, too, the press had begun to frame them as an item, which had put things well into the public sphere and moved them forward. The wedding, I am certain, even in your time, remains the standard by which others of its kind are judged. Truly, it was everything we could have hoped for.

There. That wasn't so bad.

DAY THIRTY-ONE

INTERESTING, how quickly a body can cease to be diurnal. This may simply be diminished health, but more and more I'm sleeping, waking, writing, sleeping, waking, writing . . . without reference to the sun. When I poked my head out just now, I see that it is dark. Pitch dark. But I begin our day regardless: the candle flickers as it must.

Norway was part of a deliberate campaign to move us up and north, away from down and south. It wasn't only Gwen. With Washington sliding ever deeper into faith-based economics – and dragging our trading partners in the Blue states with it – it just didn't make sense to stay hitched to a wagon whose wheels were so clearly spinning out of sync. Parliament was more than half convinced of this already, and Canadians – ordinary citizens, I mean – were more than willing to hear a voice of reason. All they needed was one strong enough to overcome the braying of the merchant class, which despite its automatic reflex had sadly choked already on a sixty-five-cent greenback.

Norway, on the other side of the coin, enjoyed the world's highest standard of living, higher even than our own. Scandinavia, in particular – and Northern Europe, in general – was leading the world by most global measures of civilization, while our neighbours to the south were heading hell-bent in the opposite direction. We'd been gazing out across the North

Atlantic, well before anyone of us laid eyes on Gwen. Gwen was a catalyst, if you like. Or, better still, the matrix.

Her fellow Scandinavians had grown almost as nervous of their neighbours as we were of our own. European union had faltered. The divide was by no means as wide as it had come to be in North America, not yet, but Pax Americana was unravelling all over the globe. Nowhere as rapidly as Red-mad America, no, but the church in Catholic countries had begun to throw its weight around in a fashion that hadn't been seen since the days of Pius XII, while back in old Byzantium the newly European Turks were grinding eager edges on reconstituted blades. The central issue, as ever, was economics. The expanded European Union had meant that the richer, northern countries paid out endless subsidies to their poorer, southern neighbours – which was all well and good, until the beneficiaries started using their newfound credit to countervail their big-browed benefactors, all the while accusing *them* of faithlessness.

When John started floating the idea of the Boreal League – it wasn't called that then, mind you, in those days we were better described as a loose coalition of nations similarly fond of hockey – the notion was enthusiastically received by the like-minded secularists nervously scrimmaging among the higher latitudes. Canada, Norway, Sweden, Finland, and Denmark, later joined by Scotland (which pulled in England and Wales, though funnily enough not Ireland), became what we might facetiously call the Original Six. Holland signed on after that, and still remains leery of Germany's admission. Then came Switzerland, to everyone's surprise but mine, and more surprising still, Japan – though the fuss over Tokyo's membership was nothing compared to the commotion when the governors of Vermont, New York, and Massachusetts requested invitations to last year's summit, along with the commanders of their National

Guards. That put ice in everyone's drink. (Russia's been quietly making inquiries too, by the way, as has China, or parts of it. But John's thinking was always that you can't play one off against the other if you formally commit to either. I suspect that will be as wise a policy in your time as it has been in his.)

Militarily speaking, things were coalescing too. I'm sure you've been taught that the rapid expansion of Canada's Armed Forces was a function of our nation's having shed Quebec. And, of course, that's true – as far as it goes. There was justifiable anxiety, early on, that Quebec's decline might lead her into folly. And yes, we had naturally prepared for the worst. But, of course, the worst didn't happen. If you want to know the real significance, it wasn't the *threat* of an independent Quebec that established our military, but the *savings* it provided. Billions. Almost anywhere you put your finger in the budget there was money staying home; transfer payments were barely the start of it. One economist reckoned that the annual savings in document-translations alone, post-bilingualism, was equal to the cost of three or four new helicopters. And of course once Quebec was off the books, the Constitution needed realignment, which under the King's benevolent chairmanship merged nine provinces into five, cancelled ancient inefficiencies, evened up the regions, and jacked the surplus even higher. We had to spend it somewhere, didn't we? What better place to start than with the long-neglected Forces?

Truthfully, though, the roots go deeper than that. Think in terms of syllogism. John loved the military. The country loved John. Is it all that surprising that we learned to love our military too?

Canada is a much more martial nation now than before. True. But having lived through the evolution I can tell you that it was as smooth and natural a transition as you could wish. *Maturation*, indeed, was John's more considered choice of words. And, of course, our allies played their part. Spanish and Portuguese trawlers had been raiding northern Europe's fish stocks as long and as avidly as they'd been plundering ours. When John began popping up in the *Hazel McCallion*, torpedoing their hulls whenever he caught them with nets in Canadian waters, our North Atlantic neighbours cheered as lustily as the good folk in St. John's Harbour. So happily, in fact, that they declared themselves perfectly willing to send out their *own* ships, to cruise in company with John's patrols. When Spain sent gunboats into the nose of the Grand Banks, their captains found it wasn't just our Osprey squadrons they were facing off against; it was Norwegian frigates, Swedish submarines, and a bristling armada of Danish corvettes. The Spaniards screamed blue murder at The Hague, naturally, but who was going to send enforcers? France? Italy? They had concerns of their own.

That was the start of our New Internationals, whose shining headquarters you can see framed in the windows of John's office. And that's what took us to Darfur. I keep saying he was lucky – I've often said that, haven't I? – but just as often I could tell you that John's luck was as much the result of stupidity on the part of his opponents as our own good judgment. And that's not to say that either he or I ever cast the United Nations in the role of opposition, ever (I can lay my hand across my heart and swear to that). It's just that the UN behaved so badly with respect to North Africa – so completely ineffectually, and on the heels of many similarly gruesome failures elsewhere – that you'd be forgiven for believing the Security Council deliberately set out to make John good by making itself look bad. News agencies all over the world had been filing stories for months about refugee camps transformed into medieval slave bazaars, with Janjaweed raiders moving in and out at will, killing the men, rounding up the women, and trading the surplus across the Red Sea to finance the next expedition. The world knew all about this, just as it had documented each of the earlier slaughters. It also was aware that at the UN headquarters in New York, meanwhile, delegates were far too busy arguing about the definition of *genocide* – which had to be agreed upon before they could agree to anything else – to even think of intervention. "Angels dancing on the head of a pin," said John, with smoking villages behind him – and the world nodded its profound agreement.

What with everyone else applauding our troops, it was hard for the pacifist crowd to find much traction here at home. People like their militaries strong, they just do. File that one away as an axiom to bank on. We were furthermore blessed with some truly spectacular weather: two class-five hurricanes down East, a string of nasty avalanches in the Rockies, and some perfectly massive flooding out on the Prairies. In the face of these emergencies, Canadians watched their soldiers behave with commanding efficiency, putting local authorities to shame: filling sandbags, clearing debris, blasting ice-dams – yes, and delivering terrified children into the arms of weeping mothers. Four troopers managed to chalk up the ultimate sacrifice – while rescuing a school bus, no less – swept away down the Red River and never seen again. They were mourned as national heroes, and their King delivered a eulogy that even now will bring tears to your eyes. He used the opportunity to savagely assault the environmental degradations he convinced us all were at the root of these catastrophes, and made great headway with that part of his objectives. John reasoned through what he was doing, made people see the connections. He was forever rousting troops out of their barracks to plant trees around the floodplains and pick garbage out of riverbeds; Canadians approved, and looked upon their soldiers with a pride that would have shocked them even a half a decade earlier.

So when we sent them abroad with guns and war machines, people lined the piers and filled the streets with maple leaves and kisses. By that time we needed them out of the country. Understand that there's a downside to anything with more than one dimension. This, too, is axiomatic. Military expansion is a perfect case in point. History warns that if you're going to build your army, you'd better provide it with something to do or face the consequence of bored young men slouching around with grenades in their pockets. Ours grew fast, very fast. We'd seriously underestimated the rate of international enlistment, you see, which was bad enough. Then the influx of Americans caught us completely flat-footed. What I'm saying is that there are only so many sandbags you can credibly fill, even in a good year. Sudan, thankfully, had tons and tons of sand in need of bagging, at a very convenient distance from home.

Policy is a text of interlinking plots. Narrative is just a means of organizing text. This is what we do: we rearrange the randomness until it works, then work it. When the story takes an unexpected twist our job is to incorporate the twist, to write it in, adapt it to the plot as if it always was, and – with a stylish turn of phrase – it is. The Great American Defection was this chapter's unforeshadowed plot development. We solved it by weaving its thread into the larger tale. If your narrative is solid to begin with, you can almost always get away with that.

Neither John nor I, I'm telling you, anticipated the rush of American deserters. Maybe we should have. Of course we should have. But we didn't. We'd expected our army to grow, sure – that was a safe bet; enlistment was up already from the pre-John days, but where else could it go but up? We'd also anticipated a healthy influx of U.S. *civilians* seeking refuge, though you could hardly call us clairvoyant for that. Americans had been coming here when things went overboard at home since the beginning. Empire Loyalists were just the first wave of U.S. citizens rejecting the Republican enthusiasm with their feet. Fifteen thousand skedaddlers poured across the border to avoid the civil war, Vietnam sent fifty thousand more, and the present, perpetual fiasco in the Middle East has them arriving still. But these have always belonged in the conscientious-objector category: hippies dodging draft, lefties making statements, the usual assortment of nebbish intellectuals and disappointed Democrats.

Not soldiers. Not hardened veterans. The career soldiers we simply hadn't foreseen – all those West Point grads who'd made their peace with Homeland Security, with the Patriot Act even, but for whom the PVPV was one step too many back from the road their fathers had laid down their lives to defend. We'd expected the civilians, yes, but we never saw the ranks of uniforms behind them.

I don't think I have to tell you that relations with Washington, by this time, were more than a little problematic. The Red states held the presidency, remember, and control of Congress. True, New England and the Blue states were now leaning closer to Toronto than to Washington, but the Union was very far from shattered. A full-blown military crisis was exactly the kind of patriotic issue that could tip the balance back again. Washington's creation of the Department for the Promotion of Virtue and Prevention of Vice, and the terrifying powers it granted, had driven a great many northerners to the brink of the unthinkable. But a perceived *external* threat could just as easily drive them straight back home again. All the Eastern governors were telling us that on no account could we permit U.S. soldiers to defect to Canadian soil. That it might indeed be *causus bellae*. At the very least it would shift much of our hard-won momentum back into the hands of the Reds. Canada's perceived absconding of U.S. assets would provide the Pentagon with a heaven-sent diversion. America had always been willing enough to send us the wretched refuse of its teeming shores, its tired socialists and huddled homosexuals. But men in uniform, that was something else again. What it was, was disaster.

Sudan saved our bacon. People like to say that the New Internationals were created in some kind of spontaneous combustion of global outrage, and that's surely how we told the story from our side of the lectern. Certainly that's how they phrased it in the NI's Articles of Constitution. But first and foremost it was a means of redeploying American deserters under a flag that hadn't any maple leaves in view. That's really what it was all about. That and the fact that it worked.

I am my own Scheherazade, am I not? My own Schahriah too. Sleep on that.

DAY THIRTY-TWO

MY HUT HAS COLLAPSED.

This is the problem with surrounding oneself in literary allusion. We make them up; they fall down on our heads. Schahriah – more fool, I – was the murderous king to whom Scheherazade whispered her thousand and one tales, night after night, and kept her head and possibly her hymen. (Was there time for sex, I wonder, during all that endless narrative? I've often wondered.) On a more literal plane, I'm referring to my roof, which has just caved in: a fine example of having one's house and burning it too. John's supply of paperbacks is now entirely consumed. I've stacked the hardcovers back together again, but the weave is weaker and growing draftier with every volume I combust. This is where analogy admits its disadvantage. Only a question of time, now, before I'm burnt down to my foundations. A deadline is a wonderful thing to concentrate the mind.

I recognize, too, that I've given short shrift to the New Internationals. But the clock is winding down and the rest you can Google – if there's still such a thing as Google a quarter-century on. It's Gwen we have to talk about today, and you.

Funny how persistently I've dodged this. Even now my hand trembles as I write. You will say it is the fever, or the chills, but today these have achieved some kind of tactful counterbalance.

Perhaps I've reached the happy equilibrium we read about: I no longer *feel* cold, though I suspect I should.

Gwen was everything a Queen should be. The people adored her, possibly more so even than John. And, of course, the press could never get enough. I doubt there's been a week since the wedding that you could walk into a newsstand anywhere in the world and not find the Queen in the pages of one glossy or another. *Guinevere; Gwen-Ever, Ever-Gwen*: Headline writers wracked themselves with twisted diction, dreaming up new ways of playing on her name. Admittedly, the endless Camelot analogies got to be burdensome – for John especially – but it *was* a storybook marriage, truly, and the two of them *did* get along together famously. The only time I remember them spatting, in fact, was over John's buffalo robes. Gwen refused to wear hers, which grieved the King sorely. By this time, the Royal Buffalo was fully entrenched in King's Cup tradition, and John perhaps foolishly expected his bride to embrace her role in the pageantry as willingly as she did most other photo ops. But Gwen was having none of it, not that. She defended her refusal on the grounds of aesthetics (buffalos are ugly and so are their pelts). But the King was not deceived. What Gwen truly disliked was the cold. He knew it wasn't the outfit she objected to as much as the event itself – or should I say the part that required her presence out of doors for three hours in the dead of winter. Somehow the King had convinced himself that a love of winter wonders went hand in hand with being Scandinavian. He could be strangely naive at times, could John. A woman with looks like Gwen's is duty bound to hate the cold if only because it forces her to cover up.

Sorry.

The last thing I should be doing is giving advice about women. Hester once went so far as to call me misogynist, though Gwen assured me later that this wasn't so. "Blue is no misogynist," she said, laughing, "only disappointed." She was in every sense John's perfect mate.

Did you know you were conceived in his office?

When you've recovered enough to think about it, I'm sure you will come to admire the symmetry. John, as I've often said, was political to the core of his being. That you should have got your start in the epicentre of his dominion is superbly, poetically fitting.

It came as an enormous relief, though, and not just to the royal couple. During that long stretch before our joyous proclamation, the Queen's failure to conceive had emerged as something of a national – then international – preoccupation. Hardly a week went by without a gossipy news item somehow involving Queen Gwen. But as time went by, these stories began to focus more and more on the continued absence of a royal heir. This was partly Gwen's own fault. She'd admitted to Barbara Walters, in a lengthy interview just before the wedding (and with that disarmingly beguiling blush), that she and the King intended to start a family *right away*. She wasn't getting any younger, after all. The tabloids picked up on it magnetically (ROYAL OVARIES TICKING, etc.), and stayed fixated right up until the week we announced that the royal couple was expecting.

This next part is delicate too.

I've promised not to lecture you on women. But I can't help it. There is something you won't understand, at your stage in life, something none of us really come to terms with until it confronts us in our own world. I had no idea myself until it happened. Nor, I'm quite certain, did John. It's this: When a woman past a certain age begins to think too much about a baby – and doesn't have one – she can start to lose perspective. I'm not saying your mother did – Gwen never lost grip of anything, believe me. What I'm saying is that she, like millions of women before her, ended up increasingly . . . preoccupied. I'm telling you this only because it will be alien to your present state of mind. I was twenty-five once too, remember. At that age, whatever thought we give to conception tends to be focused entirely on prevention, not the other way around. This will change, especially from the woman's point of view. I'm advising you, is all, that when you reach the stage when the women you're with are on the nether-side of thirty, you'll be wise to gird your loins more carefully than ever.

For Gwen, the crisis arrived a little younger than usual, but of course the ticking in her ear would have seemed much louder. The thing about Gwen, like the thing about John – and Hester (and me too, for that matter) – is that she's very much the proactive kind of personality. Not a feather on the breeze of karma is our Gwen, not the kind of girl to sit around and wait for nature to take its own inscrutable course.

Neither is she one to wear her heart on her sleeve, unless she's decided it strategically belongs there. I doubt that John was more than vaguely aware, and perhaps not even that, of where his wife's preoccupations were guiding her. Not that he'd have told me, even if he was. But I think I would have picked up on it. Yes, I'm certain I'd have had some inkling if John himself had been alarmed. I'm convinced he wasn't any more consciously aware of it than I was.

By the time you read this, what we now call the modern fertility industry will, I am certain, have made itself quite a lot more fertile still – and your generation will be coming to grips with the consequences of mine's recalibrated loins. Things are confusing enough at present, and I wish you all the best with it. In any case, it's my belief that Gwen would not have waited very long before availing herself of medical science. She was brisk about that sort of thing. This must surely have involved a danger. If the press had got wind that the Queen was consulting a fertility specialist, it would have sunk every other headline for weeks – but the story never broke, so whoever did the labwork must have done so with discretion. My guess is some small and well-financed outfit somewhere deep in the arctic night of Norway; she travelled back and forth a lot around that time, and it was home. But it might as easily have been a private clinic in some Scarborough strip mall – we'll never know. I won't. What I *can* tell you is that at some point the Queen began believing that the problem wasn't with her end of the Fallopian tubes. You have proven her correct in that assessment.

It's the next part that presents the greater mystery.

How did she verify that it was John, without John's knowledge? I'm certain that she did, and I'm certain that he never knew. I have faith enough in Gwen to know that she would never have done what she did without the facts lined up incontestably behind her. Gwen was loyal, that's important to remember. Yet loyalties have their hierarchies too.

Please forgive me, but I'm doing it again. I'm about to impart another fact of life (although the facts may have changed in the decades between my time and yours; it's possible). Know this, though: once you release your sperm to a woman, it's hers to do with what she pleases. This truth applies as much to kings as to anybody else. Gwen, I'm certain, smuggled out a sample of the royal seed and sent it off for testing. How she managed this is a puzzle I prefer not to address. Suffice to say she would have viewed this as entirely within her rights – both from her perspective and the law's – and yet she must have carried it out in secret. Women have unique perspectives on their husband's egos, hereditary monarchs especially so. There were politics on politics, as always. You must understand this.

Everything that follows, flows from this: Gwen was certain that the King was infertile.

DAY THIRTY-THREE

IT'S DARK AGAIN, colder, and the dog is growing hungry. We're out of food but I'm afraid he's going to have to wait.

Everyone is said to have a private haunt, so the theory goes. A seat of inalienable sovereignty, a sphere of personal dominion – a room of one's own, according to the cant – a sanctum sanctorum. John was more fortunate than most, in this regard, in that his was shielded with the full authority of the state. The King's Osprey Elites defended the door to his private office as zealously as they did their commander himself. No foreign heads of state, no deputations from the Privy Council or His Loyal Opposition, no cozy year-end interviews with CBC-TV shot before the granite hearth. Even the Prime Minister was never once permitted to set foot inside that room. Entrance was restricted to everyone but Gwen, who came and went at will, and me. In the normal course of events, the Queen seldom had cause to visit – she had other rooms and other venues – so when I received word that I was expected in John's office, I naturally assumed the summons had come from the King. We would sit there by the fire, he and I, sipping Scotch and parsing policy.

The hearth was burning that morning too, but John was nowhere to be seen.

"Hello, Blue," she said as the door swung shut behind me.

"Gwen!" I said, glancing around. I think I assumed that John had just stepped into the bathroom. Mostly, though, I was startled by the sight of Gwen herself. She was standing in the middle of the room, smiling, wrapped in one of John's buffalo robes.

"You like?" Her hands were buried in the pockets and she swayed to make the hem sway with her.

I'm ashamed to admit it, but what flashed through my mind was that John had somehow convinced her to wear the fleece, which would have been wonderful news for me. The Queen's refusal had made things difficult, from a PR point of view. Getting us over that little hump struck me as the morning's unexpected bright spot.

"It does you proud." I told her, smiling back, wondering how he'd managed it. I was still expecting John to pop out through the door behind his desk.

"He isn't here," she said, taking her hands from the pockets.

Remember. Remember. Please remember this if nothing else. Clichés work. That's why they're what they are.

It's cliché for me to tell you that time decelerated, starting from the moment Gwen withdrew her hands from John's pockets. Its cliché to say that the memory I keep of those few seconds, of those few seconds at least, is cinematic in its clarity: Blue standing there in hackneyed stupefaction as the Queen undid the buttons of John's robe, one by one, until it fell around her feet. Cliché to write that there was nothing underneath but Gwen.

Everything that follows is cliché: what I said; what she said in response; and then what happened after that. That is all ye know and all ye need to know on Earth: Cliché is Beauty, and Beauty is Cliché. I won't record the details here because these you will imagine too.

Over the next several months the summons was repeated. The terror of it was that I would never know which of them was calling. She used his name, you see, to command my attendance. Most often it was the King, as always, and I would struggle with my breathing and the weakness in my knees and wonder if he noticed. But other times it wasn't. I wouldn't know; I'd never know until the guards saluted and the door clicked closed behind me.

What I failed to see – through all that time I swear I never saw it – was the pattern. This was obscured, deliberately, by certain anomalies intended for exactly that purpose (freebies, you might call them if you intended to be crude, though on her account or mine we'll neither of us contemplate). But of course I didn't recognize this either. Sometimes weeks went by in normalcy – I would tell myself that it was over, that the Queen decreed that it was over – then the call would come again and I would point my head upstream like any salmon, and swim. It never once occurred to me that my visits to John's office were orchestrated to coincide with the Queen's ovulations.

And then it stopped. Simply ended. Months – three or more – while I schooled myself to believe that this time it was permanent. One afternoon when the King was supposed to be down at the docks inspecting a new frigate, the message found me again – and I fought against the beating of my heart throughout the long walk down the corridors and up into the Silos' heights. But it *was* the King this time, back early, embracing me joyously. And it was not our old decanter of Macallan standing by the fire, but an iced bottle of Vueve Clicquot, the *Grande Dame* year I knew to be Gwen's favourite, with frosted flutes arranged around it.

Three, I counted.

"Gwen's just stepped into the loo," he said, gesturing behind his back. He gazed around the room and took me by the hand, eyes brimming. "*We have news,*" he said, "*real news!*" Then he gripped me by the shoulder and whispered, "You may have noticed she's been a little out of sorts, this last month or so . . ." He glanced back nervously toward the bathroom door – and right on cue it opened and the Queen emerged. She did indeed seem pale. I hadn't noticed that either. John put a glass into her hand. "Just a sip," he said, "you're drinking for two." The Queen smiled at him, and looked at me.

"We're *pregnant!*" whooped John. "That's the news!" And the cork went pop.

I don't remember much of the rest, except that I drank my champagne like a man and hardly spilled a drop. I do have an image, though, of Gwen's hand resting on her husband's shoulder. He was sitting in the wingback chair beside the fire, Gwen had moved around behind him, watching me. John was detailing his plans for how the announcement was to be spun. It was going to be a doozie of a press release, that was for sure, and he wanted it pitched for maximum impact. "And put in too," murmured the Queen, "when you write it, be sure you put it in that I'm planning not to cut this off at one."

John touched her hand affectionately. "Gwen has her heart set on a houseful of children." He was shaking his head as he said it, staring blankly at the ceiling, enraptured with the wonder of it all.

The rest I'll piece together from glimpses captured now and then obliquely. The conjugal visits stopped, of course, you having made them redundant. Gwen avoided me until I'd proven I could play my part responsibly. She would not tolerate Blue's making a nuisance of himself, and Blue – clearer now about the way of things – did not disappoint. He tapped the depths of discipline these many years at his disposal, and never once stepped beyond the threshold of intelligent discretion; there was the future to consider. But little bits and pieces came to light, fragments of insight offered as it were in passing.

Morsel by morsel, I believe I've spliced together the sequence of Gwen's thinking.

To put a word on it, she proxied.

Confronted with the knowledge that John's child was not to be had – and had to be had – the Queen shifted to the next-best available option. Leaving aside for a moment the ineluctables, I must admit it's difficult to fault her reasoning. You will interpret this as grotesquely self-effacing, or profoundly self-obsessed (I argue for a share of both). But in any case, it doesn't matter. Her choice of me was Gwen's means of remaining as faithful to John as she could, under the circumstances, while still producing you.

And you, of all people, will not blame her for that.

Therefore, neither will I.

But me? There's still me to consider, isn't there – the ghost-writer's commission? I'm afraid that doesn't matter either now.

I know this will have come as a shock. The ironies are piling up already, I can see them: all those times someone's clamped a hand on your shoulder, saying you're the spitting image of your dad. I have no doubt of it. You are – because John resembled me. Can you bring yourself to understand this? There's only one degree of difference, do you see? As far back as Malaga, people were taking John and me for brothers. Years of common interest have, if anything, increased the likeness. It's fair to say we even thought the same. She could not have made a better fit, or closer fix.

And tell me, what else would you have had her do? Shop for the anonymous? Browse through vials of retail spunk like a savvy shopper tracking down the ideal shade of blush? Hook up with a likely stranger in some murky bar uptown? There *were* no other options. Nothing else could possibly have worked. Gwen would have understood this, absolutely.

Observe that even in her choice of setting she was faithful to design. You were conceived in John's office. There was no other place you could have been. As an act of composition it's fidelity itself.

Now I'm being sentimental.

And flattered? Yes, that too – on the nation's behalf as well as mine – not to mention grateful. It always comes down to the nuts and bolts of resolution in the end, doesn't it? That's the tale within the tale. There's the covenant between us.

Hundreds of pages, thousand of words, only now written.

How is that for resolution?

DAY THIRTY-FOUR

THE KING WAS ASSASSINATED. You and all the world are perfectly aware of this. You will also be informed by years of scholarly reflection on the fallout from his murder – whereas I can only guess. But I will make a fair assumption. I'm betting that the realm you inherit is larger than the one he left you when he died.

Yes?

As with so many fundamentals of his life, the circumstances of John's death could hardly have conspired to induce a greater convulsion. While I sit here in the ashes of his library, our neighbours to the south have reached the brink of civil war. For all I know, they've passed the brink already. There's a silence out there lately I can't otherwise account for. An absence of usual motion. No roar of snowmobiles; no moving lights among the stars; no jet-trails threading through the clouds. People are hunkered down, I think, watching. Waiting. Which may explain why no one's come looking for me. Times are too chaotic for anyone to give much thought to Blue. There's a rupture in the fabric of the continent; I can feel it even from here. Your country has always been the beneficiary of fractures to its south. These have bled out people mostly, according to tradition. But this time I'm betting they'll have brought you territory too. Old America has faltered.

Your legacy.

And by the way, you'll note that I've observed John's wishes in this matter also – in the timing of its delivery. The King was troubled with a growing conviction that childhood in recent generations has been deliberately eroded, even as longevity steadily increased. It always seemed to him the reverse of what was reasonable. The present threshold for adulthood, John argued, is set ridiculously low. Back in an era when most people were lucky to reach sixty, the voting age was wisely pegged at twenty-one. But when higher living standards increased the average life expectancy to over seventy, governments of the day responded by *lowering* the age of majority, not adjusting it upward. Since then the equation's only got more lopsided. Now that your generation can comfortably aim for one hundred, there's talk of cutting the voting age down to just sixteen. Pretty soon, said John, we'll be sending out enumeration cards on the backs of Cheerios boxes. The King was convinced that the best way to deal with low youth turnout at election time was simply to accept the fact that human beings with seven or eight decades of life still ahead are very reasonably aware that they'll have plenty of time, later, to think about all that. His goal was to bump majority up to twenty-four or twenty-five, and I'm certain he'd have made it happen if he'd lived. I've respected his wishes, as ever. I have made arrangements ensuring this document reaches your hands the day you turn twenty-five.

Happy birthday, son.

I'm assuming that you're King. Anything else is simply unimaginable. It's a safe bet, though – if for no other reason than I trust your mother to cut the legs out from under anyone who stands in your way. Catherine de' Medici was a schoolgirl compared to our Gwen. A far more intriguing speculation, from where I sit, is the present span of your dominions. I'm guessing that they now take in the Eastern Seaboard down to

Washington D.C., and very likely Washington, Oregon, and California too. Though I'm not so optimistic about the status of the Central Border States around Chicago: a safe bet, I think, but not a sure one. And Alaska remains the enigma it always was (I'd love to know what's happened with Alaska – such an oversight).

That is what his death has bought you.

How long have I been here? Thirty-three entries. How long is that? A lifetime of fatherhood crammed into weeks, deliberately, paternally, sequestered. But I have some skill in this (anticipation), and here's my prediction: If she has not done so yet already – and odds are she has – Gwen will any day now be demanding Parliament's confirmation of you as John's successor and heir to the throne. She will certainly succeed in this. As the brave and lovely widow, as the tragically defiant mother, the Queen will be sublimely well positioned to force the government's hand. But of course it won't need forcing. With all due modesty, governments don't get to be governments these days without the seal of royal blessing. I have every confidence in the present Privy Council's political acuity. They'll be sure to see the advantage of striking while the iron's hot.

It couldn't get much hotter. The Blue territories were close enough to outright rebellion *before* John's assassination. The methodic callousness of regicide – the brutal, calculating cowardice in the act itself – the sheer, prodigal malignance of John's murder will have sent them shrieking over the edge. By now there will be documents in open circulation (and savage efforts to suppress them) confirming rumours of the King's now ruined peace. The Blue press will have whipped itself hysterical with shame and rage. Every furious denial of Red involvement, every ravening demand for calm and lunatic appeal to patriotism will serve only as reminders that the patriots have left.

Moved on. From the moment of John's death, the copy began to write itself:

The King is dead. Long live the King.

Gwen will see to this. The cameras always loved her; they will love you too.

You are King, and mighty in your realm. I hold this as an article of faith.

What I'm less certain of is your schooling. There's another odd card. There wasn't time to see to that. Consider these pages therefore as my contribution to your education: I hope you accept them in the spirit they've been tendered. We've almost reached the end, you and I. Your patience is commendable.

If you can picture me at all, picture me smiling.

It works the other way around as well, you know, the uncertainty. It's as difficult for me imagining *you* as it must be for you imagining *me*. More so. You at least will have access to a smattering of history: photographs, film footage, public archives, and the like. There are relics of me out there if you choose to look. But of *you* there is nothing, not for me. You haven't yet existed.

I shouldn't say that. You exist in larval form, in infancy, and I have held you, yes, and soothed you with these hands. There is no use denying the force of this connection. If I close my eyes even now I can summon you – who'd have thought a swaddling child could penetrate so deeply? I will shut my eyes tomorrow, and call you up again. But strategically speaking, right now you're not that much to go on. You are the abstract sum of all potential – that's a lot, admittedly, but hard to deal with in the present tense. It's the man you have become I need to speak to. Who is he? I have no way of knowing this, and so – in the absence of any other useful model – I imagine you as being me, and extrapolate from there. I suppose that's what every writer does, and every father too.

It occurs to me we humans have two paths upon which to hang our hopes for life immortal. We can carry on through DNA – there's the standard option. The other is to persist by means of living thought, to pass on strings of ideas conceived to outlive us. John and I have mixed these streams together, admittedly. But I think you're none the worse for that. Far too late now, anyway, to fuss about genetics. It's your thinking that I need to channel.

You will know that John was poisoned. All the world knows John was poisoned.

Remember long ago I told you how often it has seemed to me as if some species of political muse was guiding the King's movements, causing him to do exactly the right thing at exactly the right time? It's my understanding that John's muse was hard at work again the day he died. There were seven capsules in the jar, I counted. Which means that there were seven different opportunities. But didn't John choose exactly the right one at exactly the right moment for his death to do the most good? Uncanny.

But it was the Reds, I hear you wailing. *It was the Reds who murdered my father!*

Your father murdered your father. I'm sorry for that too. History's not reliable. I have mentioned this before.

Yes, John attended that fateful session in Washington, and yes indeed he died there. It was his last-ditch effort to broker a peace, though no one expected a peace to result. That's true as well. His advisers urged him not to go; Gwen in particular pleaded that he stay at home. Send Blue, she said, you keep house here with me. Osprey Intelligence tried to force him to decline, as did the RCMP, and virtually every Blue state governor. But John, being John, insisted that these were civilized people, fundamentally, and with so much at stake cooler heads must necessarily prevail.

You will know all this: You will know how the thousand miles of suburb otherwise known as America's Southwest had pumped itself completely dry by this time; you'll know how those yellow putting greens of Texas had sucked out the last of Texarkana's water and now were drying, dying, grasping upward – demanding wholesale diversion from their Great Lake neighbours. You'll know how the Northern governors had banded together to stop the pillage, and how the President had vetoed their objections – to which the Northern Coalition responded by mustering their National Guards. You will know that this was the mix John had thrust himself into, that eventful day in Washington. I really think he did believe, our John, that peace was still the better option. The day after the meeting – where cooler heads did not prevail – the King was lying dead in his hotel suite. All this is familiar history. John died of anaphylactic shock; the King's body was discovered in the bathroom; the reaction to the drug came on so suddenly he never made it out again, although there's indication that he struggled with the door before his throat closed and his breathing stopped.

And yes, it is also well beyond dispute that a cell of Southern Reds was plotting his assassination. This was the earliest and most significant piece of intelligence to emerge from the investigation, and directed the course of everything that followed. Last I heard, even the Reds were convinced the killer was one of their own. With their customary wisdom, they were calling the assassin a patriot.

We must back up a little now, to the parts you will not know. You may be surprised, for instance, to learn that you were present for the murder. You were all of eight days old and barely able to open your eyes, but already you were exerting considerable influence on your mother, and consequently everyone else inside the Silos. Like many mothers of her time, Gwen held it as a matter of principle that a baby's father should be every bit as responsible for child care as its female parent. In her case, the process of equalization was expedited not only by the physical proximity of the father in question, but also by the fact that there were, for practical purposes, two.

It goes without saying that the Silos employed a large staff of nannies and nurses and various child-care professionals to relieve the Queen of any parental burdens she might wish to be relieved of. But insofar as John was concerned (and, by extension, me), anything less than hands-on involvement was tantamount to shirking. Within days of your birth, the Queen adopted the habit of appearing unexpectedly in the King's private office and leaving you there. The tricky part was that she would never say how long she intended to be gone. There was hell to pay, believe me, if Gwen popped back in half an hour's time and found the baby gone off with the nanny and John delinquently attending to affairs of state.

At first he was mortified, on my behalf, and kept up a string of apologies. It was one thing for *him* to be caught up in the dogmas of paternal orthodoxy, but John was genuinely pained to see *me* trapped there too. Of all the grounds I have for guilt, and I damn myself even for writing this, I'm ashamed to say I feel the guiltiest for this. Naturally I assured the King it was no hardship at all, looking after you, that really you were very good, as babies go, hardly any trouble – that I could decode the morning's memo from the Bank of Canada while rocking you as easily as otherwise. But John was convinced I was only saying this, that it was just another illustration of his friend Blue's unstinting loyalty. It wasn't. It *was* a pleasure, once I learned to flow along with it, and before long John was learning to relax as well. In retrospect, it's fascinating to reflect that *both* of our lives with you spanned the same eight days. What a testimony to adaptability. How quickly we all fall into our roles and routines. *Homo adaptans.* Well before our eight days were up, John had more or less assimilated the notion that I was perfectly willing to change you when you needed changing, or soothe you when you needed to be soothed. Not to say he didn't still resent the necessity. John assumed the job of grumbling for both of us: it wasn't like being King was not a full-time job, after all; and would it kill her to mind the baby while we did our best to see to the country's affairs? Gwen's inflexibility, I think, irritated him to the point that he began to find excuses to work outside the office.

I'm pretty sure that at least one of the reasons the King was so keen to make the trip to Washington was to put some distance between himself and diaper duty. History's a bitch, truly.

I wonder, Did you know that you were born with a blue spot? I can't decide if this would be the sort of thing your mother would have bothered telling you. In the normal course of events, it should have been without significance, long gone before you reached the age of self-awareness. I have no memory of mine. A Mongolian blue spot – in case all this is news to you – is a bluish, bruise-coloured pigmentation that shows up on the skin of certain newborns. It's often mistaken for a bruise and frequently presents around the buttocks, as in your case (and I believe mine). Typically it vanishes within a year or so. It's completely harmless and benign. The interesting thing about the blue spot is that it tends to be more common among darker-skinned people, Africans, Chinese – and of course Mongolians, which I'm assuming is how it entered the pool of genes you share with me. Remember I told you that for two or three centuries the Mongol Empire occupied the part of Ukraine where my own ancestors lived? They were industrious rapists, those heirs to Genghis Khan, and very keen for fatherhood. The Mongols left a deep genetic legacy: Blue spots are common, even to this day, among people of Ukrainian decent.

It worried Gwen at first. She fretted for appearance's sake as any mother would. But the doctors assured her there was absolutely no cause for concern, and otherwise you were perfectly fine, splendidly healthy in fact. And sure enough, half-a-dozen diaper changes in and we'd all stopped noticing. Within the span of just eight days, the four of us evolved what I might have been content to call a state of willing equilibrium. I was daring to think that perhaps our deception was achievable – that the strain was actually tolerable – that I really did have it in me to see this through. Your mother, of course, had reached that conclusion much earlier.

And then it happened. Another torque in the arc of John's narrative. Just like that.

Gwen was still lobbying to keep John home, but by now the effort was largely pro forma. This would have been eighteen or twenty hours, say, before his death. The three of us – no, the four of us, because you were there too – were assembled together in John's office. Even the dog was present. The King's bags were packed and ready by the door, the helicopter idling on its pad. All the necessary documents were coded, or gone to the shredder. The Prime Minister had delivered his Cabinet's heartfelt wishes for success of these negotiations, which the King had insisted could be undertaken by no one but himself. Gwen was still trying to talk him into staying, but I think she'd pretty much given up on changing his mind. She'd brought you with her, though, and in a last-ditch gesture of maternal suasion she'd trotted in the dog as well. I must tell you that Gwen was adoring motherhood. She loved parading you up and down the Silos' many-windowed chambers. It was a joy to behold her wheeling your pram among the gardens on the rooftop, or carrying you papoose-style through the wooded walkways of King's Island. Gwen was convinced that John cherished these occasions also. And he did. It's just that there were other things he cherished too.

I suspect that what the Queen was doing, that morning, was imprinting a sense of normalcy. She had resigned herself, I believe, to bridging the gaps. Gwen was braced against the tension. But I also think she'd decided to bypass anxiety as much as she possibly could. It struck me that morning that Gwen was behaving as if her husband was already safely back in her bed. My job was to look after the Silos. This was our custom. Blue held down the fort when John went abroad, kept the home fires burning while the King took the battle out into the field. But there were one or two last-minute details – there always are – that needed finalizing. We were in the midst of these when Gwen sailed in with you and the dog.

The King had made his farewells, at least he thought he had. He certainly believed he'd taken leave of you; I don't know what parting rituals he had with the dog. But if he was exasperated, John didn't let it show. He was above all things a kindly man. I hope you will retain this. There were many times his work obliged him to put aside his kindliness. It will for you as well. But John understood that his wife was worried on his behalf, and what man could not be touched by that?

So it was John – when you chose that moment to turn red and fill your diaper – who took you from your mother's arms and set you on the change table. (Yes, one had been installed, of course.) Is it possible that there's something contagious in this process? The question is absurd, I understand, but more than once I have observed that changing your diapers often inspired a visit of my own to the men's room. It seemed to have had that same effect upon the dog, more to the point, who decided just then that he desperately needed to go outside. His housetraining was not entirely reliable (still isn't, truth be told); this was a warning we all took very seriously. Gwen poked her head out the door to yell for one of the Osprey to take him off our hands, but dutifully they replied that they could not, that would have compromised the King's security. As it happened, there was no one else in sight, so Gwen escorted the dog out into the hall to whistle down someone who couldn't say no.

There wasn't much else to be done then but stand beside the change table with you and John and pass the King the handy-wipes. I'm guessing you will not have had much experience with diapers. The most effective way to change a diaper, as we had both so recently discovered, is to grasp the infant's feet and pull them up out of the way. You were duly cleaned, wiped down, dried off; John had just asked me to hand him a fresh diaper. There's something about a baby's bottom, you know, something that almost irresistibly demands caress. You won't understand. John was patting your bum, just then, in the fond way of fathers, his fingers absently brushing the spot of blue pigment. "Blue," he said, "pass me the talcum powder?"

And that commenced our moment.

I can see him even now, gazing at your blue spot. I can see his mouth silently forming my name. I see him looking at your bottom, then looking up at me, then looking back at you. I can see the workings of his mind, as clearly as if it's written out in pictures, travelling back through the years. I see myself at my desk at our Spanish school in Malaga, declining irregular verbs. John is sprawled across his bed, reading a letter. But the letter isn't his, is it? It's mine. A letter from my father. "*Blue?*" John is saying, "Why is he calling you *Blue?*" Then I snatch the letter from his hand – remember? – telling him to mind his fucking business. But he teases me, doesn't he? For a long time afterwards, a lifetime, promising that he'll get to the bottom of this "blue" business some day.

And I can see what else is happening, something in the angle of the head and the tilt of the shoulder; I have witnessed this before.

"Oh, Blue," says John, "oh, Blue."

Then Gwen burst through the door with the dog, hollering at John to do something about these traitorous Osprey – and maybe also get someone to clean up the mess outside in the hall. John closed his eyes and opened them and very gently handed me the baby.

"I'm coming," he said.

For the next several minutes, you and I and the dog were alone in the King's private quarters.

Have I mentioned he had recently been neutered? The dog, I'm referring to, which may in part explain his presence there that day. Gwen was feeling guilty; pet owners often do in the wake of this procedure. By way of atonement, she'd decided to take on the duty of dog-walking herself. She had also insisted on personally administering his post-op medication. The vet had prescribed antibiotics. I can tell you all about this, because at least once a day the Queen reminded me not to let her forget to give the dog his pill. One was administered in the morning, another in the afternoon – and a third one at night before bed.

Mornings were never a problem.

John himself took a pill shortly after rising each and every daybreak of his life. This reminded him to remind Gwen to give the dog his. He was a great fan of vitamins – had been for as long as I had known him. John had learned from childhood that keeping his own immune system in tip-top working condition was the surest way of preventing infections before they began. Even back in Malaga, he swallowed his daily dose of supplements with near-religious discipline: a single capsule every day before brushing his teeth. As far as I know, the dog never once missed his morning medication.

Afternoons, on the other hand, presented a challenge. This was the part of the day Gwen was likeliest to be distracted. In consequence of this, she had appointed me that week as royal afternoon-reminder. And just to be sure that *I* would not forget, the Queen gave me the pills for safekeeping. If she hadn't summoned me by midafternoon, she said, I was to find her, hand over the bottle, and remind her to give one to the dog. I'd kept the amoxicillin tablets handy in my pocket, all that week.

The other receptacle germane to this story – the one containing John's vitamins – was in the King's overnight bag standing by the door. You'd begun to fuss by this point. I'd put you back into your pram and you didn't like that. You were vocalizing, not yet outright crying, but getting close. I popped a soother in your mouth and unzipped John's bag. The vitamins were the kind manufactured in capsule form, big ones; it always amazed me that he could swallow them. I removed a single capsule from the bottle and took it to the bathroom where I carefully twisted it open and flushed the contents down the sink. Then I filled it up again with crushed amoxicillin. When I was finished, it looked no different from the others in the jar. There were seven capsules in there altogether, including the one that would kill him. I counted.

I'd seen the consequences of that look before, remember. John knew. How would history have turned out, I wonder, if he'd chosen any of the other six? Destiny is destiny. He would have recognized that too.

By now you were howling. You were still howling, a few moments later, when John and the Queen and the dog re-appeared – though by then I was holding you again, singing you a lullaby. Gwen rushed over to take you; no mother believes that anyone else is capable of soothing her baby. By the time we'd got you settled, the King had recovered his luggage and was on his way to that historic rendezvous in Washington, D.C.

After a while, you stopped crying. Not long after that, you fell asleep. I reminded the Queen that it was time to give the dog his medication.

DAY THIRTY-FIVE

SINEEY IS THE WORD FOR *BLUE* in Ukrainian. My father's
boyhood name was *Sineey*. Blue spots run in the family; I'm
sure you've worked this out by now. But *sineey* has unfortunate
connotations – doesn't it? – when pronounced in English. My
father never liked it either, and gladly left the name behind
him in Alberta. Yet it must have caught up with him again, I
suppose, when his son was born with a blue spot too. It must
have tugged some ancient ear for echo. Blue is what he called
me, which sounded not so bad in English.

It never sounded good to me. Even as a child I insisted that
people never call me by that stupid name, and – by the time
I'd reached adulthood – I believed I had succeeded. No one
called me Blue by then except my father, and only in moments
of affection. I had thought that I was shed of Blue until John
resuscitated it in Malaga, and then again here.

We all have our childhood afflictions, though, don't we?
John's youthful trauma was his allergy to penicillin. As a child
he'd picked up a common infection – in the sinuses, I think, a
flu bug, if I'm not mistaken – at any rate a fairly common
variety that doctors routinely killed with antibiotics. His
mother had dutifully filled the prescription and John had
washed down his pill with a bottle of Canada Dry on the way
home from the drugstore. Minutes later, he was having trouble
breathing. He always said the only thing that saved him was the

fact that they happened to be just a block south of Sunnybrook Hospital when the first seizure struck. His mother had the presence of mind to wheel straight into Emergency. The triage nurse recognized anaphylactic shock when she saw it, and within minutes John was pumped full of antihistamines, which saved his life. Ten blocks farther on, one red light instead of green, and we'd have never had our King, or you and me our compact.

For the rest of his life, John wore an Allergy Alert bracelet. The inscription on the back stated that he was allergic to penicillin and all related drugs, including amoxicillin. As a child he'd resented having to wear it, the other kids had teased him – this was before allergy warnings were as ubiquitous as they are today – but, of course, in later life King John of Canada became global spokesman for the Allergy Alert Foundation. I'm acquainted with the story because I helped roll out that campaign. It caused quite a buzz when it aired, and not just in the advertising world. Never before had a reigning monarch been so generous with the use of his image. When the commercial first appeared, a good many royalists pronounced themselves aghast. But John was a different kind of royal, wasn't he? – and today his face is among the most widely recognized on Earth. Anyone who owns a television has seen the King of Canada reassuring boys and girls across the globe that they should *never* be embarrassed about wearing something that could some day save their lives. "Look," says the King, jangling a royal wrist, "I wear one too." Variations of this message have been translated into more than a hundred languages. Hundreds of millions of viewers have watched John tell his story. The whole world knows exactly what King John was so allergic to. Which makes the method of murder that much more despicable.

Of course it does.

Heads will roll, I promise. They've likely rolled already. This will have been the final straw, a death knell to the Union. Any

Red conspirator unlucky enough to be captured will face a hasty execution, and probably quite a few others as well. We have come to the end of an era. Blue values are ascendant. That is worth the cost of everything.

And your mother's still alive! There's another thing to make me smile. Gwen, I am certain, remains a forceful presence in your life. I would ask you to send her my regards, but I think it best we keep this just between the two of us. Before you judge too harshly, please understand that there was nothing she could have done. If she'd acknowledged anything, anything at all, she would have denounced herself as well – and you; most importantly, you. I needn't remind you that if you were not John's legitimate heir, you could never have been crowned. Simple as that. It's possible even that Gwen may have found herself obliged to help cover my tracks. Poor dear. It's still surprising that the investigation never came anywhere near me. That must have been awful for her. I feel very badly for that.

It seems that I have timed my finale rather neatly. The last of John's books has just now gone into the fire. Fate attends the King even when the King is dead; his biographer has reached the end at precisely the moment it's safe to let the flame expire. And while I'm thinking on it, let me say how sorry I am to have combusted this part of your inheritance. At one point, I considered torching the cottage itself. I'm very glad I didn't. This place is willed to John's heir. It pleases me to think that some day you might visit. I think John would have liked that. If you do come, please let it be in summer. It's the only sensible time for people to be here. You will arrive by boat because this is an island. On your way you'll pass a boathouse. It's a white boathouse, classic Muskoka design with double doors swinging out across the water, bedrooms above, and a broad bay window overlooking the lake. I hope the boathouse is still standing. The point of land it's built on will surely still be there. Draw a line from that point out into the channel where, according to John's map, the lake is at its deepest.

That spot marks the end of our story. Now you will accuse me of manipulation. Fair enough.

In a little while I'll seal these yellow pages into a mailing box I packed in with me when I arrived. I've also put aside a good supply of postage stamps, plenty to see this through the first leg of its travels. There's a mailbox by the public dock in town. The great virtue of monarchies, as you must surely understand, is their ability to see ahead. Elected governments come and go, five-year plans are reduced to two and then forsaken for the next campaign, but a King oversees a lifetime. As a dedicated monarchist, Blue is better adapted than most at taking the long view. What I'm saying is that making sure this document reaches you is easily within my field of expertise.

But I can see you're curious:

There's a house in Switzerland – the Swiss are good at things like this – that deals in long-range contracts. The firm I'm speaking of has been in business quite a number of generations. Associates in Zurich will store this package for you and deliver it on the date I have specified. Satisfied?

Later tonight the dog and I will set out on our final trek to town. My foot is bad – I'll be happy to escape the odour – but it will bear me this last time out. It's cold again, the ice is firm. The dog will help me pull; he's settled down these last few weeks and the moon will light our path – it's nearly full tonight. Before dawn I will kiss this – and you – goodbye, my son. Canada Post will speed it on to Switzerland, where it will spend the next quarter-century in the keeping of our helpful gnomes in Zurich. (You'll be hearing from them, by and by, in connection with other matters – rest assured your assets are greater than you presently believe.)

But now you're worried for the dog.

Please don't be. The dog will survive, that's what dogs do. I'll tie his leash off to the mailbox. When the town awakes tomorrow someone's bound to find him. He has a winning disposition, despite what I've been telling you. It shames me to admit it, but I'm expecting that goodbye to be the hardest. He's been a consolation, these final days, having him around. I wish him a long and unremarkable life.

In due course the tracks we made going in will return me to the place I left the toboggan and the chainsaw. The moonlight in the windows of the white boathouse will let me know I'm where I should be. Then it's a matter of simple execution. It's bitter cold tonight. Long before daylight the hole will have refrozen. Ice renews itself, as John reminds us. That's its nature.

I believe it is customary, upon reaching the end of a manuscript, for the author to acknowledge full responsibility for any errors and omissions in his text. If you're reading this, it stands to reason none has been committed. All history is accident.

The Reds drone on about their favour in the eyes of God. It's always been the thing about them I've despised the most: a founding poison to the very notion of America . . . and yet . . . it's hard – isn't it? – not to feel the breath of it oneself. From John's death is born a new beginning; a newer, stronger, brighter beacon on the hill. What founding father wouldn't sacrifice for that?

I wish I could have known you, son. But we'll settle for this.

Goodbye, my boy, my son. My King. What a joy it is to write these words, and to know you know I have existed.

Be brave.

– The End –

ACKNOWLEDGEMENTS

The narrator in this novel often speculates about the role of serendipity in human affairs. His creator has cause to do the same. As my wonderful agent, Hilary McMahon, so rightly points out: this book could not have found a more propitious publisher than Douglas Gibson. For the depth of your political wisdom, Doug, for your predatory eye as an editor, and for the breadth of experience you have brought to these pages, I thank you. I'm grateful, too, for the brutal mercies of Heather Sangster's copy-editing. The scrutiny of two such formidable minds is cause in itself for thanksgiving.

While on the subject of gratitude, I warmly acknowledge mine to both the Canada Council for the Arts and the Ontario Arts Council. VISA does the same on my account. To Leah and Alan Macpherson and others: I know that you know how much your advice has helped through the long and solitary stages of this manuscript. Thanks also to my nephew Brent Feniak and his distant ancestors among the Golden Horde for the device of the Mongolian blue spot, and to the Haligonian Harpers for providing a name for their CFL team. I'm obliged to Dr. Jaroslav Grod for his lessons on shades of meaning in Ukrainian.

Ornithologists will note that I have confused the northern shrike with the loggerhead shrike. I hope they will forgive me. One name suited my purposes much better than the other, and the ends – ecologically speaking – I hope will justify the means. Speaking of Machiavelli, I acknowledge my debt to his *Prince*, as I do to John Steinbeck, whose *The Short Reign of Pippin IV* got me thinking about a Canadian take many, many years ago. Everything else in this book comes from the pages of Toronto's daily newspapers.

That being said, it's all made up.

OTHER TITLES FROM
DOUGLAS GIBSON BOOKS

PUBLISHED BY McCLELLAND & STEWART LTD.

THE WAY IT WORKS: Inside Ottawa *by* Eddie Goldenberg
Chrétien's senior policy adviser from 1993 to 2003, Eddie Goldenberg gives
us this "fascinating and sometimes brutally honest look at the way the
federal government really operates." – Montreal *Gazette*
Non-fiction, 6 × 9, 408 pages, illustrations, hardcover

RIGHT SIDE UP: The Fall of Paul Martin and the Rise of Stephen Harper's
New Conservatism *by* Paul Wells
Canadian politics were turned upside-down between 2002 and 2006. "Wells
tells both sides of the story in his trademark style – bright, breezy, accessi-
ble, irreverent and insightful." – Montreal *Gazette*
Non-fiction, 6 × 9, 336 pages, hardcover

YOUNG TRUDEAU: 1919–1944 *by* Max and Monique Nemni; *Translated
by* William Johnson
A disturbing intellectual biography of Pierre Trudeau that exposes his
pro-fascist views until 1944, completely reshaping our understanding of
him. "I was extremely shocked." – Lysiane Gagnon, *Globe and Mail*
Biography, 6 × 9, 384 pages, trade paperback

STEPHEN HARPER AND THE FUTURE OF CANADA: *by* William Johnson
A serious, objective biography taking us right through Stephen Harper's
early days in power. "The most important Canadian political book of the
year." – *Calgary Herald*   *Biography, 6 × 9, 512 pages, trade paperback*

SORRY, I DON'T SPEAK FRENCH: Confronting the Canadian Crisis That
Won't Go Away *by* Graham Fraser
The national bestseller that looks at how well official bilingualism is
working in Canada. "It's hard to think of any writer better qualified to write
about language than Mr. Fraser. . . . He is informed, balanced, judicious and
experienced, and a very clear writer." – Jeffrey Simpson, *Globe and Mail*
Non-fiction, 6 × 9, 352 pages, hardcover

SAILING AWAY FROM WINTER: A Cruise from Nova Scotia to Florida
and Beyond *by* Silver Donald Cameron
"Silver Donald Cameron is a wonderful chronicler of small-boat sailors," says
Farley Mowat. Armchair travel at its best, this 3,000-mile voyage "offers an
exhilarating experience even to the most sedentary of landlubbers."
Non-fiction, 6 × 9, 376 pages, illustrations, hardcover

THE VIEW FROM CASTLE ROCK *by* Alice Munro
The latest collection of short stories by Alice Munro is her most personal yet, based loosely on her family history. "When reading her work it is difficult to remember why the novel was ever invented." – *The Times* (U.K.)

Fiction, 6 × 9, 368 pages, hardcover

CHARLES THE BOLD *by* Yves Beauchemin; *Translated by* Wayne Grady
An unforgettable coming-of-age story set in 1960s and 1970s east-end Montreal, from French Canada's most popular novelist. "Truly astonishing . . . one of the great works of Canadian literature." – Madeleine Thien

Fiction, 6 × 9, 384 pages, hardcover

MAGNA CUM LAUDE: How Frank Stronach Became Canada's Best-Paid Man *by* Wayne Lilley
An unauthorized biography of Frank Stronach, the controversial man behind the country's most famous rags to riches story. "Lilley, a versatile business writer, has produced a judicious, balanced, lively trip through Frank's balance sheets." – *Globe and Mail*

Biography, 6 × 9, 376 pages, hardcover

WHAT IS A CANADIAN? Forty-Three Thought-Provoking Responses *edited by* Irvin Studin
Forty-two prominent Canadian "sages," including Roch Carrier, John Crosbie, Joy Kogawa, and Margaret MacMillan, provide essays beginning "A Canadian is . . ." The result is an important book for all thinking Canadians.

Non-fiction, 6 × 9, 283 pages, hardcover

STILL AT THE COTTAGE *by* Charles Gordon
The follow-up to the classic *At the Cottage*, this is an affectionate and hilarious look at cottage living. "Funny, reflective, and always insightful, this is Charles Gordon at the top of his game." – Will Ferguson

Humour, 6 × 9, 176 pages, illustrations, trade paperback

CRAZY ABOUT LILI: A Novel *by* William Weintraub
The author of *City Unique* takes us back to wicked old Montreal in 1948 in this fine, funny novel, where an innocent young McGill student falls for a stripper. "Funny, farcical and thoroughly engaging." – *Globe and Mail*

Fiction, 5½ × 8½, 272 pages, hardcover

THE QUOTABLE ROBERTSON DAVIES: The Wit and Wisdom of the Master *selected by* James Channing Shaw
More than eight hundred quotable aphorisms, opinions, and general advice for living selected from all of Davies' works. A hypnotic little book.

Non-fiction, 5¼ × 7, 160 pages, hardcover

ALICE MUNRO: Writing Her Lives. A Biography *by* Robert Thacker
The literary biography about one of the world's great authors, which shows
how her life and her stories intertwine.
Non-fiction, 6½ × 9⅜, 616 pages plus photographs, hardcover

MITCHELL: The Life of W.O. Mitchell, The Years of Fame 1948–1998 *by*
Barbara and Ormond Mitchell
From *Who Has Seen the Wind* on through *Jake and the Kid* and beyond, this
is a fine biography of Canada's wildest – and best-loved – literary figure.
Non-fiction, 6½ × 9⅜, 488 pages plus photographs, hardcover

ROLLERCOASTER: My Hectic Years as Jean Chretien's Diplomatic Adviser
1994–1998 *by* James Bartleman
"Frank and uncensored insider tales of the daily grind at the highest reaches
of the Canadian government. . . . It gives the reader a front row seat of the
performance of Jean Chrétien and his top officials while representing
Canada abroad." – Ottawa *Hill Times*
Autobiography, 6 × 9, 376 pages, trade paperback

DAMAGE DONE BY THE STORM *by* Jack Hodgins
The author's passion for narrative glows through this wonderful collection
of ten new stories that are both "powerful and challenging." – *Quill & Quire*
Fiction, 5⅜ × 8⅜, 224 pages, hardcover

DISTANCE *by* Jack Hodgins
"Without equivocation, *Distance* is the best novel of the year, an intimate
tale of fathers and sons with epic scope and mythic resonances. . . . A mas-
terwork from one of Canada's too-little-appreciated literary giants."
– *Vancouver Sun*   *Fiction, 5⅜ × 8⅜, 392 pages, trade paperback*

ON SIX CONTINENTS: A Life in Canada's Foreign Service 1966-2002 *by*
James K. Bartleman
A hilarious, revealing look at what our diplomats actually do, by a master
story-teller who is a legend in the service. "Delightful and valuable." – *Globe
and Mail*   *Autobiography, 6 × 9, 272 pages, trade paperback*

RUNAWAY *by* Alice Munro
The 2004 Giller Prize-winning collection of short stories by "the best fiction
writer now working in North America. . . . *Runaway* is a marvel."
– *New York Times Book Review*   *Fiction, 6 × 9, 352 pages, hardcover*

A NOTE ABOUT THE TYPE

King John of Canada has been set in Garamond BE, a modern type family based on types first cut by Claude Garamond (c. 1480–1561). Garamond is believed to have followed classic Venetian type models, although he did introduce a number of important differences, and it is to him that we owe the letterforms we now know as "old style." Garamond gave his characters a sense of movement and elegance that ultimately won him an international reputation and the patronage of Frances I of France.